LAST BEAR McCAIN

BY

BILL HOTCHKISS

*For my beloved wife,
Lee-Marie

Much love,
as ever
— Bill*

Castle Peak Editions 2004

DEDICATION:

For James B. Hall,
master craftsman, inspirational teacher, loyal friend

Front cover design by Dick Hotchkiss

Author's Note:

I began *Last Bear McCain* during fall term, 1962, at the University of Oregon. The book came as the direct result of a conversation I had over coffee: Jim Hall was my advisor, and I was a graduate student casting about in search of a subject for an M.F.A. thesis. I found myself telling Jim the legend of the Wild Man of Deer Creek, a tale I'd heard my first summer with the U.S.F.S., on California's Tahoe National Forest. Jim nodded and said, "Mr. Hotchkiss, there's your yarn." By June I'd completed two versions of the tale, then titled *Fever in the Earth*. The following year, as matters turned out, I wrote something quite different for my degree and then returned to the McCains. I'd already transformed the figure of the Wild Man into the eccentric hermit printer and poet Abram McCain, Isaac had emerged as well, and by 1977 the book had gone through several revisions and was published as a long narrative poem. Even then the fable kept drawing me back. I turned it into prose and revised that—then once again into poetry through two further full reworkings, and finally, during summer of 2002 (at the urging of my wife, Lee-Marie), the book became a novel once more, its title transformed to *Last Bear McCain*. The following summer found me at it again, fiddling with details. As poet Ken Hancock said to me one day, "These things take time." But Jim Hall? My lifelong friend and mentor may possibly be proofing a portion of the revised manuscript even as I write this note concerning the book's seemingly endless period of gestation. Thanks also to Monte Schulz, whose careful reading brought about a final series of editings, holiday season, 2003. Total elapsed years: forty-two. Abram, Isaac, Mack, Iphigenia, April, Burt, Sheriff Hutchings, the others—these purely fictional beings have all become part of the family. With this present publication, however, I hereby turn them loose. An author, after all, cannot spend an entire lifetime working on one book....

—Bill Hotchkiss
Munger Creek, Oregon
January 1, 2004

OTHER BOOKS by BILL HOTCHKISS:

I Hear the Coyote (poems, Castle Peak)
Who Drinks the Wine (poems, Castle Peak)
Yosemite (novel, Bantam)
Sierra Santa Cruz (novel, Bantam)
To Fell the Giants (novel, Bantam)
Great Upheaval & Other Myths (poems, Castle Peak)
Sancho's Guide (with Ray Oliva, grammar, Castle Peak)
Dance of the Coyote (novel, Bantam)
Fire Woman (novel, Bantam)
People of the Sacred Oak (novel, Bantam)
Mountain Lamb (novel, Bantam)
Spirit Mountain (novel, Bantam)
Pawnee Medicine (novel, with Judith Shears, Dell)
Shoshone Thunder (novel, with Judith Shears, Dell)
Ammahabas (novel, W.W. Norton)
Soldier Wolf (novel, Bantam)
Crow Warriors (novel, Dell)
The Medicine Calf (novel, W.W. Norton)
Middle Fork Canyon (poems, Blue Oak)
Poet from the San Joaquin (criticism, with Campo and Carpenter, Blue Oak/Capra)
Climb to the High Country (poems, W.W. Norton)
Fever in the Earth (longpoem, Blue Oak/Capra)
Jeffers: The Sivaistic Vision (criticism, Blue Oak)
The Graces of Fire (poems, Blue Oak)
To Christ, Dionysus, Odin (poems, Blue Oak)
Tilting at Windmills (grammar, with Ray Oliva, Castle Peak)
Steephollow Poems (poems, Ponderosa)
Into Autumn (poems, chapbook)
Black Flowers (poems, with James Petras, chapbook)

TABLE OF CONTENTS

L A S T

B E A R

c C A I N

LAST BEAR MCCAIN

Canto One:
RETURN TO DEER CREEK

THE ROPES WOULDN'T HOLD.
WILLOW ROPES,
THEY FELL RIGHT OFF HIM, OFF
ARMS AND LEGS.
HE SMILED AT THE CREW,
MOTIONLESS
IN HIS DARK EYES.
THE HELMSMAN SAW THIS,
HE IMMEDIATELY CRIED OUT,
HE SCREAMED TO HIS MEN:
"YOU FOOLS!
WHAT POWERFUL GOD IS THIS
WHOM YOU'VE SEIZED,
WHOM YOU'VE TIED UP?
NOT EVEN OUR SHIP,
STURDY AS IT IS,
NOT EVEN OUR SHIP
CAN CARRY HIM...."

["FIRST HYMN TO DIONYSUS,"
THE HOMERIC HYMNS]

*

Interstate Five wound south, out of the mountains and then down the big valley of the Sacramento River, the *Daha* as Ishi called it. Past Red Bluff old U.S. Ninety-nine veered southeast to Chico and on to Yuba City and Marysville—from whence California Twenty twisted through low rolling oak woods and across Yuba River and onward into the mountains, where a new roadside billboard proclaimed *Deer Creek Park Estates—This is Bullardi Country, Zone of Opportunity—Ranches, Cut-over Timber Lands, Retirement & Recreation—Burt Bullardi Enterprises, Inc., Diggins, California*.

The blue and gold message took a moment to register—and Ike was well beyond it before he began chuckling.

"The Bulldog's into self-promotion," he told Doom. "Guess he's a full-fledged entrepreneur these days—as well as a dirty sonofabitch."

From Grass Valley there was a stretch of freeway: four lanes looped past Brunswick, over the hill once known as Town Talk, and across the county seat of Diggins, setting him down on two lanes at the base of Harmony Ridge. He'd known the new road was in place—someone had told him about it. Nonetheless, Isaac McCain felt disoriented, as though this were not indeed his hometown at all but some other place, similar in appearance, ultimately foreign to him. Perhaps that was partly the reason why, along with dazzling haze of late afternoon sunlight, he missed the side-road he was looking for a dozen miles east of Diggins.

"I seem to have trouble with turnoffs," he mumbled.

Isaac reversed directions at Crooked Pines, made note of what appeared to be a new mess hall and a barracks, turned westward on the highway, and this time caught the dusty one-lane road leading down to McCain Flat. A nearly full moon was already rising, and the night, he thought, would be full of magic—cries of owls and coyotes. He pulled to the side of twin ruts of dust beneath pine and fir forest, shut off the engine, opened the door, and let Doom jump out.

McCain made a sandwich from chunks of French bread and a thick-cut slab of bologna, food purchased in Ashland that noon. He opened a can of warm beer—ate and drank.

Doom, smelling meat, suddenly lost interest in the new area and came loping back to the Buick.

"Hungry, White Brother? Think your master's going to share his chow? Why don't you go catch a slow jackass rabbit? That's what any real dog would do, you know."

The English setter's tail rattled back and forth in dry grass by the open car door.

"You're a failure, old fellow, just like me. Here...."

But now that McCain had driven five hundred miles on an impulse—a need to return to what had once been his home—he felt unaccountable reluctance to continue along the pair of ruts to Abram's old cabin. He could feel the beat of his heart, anticipation and reluctance all at once.

Nineteen years.

Abram McCain, after all, would not be home—for he was buried in the cemetery above Diggins. No, the cabin and printshop had been vacant for a long while, the same length of time that he,

Isaac McCain, alternately named *Last Bear*, had been away from the sound of Deer Creek's swift-flowing waters.

"A lifetime ago, Doomer Dog. Your speckled granddaddy probably hadn't even been thought of yet. This is where I lived then, just down below. Used to walk the road every morning to catch a half-pint school bus sent to fetch me and three or four other kids from over on the river—at the little town of Washington. If we had snow, the bus didn't even try to come up. Those were the days I liked best, I suppose—or else when my pal Mack Madison and I were helling around together. Well, that was then."

Isaac got out of the Buick and walked about, trying to achieve his bearings. He began laughing and set off through the trees at a slow run, his dog trailing him, then flashing past as a covey of quail chirred into the air and over some low brush. Chill air felt good against McCain's face, and he breathed deeply as he jogged along. He wasn't heading anywhere in particular, wasn't even sure why he was running. Just felt like it.

Past sundown he returned to the car. The moon hung over the treetops, and Isaac smiled into darkness as a single coyote howled somewhere up the canyon. Then man and dog got back into the coupe, and they drove down the rutted road that twisted through dense growth, along a canyonside toward Deer Creek and a meadow where he'd grown up, a boy and his father in a house lit by lantern light as well as some six volt fixtures from current generated by flume and water wheel and automobile batteries.

At the upper clearing, Isaac McCain shut down the Buick, got out of the car, and stood in cool air. Pines and firs were bleached to watery silver.

*

The other two women assisted in subduing their unfortunate sister, laughing hysterically as they did so. Coyote-Head was poised above his victim.

*

By moonlight the cabin and printshop appeared just as they'd always been in his memory. The entire meadow, in fact, had about it something of a timeless aspect—an *eidólon* rather than a real place, an archetypal presence.

"Well, Abram, I've finally come home. I'm your son, and you've drawn me back. I've got my degrees—have paid those debts—have even gained some reputation. Now my isolation's almost as great as yours was. Hell, Dad, I'll phone the university tomorrow. Plead sickness, plead insanity, plead broken legs. Taking off this way without prior notice is cause for a reprimand, not more."

Isaac continued to stare at two small buildings huddling in moonlight. Something.... Something was different—he recognized it now but remained uncertain as to what.... A thin, papery wind scratched among trees; and over across Burlington Ridge to the south, a couple of coyotes were yowling, pointlessly, mournfully.

"Doom Dog, your feral relatives are out tonight. Maybe some wild sisters, ladies in heat.... You're not interested? If I were you, I think I'd be."

The dog's tail slapped against Isaac's leg.

"Tell you something, though. A hell of a lot's changed from what it was. I swear to God, I'd never have recognized Diggins at all, except for that ugly, square-faced courthouse and the little white church with its pinnacle. A freeway right through the middle of town, for God's sake! Civilization's worked its way up into the hills, no question about it, and there's subject to be a lot more before long if Bulldog Bullardi has his way. We went to high school together, did I tell you that? And I'll wager there are dope farmers hidden in half the canyons—wherever the stuff'll grow. What's the world coming to? Dig out the kitkitdizze and plant marijuana. Close to harvest time right now, I'd guess. What do you think, Doomer, old friend?"

The dog did not reply.

Isaac got into the Buick, fixed another sandwich, drank another beer.

The dog raced off in pursuit of a deer or a shadow, returned, was admitted to the car. Isaac lowered the hinged seat back, an improvisation designed to allow him to sleep in the car if he chose, those times when he and Doom took off for the mountains or high desert country to the east of the Cascades.

Now McCain sprawled as comfortably as possible, felt suddenly drowsy, and fell immediately asleep.

The dog also slept, chin resting on his master's stomach.

*

Isaac awoke well past dawn. Sun burned an autumn heat over the eastern rim of the mountains. He crawled out of his car, the dog bolting past him, stood up, stretched, relieved himself—then realized a thin line of smoke was rising from the chimney of the cabin below.

"I'll be a double-damned.... A man goes away for nineteen years, White Brother, and when he comes home, he's got squatters in his cabin. You ask Old Man Odysseus if that's not true. Well, probably some of those pot farmers I was telling you about...."

He removed a twenty-two pistol from the glove box, fastened the holster to his belt—feeling a bit absurd, a man in tweed jacket and slacks, a professor wearing a gun.

"Guess we'd best see who's moved in over the weekend."

He skirted the meadow, staying under cover of trees, and came up from below. The building had been painted, stained silver-gray—and flowers, zinnias and petunias were planted along three sides. Curtains in the windows. Close by the printshop was a fifties-vintage Volkswagen, faded yellow paint peeling, right front fender smashed and the passenger-side door caved in, held shut with a portion of what appeared to be a bicycle inner tube.

A distinct feminine presence....

"Peculiar," he said to the dog. "Downright peculiar. Must be a family—abandoned cabin, pry loose the door, just move in—hippies, without question—wretched members of the counter-culture, no doubt on food stamps and otherwise sucking the public teat. Well, folks, I'm afraid it's move-out time."

Isaac glanced across the meadow, *his meadow*, half expecting to discover some neatly planted rows of marijuana bushes, but none were visible. Then he walked around to the front door, hesitated a moment, felt like an intruder, and knocked.

A voice from within, a young woman's voice—melodious, surprised, perhaps even hostile:

"Who's out there? What do you want?"

"My name's Ike McCain," he answered. "I own this place. Open the damned door."

No immediate response, and he thought, *Maybe she's dressing...it's still early.*

He knocked once more, and this time louder.

"Just a minute, please. I wasn't expecting anyone—what's your name again?"

"McCain. Isaac McCain. You happen to be living in my cabin, without authorization, I might add."

She threw open the door then and stood facing him, a rifle in her hands.

So that's why Odysseus came home in disguise....

"What do you want, mister—you've come to throw me out? If you're really McCain, then you're loony as your father was. That's what the old-timers in Diggins say. If you're McCain, then prove it. He's supposed to be living up in Washington someplace...."

"I just moved home from up in Washington someplace...."

He shook his head, grinned at her.

But she was startled by the size of the man in front of her—the deep-set eyes, black beard, the huge frame of the man.

He, too, was stunned—this bit of a girl facing him down with a rifle—drawn-back, auburn-colored hair—and the eyes, yellow or nearly so, intense, a slim, sinewy little lady in Levis and sweater, her hands trembling slightly as she held the gun, high cheekbones and a trace of freckles.

Without thinking, Isaac reached out for the barrel, twisted it away.

The shot, missing, rang in his ears.

The girl clung to her weapon, and he shook his head and erupted into laughter: relief and absurdity all at once.

As she attempted to kick at him, he asked, "Have you got a cup of coffee?"

She stood still, released her grip on the rifle.

"McCain? You're really him? Guess I made an ass of myself, huh? I knew this was your place—checked it out at the county courthouse. But I haven't hurt anything, honest. The house was empty, and I was told you hadn't been here for years—just paid the taxes on it. Since I didn't have anywhere to live...."

"Coffee, Yellow-Eyes?" Isaac grinned. "Bless my soul, Little Athena, I *need* a cup of coffee. The last time I was shot at, the guy didn't miss. This old bear of the woods figures you owe him—breakfast and coffee as well."

Doom sniffed at the girl's feet, slipped into the cabin, looking for food.

"You're going to kick me out, aren't you? This place don't matter a rat's ass to you, McCain, but it's my home. I've been living here for three years now—doesn't that mean I've got some kind of rights?"

"Rights, you say? Well, maybe if you'd been paying rent—but I don't recall getting any checks lately; let's have a spot of breakfast, and we'll talk about it. I'm hungry as an old cougar with bad teeth.

My dog's hungry, too—perhaps stale bread and some canned milk? His name's *Doom*. We drove down from Oregon yesterday, spent the night up on the ridgetop."

But Last Bear McCain was dizzy now. Amber streams of fear and nausea rose and nearly choked him.

The shotgun...the rifle...the near miss...old pain, a downward spin, a horrible scar....

Isaac's hands were shaking as he lit a cigarette, spasms in his chest, shortness of breath. Nearness and repetition, blank fear....

*

The young woman was not at ease as she cooked breakfast, but neither was she frightened—kept glancing at this stranger in her house, *his* house—this tall, burly stranger whose form was draped in a chair, smoking. He was watching her from behind, the way men do, and she mildly resented it. She realized he was also uneasy, however, and there was comfort in that observation.

"So what's your name, Yellow-Eyes?" he asked. "If I'm going to eat breakfast with a lady, I feel I ought to know her name at least. A man takes a terrible risk at times—you know, predatory female nature and all. Well, you must have a name?"

She turned from the stove, faced him. But he was staring at her, and so she looked away, annoyed with herself for not being able to meet his eyes. Then she forced herself, looked back at him.

I think I could like this McCain a little, she mused—and then remembered trying to kill him when he grabbed for her rifle.

Isaac nodded.

"I'm sorry I shot at you," she said. "You surprised me. Hunters come wandering around this time of year."

"It's nothing," he replied. "I'm used to it, I guess. Main reason I've got a beard, in fact—for what it covers. Last time I caught birdshot in the face, took half my jaw away. The plastic-sawbones put me together again. Come on now, tell me your name. Then I'll give you the whole sordid story of the Great Disfigurement."

She looked more closely at the beard. Was he lying, just talking bullhonky? But she could tell nothing.

"Were you over in Nam, then?"

He shook his head, shrugged.

"Ginny," she said. "Iphigenia Singares. My father's Greek, and my mom's Irish—so I'm kind of a Halfbreed. You too? That's what some of the fellows down in Diggins told me. You look Indian almost. I shouldn't have said that, no offense. What happened, I mean about the beard? Actually, it looks good on you, McCain. Here, your eggs are ready. Am I getting too personal?"

*

Are you tormented, Isaac McCain? This vision, an illusion you can't really see, it's been with you for half of your life.

Often he dreamed distortions of those past times, but this morning a sequence rose before his eyes like some half-remembered black and white movie he'd viewed as a boy—yet those others were remnants, sheer celluloid fantasy, actors and actresses, appropriate music, while the vision was real—more real, perhaps, than if he'd actually been there. Had he not, in waking awareness, played the scenario over and over, and each time thinking, surely, surely this time he'd catch a glimpse of the pursuer, not beast, but a man, after his prey?

Instead, the seasons slipped past, that fatal drama in the rain ever fainter, more fleeting—until now, re-emergent into consciousness, and without cause.

"Bullardi," McCain blurted, "you filthy sonofabitch. Burt...."

But it wasn't, couldn't have been. Such explanation was too simple, too pat. McCain's anger toward a boyhood rival, he was well aware, had the capacity to cloud his vision, blunt judgment. That world, long vanished, a stream of recollected images, a child's constricted awareness, not much more. He and Burt—they'd been just boys really, although deadly earnest and intent upon braining each other that night, with sections of two-by-four from the scrap pile close to big hinged corrugated metal doors of the mill burner. Even these torches were gone now, things of the past. Now every last bit of scrap utilized, chipped for particle board, shiploads from the West Coast mountains, leaving places like Coos Bay, on their way to the Orient.

Possibly, just possibly he and Burt had not been *thinking* at all. No, it was conflict, male rage, two young fellows just coming into the full strength of manhood, rivals for the affections of a woman child. But they were also driven by something dark, uncivilized, fierce.

Sparks drifted upward from that ghostly wigwam shaped, sixty-foot tall burner, swarms of bright orange fireflies spewing into the night.

Then images faded, and Isaac McCain realized he'd missed a freeway offramp—and the English setter, curled up on the front seat beside him, slept on, oblivious to mere human purpose.

*

Something touched at her face: she screamed, ran. Her lungs burned with cold, wet air. She stopped to breathe, gasped, closed her eyes. Numbness, the rain in her mouth. Footfalls again, pursuing; she raced away once more, veered from the path she knew even by darkness, turned toward heavy woods, as a deer flees through the deepest fastness and into the black heart of the forest. But she was no doe, strong in the withers and, with a moment's warning, capable of outrunning dog or bear or mountain cat: no, a young human female, her blood fevered with fear, she was clumsy, she fought for breath. Twice fell, struggled to her feet, plunged onward, and finally in desperation hid among boulders near a big creek pouring westward, its current timeless. Years before, a child then, she'd played here....

*

This day in September marked the opening of fall term at the university where he taught; he was on his way to an eight o'clock graduate seminar dealing with the one academic subject dearest his heart—the theme of wilderness, *of wildness*, in American writing, the impact of feral landscape upon the collective psyches of the those who'd attempted to chronicle the settling of the nation, presumed conquest of a continent—the seminar was a course he himself had struggled to get through committee, deflecting liberals and conservatives, nodding wisely, was deferential and willing to listen to rant and drivel directed toward him. Confrontation was clearly no way to deal with these more or less hopeless academics.

The West of which I speak is but another name for the Wild, and what I've been preparing to say is that in Wildness is the preservation of the World.

Thus a certain pencil-chewing Yank named Henry David Thoreau put the matter during a momentary reflection of genius. Indeed, a genuine academic future was possible for a literature of the earth, of earthscape, environmentalist literature, and for the students thereof—if the tree-hugging contingents would graciously continue to avoid courses that required a semblance of thought, and if the curse of oxymoronic political correctness (since that's what it was now being called) and collateral neonatal socialism could be kept out....

"Individuals," Isaac McCain told his dog, "not pale gray collectivists, took possession of the continent, fought for the old ways until crushed by model A Fords and locomotives and more recently by hordes of young women in patchouli oil but no panties. Take notes, damn it, Doom. Quiz on Friday...."

The dog thumped at his ear, the footless right-rear paw lost years earlier, caught in a cougar trap and held there several days, then released by a government trapper who read the tag on the collar and called the university: the paw had to be amputated, but in the aftermath the English setter, Isaac noted, ran just fine on three feet.

In truth, Ike McCain resented the Twentieth Century—an era of great foreign wars, electronic devices, asphalt roads leading everywhere.

The beautiful land....

"Dad always said I didn't have sense enough to come in out of the rain—that my head's in the clouds," McCain continued.

The black-and-white dog on the seat next to him was now staring ahead through the windshield, doubtless on the lookout for jackrabbits, house cats, Bengal tigers....

"Aren't you going to say a damned thing?" the man persisted. "Well, as far as you're concerned, I suppose Cottage Grove's as good a destination as Eugene—if you can find a squirrel to chase, your world's complete."

The English setter snorted, lowered his head to bite chest fur, then stared again out through the windshield.

At the next offramp approach, Professor McCain simply depressed the accelerator, laughed gleefully, and sped on by, knew he was being perverse, took joy in perversity. He was, and knew it, playing a small joke on himself.

"Hell, I can catch Oak Ridge turnoff," he said. "Head back to the U. What thinkest thou, Brother Dog? I'm a few minutes ahead of schedule anyway...."

Nineteen years.

The phrase erupted, and it took McCain a moment to realize its significance.

"My damned mind's playing tricks...."

It was just that he'd stared into the bathroom mirror that morning—really looked for perhaps the first time in several years—

and the face he'd seen wasn't his own. Thus a moment's perception led to a series of questions, all of which, upon analysis, came down to just one. *Who the hell am I?* Clearly, the query was one he needed to make of someone other than himself. But Doom the English setter wasn't about to reply—wasn't concerned in the slightest with philosophical musings.   Nor was McCain's pot-smoking lady friend, Thomasina Wentworth, a.k.a. *the Art Student*, at that moment doubtlessly sleeping off her previous night's jag and curled nude beneath a bright red blanket.

Obliging Thomasina's wish that she should be allowed to move in (a week or so earlier), Isaac now realized, had indeed been a serious mistake. Despite the best of intentions, the girl was in fact half-frigid, one who viewed the matter of sexual congress essentially as a contest of skillful manipulation, something one did to and for a man without herself being more than passingly involved.

In return, as she saw it, she should be provided with a place to work at her paintings, to indulge in marijuana and half a dozen other drugs, and to listen to rock music played at an astonishingly high decibel level.

Now, McCain reflected, would come the messy business of trying to get the Art Student to move out.

"*In*'s easy," he grumbled. "Sometimes *out* isn't. *Vagina Dentata* has the teeth of a serpent." Drugs, music, detachment, and the odors of oil and acrylic paint—those were things that might have been tolerable. But one condition wasn't: Ms. Wentworth's brain, as he'd come quickly to realize, was almost blissfully empty of serious thought.   *A damned new-wave liberal, stuck on a matriarchy that never was....* The utter shambles of her paintings certainly displayed a similar shambles within—complete chaos, no two things connected, all arbitrarily placed in a sort of kaleidoscopic stew.

Who the hell am I? Burning-Man, Kakini Busda, the spirit within. Stitched wildcat skins stuffed with pine needles and oak leaves: a human form created and adorned with woodpecker scalps and strings of dentalium and elaborate designs wrought with porcupine quills. At the conclusion of the Ustu ceremony, this "Burning-Man" was walked forward and thrown into a cone of flame so fierce that none could stand near it for fear of blisters on face and arms. One who was actually named Burning-Man had a son, Ishi-Pano, Last Bear. Last Bear McCain. Indeed, the golden grizzly, old cinnamon bear, had become extinct twenty years before this boy was born. In any case, he did not use the name—since the

*world he lived in would not have understood or approved. Isaac—
Ike—would have to do for the Halfbreed son of Halfbreed parents.*

He'd been toying with that question when he missed the offramp. "I," he informed the English setter, "am Isaac McCain,
Ph.D., Professor Last Bear—teacher, scholar, and putative expert
in the area of Western American literature. Pay attention now,
Doom. It's time you learned something about your master. I've
written some pretty fair poems, and now that my critical volume's
been published, I've got a Goddamned growing reputation, and
don't you forget it, White Brother. I'm allowed to autograph
copies, the whole nine yards. Papa McCain didn't raise no fool."

The Influence of Landscape Upon the Literature of the West.

"Hell of a appellation, don't you think? Certain to make the
New York bestseller list, a virtual Gawddamned certainty...."

The dog growled softly, said, "Stop cussing, ike, you're taking
the name of the Lord in vain," then curled up on the seat and
closed his eyes.

"Mt. Shasta, Seedskeedee, and South Pass," McCain muttered.
"It's like water on the brain...."

All this was true, but there was more, and that was why an
image reflected at him from a steamy mirror had made such an
impact, for the face, though strangely familiar, wasn't his own.
"When thou hast done," he sang, "thou hast not done, for I have a
scar...."

Isaac McCain was a man who lived behind a façade of whimsy
and occasional sarcasm and cynicism, a man peculiarly misplaced in
a world of books and students and polite academic conferences, the
perpetual bickerings of departmental politics. He considered
himself an anti-academic academic, Inhumanist in the midst of a
humanities division, a Jeffers-derivative ecology nut who'd damn
well *rather kill a man than a hawk* and who, indeed, if he had his
way, would cut the earth's population in half, then halve what
remained. Such, at least, would be a first step in the direction of
possible human survival on the planet.

Despite teacher's garb, McCain looked as though he belonged
out in the woods somewhere, and no doubt he did, perhaps
running chainsaw or driving a logging truck—except that he hated
loggers and logging trucks as well. A large man at six foot six and
two hundred fifty pounds, his colleagues called him Isaac the
Whale. McCain was a former collegiate wrestler and an income-
petent second string forward on the basketball team until he'd lost
all interest in athletics and summarily retired from the world defined

by U.C. Berkeley's Harmon Gymnasium.   A fraud, then—a bookworm who despised other bookworms. He was a man who liked to climb mountains, photograph waterfalls, explore ice caves, swim in tarns above timberline. He enjoyed whitewater rafting and aimless wanderings through fir forests. He supposed black bears to be, potentially, his best friends—and yet the sonsofbitches refused to socialize with him.

But he was also a man without a landscape of his own—so he imagined—and that was why he'd created in writing the very thing that he himself lacked. Furthermore, he was a man who enjoyed severe problems with women—a man who more or less seriously supposed himself incapable of genuine love and so settled for seemingly endless arrangements of one sort or another, invariably to his own ultimate grief. He sometimes considered it a matter of arrested development. He'd learned how to copulate with some degree of finesse—but mastered nothing beyond that elemental skill. He even supposed he knew why.

Somewhere, somewhere he'd lost the one thing most vital—the sound of a particular stream rushing amidst dark-colored rocks and overhung by firs, alders, and pines. Inextricably bound to this sense of loss were the yells of coyotes on moonlit nights, as well as storms driving in over mountains, different mountains than these fir-choked Cascades where he lived. Oregon country was beautiful, but it was the wrong terrain. It wasn't Mother Lode. A few miles above his home on the upper McKenzie River, The Three Sisters loomed high and white, magnificent peaks.   The canyons and ridges that rose to shoulder the Sisters and their ice fields were wild, a region of volcanic landscape, lush forests with rhododendrons blooming through half the summers, waterfalls bursting out from porous banks of cinder and basalt.

Nonetheless, something was missing, had always been missing.

Bullardi's image flashed across McCain's mind once again. Burt, of course, was the one who had *motive*—a conjecture that occurred to Isaac more than once over the intervening span of time—Burt, in jealous rage.

Who am I? Where did I come from? Where am I going? Ah yes, Gauguin's natives, and all other sapient critters as well....

Nineteen years ago he'd left himself behind, abandoned himself without realizing he was doing it—left behind a place and an identity that were his by right of birth. He was, after all, the last remaining member of his own lineage, a different sort of Ishi, rather a family that sprang from Judge William Goffe the regicide—

and from Ben, True Bear, and Abram McCain—yes, and from
native earth as well, Acorn Girl, Fire Woman, Lucinda Septien....
He was Last Bear McCain.

Yet at one time he'd seriously considered having his surname
legally changed—perhaps back to Goffe, for hadn't that been the
actual family denomination prior to the time of old Benjamin, his
great grandfather? Ben, who'd come West during the Gold Rush
and turned outlaw and married a hell-raising Maidu woman named
Ooti.... Isaac's father, Abram, told him the story—had in fact been
fascinated by the whole family line, clear back to the Judge, who'd
fled to the colonies at the time of the Restoration and hid along
with Whaley, hid in caves and root cellars to avoid being
apprehended by royal officers. Almost from the beginning, European and North American bloodlines mixed, for Goffe took to wife
one of Massasoit's daughters—they were married in Wampanoag
fashion, not according to the Whiteman's rituals—if any of that
mattered at all. Indeed, old Goffe actually plotted invasion of
England, where his other wife lived, the wife he was never to see
again in this world. Under Cromwell he had defeated one King on
the field of battle. Perhaps he could do it again?

So. He, Isaac, genetically more Indian than White, a truth
perhaps utterly irrelevant, for the tradition of university education
was also dominant in the Goffe-McCain manner of dealing with a
changing cultural landscape. Perhaps the tradition went back to
Massasoit's son King Philip, Metacomet, younger brother to Wam-
sutta, in the more or less peaceful days that preceded King Philip's
War, a conflict that devastated Pilgrims and Indians alike and
enforced a schism between Goffe and his Indian family, even as his
Puritan loyalties severed him from his family in England.

But one son to William Goffe and the Wampanoag woman
survived, and from that line old grandfather Benjamin eventually
sprang—Benjamin, the *Bear Who Does Not See Well*, husband to
the Maidu *Ooti*, the acorn maiden.

Thinking: *One way or another, we're all descendants of Adam
and Eve, but the paths that lead us from Eden are a maze running
through time, an utter complication. Yet the past does not control
us, does not determine who and what we are. No, by God, that's
our responsibility, ours alone.*

Not totally, at least, for there had been compensations. In the
case of Isaac McCain, once the forests and canyons of California's
Sierra Nevada were behind him, he took deep solace in the realm
of his own mind—endless reading, challenge of examinations, slow

but certain climb to a doctorate. Then a position with the university, temporary replacement at first. He'd entered, so to speak, not by the door—at least not the front door. But a sought-for appointment as assistant professor was eventually forthcoming, then promotion and tenure, the excitement of teaching, years passing by, full professorship, publication of his book....

"Perhaps," McCain told his English setter, "if there had been a woman, the right woman.... Perhaps then it would have been different, complete."

The dog lolled his tongue, panted.

Instead Isaac recalled a blur of faces and bodies, himself involved in a self-destructive dance: grade-grubbing co-eds, dopers, innocents, wielders of female weapons, open wombs, open mouths, an occasional older woman appreciative but with psychological problems and usually two or three children and a husband or ex-husband in a closet somewhere—one after another until identity was lost, theirs and his as well.

No: it wasn't their fault. It was his own, and he knew it—an indecent flaw in a black emptiness inside himself, an emptiness both bitter and voracious, incapable of being satisfied, a cynical void. In the bleakness of his own vision of things, Isaac McCain saw the sexual revolution of his time and the drive of young women toward what they imagined to be freedom as little more than an open-ended invitation to the satisfaction of his own desires. It was perfect. But if that were so, then why did his emptiness remain, why did his darkness persist? Had the little nymphs not, in fact, used him? Was he indeed incapable of love, or was that idea simply conjured to justify his own actions, no more?

But something inside him died, and that had happened, he realized, almost precisely nineteen years into the past.

*

Thomasina was asleep in the adjoining bedroom, and he was ready to leave for Eugene. Through the open bathroom window he heard the subdued roar of the McKenzie River, and perhaps that had been the cause—something about the noise of running water, a congruency. His image in the mirror exploded. Black beard and bushy eyebrows: not his own face, but his father's, the face of Abram McCain.

"Isaac, son of Abram," he muttered. "Isaac becomes Abram, but there's no covenant, I have to have my own covenant."

He'd been clean-shaven all his life until after that shotgun blast, and the memory of a night at Tex's Tavern came flooding over him. He heard again those intertwined roarings of noise and pain all at once, pellets ripping into his shoulder, most of the lead cutting into the throat of a young woman who was tending bar, a blood-splatch, and her mouth momentarily open yet wordless as she crumpled sideways into neatly stacked empty bottles that formed a small pyramid in front of a suddenly shattered mirror. He'd lunged toward the man, realizing only at that moment the weapon was double-barreled, and he thought, *This is it, Isaac old fellow. It's come quickly. It's over....*

A second blast took him in mid-career, and the strength went out of him. He was sprawled on a sawdust-littered board floor. Blue light and a spinning to blackness as his inner mind cried its vain denial.

*

A large, bearded man in an old Buick coupe, a man wearing a tweed jacket and a string-tie: the dog sat beside him, intent, shoulders high, as though he, the dog, were actually driving the car.

The man had once been a boy who grew up with the sound of creek music in his ears, a boy who ran traplines and wandered endless woods, who climbed high ridges and, not satisfied yet, pulled himself hand over hand up through limbs of pines that rooted themselves along crests, a boy who caught trout with his bare hands and who'd seen long vees of wild geese trailing southward through blue October skies, who'd listened to the clatter of pigeon wings among oak leaves as he walked home through forest at night to his father's house, a boy who'd hunted deer and once even drank the hot fresh blood of his kill.

*

In some ways, he knew, he'd been a savage—had lived something of the life of his Indian forebears, felt easy and natural with it, alone up on Burlington Ridge. Yet behind his father's house, a hundred yards distant, was a gravestone. His mother was buried there, the mother he but vaguely remembered, for he was only three years old when a gasoline drum exploded, shattering the side of the house and leaving a child buried beneath a tangle of broken boards. That much indelibly etched. He'd not even been frightened, wasn't injured at all.   But from that instant onward, Isaac would recall everything—everything, day by day, if it were possible.   He saw again Abram, his father, digging the grave.   His mother's body was mangled—she...it...was in the printshop, behind a locked door.   The sound of his father's hammer and saw—the building of a coffin.   Later a sheriff and his two deputies came, the three of them arguing with Abram, who finally ordered the men off his land.

After an interval, Abram began to rebuild the house where the boy—he, Isaac—grew up.

Now Isaac spoke to the dog.   "Doom, old friend, your master's half asleep.   Mind's wandering.   My students will rebel—they'll break out the windows and defecate in the corners of the room.   What do you think about that, White Brother?"

The English setter yawned, stretched, placed his paws against McCain's leg, wagged his tail, and sighed.

Isaac rubbed a big hand over his beard, touched at rough scar-tissue beneath.   Brought it all back.

The sequence of events played endlessly through his mind these past few years since that night in Tex's Tavern.   Sometimes memory caused him to awaken in the middle of the night—his own voice, shouting, memory fragments that gradually drifted away—but which had of late begun to emerge once again as real and immediate presences.

He was drinking beer.   He'd won several games of eight ball and was in an exceptionally good mood.   When a lanky young logger challenged him to an arm-wrestling contest, Isaac laughed and pretended weakness.   The logger persisted, however, needling him with minor insults until McCain gave in and proceeded to thump the smaller man's fist heavily to the table.   Onlookers laughed, but the logger took a swing at him, missed, and stumbled to his knees.   Friends dragged the tree-butcher away, but he was still cursing as he left, and Merle Haggard howling from the juke box.

Half an hour later the fellow returned, double-barreled twelve gauge in hand.

Isaac awakened in a hospital, uncertain where he was.   He lay dazed, tried to speak.   Pain.   Bandages over his face.   Something in his mouth, something that tasted like rubber.   He could not speak.

Darkness.

Then, later, the doctor's voice:

State trooper had to kill him. After he shot you, Prof, he went out into the parking lot and began to blast away at customers' cars. When the patrol vehicle showed up, he fired at that. Well, university teachers shouldn't spend their time in redneck taverns. The Old West's still alive in mill towns. Loggers and mill hands are a rough lot—the uncivilized bastards haven't figured it out—the frontier's long past. You're lucky as hell, McCain. You're going to survive. It's pretty bad—I'll level with you. Half your jaw's shot away, but we should be able to rebuild the cheekbone and mandible. I think your eye will be all right—I took out one chunk of birdshot, but it missed the cornea, thank God. Scars, yes, but perhaps with plastic surgery.... In any case, you're going to make it. Could have been a lot worse. You could be dead, just like that young lady who was tending bar, you remember her?

The voice in his mind trailed away—then another, more immediate voice: *the path that leads up and the path that leads down are the same path.* Not his own words. Whose, then?

Isaac McCain stared into the rearview mirror, looked at the bearded face that seemed to him now so much like his father's.

"Abram," he said, "My God, Abram McCain, what are you doing in the looking glass?"

"How's it going, Last Bear? What happened to my damned mule?"

Isaac sped by the Oak Ridge turnoff. His vision blurred, and he realized he was sweating.

"What am I up to, Doom?" he said aloud. "What in the crazy hell am I about?"

But really he knew. He knew where he was going. He laughed so hard the tears came to his eyes. He rubbed his hand over his face and beard.

"Nineteen years, and I'm going home. A plague upon such stuff. I'm going home. We're going home, Doomer Dog—home to our hills. Your home, too, and you've never even been there."

*

Autumn, scales drawing to balance. Snow had melted from all but the highest peaks, and granite and red cap-rock were bare. Nights grew colder, even as the days remained hot, leaves were beginning to fall. Soon frost would fret the grass along Woodpecker Creek, and wild grapevines would burn to gold.

Winter was coming, yet no man could say what kind of spring would emerge beyond the far turning.

Numunana, Isakawuate, Old Dreamer, Great Spirit of the Inyo, Coyote who put the rocks into place: green essence of river and forest, germ of hunter and hunted, mystery of meristem and the flight of birds and of cougar tracks in damp sand by a stream, quiescence of fall, swirling white semen of winter, upthrust of delicate grasses in springtime, green rush of summer, bounding mule deer and crowning forest fire....

A whirlpool inside Ike McCain's skull.

A few weeks earlier a president of the United States had resigned his office, and afterward the new president unconditionally pardoned his predecessor—for whatever wrongdoing might have occurred, then a few days later offered conditional amnesty to deserters and draft evaders—the protracted agony of military involvement in Viet Nam had come to an end.

"And by God," Isaac McCain mused aloud, "Hank Aaron's broken Babe Ruth's home run record.   There's significance in practically everything.   Maybe Muhammad Ali's even got a chance of whipping George Foreman, who knows? And a time will come when no one will remember, no one will care to recall what happens this year or next, mere bloodstains in Yuba water rushing westward to the valley, to Río Plumas and Nem Seyoo, and trails of vapor rise from the jumbled peaks of Middle Hills, from Estawm Yan, the souls of the dead rising toward the star-path, to *other side camp.*"

The road south continued to spin from beneath the humming tires of an ancient 1940 Buick coupe.

For three days they tried to track him down with dogs, and he killed the dogs and got away....

Abram McCain winked and nodded.

"This human life's a little madness turned in at either end with darkness."

A flight of images as Isaac drove toward California.   Images and a voice.   His own? He envisioned the mountains where he'd grown up, high ridges below the granite spine of the range, streams flowing down through deep canyons—Steephollow (where Benjamin Goffe and Acorn Girl and the Pano Maidu struck back at miners who'd annihilated an Indian village), Woodpecker, Greenhorn (feeding from Gold Rush boomtowns Of Red Dog and You Bet), Deer Creek (where he'd grown up), the forks of the American River (*Ko-lo-ma* village where Marshall found gold in a millrace),

Screwauger Canyon, Bear River, the branches of the Yuba (possibly *Grape River*), the Rubicon flowing from bare, glacially polished granite in Desolation Valley....

Northern end of the range, Pyramid Peak to Sierra Buttes....

Isaac could hear water purling among stones, he could see an ouzel where it dived beneath the surface, out again, to stand pulsing on a shaded rock, he could see a great blue heron stilting the shallows, head cocked to one side, eyes clouded with passing time, he could feel soft weight of winter snow wrapping itself about ponderosas, sugar pines, Jeffreys, could smell dry grass of autumn. Brown deer glided among Douglas firs. A coyote yowled from a ridgetop in twilight. Autumn, rest, balance in the cosmic flux of things. Rainstorms and the long coils of mist running through canyons, dusty woods transformed to a glistening....

He could not comprehend it.

*

By early afternoon the Buick crested the Siskiyous and began a long grade down to Klamath River. Off to the south rose the great white-streaked sentinel of Mt. Shasta—Joaquin Miller's mountain, his because he loved it, worshipped it.

"Big," Isaac said. "Damned big. I always seem to forget that somehow...."

When he crossed the Klamath and urged the old Buick straight-eight up the grade beyond, he thought: *Why do you torment me still and force me to speak such abominable lies? After all this time, am I not innocent? Why must the forest be ravaged by fire again and the stillness be destroyed?*

He burst out laughing.

Doom glanced sideways, huffed, growled softly, slept again.

Without his having willed them, the words formed in a series of small blue explosions: startled—he gripped the steering wheel more tightly.

Crazy. Crazy just as your father was crazy. You never had the slightest chance of running away—can't run from what's inside you.

But now the vision sequence altered, and McCain became aware of falling water. Flute music. Through black light he could discern dripping ferns and azaleas in full bloom. Behind these was a waterfall, mist rising in sworls from its base. On a large rock below the falls sat a god-figure, coyote-headed, body of a man,

muscular, naked, luminescent green. The music stilled. Motionless. Only the twitching of muzzle whiskers.

McCain shook his head, but Coyote-Man spoke anyway:

*Earth itself must shudder to its base, for what are we but raw
emotion laced with cunning intellect, and that so slight our fingers
trickle fire? I am a man, and yet I neither live nor die, but am
instead the sap that eats the earth, roots that claw between the
grains, leaves that pierce the sky. I live here in the forest—these
woods have always been my home. Oh, I've slept for ages awaiting
this time: my blood's as red as yours, my heart is tuned to that
same metronome. My other name is Fire, and when let loose, I'll
burn the cities down.*

Flute music returned, wilder and louder than before. Three
naked young women, a blonde, a redhead, and a brunette, their
bodies brilliantly green: they danced into the clearing from the
forest. They gyrated to the music, at the same time cupping and
massaging their own breasts. Their eyes were half-closed, their
mouths sensuously open. Coyote-Head turned to watch, his dog
whiskers twitching. After a few moments he entered the dance:
music louder, rising to intolerable intensity. Coyote-Head grasped
the dark-haired one about the waist and wrestled her down into a
thick growth of brackens. She screamed soundlessly, but the god
was determined. The other two women assisted in subduing their
unfortunate sister, laughing hysterically as they did so. Isakawuate
Oleli was poised above his victim.

    ***

Canto Two:
ABRAM'S JOURNAL

THE FIRST IN TIME AND THE FIRST IN IMPORTANCE OF
THE INFLUENCES UPON THE MIND IS THAT OF
NATURE. EVERY DAY, THE SUN; AND, AFTER SUNSET,
NIGHT AND HER STARS. EVER THE WINDS BLOW; EVER
THE GRASS GROWS. EVERY DAY, MEN AND WOMEN,
CONVERSING—BEHOLDING AND BEHOLDEN. THE
SCHOLAR IS HE OF ALL MEN WHOM THIS SPECTACLE
MOST ENGAGES. HE MUST SETTLE ITS VALUE IN HIS
MIND. WHAT IS NATURE TO HIM? THERE IS NEVER A
BEGINNING, THERE IS NEVER AN END, TO THE
INEXPLICABLE CONTINUITY OF THIS WEB OF GOD, BUT
ALWAYS CIRCULAR POWER RETURNING INTO ITSELF.

[RALPH WALDO EMERSON,
"THE AMERICAN SCHOLAR"]

*

And Isaac thought: *Abram, my father, you've raged through
my brain for years—you haunt my imagination just as you haunt
the pine hills and the streams that work down through the ridges.
That big voice of yours bellows the canyons, is caught in the
ululations of coyotes, spins webs through starry skies. Even now
I'm not sure I know you, you chorus of voices, you bringer of rains,
you silence of snow, you forest fire. Must we wrestle again? Your
strength is too great, your arms like trees. Your curses break
through rocks, burn manzanita and chaparral in a torrent of noise.
I suppose I'll have to outwit you....*

Words from some book or another: *Mythic exaggeration, the
way in which the dead invariably come to take on attributes of
titans. Whatever virtues may have been possessed in life are vastly
magnified in death, vices become equally overdrawn, and mad-
nesses come to approximate the insanities of divine beings.*

But Abram McCain said: "The shimmer in leaves and shadows
in moving water—ah, leopard lilies by the stream, are these not a
proof of the only Lord Who exists? I have seen great torrents of
fire sweep the hills, I've seen two-hundred foot trees flame like

matches, red and yellow clouds drawn from earth's fever. I've seen
snows lock the mountains in winter, I've walked in blizzards and
seen pines explode in white fire in a soft, violent dimness. And I've
seen you, my son, as you ran to catch a spinning demon of autumn
leaves twisting down from an oak grove in a yellow meadow. I've
lived my life and not always kept madness at bay. Sometimes it's
mastered me and driven me to frenzied, violent acts. Yet there
have been times when the shimmer and the fire and the snow and
the whirl of autumn leaves have perfectly melded—and I've enjoyed
in such moments a wonderful vision. I tell you, sir, the mountains
all exploded. Walls of water and thick debris came crushing down
these slopes. Ours is the remnant of a world. Oh, we Indians
knew, the Maidu people knew. Our legends speak of the last time
the skies changed. All a man has to do is look, and the madness is
there. No one's sane who's worth a damn. Let it be a lesson. I
climbed up Shasta once, up past the Red Banks and the tongues of
ice, past boiling springs (where John Muir huddled in a blizzard) to
the high summit. Mist spume trailed from the peak, and sunlight
came through in gusts of clear brilliance. Then it was all at my feet.
You can see the world from there...."

*

They talked for nearly two hours—Isaac talked mostly, for
Ginny seemed willing to listen, and that, he concluded, after a few
weeks in the company of Thomasina Wentworth, was a welcome
change. He spoke of his mother's death, how he'd been raised
here on Deer Creek, raised by his eccentric father. Isaac mentioned Abram's death but supplied no details, then talked about
Berkeley, graduate school, and his job at the University of Oregon—how he'd decided to cut class, drive *home*, that he'd get in
touch with his department head, would probably leave that night so
as to get back to being a responsible, class-teaching citizen.
   *But even as his words flowed, he knew, knew somehow that he
was not going to do it—that he'd come home, would probably not
leave again.*
   "Hell," he concluded, "maybe my academic alter ego's dead,
who knows?"
   "I don't understand."
   "Enough years of institutional horsecrap—excuse me—but
enough years of it, and a man either turns into what's around him,
or he gets away from it. Old Doom here, he was ready for an

adventure. Talked me into it. Well, freedom and security, Ginny. One condition won't allow the other, mutual exclusion. Guess I've learned that much from my books anyhow. Or maybe it's just that I need time to get my wits together. Teacherly burnout. I needed a sabbatical, and maybe this is it. I suppose it's nothing you're much interested in."

"So what are you going to do now?"

He squinted at her, as though attempting to absorb the apparition-like, flame-haired, yellow-eyed creature before him.

"I don't know, don't know. I imagine I'll probably head back. Look, Ginny—Iphigenia Singares. Since I've had a chance to think upon the matter, it seems like a pretty good idea to have someone living in the cabin. If you're here, at least no one's going to vandalize the place. I guess you can stay as long as you want. Actually, the old homestead looks better than it did when Dad and I lived here."

"I could pay rent if you want...."

"No. Hell, no. Just drop me a line once in awhile, let me know how things are going. Will you do that? And no roommates, please. You don't have any kids? Here, I'll write my address for you. Tell me about yourself. What's a nice girl...?"

"That's a dumb line, McCain. But thank you—it's lovely here, and I.... Why would I want to live here? I'm a hermit, I guess."

"Was it always that way?"

"No, not really. Mom and Dad live in Seattle, but I split right after high school graduation—came down to Sonoma State to study psychology, that mostly. Didn't quite graduate, though. You want to hear all this? Okay, okay. I hooked up with a guy in grad school, and that was good for awhile. Then he got into heavy drugs, and one night he nearly killed me. Things were going downhill anyway, so I just left. I wandered around for a month or two and then ran my VW into a pine tree just outside of Diggins. No insurance, naturally, not the kind that would pay for repairs. So there the bug sits, a one-headlight wonder. Still runs, though. Anyhow, this area seemed like a good place for me to stop for awhile. I found a part-time job and...."

"Decided to squat in my cabin," Isaac nodded.

"Something like that."

*

The conversation drifted on, but at length Isaac McCain rose to his feet.

"I've got to be going, young lady. It's nearly noon already, and I have a long road ahead of me. Nine, ten hours if I push it. I'm glad I came down, and I'm pleased to have met you, Ms. Singares, rifle and all—old Doom here wanted to see the home place—I'd never brought him here before."

Isaac moved toward the door, then turned and shook hands with Iphigenia, raised her hand, kissed it.

"My lady," he continued, "you've got to get over this bad habit of yours—shooting at your landlord. Drop me a line, you hear? Maybe I'll come down this way next summer. Right now, I have some serious thinking to do."

She nodded, smiled as he exited. From the window she watched as the tall man ambled up the old road to where he said he'd left his car, and once again she thought, this time out loud, "Yes, I like him."

*

A few hours later he returned.

"Didn't really think you were leaving," Ginny said as she opened the door for him. "I don't know why, but I guessed you'd return. You decide what to do?"

McCain sat down by the fireplace, leaned forward.

"Iphigenia," he said, "I've just resigned my damned professorship. I want to stay here. Well...I simply can't go back to that life. I lost myself somewhere along the road. You keep the cabin, though, just as I said before. I'll stay in Dad's printshop for a time, then maybe head on over to Colorado country. There are one or two mountains I haven't scrambled up yet. Plenty of room in the printshop, and maybe my father's presence is out there. This cabin's much newer. Dad built it the last year of his life—the old one burned down the summer of '54. The woman he was living with was killed in the fire—don't suppose you needed to hear that. Anyway, it's okay. I'll try not to bother you. If necessary, I'll build on another room. Don't want you to have to move out—because I probably won't be here all that long. Just need time to get my addled wits together."

She studied his bearded face, deep eyes.

"Could we be friends, Isaac? I mean, *just friends*? I'd like that very much. I don't want another old man right now...."

He grinned.

"I'm not precisely lapsing into senility, not yet anyway."

"You know that's not what I mean. It's just...I think we could be good friends."

Isaac McCain leaned back in his chair until it strained with his weight. He stroked his beard and smiled.

"Well, Yellow-Eyes, I've never had a *genuine* Platonic mistress before, but perhaps it would be a change for the better. One condition, though. No more shooting?"

She wanted to hate him for his smartass attitude—instead she tried to smile. But she couldn't actually look at him.

"Why are you laughing at me, McCain?" she demanded.

*

That evening he lit the old Coleman lantern. New mantles, and it worked perfectly.

Iphigenia Singares had never opened the printshop, and apparently no one else had either. A mildew-like dust was on everything. Rats had chewed stacks of paper which, upon examination, turned out to be ungathered signatures of his father's poems. The rubber ink-rollers for the antique Colt's Armory letterpress had fallen prey to rats and to the sun as well, chewed and partially melted. Rubber had peeled from the steel spindles like flesh from an arm bone.

Isaac gave the flywheel of the press a spin. It creaked as it turned. The one-cylinder steam engine that formerly powered the press, connected by pipes to a makeshift boiler outside, also appeared to be in more or less working condition, a twist on the heavy wheel suggesting that no parts were frozen up.

A pile of cotton padding was scattered in front of the sofa where he and his father had many times sat talking. Isaac walked to bookshelves that literally covered one long wall of the printshop, these laden with volumes to the limit of their capacity. A section of the uppermost shelf was filled with books Abram McCain himself had printed, nearly thirty of them, printer's copies, a collection no doubt rather valuable, the McCain Press archives. Rats hadn't touched these, though the rodents had chewed, seemingly at random, the bindings of other volumes nearer the floor. Isaac scanned the shelf left to right, over to the book of etchings his father completed the summer of his death.

One volume caught Isaac's eye—a shelf lower, thrust in between a *Complete Byron* and a copy of *Walden*. The leather cover was clearly the work of Abram McCain.

Isaac wiped dust from the binding, opened the book. It was a journal, hand-lettered in black ink. He thumbed idly through the pages, noting that most of the leaves were blank. Only the first few had been written on, and the introductory was dated June 13, 1955, the final entry inscribed July 11th the same year.

For a moment Isaac's vision blurred, his breath caught in his throat. These few pages apparently represented the final words his father was ever to write, for indeed July 11, 1955, had been the precise day when Abram McCain had committed suicide.

Isaac's hands were trembling as he lay the book down, for he realized the pages could contain proof of the last thing in the world he wished to know with certainty.

On the other hand, such a testament might well substantiate his father's claim of innocence.

"I'm not ready for this at the moment," Isaac said aloud, half addressing Doom and half himself. "Later. Later I'll read it through. Why didn't Hutchings and his men find this journal? They never thought of looking?"

*

The following day Isaac drove in to Diggins, the town much changed from his memories of it—with many of the old Gold Rush structures either refurbished or in the process of transformation. Whatever the cause, whether from tourist trade or the presence of a considerable enclave of counterculture people, artists, writers, musicians, dope farmers, and the like, there was an air of money and the odor of espresso coffee, with numerous antique stores, art galleries, and souvenir marts. The old Quonset-hut Purity Market was a market no longer, and Isaac resorted to a homegrown shopping complex, purchased groceries, and drove up the grade toward home.

Ginny wanted to refuse his *Santa Claus* gesture, but finally accepted, agreeing to cook dinner for the both of them.

"Hoping you'd offer," he laughed.

She pointed a finger at him and said in a low voice: "You sonofabitch!"

He entered the printshop, intending to put out rat poison— then realized he actually held no grudge against the rodents and, in any case, there was always a danger that Doom might get hold of the stuff.

"If you're still in here, Rat People," he intoned, "listen to what I'm saying. I'll grant you a reprieve, but you've got to get the hell out of my house. Go build your own bungalows in the woods. You're supposed to be wood rats—act like it...."

Only then did he think of the mule, Oliver.

And yes, the coyote, Abram's young coyote. What happened to them? The pup, of course, went wild again. About the mule—who could say? Perhaps a hunter had gotten it. Perhaps someone stole it. Isaac tried to imagine why anyone would wish to steal Oliver, for the beast had certainly been the most spoiled, cantankerous creature alive.

After a time Ginny called him to dinner. As they sat together, eating, Isaac attempted to maintain a pleasant conversation but was uncertain of the success of his efforts. Ultimately he pled exhausttion, thanked the young woman and complimented her cuisine, returned to the printshop.

He strode immediately to the bookshelf, took down his father's journal. He lit the Coleman, pumped it to white brilliance, hung it from a nail, and sat down in Abram's rocking chair. He turned to the first page and began to read.

But Doom was scratching loudly on the board-and-bat door.

"Damn it, sir," Isaac called out, rising, "is nothing sacred to you?"

                    *

June 13, 1955:

This morning it seemed to me a fire was burning, but the haze was apparently only within my skull. The past year, in fact, has been little more than a blur and a haze for me: but now, I believe, for reasons I cannot comprehend, I'm returning to clarity.

Throughout my life I have never followed a well-worn path if I could help it; and hence, I suppose, those who have known me have always considered me an eccentric. But this year in particular, ever since Elizabeth was burned to death, my mind has not been my own. Some of the things I have done I do not wish to recount, not even to myself. The horror of it is that my actions have controlled me rather than the reverse. It's entirely possible, even, that I've done things which I simply do not remember—so fragile is a man's mind, so powerful his innate drives. My son Ike came

down from the fire camp this afternoon, and we dry washed some
black sand—good ore, and we got a couple of ounces. I felt happy
again, for my son's a fine young man—such shoulders on him, and
nearly as tall as I am—ha! ha! He's proud to be able to look me
straight in the eye. I think maybe he'd like to try me at wrist-
wrestling. Well, he's watched me practice the art on numerous
occasions.

Then it's only a matter of time. My strength is waning, and his
increases. Sometimes, though, such strength is not a blessing—as
my own father, True Bear, told me once or twice.

Elder brother, Axe, I don't think he ever got that figured out.
Requiescat in pace, both of you.

May my son Last Bear be protected from the demon that
sometimes possesses me—and no doubt upon occasion possessed
all the McCain and Goffe men before me.

I guess it's a certain vile worm that lives in the brain.... But
now my mind is clearing: and so I begin this book, which, in itself,
should effect a kind of therapy. Yet I know well enough there's no
substitute for the blessed company of other human creatures.

Isaac's away at Berkeley during the school year, so I see him
now only on holidays and weekends in the summer. I think I'd be
all right if he were with me, but my problem's my own, and he
must live his life.

So now I propose to write a bit each day, to keep a most
exacting record of the rhythms of my mind. Whether I shall mark
each passing day's events, or whether I shall ramble, and thereby
synthesize the pattern of my life, I cannot at this moment determine. But write I shall, so long as my intellect is what I may fairly
call my own.

It is begun.

*

June 14, 1955:
These hills are endless in their delights: for all the shades and
colors of the Lord and Olelbis the Dreamer alike breathe over
them. I rose up early this morning and shared my breakfast with
Horse, my coyote pup. We went out together to watch the
sunrise—though I was half afraid, since this was the first time I'd let
him out of the house since I captured him, that he might well run
off into the forest, and I should have seen the last of the little bush-
tail. But he's becoming a dog by degrees, and he stayed close at

my heels. It's almost as though he has forgotten the out-of-doors, the wildness that was his by birthright and I guess mine too.

Well, it's true. I was born and raised in Upper Eden, and there's a certain poetic justice in that fact, I suppose, for I was the late offspring of distinguished parents, both of them Halfbreeds: True Bear, a cattle rancher and gunman, a man who went to Harvard, and Fire Woman, one of Ishi's kin—her mother raped by a Whiteman she later killed—Fanny they called her, she was an ally to Captain Jack, later chief madam for Huntington's operations, *yclepped* "The Queen of Reno," a little hell-raiser.

Poems. If the Lord gives me sufficient time, I may well have another volume of verses left in me, for indeed there's yet much to describe, such a grand variety of things to paint into words.

When I was still young, I used to fear that I might eventually run out of subject matter, but it hasn't happened.

Horse and I saw two large mule deer at the far end of the meadow, their antlers still in velvet. And all along the creek, grapevines are in a profusion of new leaves. The azaleas bloom: their honey scent is all but intoxicating. On the first day of creation, the Grand Dreamer must have told azaleas to grow.

But sunrise this morning was exceptionally beautiful. It seemed to flow down the eastern ridges like a tide of burning white metal. What proof more than this does a man need—proof of the existence of God? The Old Man, as one poet claims, is a lover of beauty. His Highness squirms in the leaves of the compost.

                              *

June 15, 1955:

This will be a day for the recording of dates—not because I vainly suppose anyone will ever be concerned, but merely because I find myself in a mood to take written note of them.

Yes, I was born in Upper Eden, close by the mountain the Yana Indians used to call *Wahgalu* or *Waganupa*, otherwise known as Mt. Lassen, the fire mountain. The year was 1893, and the date October the 13th. I don't actually know whether it was a Friday or not, though a more systematic historian than I myself would no doubt do his proper research. My mother and my father were both in their forties when I came screaming into their world.

My older brother Axel was eighteen years my senior and a logger when he wasn't being simply a wanderer—a grand rebel, I suppose, for he was the only McCain [Goffe] in several generations not to have done significant time in the proper correctional facility known as Harvard College. Indeed, it was during one of his periods of helling around that he met and courted Yuba Sue Skillman, who became very much a loving older sister to me. They were a pair of thieves! Yes, but happy together, as though time were without end, and each day an invitation to adventure. Axel— Axe. Mother and Father must have sensed from the beginning what his fate was to be.

When I was exiled to Massachusetts, it was clear that True Bear saw in me the last hope for the family tradition. By sending Isaac to Berkeley, I suppose I've violated some kind of sacred trust, some family obligation or another. Yet if that's so, I was never fully informed—and besides, Ike's got a mind of his own.

My father returned to California in the eighteen-seventies and married my mother, *Auna-yi*, one of the few remaining Yahi Indians. True Bear (the name Dad went by rather than the more prosaic William) was reputed to have had a lightning-fast draw as a young man, and I gather that reputation got him into difficulties more than once. He was also a remarkable tale-teller, one given to a certain degree of mythic elaboration, I'm sure. But the stories he loved most dearly were about his own father, Old Benjamin, who'd come to California just after gold was discovered, turned renegade, fought with the Maidu against the Whites, and ended up as an Indian agent. If True Bear's stories are to be believed, Ben knew Sutter, Brannan, Marshall, the Greenwoods, Lassen, Bully O'Bragh, H.V. Olivo, Califia Beard, and Jim Beckwourth.

This madness of mine—I think my father planted it in my brain and may even have known exactly what kind of seeds they were. Young boys are impressionable, to say the least.

After I'd spent my time in Boston and returned to California, I foolishly decided against continuing my life at Upper Eden. Instead, I opened a printshop in Los Gatos, thinking to produce books—perhaps even works of literature. I mastered my trade in due course and, as chance would have it, met Lucy Septien, a dazzling young woman of Spanish and Indian blood, an exceptionally loving nature, and a quick temper: too much like me for her own good. Even now I'm not sure who seduced whom that night on the beach near Point Sur, though at the moment I imagined myself the *agent provocateur*.

Thus ever the male of our species persists in delusional theory—while the woman brings the moment to crisis, then plays out the threads of fate.

We were married, and I took her to Upper Eden to meet True Bear and *Auna-yi*-Fanny. Lucy fell in love with the mountains and demanded that we relocate. I was still unwilling to go home, however, and so we began to look for a piece of land of our own.

We found this meadow, quite by accident, on July 4th, 1920—and that day, in all real ways, was our independence. Here we lived, happy as your proverbial raccoons in a vineyard—until the moment of her death.

Those who believe lightning strikes but once in a place are wrong, quite wrong. The ruins of my life are proof of this unfortunate truth. In any case, from the time of Lucy's death, I might well have entered a desert and not returned—except for my son Isaac.

In the aftermath of Lucy's death, I was broken, helpless, used-up—but I had a child to raise. My sister Jessie came to help out and stayed for two years, after that returning to Upper Eden and there presiding over the deaths of True Bear, *Auna-yi*, Yuba Sue, and Axe—in that order. Thereupon she herself committed suicide.

When Big Sis left, I was father and mother to Isaac as well as I could be. Those were the war years, and finally I took another mate and learned about lightning. I grasped toward life and am punished for it.

So here is the desert—it's come to me, takes possession of my bones and brain, and I'm alone with Horse the Hound.

                              *

June 16, 1955:

The Mexican Spanish came into California to establish great ranchos and a string of missions whose task it was to Christianize the native peoples, something intended through slavery and the crushing of indigenous cultures.

The first Anglos, Bostons rather, on the other hand, were adventurers—men in search of new lands for trapping beaver—Jed Smith, Joe Walker, Joe Meek, Jim Beckwourth, Kit Carson, John Frémont, the latter no doubt with American territorial claims clearly in mind.

Next were the Argonauts, Benjamin Goffe among them, whose minds were compelled by a vision of gold. Indeed, most of these men apparently saw nothing beyond the gold under the rocks. Greater riches eluded them, so obsessed they were. I've tried to imagine these hills as they must have been on the day of my own birth, but already there were far too many humans—and already the great hydraulic mines had ceased to operate and seedlings had begun to sprout among the diggings. In fact, the ravishment began almost immediately, madness of '49 and '50 and the decades afterward. The turning of rivers, blasting down after quartz veins and what they held, washing away of entire mountainsides.

When I look backward in time, I always seem to see an autumn landscape. I perceive men working with sluice and rocker box— every stream bed, then the sands and gravels higher up, even thin auriferous veins deep in the earth. Monitors and whole rivers of water directed against the hillsides! The cliffs at Malakoff are nearly four hundred feet high....

Such men they were, the ravagement of Terra, of Queen Caliphia herself. Is it not strange, though? For the earth springs forever virgin and untainted. In my lifetime I have observed two world wars drift obscenely by, and yet the old equation holds. Mankind, in the end, will be eroded from the hills. Give the planet a few thousand years, a few million at most, and all will be silent again, at least to human ears.

Ben, grandfather that I never knew, tell me what it was like! Ah, you came too late. The gold, the gold had already been found by then. But there are worse things, and those lie in the other direction—down the waves of the future. You know, in the space of a century or a little more, our West-faring pioneers destroyed vast herds of buffalo, perhaps seventy million of those fine ani- mals—or were their numbers already diminishing in a perverse lemming rush to death? And here in California, our grizzlies have vanished, our tule elk nearly gone, the condors winging away into black extinction. Many, many other creatures besides—the beavers, the whales, God knows what all. We've destroyed damned near everything we've touched.

But if you want bad dreams, I mean really bad dreams, sir, then take a look down the future with me. All over the planet I see wilderness vanishing. I see cities growing ever more monstrous. I see us pitching nuclear bombs at one another, the new ones made from unstable hydrogen. I see millions starving. I see anarchy loosed, prowling mobs, hysteria beyond all bounds. Something even more strange and wonderful: millions dancing, millions dying, bodies lying about like drifts of windblown snow, a terrible stench, overpowering, throughout the land. I see bodies everywhere—men and women and children. Fires are burning. Mother Earth moves, shifts her plates about, and cities fall down. Vast waves of water pour over the land. A sea beyond the Cascades and Sierra, and new canyons gorged to the sea. Then I see a good thing: it is quiet again. Whole forests regenerate, and the rivers run clear. By God! It takes strong vision to see that far.

As for myself, Lord knows there are plenty who think I'm crazy, and I suspect they're right.

*

June 17, 1955:

How often we human critters confuse material holdings with inner quality. Is not almost precisely the reverse the truth? Do we not grow ever more corrupt with each single material object our madness forces us to possess?

The passage of time smooths memory.

Lucy Septien! My dark-skinned, raven-haired beauty, the mingled blood of Mexican Spanish and Ohlone, her people drawn into the Missions some generations ago, neophytes with numbers assigned to them—immortal souls given numbers, and mortal bodies set to the tending of vines and the raising of cattle.

A girl growing up in a patched-together shack high in the coast mountains, close by the Ventana Cones—eleven brothers and sisters in all. Fire in her veins, that one! Even now, after all these years, it's virtually impossible for me to believe she's gone— vanished into the Spirit World of her people and mine, whoever they are, genetic threads interwoven, the European and the North American, Halfbreeds both of us, and both of us wanderers in a world we were never capable of accepting. At times I considered us as representative members of a new race, but that's simply foolishness. Both worlds are dead and gone.

What did that poet say? *Where are the snows of yesteryear?*

Now we've got lightning in a bottle. The woods are dry, and those who guide the world's master-nations are fond of striking matches—like insane children who've found an old powder shed, complete with dynamite, caps, and fuse. In a little while, in a little while....

Lucy, dark-eyed beauty, Salinas Valley loam stained into the palms of her hands.... She accepted my quirks when another would not have, and she worked like a man as we built our cabin here in the meadow. She followed me always with a blind and loving faith, followed when I had no genuine idea where I was leading. Such, perhaps, was her greatest flaw—she was inexplicably set upon following this half-crazed vestige of a century past, this hulking creature born out of his proper time.

Ah! We made love, though. At times I wondered if we might not wear out our sexual parts. A few years of utter abandon....

Then our son came—pilgrim from one huge night to another— and you, *Señora Septien*, you sat there and strummed a guitar and sang, and damned if it didn't work. He always stopped crying.

Lucy, I've done my best. It's been difficult without you, for Isaac has not known the kind of love that only a mother can give. But love he's had, for you live within him.

Sometimes at night I awaken to find you've vanished from beside me. My bed is empty now.

Our son, Ike McCain. I'd fight Old Man Gawd before I'd hurt that boy. You remember how it was, Lucy—Lucinda Brown Eyes—the one ragged edge to our happiness was that we came to believe it impossible for us to have children. We took our pleasure and preferred not to worry the matter. Fifteen years passed here on Deer Creek, and then after dinner one night you smiled at me in the mysterious, private way of the woman, and I knew even before you spoke. Surprise and elation—you were with child. You were thirty-nine when our son was born, and I some four years older.

The blessing came, but not ours to enjoy together long—for there's fire in everything. It spurts out at times, burns to the quick, to the core, to the bone.

*

June 18, 1955:

The madness I fear came upon me once more this morning. Unhappy wretch that I am, I believe I have butchered some more of that fellow's sheep. I'd think it a dream, but I had blood all over my shirt when I came to my senses this noon.

It's fortunate for my own sanity that I have to deliver books to the bindery in San Francisco. I imagine Mr. Hutchings, a very fine man and I think my friend, will no doubt be up to talk with me this afternoon. He'll guess correctly that I was responsible. I'll not be here to meet him, but I will leave sufficient money to pay for what I've done.

*

June 19, 1955:

I was twenty-three when I received my M.A. from Harvard, thus playing out whatever ritual or tradition was established at some indeterminate point in time between old Will Goffe in Restoration days and Grandfather Benjamin—and no doubt his father before him—and his father as well. New England's all right, as they say, but I never wished to live there—though the region, away from the Hub at least, is certainly archetypally American. Henry David & Ralph Waldo & and old Judge Hathorne & fair Bradstreet & King Philip and the vanished tribes—the ghosts of Indian dead, indeed, everywhere across this entire continent.

William True Bear Goffe McCain, he talked me into it. That wild-eyed old gun-slinging renegade and probably none other than Oleli Coyote in disguise. It's a terrible responsibility—having a man like that for a father: and here I am, halfway grown up and past sixty, the Halfbreed son of Halfbreed parents of highly questionable sanity. *Homo halfbreedus*, an American subspecies....·

New England. Mostly I think of proper young women with parasols and small, high-pitched voices. That and the wind running in off the ocean and across the woods and marshes of Cape Cod.

No, it all started when Lucy Septien and I bought that Model T and quite by chance found this meadow. We laid a mining claim on it and eventually got patented title. Gold enough on the hill above the creek to make the whole thing seem reasonable, and we went to work to build our little house and a workshop for the presses we intended to buy. We labored together, hauling in the lumber, driving nails. Then the Colt's Armory we bought from the Grabhorns themselves. It was a joyful time for both of us.

Not even Adam and Eve dreamed so together, yet mankind swims against a steady current. The Maidu people speak of Land Above, the Upper Meadows—and perhaps that was the reason Ben McCain called his place Upper Eden, I don't know. Well, our Upper Eden was at the bottom of this canyon, and damned if I know of a better place. After death, I want to come back here, but there's a condition. You listening, Old Coyote Man? Lucy's got to be here too.

*

June 20, 1955:

Even this morning at sunrise (Horse and I out in the fields once more), the hills were blue-gray with smoke. We climbed the ridge to the rocky outcrop, and I could see a plume off to the north, perhaps fifteen miles away as your proverbial crow flies. I imagine Isaac's working on that fire—he and his friend Madison and the others. I hope the blaze is controlled soon—the weather's hot and dry, and a strong wind would eat the mountains for miles around. Some kinds of fire purify, assuage grief—as in the old *Ustu* ceremonies of the Maidu. But there's another kind of fire, and that's a primal enemy: fires outside and fires within.

I detect some jealousy in Oliver, my mule. He tried to kick Horse this morning at feeding time. I swear, there's a good deal of human in that long-eared beast. Who but I would put up with him? If ever there's work to do, the wretch rebels. He likes sugar, though, and will often accept that as a bribe. It's not the best wages, but better than none. Oliver's pride requires payment. Too much like me for his own good. A truism here, perhaps. Let's call it the McCain Function.

To the extent that man, beast, tree, or rock resembles Abram McCain, to that extent trouble's inevitable.

Well, I make a damned poor Job. I'd suspect Old Man Coyote of some kind of droll jest, but the God-Dog is probably off hunting mice.

*

June 21, 1955:

I can still see smoke to the north, but less of it today. Apparently the demon is being quelled. And today is the longest day of the year, solstice. Elemental truth: longest day or not, today's twenty-four hours in duration, just like all the rest.

Horse and I were out again this morning to watch the sunrise. I didn't check the time, though perhaps I should have. I've always had trouble with time and ought to keep better track of it—my Indian heritage, no doubt. Well, contemporary humans kill themselves with clocks and schedules and calendars, ignoring the obvious rhythms of the seasons. In any case, sunrise was beautiful, the entire eastern sky a dull red color—owing to smoke in the air. What irony that destruction breeds such beauty, the rules etched deep into the metal plate.

Oliver followed me down to the creek, and I splashed water on him. He may well be angry now and nursing a grudge.

Leopard lilies are up all along the stream bottom, and buds are forming. I dug one up once: their bulbs look like green pine cones and hide deep. I don't think they intend to be unearthed, and don't like it at all. Wildness ever resists domestication.

*

June 22, 1955:

The feral element's inherent, and no man can resist it—not face to face. This so apparently peaceful earth is in reality an unending sequence of living and dying—and there, perhaps, is the quiet and unbelievable beauty of things, as the poet says. Even trees fight one another for sunlight. Pines grow upward for survival, and yet a wondrous balance is somehow maintained, ever shifting slightly about and dynamic, but constant in that dynamism. I did not know this truth when I first came to Deer Creek, Lucy and I—though I should have known. After all, when a boy's been raised at Upper Eden and has had his head filled with lying tales by Brother Axe and Papa True Bear....

I remember an early autumn, years ago, about a month before Isaac was born. Up on Burlington Ridge I came upon an old stag mule deer, stumbling and blind and ready for death. Three coyotes were following along, alert, waiting, their tails whipping back and forth. The mule deer knew, but he wasn't quite ready yet, I guess. I shot the deer, and the coyotes slunk off, none too happily, into the brush. I dressed out the carcass and hauled it down the mountain, hung it up on the side of the printshop. But by morning the body had been shredded—those same coyotes. Who else? Why did the little brush wolves do such a thing? They wanted their meat, and I had stolen it from them. I turned the matter into a game without realizing. So they followed me and watched and waited. Then, as I slept, they despoiled the carcass, no doubt having a high old time in the process, though they didn't actually get much to eat. A hell of a game.

Is it possible that Old Man Coyote, imperfect agent of the Perfect Dream, urges his younger brothers on? Let's see now: if I had taken their meat, then I became their meat. It wasn't just the remains of an aged mule deer that was left hanging on the printshop wall. It was none other than Abram McCain, crucified, desperately hoping to learn something. Those who play Odin take chances. It was me the brush wolves tore down, and I learned the lesson of all crucifixion.

Joyful, merciless cunning of wildness. Utterly amoral—because that don't apply. Utterly non-human. Living and dying and fierce and happy.

*

June 23, 1955:

Fire has killed the two women I've loved, Lucy Septien and Elizabeth Collingwood too, she who came to me at a time of great need. Three times I have built this cabin on the same foundation, but the run of future seasons, I now realize, has grown much shorter for me.

Perhaps I should learn to use fire myself. Perhaps a failure to learn the proper use of fire has been my undoing.

It's true that the forest actually desires the caress of flaming tongues. I believe so. Flames play their part, are the agency of some force beyond them, a force given to whim, utterly patient and at the same time impatient. Old Man Gawd: he's a sculptor who never rests, is never satisfied and yet is endlessly satisfied, who ceaselessly alters his creations, oblivious to time and exempt from it, so that His grand *mobile* is forever in motion, in change, in flux. The process is constant, and its component elements consist of change, alteration, and transformation.

Elizabeth Collingwood, you were my companion for a year and a half. You needed a man, and I needed a woman—the male *I* and the female *O*. I could not care for you as I cared for Lucy, and yet, in the time allotted to us, we drew close. Isaac brought you here, and together we sought wild honey.

These things just happen. I haven't been punished, and I've not been abused. No, it's a trick in the human brain—the curse and blessing of sentient memory. The living and dying: we are part of *IT*. Our flares of consciousness should be strong enough to accept, but they're not. In quiet moments of solitude and vision, perhaps, we are able to accept the conditions of our existence, but at other times we rage at the unalterable stars.

So here I am, a maniac citizen in the realm of King Dwight Eisenhower, a monarch benign by nature and yet one who, like old Marcus Aurelius perhaps, has accepted his public role and otherwise kept quietly to himself. The man has been a leader of armies and architect of the great invasion of Europe, just as it is now given to him to guide the destiny of what we foolishly call the *civilized world.* Yet what does it all amount to?

That sow black bear up canyon is more civilized.

In another age, I might also have been a leader—but not King Dwight's kind. No, I might have been a Thomas Moore or a Ben Franklin, though. Better yet, since I'm playing the child's game of pretend, a healing priest in a Maidu village, *Kuksu,* leader of the Big Head religion, one capable of expunging *omeya* and directing the *wulu* dance, wielder of *yompea.* I might have communed with *Olelbis,* The One Who Sits Above, and made wise pronouncements to the people of *Kul-kumish.* My grandmother, after all, was *Kuksu,* and so was her sire before her—according to my father, True Bear.

Well, the present's the present. And what I meant to say: Elizabeth, I loved you well, and I think you knew it.

Why was it that you didn't find a man when you were still young?

What beautiful thighs you had!

Oliver's nuzzling the door—I suspect he wants me to pull him some more carrots. He's ravenous for the yellow roots. Long Ears has a host of vices, but most of them are harmless, I'd say.

                                    *

June 24, 1955:

I drove to Diggins this morning for supplies. It irritates me sometimes the way folks seem to draw away from me now. I suppose I'm becoming a legend of sorts. *Madman McCain.* Thus. It's all right. We put up with one another, the human race and I. But will my son eventually draw away from me also? That would be the final and worst blow.

Well, Louis Kelly still talks to me, Old *Lalook,* theoretically the chief of the Nisenan Maidu, you know—Lou must be about seventy now. He's a good fellow, but hard to communicate with owing to the fact that he's deaf as a granite boulder. I bought him a beer, and he nodded and pretended to understand what I was saying.

I heard Oliver bray: he came clopping to the door, stood close by the house. I took my thirty-ought-six and went outside, the coyote with me, his hackles up. An odd odor hung in the air, faintly discernible, just for a moment—a breath of wind up from the creek.

"It's that bear, Ollie," I said. "Old black bear, she's hungry."

I found her down in the shallow pool, and she rose from the water when she caught my smell.

"Hey, ugly woman!" I hollered. "You're giving my mule fits. You get on home now, you hear me?"

She backed out, stood up, moved her head one way and then the other, looking for all the world like Hugh Glass' friend when she got ready to hug him. Black bear was trying to get me in focus. I've read that bears are abominably nearsighted, but I'm not certain I believe it. I shouted and moved forward, but the bear didn't retreat.

I thought best to stop.

Horse was hissing, half-growling, but he was safely behind me—or so he supposed.

And the sow said, "McCain the printer is it? Well now, old man, if this ain't my home, then just where in hell is my home? You answer me that."

She settled slowly to all fours, turned, moved in bear-fashion off into the woods. She didn't hurry, and she didn't look back. I know the condition of amused disdain when I see it.

Human beings are mostly an annoyance to bears, and that's why there aren't any more California grizzlies. Blacks have better dispositions and are more given to simple avoidance, and hence they've survived. Problem is, blacks and grizzlies both lived too long in a world without rifles, and they couldn't really believe the two-legged apes could harm them. In old Maidu days, *Pano* the Grizzly was a chief god, and it's hard to say whether the furry people or the hairless people were more successful in killing the other. Any spot where a bear slew a man was sacred, though.

The grizzly's gone, but the black isn't afraid of us either. Bears haven't adapted too well. Traditionalists, that's what they are.

*

June 25, 1955:

I spent this morning re-reading Plato's *Timeus*. I find it difficult to believe the ancient stories could speak so consistently of catastrophe, of oceans overwhelming the land, of mountains rising, and the like if there were not a grain of truth. Possibly this Velikovsky fellow will cause our geologists and historians to do some thinking.

Well, not likely—now that I consider the matter.

True Bear loved the tale of how waters covered the world and how Turtle and Clown-Coyote floated about on a raft until World

Maker came and caused the Yuba Buttes to rise out of the gray waves. Then the man from the sky planted *Ootimsaa*, the Maidu *Yggdrasil* tree. All twelve kinds of acorns. After that, everything else was created.

I've long pondered the meaning of Homer's phrase, *wine-faced sea*. The brine must have been red to red-gray, for the references are general in ancient texts. Even these mountains of mine bespeak tremendous upheavals in the not-too-distant past. A man would have to be blind not to see and know that ice lay over these peaks to depths of perhaps several thousand feet—and blinder still not to realize that these gravel ridges we wash down for gold are the remnant of some tremendous flooding. Why is it, I wonder, that all the gravel is quartz, and yet there's precious little quartz in the high country? Evidently, then, the gravels came from somewhere else. But where? And how?

North of here the mountains change, fan out, the rocks are different. Beyond Feather River the forms are volcanic and much more recent, Cascade volcanism—and Mt. *Tehama* where I grew up, is just a huge hole to the south of Lassen, *Wahgalu*. But sixty miles east, across the valley, the rocks are like the Sierra again—same granite, same dirt. I'd say the range was sheared in two, the northern part thrown westward and left there, with new rock bubbling up from inside the earth to replace mountains that were torn away. New peaks forming—*Tehama* that blew up, Lassen and Shasta, Medicine Lake Crater pouring out a thousand square miles of lava, and a long string of snow peaks running up into Canada....

But what do crazy old hermits like me know? Coyote Gawd, fiddling with the sculpture. All the mysteries of creation lie about my feet, and I am blind. The Green Must impregnates, and the flow continues. But now is the time of its ebbing.

No. Only a human ebbing, a minor matter, and that won't come for a while—not until there are so many of us we all go mad, and I won't be around to worry about the matter by then.

Ha! ha! The mountains will spew fire again in time, and the skies will come down to touch the earth. Then Coyote will use pine trees to push the heavens back into place, just as he did once before.

*

June 26, 1955:

I wonder why the salmon return? To die. To lay their eggs and die.

Summer continues, and I'm waiting for something to happen.

Smoke.

Afternoon light is a dull yellow.

Sister Jessie, why did you commit suicide? There was no reason, no reason—just too much of death all around you. But darkness comes soon enough for all of us. You and I, Jessie, son and daughter to a pair of rebels. By God, they loved life more than any of us. True Bear McCain and Fanny Bitler, she was Queen of Reno in her youth. We came from good seed, good earth, both of us, Jessie. Damn it, I wish big brother Axe were here with me right now. That lanky tree-killing stump-humper had a sense of humor and knew how to use it, too.

There's no one at Upper Eden these days—just a couple of Maidu boys running cattle on the old spread, Big Woodpecker's grandsons. Their lease money pays the taxes, not much more.

*

June 27, 1955:

More gold's in the mountainside that I had suspected. I seem to have hit a rich vein. Well, I'll blast deeper into the earth to see what's there. I've no use for the gold, of course. It's an irony—I'm halfway a rich man by the world's standards, but that's if one counts up worth in dollars and land. Yet I know well enough the only riches that matter lie elsewhere, and on those grounds I'm wealthy and poverty-stricken at the same time.

If I have no use for the gold, then why do I seek it?

Is it not the mystery of the darkness, the coming into contact with earth itself, on its own granular terms?

Let's call this a day's writing. Old Halfbreed Injun, he's tired. Heap tired. Wagh!

*

June 28, 1955:

The little spring's nearly dry. In all the years I've been here, that spring has never failed completely. But this summer, that's something else. Nearly two more months before the first rains come....

I find it remarkable that in my sixty-second year, I feel no different, so far as I can recall, than I did at thirty. In truth, sixty-one isn't all that old. The big black oaks and ponderosas on the ridge, they're older than I am. If they complain, they do it quietly.

Hell.

Maybe what I'm really saying is that I need a woman: the primal heat runs through me, and I find myself daydreaming of breasts and buttocks—so strong the warm tide of life. Famous men, celebrities and that sort, most all manage to find young women to sleep with them. Guiltily I make note of nymph-like females who wander aimlessly along the streets in Diggins, their movements shouting out sexuality, shouting in voices they cannot themselves even hear: *Ravish me! Give me release! Prod me into life! Put life into my womb, you dim-witted male animals. God gave you the job, then do it....*

But they look at me and laugh. With this big carcass of mine, I look more ancient than I am. No, they're after slim-limbed boys—when they aren't daydreaming about Elvis Presley. Well, I like listening to the kid sing myself.

Part of me's grown old at least, otherwise I wouldn't wonder whether it's wrong to have such thoughts. Coyote Lord, he keeps the fires running through my frame. Maybe I'm supposed to get another child.

After all, a Maidu chief might take a young wife—someone to nurse him when he grew old and his other wives died or perhaps also needed nursing—though I don't detect any young ones trying to climb *Lalook*'s bones. On the other hand, if they called to him, how could he hear them? But just between you and me and the bedpost (dear Imaginary Reader), I know well enough there's not a woman alive under forty who's got her wits about her—and the same's true of men.

The Coyote-Dionysus Factor—that fire's got to die down a bit before we're capable of seeing anything very clearly.

The questions I ask myself are meaningless, of course. In any case, it isn't a matter of growing old. It's just that I'm like a gray-muzzled bull buffalo, and the herd's left me behind. I wander my prairie, bellowing.

Fair enough. These mountains, at least, are mine. I earned title years ago. I should have wrestled that black bear. Might have been a good way to go. Nothing that lives lives forever, and there's no *forever* in any case, not for the varmints that wander about on

the earth—only the *forever* of incessant change, and it's our
challenge to accept what is. But something's about to happen. I
can feel it coming. Whatever it is, I'll face it. Better to hug death
to one's chest than to die running. That maverick, Axe McCain, he
put the idea into my head years ago.

How is it out there in the darkness, older brother? Chances are
you're up in the White Mountains, sharpening your misery whip,
staring at the biggest damned bristlecone in the world, and looking
sex-crazed—and probably drinking an Acme beer to boot.

There's a certain inevitability about things, and a man should
go down grinning. That poet over in Carmel says so. He sits on
his ledge, I on mine.

These mountains are beautiful beyond description. I shall walk
the high ridge tonight after the flaring of sunset. Horse and I, we'll
do it.

A big buck mule deer was drinking at the creek this morning,
his antlers still with the velvet upon them. He glanced up, sensed
my presence, and was gone.

So it is.

*

June 29, 1955:
There are loggers up the creek. I believe they intend to take
out that huge grove of sugar pines and firs. Such ravishment of the
forest should not be allowed. Those trees have been growing for
more than two centuries, and that's longer than this Republic's
been afoot.

How needlessly destructive man is, and for what? The magnificent trees will become beams, boards, plywood—houses, at last,
in Sacramento and Bay Area suburbs. But the worth of what the
simple loggers destroy is so great! Shouldn't be allowed, shouldn't
be tolerated.

This fall when the rains come, I'll walk over to that grove and
find—a hillside of stumps, piles of slash, and raw and bleeding
earth. I have ever hated all loggers on principle, even though my
older brother was precisely that, and I loved him dearly, needless to
say. Even Axe, archetypal bull of the woods that he was, eventually
grew sick to the soul with what he was doing and turned away from
it all.

What a strangely perverse urge this is—to lay out the last of the
virgin timber, as though that were indeed the ultimate purpose and

goal of logging. Those who would copulate with Persephone in this utterly perverse manner, tying her up and whipping her first, they are mouths without minds, totally insensitive to the forest, to the beauty of stillness and vegetation. But I give them too much credit—those with the great fortunes, intent merely upon making their fortunes larger. They've never looked for Artemis, naked, bathing—and aren't interested in the slightest. If anything, they worship the gods *Money* and *Progress*.

Come to think of it, I'm not overly fond of cattle ranchers, sheep ranchers, or real estate developers either—nor the government boys with their compulsion to build dams. Given the chance, I'd stake them all out over hills of red ants. What it is: too many people upon the land. Too many machines. Ii half the world's population went under all at once, it would not be too much. We've been tree-eating locusts, mountain-eating gophers for as long as we've been here. When only the Maidu hunted deer, it was all right. Their lives were simple and good—and often short—but they were one with the bears and coyotes and vultures. This land was theirs, and they belonged to the land. My people.... Their ghosts are still around—one can see them flitting among the trees at twilight. Just necessary to look closely, that's all.

Quite possibly I *am* one of those ghosts—and so is Lou Kelly. Those people, our people, stepped off the edge of time. Even Yuba Sue Skillman, Axe's wife, was Indian only in the sense of genetic linkage. Her culture had already vanished behind her. Hers and mine and Lucy's and Jessie's and Axe's.

I'd have bought that big grove of trees years since if that had been possible, simply to protect it from the intrusions of Sacramento housing developments. But the trees are on government land, and we all know the government's looking out for our best interests.

Consider, for instance, what a fine job they've done with the national parks. The miserable, city-bound fools! Farming trees, are they? I tell you, there's no sound in the world more hateful than the snarlings of chainsaws.

I exaggerate. Maybe there are one or two others.

                              *

June 30, 1955:
This evening I have committed an act of violence, and yet I have no pangs of conscience. My mind was my own. The loggers

have indeed cut some of the most beautiful of the trees, including that huge sugar pine with the great bent top. My action will not, of course, save anything, but a little constructive destruction is about the only thing that, in the long run, may save the damned human race.

Homo stupidus.

In his lust for money and in his hatred for nature, he's hellbent on destroying every beautiful thing. Wherever he walks, the grass dies, the animals die, and a sterile desert spreads out behind him. No, not a real desert—for there are few places that possess the possibilities for solitude or that embody the vastness and scope of Nevada's basins and ranges, for instance. What I'm talking about— a totally different kind of thing. It's time for the mountains to erupt. Lassen sputtered and blew for a time when I was still a young fellow and World War One was pulling down cities. Damned impressive, all in all. Come on, old Wahgalu, wake up! It's time for man to be wiped from the face of the planet. It'll come, soon or late, for I can feel the energies gathering. Jeffers saw it, and the critics ate him—or are doing their damnedest.

God curse the paltry lot of them, stupid little hothouse plants that they are, and may they all die of indigestion. Arbiters of taste, are they? A great job they did of preventing two world wars. The religion of the humanists! I can think of nothing that fits the human race less gracefully. Sometimes truth doesn't go down well. I feel the great Sierra shudder and tense. Put your ear to the ground near the Mono Craters....

Primal Force is in abeyance just now, but it's patient.

*

July 1, 1955:

I've spent this entire day working with my presses, cleaning them, oiling, putting trays of type into order, fiddling with the binding equipment. Yet I have no further projects in mind at the moment.

I'll need to get into touch with my friends in San Francisco—I need work. Voltaire was right, no question. Through a man's work alone he derives his identity. The madness is always there, waiting, waiting for a fellow to rest. Oh, the greatest rest is labor.

Yes, *Homo stupidus.*

We came down out of Eden to build the forge from whence would issue sapient man. Quick brains and facile hands. I think of the Maidu creation story—the animals argued about what man should look like. Old Elk, he thought we should have great antlers. The Goose that we should have long necks and powerful wings. And so forth. After much argument, all the animals except Coyote fell asleep. Thus Bush-Tail created us, made us look the way we do—so the other animals would cease their debate. But he gave us brains like his own—we're supposed to look like Coyote on the inside, but Old Man, he never does anything very carefully. I think some Weasel got into our skulls along the line. *My apologies, Master and Madame Weasel.* But something must have distracted the good Song Dog at a crucial moment, and if we're to amount to a hill of beans, we have to finish the job ourselves.

I imagine Sheriff Hutchings will be up to see me soon: good law officer that my old companyero is, he must have some suspicions about that busted-up logging equipment.

But I have no intention of paying a penny. I was careful to cover my tracks, and you know, loggers insist on using those saws. Sparks will fly. In weather like this, the duff rotten and dry, a red seed in the leaves can become an instant inferno.

*

July 2, 1955:

That young woman my son's so obsessed with is indeed a beautiful creature. Down town today, I noted her picture in the newspaper. She's lovely, no question. I can only wish that she has a mind as well as a body. Such women, I fear, often do not—or if they have minds, they discern no need for them. Old Gawd Coyote's careless in his acts of creation. Why doesn't he exercise a bit more foresight? And a bit more restraint? Probably takes time off to catch squirrels.

*

July 3, 1955:

Here's a parable for you: or perhaps it's a species of metaphorical autobiography. Well, a verse, in any case—

> I planted an apple tree
> And cautiously watered the thing.
> Indeed, the leaves came out—
> But they do not thrive.

Yet where I have watered,
Seven slim sunflowers have grown,
Uncalled for.
This morning
One is in bloom,
Facing east.
And I am bathed in tremulous vines
This day of killing heat,
My head garlanded by thorns.
Beads of sweat run into my eyes.
My winged horse
Is a stumbling Percheron—
I ride and eat and drink
Enormously, the heavy-footed beast
No doubt as drunk as I
And threatening to pitch me
Into the road, a sotted Caliban
With eyes of gold and cloven hooves.

Grandfather Benjamin, if I recall correctly, was supposed to have ridden a Percheron. He was a big lout, like me, I guess. Call it the McCain curse.

Are you at me again, Coyote-Head? Green fellow?

Go find a prostitute. Perhaps she can take care of you, can give that heavy body of yours some rest. Comb your beard, my friend, and scent yourself. Your blood can simply never be denied. Take a trip to Nevada. Mustang's a good place, all things considered. The professional ladies, they know how to milk one dry.

All right, then.

But for just now, I think I'll walk down to Diggins tomorrow and watch the parade. That should be a harmless pastime. I haven't been past Scott's Flat for some while. Maybe later in the week I'll drive to Nevada. Be ritually washed, manipulated, taken care of. A man my age shouldn't be possessed by such an urge. I tell you, it isn't fitting at all.

Ah, hell.

That's another myth. We learn more, but we do not grow wise. Neither are the sexual fires turned off.

*

July 4, 1955:
Got home late.

*

July 5, 1955:
I had just returned from a walk with Horse and Oliver, had fed the pup, fixed myself some coffee, then turned on my little battery-pack radio, something I seldom do.

That girl is dead—April Incendie.

I wonder if Isaac has heard? I hope he's strong—I know he loved her dearly, and the two of them might even have married eventually, once they got beyond the fighting stage. My son, I hope you're stronger than I am, for these are the body blows of the Lord. They're delivered, I sometimes imagine, to test us—to see if we'll break, to see if we're worthy. But worthy of what? And for what? The comedy goes on, this process of living and dying, of begetting and of losing. The pines struggle silently upward toward light. If it were not for the beauty, the shining out of things under stress, there would be no meaning.

God Dog. We laugh at your antics, muse when we hear you singing at night. But you're a *terrible* presence.

Horse sleeps on his pallet in the corner. He too has heard the words of the local radiocaster, but for him it is *sans meaning.* The Great Annihilation and the Great Compost do not affect him so far as he knows. He'll live out his little span in oblivious and non-conscious awareness. An animal, I observe, does not forget, but it doesn't remember either. The animal people appear to be unaware of time except for the passing of moments and the natural rhythms of the seasons and the sunlight and the darkness—hunger suggests and demands eating, and there's neither right nor wrong.

These are lies I tell myself—and predictably human lies at that. Are the words supposed to comfort me in some way? Have I not seen creatures experience grief, remorse, anticipatory joy? Have I not seen them plot things ahead of time, and do they not hate the idea of death just as much as I do? Get right down to it, there's precious little difference between creature-awareness and human-awareness. Friendship, love, high disdain, spontaneous antagonism—it's all there. And here am I, an old man, still spouting the lies my professors told me long ago—pretending not to hear the voice of my own blood, the whisperings among rocks, the thin cries of birds and the silent conversations of spiders.

But humans. Apes of consciousness, we're pulled constantly forward and back—so that the present moment, all we have of life, forever eludes us.

Be strong, Isaac my son. Grit your teeth and face into the light. The designs of Lord Coyote (or whatever we wish to call that perverse, centralizing force) are long and twisting. But somewhere, up ahead in the dawning, we will discover his reasons. Or the generations—the generations—will discover purposes, create and will become those purposes. Ike, for all I know the government's sent you off on a fire somewhere. You're swinging an axe, shoveling dirt, clearing out fireline. And thinking, yes, anticipating the next time you'll see *her*, rehearsing a conversation that will never take place, imagining kisses and embraces that will never....

I have heard sounds over a radio, and so I know. You may not have heard those synthetic syllables, and hence the world inside your head may not yet have undergone this transformation, one of thousands, even millions (greater or lesser) that lie ahead for you, their number determined only by the number of seasons your fate has set aside for you.

Son, I don't know what to say, how to act. I could drive up to Crooked Pines and tell you—be with you. And yet I might be intruding upon a time that's as holy as it is painful, a time when a man simply has to be alone.

Gawd's purposes....

Perhaps it's not humans, after all, who will discover them. Perhaps the little coyotes of the world will rise up on two legs in the time after human creatures have passed the way of buffalo and whale, and bark at dawn and discover they've barked out words. Can they be far from it now? Perhaps they're the ones, all along, who were chosen—and it's no simple coincidence my Indian forebears have revered the Big Coyote, the Old Man Who Does Everything. He's picked those who are more nearly like himself, in bodily appearance as well as intellect and cunning deviousness.

How did the blind poet at the beginning of all this damned civilization put the matter?

Grin and bear it. The phrase is a cliché now, but only because we lack the strength to bear, we lack the will to carry. This wandering down out of Eden is not an easy business, and that's why Grandfather Ben dubbed his special place *Upper Eden.* The motive was simple. He wanted to return, to reach out to an approximation of the prelapsarian condition—the Eden of Adam and Eve, the Upper Meadows of Maidu tradition, a place real and tangible to *Ooti*, my grandmother. Ben and Acorn Girl, they sought to join disparate elements, and thus the genetic threads descended to True Bear, to Abram, and ultimately to Isaac. A new race might have come of that except for the simple fact there was but one race all along.

Yet I believe we shall arrive at the source of things in time to come, whether human, coyote, or leapfrog. It's all one.

Pain is apparently a vital portion of the equation.

The great oak still grows on Estawm Yan, *Ootimtsaa*, the oak of creation. On a clear day, if I climb to the crest of the ridge and look westward, I can see the mountains of Estawm Yan, the buttes where they rise out of the valley floor—shattered remains of an ancient volcano, a Shasta-like being whose ideal structure, in Plato's sense, exists only in the minds of those who have chosen to imagine it—yes, and in the vast potential of ether.

On such a clear day I look—and though I cannot see the Great Oak, I know it is there. Neither was it ever given to me to witness the night fires of an *Ustu* ceremony, yet I know well enough the meaning of grief for the dead.

Isaac, you've just stepped into a new world, whether you're aware of it yet or not.

*

July 6, 1955:

*

July 7, 1955:

*

July 8, 1955:

*

July 9, 1955:

*

July 10, 1955:

*

July 11, 1955:

I have been run by dogs. I have eaten little in days. But I have passed beyond insanity now. The demon is at bay, and not the man.

I did not suppose such strength remained to me.

My son, Isaac, one day you will probably read these hand-scrawled pages, the only particular testimony, as it turns out, that I have to leave you. So let me tell you again what I told you last night.

Don't listen to them. I have been guilty of much in my life, and yet I have tried to live well. I've loved you sincerely, raised you to be a man. What else can I say?

Great God, Ike, I'd never do a thing like that.

For your own sanity, you must believe me. I am not innocent, but of this I'm innocent. You're strong, you have to be. You must accept. Neither humans nor any other animals are given choice in the matter.

Aut prodesse aut delectare. Morituri te salutamus.

I'd intended to say more, Isaac, but now there's another Demonic Presence that calls me, and the calling is such that I cannot resist it. This is my decision, my way, my solution to a problem that's gotten entirely out of hand.

Find strength in those things which are worthy of the best in you.

—A.McCain

***

Canto Three:
THE INTERLUDE OF ISAAC

IT SAW FROM THE HEIGHT AND DESERT SPACE
    OF UNBREATHABLE AIR
WHERE METEORS MAKE GREEN FIRE AND DIE,
    THE OCEAN DROPPING WESTWARD TO THE GIRDLE
    OF THE PEARLS OF DAWN
AND THE HINDER EDGE OF THE NIGHT SLIDING
    TOWARD ASIA; IT SAW FAR UNDER EASTWARD
    THE APRIL-DELIGHTED
CONTINENT: AND TIME RELAXING ABOUT IT NOW,
    ABSTRACTED FROM BEING, IT SAW THE EAGLES
    DESTROYED,
MEAN GENERATIONS OF GULLS AND CROWS TAKING
    THEIR WORLD; TURN FOR TURN IN THE AIR, AS
    ON EARTH
THE WHITE FACES DROVE OUT THE BROWN. IT SAW
    THE WHITE DECAYED AND THE BROWN FROM ASIA
    RETURNING:
IT SAW MEN LEARN TO OUTFLY THE HAWK'S BROOD
    AND FORGET IT AGAIN; IT SAW MEN COVER
    THE EARTH AND AGAIN
DEVOUR EACH OTHER AND HIDE IN CAVERNS, BE
    SCARCE AS WOLVES. IT NEITHER WONDERED NOR
    CARED, AND IT SAW
GROWTH AND DECAY ALTERNATE FOREVER, AND
    THE TIDES RETURNING.

[ROBINSON JEFFERS, "CAWDOR"]

*

The mountains celebrated their own *Ustu*, ritual moments of mourning for all who had died in the past year and in all the years that came before.

"Earth will heal," he said, "and after a time.... Nature is a becoming. We are not alone. I have just learned that. We are not alone."

The next day dense smoke settled over the hills, heavy, like fog, until a man's eyes watered and he coughed, while sun glared down a dull lifeless orange, everything withering before the heat—a cool breeze late in the afternoon, driving in from the west to disperse heat and smoke, the fire-demon held and eating in upon itself until nothing remained: inches of powdery ash settled in over the scar. But still there were little tongues of flame licking up out of stumps and fallen logs and places where duff had lain heaviest, small blue trails, exhausted, wavering, rising like steam from a high mountain lake in the first rays of morning, and burned-over earth was steaming and dead, waiting until the end of August and a soft rain, so that the next morning when people in Diggins arose, they would have to turn on gas heaters or light fires in trashburners or cast-iron stoves—for the heat would be gone.

Deer gliding through damp brush, ghost-like, soundless, they would shiver droplets on wild lilac, then stop, stand on hind legs like so many brown-skinned dancers, to nibble at red manzanita berries.

A chill in the air, morning and blue sky as hawks and vultures spiraled on currents of air—raccoons scuttling along creek bottoms, skunks rattling crisp leaves that dried in sunlight, a bluejay screamed and another answered, while a young coyote scattered quail into the air, a whirring of wings.

Something was changed. Wind said it in the soughing of pines. A turning reached, a point passed. The smell of the woods said it. An alder leaf fell, floated on stream water. The year transmuted to autumn, and that brought county fair time, cattle in stalls, sheep bleating, jars of home-preserves and vegetables displayed and judged and awarded ribbons, baskets of strawberries, lugs of polished apples and pears, purple plums, green vegetables, twists of alfalfa.

Carnival. Ferris wheel, fun house, penny arcade where young boys dropped in coins and turned a handle and witnessed a woman undressing, baseballs at lead-weighted milk bottles, stuffed pandas and cotton candy, snow-cones and candied apples, hot dogs and hot pasties, bingo games where one might win cans of coffee. Tacos and beer and square dancing.

*

Mother Lode country, west slope of the Sierra Nevada, peaceful since the gold fever had gone, unless fire got loose—or some demonic force within the human skull. Yet there was still gold, so old prospectors insisted—if a man just knew where to look for it and worked out the right potholes after the spring run or the

right stretch of gravel on the right river, perhaps a gravel bar just
below a steep ravine, outcroppings of cinnamon-colored sand high
up on ridges. People enjoyed thinking about hundreds of millions
of dollars worth of gold hidden in the till of Harmony-Washington
Ridge, of Malakoff, of Red Dog and You Bet, locked in by laws that
precluded further hydraulic mining. Those same people chose to
forget about what happened to Abram McCain.

*

Deer Creek flows thirty-five miles, from Big Tunnel Spring to
Narrows Dam, from dense fir woods down to buckeye and scrub
oak and digger pine, where the Yuba is checked and held.

Oh, the government boys would build bigger dams, huge arches
of concrete, and the curling green length of *Uva* or *Ubo* River
would no longer twist its green waters out into the Great Valley.

*Tame that tricky, hell-raising sonofabitch Yuba. Tame all of
them. There's a glacier of mining debris moving slowly down out of
the canyon and onto our croplands, red muds cover wheatfields and
olive groves. Dam the river for summer water, chase those miners
to Montana or Alaska....*

Midway along Deer Creek is the town of Diggins, California;
and upstream the water is clear and sweet, but below for several
miles it's better not to drink. Arm-length pike swim idly in pools,
and there are at least a hundred old mines along the creek, for the
streambed's been worked out nearly from one end to the other.

But the hills grew mellow and sleepy as autumn came, and sun
weakened through blue haze of late September. Orchards turned
rusty red, while oaks and poplars stood out a fine rich yellow
against green of big pines and cedars. Pine needles fell and
covered blackened earth and powdery ash. Aftermath of fire
melted and dissolved into earth again because of cool, steady rains.
Even in the heart of the burn, there were small groves of trees
where fire did not reach, these in contrast to bleak gray poles of
flame-killed sugars and ponderosas and firs. Squirrels chewed the
fallen cones to get at sweet, oily pine nuts—and grass appeared
mysteriously on bare earth.

In the cemetery above Diggins were two graves, one for a crazy
man, the other for a blond-haired young woman. Already no one
seemed to remember very much about them, for it's easier not to
remember. But the one grave would be tended regularly, while the
other would go unvisited for nearly two decades.

*

Coyote-Head took the hand of a girl in a white dress. She'd been tending cattle in the stalls, and he led her up through open steel gates, along a path out into a pocket of woods. There he'd stroke and kiss her breasts and finally strip her naked and turn her over under a thicket of birch, so that all one would see was a green haze of light. He would plunge into her, muffled screams and wild thrashings of arm and leg—until she bit into earth and endured forbidden ecstasy of violation.

"It isn't rape," Coyote Man winked, "not if the lady's willing."

*

Then there were just three children. They followed the stream into the forest until they came to a narrow ravine shaded by thick overarching arms of liveoak, leaves gray and black-green as in the middle of summer. The children paid scant attention to distance as they walked.

Isaac hummed a nondescript tune as they passed an abandoned mine, two strands of iron track twisting out into space at the end of a rock dump.

They sat beside the stream, and Betty Sue took off her shoes and stockings and splashed her feet in the water.

"I wish Tommy was here," she said. "Tommy can always think of something exciting."

A bird was perched on a knurled gray rock in the middle of the creek. April Incendie watched, noticing that every few seconds the body pulsed, small head mechanically moving up and down like a toy bird her father had bought and placed over a glass of water atop their console radio. She laughed. The ouzel started, skipped into air, whirred over the stream's still surface, and plummeted into the water. Then it repeated its performance, as if showing off.

All three children were watching as the bird disappeared into a copse of young cedars. Its song came then, clear and expansively melodious, a liquid whistle lasting only a few seconds. The two girls and the boy glanced at one another, but no one said anything.

At length they rose and walked away in the direction from which they'd come.

Once April returned alone, came back to see if the magic bird would appear again, waited under liveoaks, their great black limbs that made sunlight dim and pleasant and cool. She hoped to find

the bird, even mumbled a small prayer. But though she searched
up and down the creek and even called out in exasperation, she
neither glimpsed the ouzel nor heard its strange cry. Instead the
woods were quiet. Finally she became frightened, looked up at
heavy black branches blotting the sky, and hurried away.

"If I don't look behind me, it will be all right," she said.

*

Joanne Duboce wore a tight-fitting tee shirt, the cotton cloth
spattered with colors, like a Jackson Pollock painting. The nipples
of well-formed breasts stood out against the fabric, making it obvious to anyone that she wore nothing beneath.

"Do I have to do all the work?" she demanded.

Isaac looked up, winked, and blew her a kiss.

"Nice tits, Joe. I tell all my friends you've got nice titties."

"Ike, you chauvinist pig, you boorish goat, aren't you going to
help me unload the car? We've got a lot of work to do."

"You make the bed yet?"

"Damn it, McCain...."

"Why don't you take off that refugee from the Stumptown
Louvre? Hot as hell in here, and I feel like bobbing for apples."

"Get serious, you oversized dwarf!"

Isaac rose, stepped toward her, his hands extended toward her
breasts. Joanne backed away, trying not to laugh.

"Be serious!"

"Ah, yes, damned serious. Why do you think I keep you
around, Ms. Duboce?"

"Because you love my mind, you goose."

"Your body, woman, your body."

"The fact is," she hissed, "you don't love me at all."

"Stick around for awhile anyway—ten or fifteen years, at the
very least."

"As we are, McCain? That's what you want?"

"What, may I ask, is wrong with the way we are? You've got
nice tits, and I suffer from an oral fixation."

Joanne Duboce turned toward him then, suddenly and inexplicably on the verge of tears. Her appeal at that moment was
tremendous: large, sad eyes, sudden wave of self-pity and righteous
yearning for middle class respectability. Her tight splotched tee
shirt....

"Didn't you make the bed, Joanne?"

"What?"

"The bed," he repeated, his voice teasing. "It was your choice, wasn't it? I didn't force you to move in with me. Didn't I warn you not to come, in fact?"

"But now they'll all think that...."

"Does it make any difference—what *they* think? Hey, this is silly, you know that? Silly as hell. Ain't you one of them *liberated female women?*"

Joanne Duboce brightened a little and even smiled at him. The smile, he noted, was almost sincere. He pretended to frown.

"Why did I have to take your damned class?" she demanded. "There are lots of other nice young instructors. So why'd I pick you?"

"Call it fate. You heard that I'm the resident, certifiable genius of the department and couldn't resist."

"Call it bad luck, *mala suerte*," she said, crossing her arms in a way that accentuated her breasts even more.

"Call it *good luck*. Coyote and his grandchildren, squaw, you've got that magnificent creature, me. What does it take to satisfy you? What more do you want?"

"I'm sorry, Isaac," she said, shrugging.

"That you had to settle for me?"

*

Isaac twisted the handle of the steam radiator.

"Would you like to go out for a cup of coffee, Joanne?"

She raised one eyebrow, smiled.

"My boyfriend might object."

"You only drink coffee with handsome young instructors if your boyfriend approves? Hell, I bet I could take him at arm-wrestling. Well, bring him along if you wish. By all means, bring the ignorant, insensitive clod-hopping sonofabitch along."

"What about my problems?"

"Foresee problems, do you? Let's get down to cases. First you do the reading assignment. Then you do the hard part: you think. Next you sit down at the typewriter. In point of fact, nothing could be simpler."

"Maybe it's that easy for you, Mr. McCain...."

"Joanne, it's never easy for anybody. Wouldn't be worth a damn if it *were*."

The co-ed looked at her instructor for a moment without saying anything, smiling perhaps just a bit, playing the game they both knew was being played. Then she turned and vanished out the door.

McCain picked up his papers, shuffled them, and thrust them into a briefcase. The room was strangely still, so that noise of papers and hissing radiator seemed unaccountably loud. Then he, too, walked out through the door and into a foggy Oregon afternoon.

Geese are on the wing. Season's turning....

*

Just after sundown the rain let up. A warm wind played over the hillside, up from the river canyon. He'd piled dry wood inside the tent and so was able to make a roaring fire.

Joanne cooked supper for the two of them—beans and coffee and pieces of bacon skewered and roasted crisp over flames. As they ate, full night dropped over the Cascades, and the couple sat near their fire and drank coffee and talked. Rather, Isaac did most of the talking—about other trips to the mountains, about trapping when he was a boy, about the time when he and his friend Mack Madison and Mack's younger brother and Red Lugie drove to Tioga Pass above Yosemite, slept out in freezing weather in the middle of August, and then spent a miserable day scrambling to the top of Mt. Dana.

She nodded.

"Was your mother an Indian?" she asked. "I mean, you look like an Indian, Isaac. That's why I fell in love with you, I think. I could imagine you on your horse, bow in one hand, tomahawk in the other."

"No," he replied. "Mom was a full-blooded porcupine. What in hell does being Indian have to do with the exchange rate for rupees?"

"You don't need to hide it, Isaac. You should be proud."

He spat into the fire and shook his head.

It would never work, not in any long-range way. Certain memories were helpful, but the mountains were the wrong mountains. Oregon country—it seemed foreign to him, probably always would—in precisely the same way that this girl, Joanne, would always be a stranger....

The longer he contemplated the matter, the more meta-phorically significant the basic fact of location seemed. But how could he ever return to...?

Somehow the idea of a man and a woman together, even when the attraction was great, required a third essential element, the element of place. The man, the woman, the inevitability of the right place.

Later, when the fire burned low, they had sex.

Lovemaking was quite satisfactory with them, as it had always been. On this night she knotted her legs about him and cried and said she was very happy.

"Women," he muttered, "are beyond all comprehension—like nearly everything else."

He put more wood on the fire, and flames threw delicate light and shadow out into surrounding rhododendrons and firs. Sky bore its richness of stars, pregnant, as if ready to explode. And later, with Joanne sleeping, Isaac walked to the lake's far shore, to a small cove, stripped naked, and plunged into the water.

He stood, neck deep in the dark lake, and pondered the nature of this relationship he'd allowed himself, willingly, to fall into.

"Contradiction, unstable compound of flesh and spirit," he whispered, shivering, "that beautiful treachery, essence of bitch and angel, damnation and bliss and purgatory. Why did you do it, Lord? McCain, dolt, thick-skulled Halfbreed and heir to infinite darkness, you babble. Here you stand, up to your chin in lake water and invite hypothermia, spouting rhetoric like one of Shakespeare's puppets. You'll become Polonius eventually, and you'll be worthy of being Polonius. That's exactly what you deserve—is even perhaps what you desire. Am an attendant lord.... Lips, breasts, bodies—that's all women are. The rest is illusion."

And what, might I ask, is a man? What but a seed sack, a cock-a-doodle-do, a compulsion to drink from the sacred fount, to lap at the mystic female zero?

Isaac slid beneath the surface, swam like a fish, came up in shallows, turned over, lay on his back in the water, shuddering with cold.

"Men," he continued, "are different. After all, we're the bearers of the vital phallus, isn't that so? Naturally we're special critters. Think of it: we can piss standing up, and they, poor dears, have to squat. Minor differences are of great importance when one essays to make fine philosophic distinctions of absolute worth.

Hell, the difference has almost turned us into two separate species—the Stand-and-Pissers and the Squat-and-Pissers. One dumb Injun made dumber by being half dumb Yengee Gringo...."

*

He stood on the porch of his little house near the McKenzie River and smelled sweet, wet odor of grass and leaves and Douglas fir. Rain, the rain fairly sizzled down. Precipitation was to blame, then.

Time—the years were beginning to run by now, and tonight he fairly resented the fact.

Professor Isaac McCain. So this is what it had all come down to—a position with the university and a gaping emptiness inside.

But energy in the rain, and that was good.

"Look at the little sonsabitches come down!" he said, wiping moisture away from his eyes. "Someone ought to compose a grand hymn to the rain. Nothing's quite so fine. Just look at it...."

He went into the house and put on old clothes. He pushed his days-overdue paperwork aside, his eventual book about landscape and literature as well, pulled on an old red jacket like the one he recollected his father having, and walked out into the streaming night once more.

Rain came in torrents, driven on the wind. At the bottom of the ravine, he crossed a swollen tributary and in so doing slipped in up to his waist. He could almost hear lyre music and the voice of an unidentified poet who related the tale of a hero coming to shore and finding shelter beneath an olive tree, half of it wild, the other half tame. Or maybe it was only the ranting of his old friend Mack Madison, a crazed poet type now, who'd come to visit a week earlier and who hadn't stopped talking for the better part of twenty-four hours.

Isaac struggled through the water, threw himself down on the bank, bellowed with laughter.

Poets, he surmised, were insane. All of them.

Then he was standing on the brow of a hill overlooking his house. Down below, bands of yellow light poured out of his study window, and for a moment he could almost see himself, slumped in a chair in front of the desk, exhaustedly reaching for yet one more book.

No, that scholar fellow has gone out for a walk in the rain. The damned fool will probably try to cross a flooding creek and fall in. Book types, they've got no practical sense.

Isaac spat up into the rain.

"Mack, you sonofabitch!" he shouted. "Get thee once more to grad-uate school. Study for a doctorate and thereby make an honest man of thyself!"

He chuckled, shook his head.

He stared down at his study window. The longer he contemplated the fact that he was not inside, poring over notes, scribbling a few lines, wadding up pages and throwing them into a wastebasket, the more he liked the idea.

"This is all a man needs, damn it," he muttered.

He continued to stare through the rain toward the lighted square of his study window.

"My prison and my awful destiny. I'm no more a scholar than the dog on the moon. Madison's up in the Tetons by now, and he's probably making love to some little counter-culture heroine he's picked up. The old coyote's drinking cheap red wine and kissing the girl and laughing at me. Books, do you know how I hate you? All this fraudulent academic world?"

Isaac walked back to the house, stood under a dripping overhang of the roof, felt steam rising from his body.

So whoever needed you anyway, Joanne Duboce? I've spent my lifetime alone, more or less, and I can continue that way. Go find that basketball-playing poker-head of yours and leave me alone! You've got your life to live, and I have mine—for what it's worth. Nothing remains to me but darkness, in any case—only I don't even believe that. Purple prose, mouthed for self-indulgent effect. Coyote, where have you hidden my stick of dynamite?

*

He remembered.

A man set his sights on a dumbass thing, like getting a doctorate. Then one day it was all over, and after that he had to live with the categorical implications of what had been done with several years of an otherwise perfectly good lifetime.

He walked across campus with the required three copies of the dissertation, thinking, "So it's all come down to this—the Anglo-Saxon, endless term papers, the rotten French and German, even the teaching of classes. Then five months spent cramming for examinations and driving myself once more through the books for final holocaust of a concluding exam, writing in bluebooks until my fingers were numb and my mind spent, and I was sick with the drivel I'd poured out, *guano accumulating upon Peruvian shores*, bird-droppings collected night and day in the library, the scribbling of bits and pieces of monstrous irrelevant supererogation onto note cards I knew I was never going to look at again even as I was dutifully filling out the damned things, then the assembling of a mash of truth and nonsense, Greek and laughter, that might yet one day become a genuine, published book—to be read by other harmless drudges who'd nod or sneer and who'd write cryptic, wise notes into the margins. It's all come down to these pitiful typed pages in blue boxes."

Isaac saw the Head of Department coming toward him, that crusty old man with intense mind and acid tongue—saw him and was for the first time genuinely happy to see him.

"Well, it's the good Dr. McCain," Department Head Svendsen said, his tone of voice perhaps slightly less derisive than usual. "Apparently you've slipped through our fingers. I gather you're to be congratulated for something or other."

"Thank you, Professor Svendsen," Isaac McCain replied, and they shook hands. Then, not knowing what else to say, he blurted, "My dissertation—do all three copies go to the library?"

"Some of our students learn how to read," Svendsen replied, "and some obviously don't. Perhaps you should look into a pamphlet called *The Graduate Bulletin*. Listen, Isaac," he continued, "in such cases I normally recommend that the damned things be thrown into the Willamette. One day that river will rise and sweep us all away."

Isaac studied the Head of Department's expression, realized Svendsen was savoring his witticism, and then shook the smaller man's hand a bit harder than was called for.

Svendsen winced, laughed, and said, "McCain, I think you might have been better off on the football team than in the graduate school. Heaven knows the lads need some help on that line. Nevertheless, remember what I said about the river."

Isaac turned and walked away, realized that Professor Svendsen was whistling.

Had the man ever whistled before?

Isaac McCain was certain he had not.

But now it was all a blur—the university with its beautiful old buildings ivy-laced, recent brick structures still far too red and

unweathered.   Friends, the stretching of the mind, catalpas and
elms and firs, the Millrace Café, the cemetery behind the women's
gymnasium, carnival theater in summer, even football games and
track meets, silence of the fine arts museum, a statue of an Indian
girl at the front door (stupidly idealized, but he was in love with her
anyway), Jan Zach's *Prometheus* statue thrusting upward from the
grass at the quad's upper end, another statue that inexplicably sent
shivers of revulsion through him, *The Pioneer Mother*, looking
smugly maternal, like a huge black widow spider—more satisfactory
memories of the old offices in Friendly Hall and then the new ones
in PLC, eight o'clock classes both taken and taught, yearly
migration of freshmen, late discussions over beer steins at Taylor's
Tavern, gray winter days, an occasional visit from the wandering
Mack Madison (visionary poet on the loose), a time of freezing rain
and then a Chinook wind coming unexpectedly at six-thirty one
evening and taking the snow with it, so that flowers were actually
blooming the next morning—all this and much more dreamlike
before him and around him as he stood there, hesitating, dissertation under arm, watching the Miltonist, Dr. Kester Svendsen,
whistling and striding rapidly toward Commonwealth Hall.

   "*Orygun*," Isaac said aloud. "Not a bad place, when one gets
right down to it. Not a bad place at all. And you, too, Joanne,
companion to me during this perverse interlude, and me never
guessing—and at the same time knowing—how unhappy you were.
Well, it all leads to a meeting with a committee and a putting on of
academic robes."

   Isaac, as well, began to whistle as he lurched toward departmental offices, whistled a pornographic little ditty called "The Old
Irish Ballad," revealed at thirty-three r.p.m. by Richard Dyer Ben-
nett, one of McCain's favored records, a clear work of high art, and
not even Mozart could match it.

                                   *

   They had given him a position after all—inasmuch, Svendsen
scowled, as the likely alternative seemed to be jail.
   "Assistant Professor McCain," Isaac said, mulling the idea,
listening to the good sound of the words. He sat in his office, feet
up on the desk. "It's time—time to begin living my life."

Then came a knock on the door, a small, tentative knock. He knew who it would be, knew though he hadn't seen her for several months, except at a distance.

Joanne.

"Is it out of order for an ex-mistress to give Professor McCain a congratulatory kiss?"

"Just a moment," Isaac grinned. "Allow Professor McCain to lock the door."

They embraced. Isaac pushed her against his desk, lifted her gray woolen skirt, and slid down her panties.

"Dr. McCain, you barbarian...."

"One last time, Joe...."

"Kiss the mountain of Venus first, then. Get me into the mood, for heaven's sake."

He kneeled before her, as in prayer.

"Oohh," she laughed. "Keep that up for another half hour, and I'll consider your request...."

They were both aware of footsteps passing by in the corridor beyond the office.

"All right, all right," Joanne whispered. "I'm ready."

Isaac stood up, grinning, and unbuttoned the Levis he was wearing.

"Is that for me?" Joanne purred.

She reached down, squeezed three times, and then drew him toward her. "Barbarian...," she repeated softly as he thrust into her.

Afterward they talked, and Joanne said, "I'm graduating. Aren't you proud of me?"

Isaac sat in his tilt-back chair and stared at her, smiling. Then, unable to exercise restraint, he burst into laughter.

"You're beautiful, Joe. Why don't you stay here with me? We'll have a big house built up on the river—we'll listen to rain on the roof and make love for the next twenty years."

Joanne straightened her hair. Her body was nearly rigid.

"You really are a barbarian," she said.

"Why not? Why do you reject my vision?"

"Because you don't mean it," she replied. "If you did, I'd stay—you know that, I think. At least, you should know it."

"I do mean it. Sincerely."

"No, Isaac. You don't. All it ever is with you is just like now, here in the office. Oh, it's enjoyable—really, it is. Having a pet grizzly bear is fun. And you're very good, you know, when you bother to take the time. But I don't think that...."

"Think what, for Chaucer's sake? Stay with me, Joe."

"Why do you persist in calling me *Joe*? It'd never work, and we both know that. I never meant to say this, so forgive me. But someone needs to tell you, and so I suppose I have to be the one. You don't love, Isaac. I mean, I don't think you *can* love. Or you love everybody the same, and you treat women shamelessly. We respond, of course, because I think some part of us wants that—to be used, abused, tossed away. I can't live with a man who's chasing after every short skirt in town, not any more. I shouldn't say any of this. You've been so good for me, Isaac, and I feel more for you than I've ever felt for anyone else in my life. But don't you see? It's not enough to base a lifetime on. I could never hold you, and I know it. I can't take that. I can't take you going to bed with others. I suppose every man does once in awhile, but with you it's an obsession."

"Joanne...."

"I love you all the same. And I don't want to be married to anyone else—not now, maybe not ever. You've given me a great deal—you've given me myself. But maybe that's exactly what no woman really wants. You dominate, but you also set free—and for me that was good. Maybe five or six years from now, maybe then it will be time to see each other again. Perhaps there's something there, I don't know. But not now, Isaac. I'm going after my doctorate too. You've proven to me that I have a mind as good as anyone's. But now I know it, don't you see? Now I have to find myself too. I have to be myself—free, as you are. Free to be a complete human being, free to have a sex life if I want, free to have an intellectual life, free to be an identity. If I were with you, I'd have to subordinate myself. I can't do that—not until I know exactly who I am and what I'm capable of. So I guess maybe that means never...."

Isaac rubbed his hand over his eyes, was silent a moment—a silence that roared in his skull. Joanne's outburst had taken him totally by surprise, though he knew it shouldn't have.

"Damned if you don't sound almost like Ike McCain," he sputtered. "How can I refute the charges, then? But what about you, Joe—Joanna Duboce? Can you *love*?"

"Yes. I do. You know that, damn you anyway. But it's different with a woman. I don't know why it is, but I know it's so. I love you and admire you immensely, Isaac, and you'll never know just how much I mean that. I'm worried about you, not for my sake, but for yours. It's like...."

"Say it, then. I know what you're going to say."

"Yes. You already know it, then. It's like something's missing or maybe something that's just hiding. Probably that. You've got such great depth and warmth, but it's in hiding. Like you were hurt sometime, a long time ago. You never got over what happened to your father and to that little snip of a—what's-her-name? April Incendie, who didn't know the first thing about any kind of fire that mattered. So now you're afraid to give in to love. That simple."

"I'm not afraid of anything!" McCain said in sudden rage, standing up, walking to the window, pounding on the sill.

"Don't be angry, Isaac. It's true. You may not be afraid of *anyone*, not as big as you are, but you're afraid of *something*. I don't know what. Perhaps in trying to be true to yourself, you're destroying something deep down inside. I've said too much, haven't I? I'd better go. I'll write. I'm going to grad school at Washington State. I've got to leave now, or I'm likely to start crying. Isaac...."

"I'll drive up to see you, then. I promise."

"You mean if you can fit me into your schedule?" she asked, standing up, her hand on the doorknob. She was clearly fighting tears.

Then she was gone.

Isaac seated himself and listened to her footsteps as they echoed from the long corridor, heard the opening of a door that led into an outdoor stairway, then the closing of the door, muffled. He sat quietly for a long moment, opened his desk drawer, took out a small red address book, flipped through worn pages, stopped.

He reached for the telephone.

*

"Not much I can do for it, I'm afraid," the mechanic said. "Compression's way down on numbers three and eight. Those in *paa-tic-u-lar*. A wonder the pistons ain't swapping holes. Second gear's got a busted tooth, and the front end needs complete rebuilding. Wheels goin' in five directions at once. I put in new points and plugs, Ike, but it ain't goin' to do you much good. Better you be thinkin' about another buggy."

Isaac drew on his cigarette and blew out two smoke rings. He could imagine his faithful '40 Buick being lowered into a large open-pit grave, a preacher intoning praises of Christian salvation, himself the only mourner.

A tree-hung grave, he decided, would be better—Cheyenne style. Redwoods might work. A *baho* or two of white feathers....

Finally he said, "It'll last forever, I tell you. I'll have it rebuilt from the tires up if I have to."

"Also needs new rubber, since you mention it," the mechanic grinned.

"Okay, from the ground up, then."

"You suit yourself, Ike. The body's in pretty good shape, but we're talking a pile of dough. Look, I got a little '61 Chevy out on the lot. New motor in 'er. Probably the boss'll give you a hundred or so for the Buick—you oughta be thinkin' about something like that unless you want to turn 'er into a genuine antique. Couple more years and you'll be there. You college professors got money. Hell, why not buy a new rig? This old horse's probably got something like three hundred thousand on 'er, don't she? Goin' to fall apart on you. Engine's maybe been overhauled three, four times already. Have to have a new block, the works. Don't figger she's worth it. A man shouldn't get sentimental about cars."

"My friend," Isaac shrugged, "you simply do not understand about this automobile. A few more years and it'll be a *genuine antique*, as you say. Then I'll sell it and retire. What do I owe the company for plugs and points?"

The mechanic used a greasy rag to wipe at his fingernails, winked.

"Guess maybe I *do* understand. I got an old International pickup I should have sent to the boneyard long ago—Cornbinder Number One. Ain't practical, though. If a machine don't work, it's no good to you. No good at all."

*

A missed offramp, and Isaac McCain had driven south, confused, remembering—a man and a dog named Doom, the animal finally messing in the rear seat of the venerable Buick coupe, McCain having to stop along the highway and threatening the dog with dire bodily harm. A winding highway south to California, toward a meadow and a printshop and a world he had not been part of for nineteen years.

Remembering.

A few months after he'd said goodbye to Joanne Duboce, that day in the office, a wedding invitation arrived in the mail.

April Incendie.

He'd told Joanne all about her, and Joe had turned jealous—jealous of a dead girl.

"And you still love her, don't you?"

"I shouldn't think so."

"But you don't know, do you, Ike McCain? You really can't say. So that's how it is."

"I don't even recall what she looked like."

"You remember all right. I hate you sometimes, Isaac."

"What the hell does *love* mean, Joe?"

"You know what it means. You should, at least."

"It was on Saturday, you see, and April and I.... Well, she was probably thinking about the wild tulips and creek azaleas, exquisite and intoxicating, burning soft fire. Or maybe I'm making it all up. It's hard to know. But she went with me and Betty Sue—my father had business in Sacramento, and he left me in Diggins, at the Incendie place. We threw stones at a swarm of butterflies, and it seems to me now as if soft music were playing, the kind of music you can't hear no matter how hard you try. Well, we wandered up the creek, the same creek that runs through the meadow at home, and we were together in the sunlight. Alders along the stream were leafing out—and Mack Madison was there too, so I guess maybe we were about eleven, all four of us. Mack was going to carve my initials and April's on a tree trunk, but he didn't. He had a new Sears Roebuck pocket knife, I recall that. Then Mack and I waded in the creek, and Betty Sue and April picked azaleas and put them in their hair and in the button holes of their blouses. Mack and I decided to have a rock fight, and the girls went looking for trilliums."

"How in hell do you know what they were looking for?"

"Come on, Joe. Of course that's what they were doing. Don't you know what trilliums are? Ladybugs were humming in the sunlight, shining, their odd musty smell quite evident. Strange how one remembers smells, even after so long. The manzanitas were blooming, small sticky white flowers that smell just like honey. I think the girls crawled over a carpet of moist brown leaves through patterns of light until they could no longer see out through a maze of vegetation."

Music even louder, the scene distorted.

"Good grief, Isaac, you make a real production out of all this. What's it got to do with Abraham, anyway?"

"*Abram*. My father's name was Abram. Only it wasn't him, it was her. April Incendie. It was what she meant to me and what she did, finally, that turned me sour. Or maybe I was just waiting for something to do it—so Madison says. But that's not it, either. I know my father didn't kill her, and yet I don't really *know*. So I've never gone back and probably never will. That world has vanished for me."

"I like your friend Mack. Next time he comes to visit, I'm going to run off with him. To hell with you, Isaac. Bacon and eggs all right? I'm pretty good at fixing bacon and eggs."

"You've got nice tits."

"Ike, you're worthless. I swear, you're really worthless."

"In a small clearing, vivid sun pouring down, producing marked contrasts of light and dark, as in a Rembrandt painting, they lay to-gether—April and Betty Sue.   After a few minutes Betty Sue probably turned over and kissed April on the mouth—and they stroked each other's hair."

"Eleven-year-old lesbians."

"Girls do that. You did it, didn't you?"

"Damn you, Isaac McCain. You're worse than a barbarian. Eat your breakfast."

Strains of Appalachian Spring, overpowering, rank in the air. Coyote-Head perched atop a boulder, smiling, whiskers twitching. A female clinging to his ankle. A ring of red-brown coyotes about them, heads back, howling, howling.

*

"Sit down," she might have said to herself, Elizabeth Colling-wood, if the world hadn't tilted off sharply to the left and filled her eyes with burning mud. "Sit down and grind your knuckles into the sockets of your eyes: for it was all to no avail. You failed him just like everyone else because you could not bear his child—or would not. You killed him just as much as they did. Yes, sit down and remember how gentle he was with you, how his huge hands moved softly over your breasts and how his callused fingers touched the quick and made you think and even believe and even want it to be for an instant that you were young again and virgin and it's Eden all over, but you killed his seed. You too are guilty of murder in the first and second and last and only degree. Abram, return to me,

please, Abram, don't leave me alone this way in the darkness. I'm
so afraid of the dark. I'll wear perfume for you, Abram, oh dear,
I'll do anything you want. I'll wait for you, Abram McCain. Hurry,
sweet Jesus, hurry."

*

The scene faded.

For a long moment the image on the screen was indistinguishable. Then they were at the swimming hole on Deer
Creek, a number of high school boys pushing one another around
and diving from the boulder in the middle of the pool. Mack
Madison, skinny as a rail and always looking for a fight with
someone twice his size, had just bloodied Burt Bullardi's nose and
got thumped to the side of the head for his trouble, but now
harmony had been restored, and Madison was swinging out over
the water on a cut-off grapevine.

Isaac didn't care much for the Bullardi boy, at least he didn't
when April Incendie was there. She was fond of Burt, and that was
reason enough. At other times, however, Burt was all right.

April and Isaac stood a few yards away from the water, under
the trees.

"You swim," April said. "I'll watch."

"You ain't coming in?"

"You're pretty dumb, Isaac, you know that? Where would I get
a bathing suit? My mother told me never to come up here again."

"Oh yeah, I forgot. Aww, come on, Ape. I don't want to swim
anyway."

"Don't call me *Ape*. I don't like that."

They walked up the creek, into dense woods. Soon they could
no longer hear the shouts and dousings of the swimmers. Grass
was dry, yellow-brown and full of foxtails that stuck into April's
stockings. Boy and girl held hands as they walked.

A buzzing sound in grass beside the trail.

April leaped backward against Isaac, and they both fell. The
rattlesnake coiled. A small black tongue flashed, and the serpent's
head appeared particularly flat, wedge-shaped.

Musical accompaniment which was strangely peaceful.

Isaac moved toward the snake, as in slow motion, and used
both hands to hurl a stone at it—a red-colored rock which floated
down to crush the rattler, now writhing on the ground. Isaac hurled

more rocks, while the slack, broken body coiled and uncoiled. Then he used a pocket knife to cut off the rattles.

April was crying, not looking.

"Shouldn't we go?" she asked.

But he replied: "Heck no. There's a place I want to show you, April. We're nearly there."

Afternoon sun a soft, gentle god, insistent, tantalizing—then a wide spot in the creek, a dark green pool with a large flat shelf of stone projecting into it. Intense gleam of sun in the water. Isaac skipped a pebble across the stream—it danced, starting ripples that moved out and crossed one another. Mirrored trees and sky swayed and twisted, grew still again in undulating greenness.

They could hear the ripples.

A hawk floated against blue sky.

Then two bodies, naked, splashed into the pool. Boy and girl wrestled playfully in shallow water close by the flat rock, and then she rolled over on the sand so that he lay directly next to her.

Flute music. Odor of summer grass, sound of running water, splash of a frog. An almost detectable sound of laughter.

A moment later they were apart, dressing quickly. They walked hurriedly downstream, not speaking, afraid to speak.

                    *

Evening, near the McKenzie River. Joanne and Isaac were in the house, sitting in front of the fireplace, drinking wine. Music issued from a stereo in the background.

"I swear, Ike, I don't know why I listen to you. You tell me all this stuff, and I know none of it's true. Have you considered insanity?"

"Straight from the Oracle."

"Well, it sounds like a tissue of lies. Maybe it is true, but so what? I'm going to bite you on the throat, Isaac McCain!"

"Get flip with me, my girl, and I'll fix you good."

"Promises...."

"No, it's true all right. And I really did love her—or maybe not love, something else. Hell, Joe, we were just kids—but it's not too damned happy to think about sometimes. Other days I don't mind."

"How old was she when Abram raped her?"

"No. No, it wasn't my father. Trying to vex me, you little bitch, and you've no right. Why do you do your best to get me riled up?"

"All right, then who did...kill her?"

"I don't know. But I'll tell you this—if I ever do find out, why I'm going to annihilate that sonofabitch. I'm going to crush him just as I did the snake that day. I'm going to pull the limbs off his body, and then cut his guts out."

"Calm down, Ike. I didn't mean to say that...about your father. Maybe I've been trying to get you to put it all together, to see it, and then to forget it. You frighten me when your eyes get that way. Besides, you've always said you were never returning to Diggins, California. Suppose you found the man and murdered him. You'd only get executed for your trouble—or spend the rest of your life in prison, don't you know that? It's all over and done with, Isaac, years ago. You were just a boy. You've got to live your life in the present. You can't go on eating at yourself this way. Forgive me for saying what I did. Please? I was wrong. Who am I to be telling you how to feel about things? I didn't know anything at all until after you found me...."

McCain refilled their glasses. His hand was shaking, and he had to be extremely careful as he poured the red wine.

"You're right, of course," he said, attempting to lighten the tone of their talk. "Joanne. My pretty Joanne. Take off your clothes. I want to see you naked by the fire, like an image from a poem—an inscape of the feminine archetype, *Aphrodite Porn*. Or the human, *Phyrne Kallipygos*, she of the beautiful buttocks...."

*

Inside the Buick coupe, heading south. A man and a dog. They'd stopped in Marysville to have the tank filled. Isaac paid the station attendant, bullied Doom into the car, started the engine, and drove out of town, heading east along Highway Twenty, across the last few dry miles of valley floor.

Late afternoon outlines of the Sierra foothills rose before him, and he glanced into the mirror at the smoke-blue profile of Yuba Buttes, *Estawm Yan*, sacred mountains of the Maidu Indians—the holy place where *Ootimtsaa* grew and where Coyote created the people.

When Isaac approached the concrete bridge spanning Yuba River where the big stream cut out into flatlands, he realized the air smelled different—different and strangely familiar.

"Don't know what the hell we're doing, Doomer Dog, but we're almost there. We're almost home."

The black and white dog placed his head on his master's lap and growled softly.

They crossed the bridge, and Isaac sped up, taking the long grade. Shadows of buckeye and oak were a blur on either side of the road. There was no traffic—only a dotted white line twisting with the curves of the highway, only the odor of digger pine and oak brush and faint trace of smoke in sharp afternoon warmth.

As they spun over a first crest, Isaac saw a blue heron, the huge bird incongruously perched on a twisted limb of a digger. The Buick sped past, and the bird flew—powerful wings cutting through air.

And then, a few short miles further on, he learned that he was in *Bullardi Country*....

***

Canto Four:
Iphigenia

HOWEVER I WITH THEE HAVE FIXT MY LOT,
CERTAIN TO UNDERGO LIKE DOOM; IF DEATH
CONSORT WITH THEE, DEATH IS TO MEE AS LIFE;
SO FORCIBLE WITHIN MY HEART I FEEL
THE BOND OF NATURE DRAW MEE TO MY OWN,
MY OWN IN THEE, FOR WHAT THOU ART IS MINE;
OUR STATE CANNOT BE SEVER'D, WE ARE ONE,
ONE FLESH; TO LOSE THEE WERE TO LOSE MYSELF.

[JOHN MILTON,
PARADISE LOST]

*

Isaac McCain sat on a stump high on a spur of Burlington Ridge. The west burned long bands of orange-red, like a campfire strewn across heaven—and below him darkness had already engulfed the creek canyon, so that only the lights in the cabin windows were visible. Chill autumn wind poured down from the high, bare spine of pinnacles and granite basins of the Sierra Nevada.

The world, he reflected, was not much changed since his impulsive departure from Eugene, Oregon, and his return to Abram's meadow on Deer Creek. His McKenzie River house was now for sale, and Thomasina Wentworth, so a former colleague informed him, had grudgingly moved out and was apparently living in Springfield with three local rock musicians.

Beyond that, Ed Sullivan had died, the Nobel Prize had been awarded to a Stanford professor who'd done vital work in plastics; Muhammad Ali had indeed fooled the boxing pundits with a stunning knockout over George Foreman in a championship match held in Kinshasa, Zaire. According to newspaper reports, Ali was now intent upon holding the crown until his fiftieth birthday.

Isaac genuinely regretted that he hadn't accompanied Mack Madison to Sacramento to view the big fight on satellite television, closed circuit.

Madison was recently back from a venture to Wheeler Peak, Nevada. He'd stopped by the university in Eugene and so learned of Isaac's whereabouts, had subsequently shown up at Deer Creek, full of news of having had a *medicine vision*, as he called it, while camped out with his new love, high up on the south slope of the mountain. He'd urged Isaac to go with him to see the fight—was certain Ali would win, probably by a kayo within ten rounds.

Even when they were boys, Mack always had an uncanny way of predicting the outcomes of boxing matches. Like Patterson over Archie Moore, for instance. Who else would have called that one? With Patterson and Liston, However, Mack had been quite wrong. So the poet's hotline to the spirit world had a few weak connections. It was good, Isaac reflected, to know his friend was human after all.

"The Lord of Chatter," he said aloud.

Well.... The English department at the university, apparently, was operating quite nicely in his absence. The pebble he'd thrown into still waters had vanished beneath the surface without stirring more than the least of small ripples.

No one's irreplaceable. Understand that much.

Whose words?

Probably Madison's. Figured. Or else Svendsen's—or J.B. Hall's—Hall, who'd given this advice: *Be like the Bank of London. Never apologize and never explain.*

Isaac, thinking: *That girl's down in the cabin. She's cooking dinner for herself. She must be lonely, she's got no lover—or so she claims. No visitors at all, and yet she doesn't seem to mind. Well, I know loneliness too. It can be endured. But it seems worse for a woman somehow—I don't know why, and the speculation's no doubt false as hell. Iphigenia—she's lovely, yellow eyes, red hair. Doesn't weigh enough to say so. Even Joanne Duboce wasn't that thin.... Joanne. Wonder what she's doing? It's been years. No, she's got children now—married and probably disgustingly middle class. Women make their male children into lovers, I think, and then they forget their men. Hell, what do I know about it? I have no children. But then, I've chosen the life I live. What it comes down to, I guess, is that I married a house full of books, and now I've divorced them, more or less. I'll build a new wing onto the printshop and then rent a truck to haul the books down here.... Still, she must be lonely. Treats me like a neighbor, no more. I'm the man who lives in the printshop—I'm part of the surroundings now, but like a tree or maybe the big rock down in the meadow. Yes, yes, that's best I suppose....*

The moon, a full early November moon low in the east, amber, almost red in the autumn haze, loomed huge above a dark line of peaks.

Shouting at the top of his lungs, roaring into the moonlight, loneliness, anger, blind desire for the promise of the glimmering scent of the promise until he heard voices below—women, struggling to get to him. Glass splintering. Green glow of vegetation.

*

"I worry about you, Isaac. Do you know that?"

"And why might that be, Miz Joanne?"

"You have so much anger in you. You live it all yourself—as though you, Isaac, were actually Abram."

"You're right, of course. Dad's merely my metaphor. He typifies a condition. In my imagination, when I was a boy, he, Abram, though everyone else in Diggins was afraid of him, became for me all that's best in man. He was the mystery and the violence. I wanted his strength. My father...."

"And his madness?"

"He wasn't mad, Joe. You've got to understand that. He wasn't, I tell you. Strong and gentle."

"But why is it so important to you? All those peculiar things you say he did. No wonder people were afraid."

"They weren't, not all of them. The last year of his life, Dad got along famously with Mack's dad—the berry farmer and the printer in the woods, a strange pair, those two, they went prospecting together. But the good citizens of Diggins, that was another matter. They had no right to be afraid."

"Yes, they did. Isaac, I would have been afraid too. But that isn't really it. I mean, it was the girl who mattered, April Incendie. She was raped—killed—and you're saying Abram wasn't guilty. You're trying to make him look innocent, but how do you know? Sometimes you act as though you aren't certain."

Isaac shrugged.

"Hell, Duboce, maybe I'm the one who raped her. Or maybe I'm the one who let it happen. Could have been my great rival, Bullardi, the Chevy dealer's wretched son. But what I'm trying to tell you, and maybe what you can't or don't want to understand, is that I loved the little bitch. I really did."

"But you don't love me?"

"That's not what I said. You know I didn't *mean that*, Joanne. One of the rules of the game. Kid-love, perhaps, but it was real as hell at the time."

"Not supposed to matter to me that you loved what's-her-name?"

"Utterly beside the point."

"I used to believe everything you said, Isaac, but I'm getting to be such a big girl now...."

*

Read your accursed books, McCain. Why did you let this female come live with you? You're not fit to abide with anyone. She's going to be a damnation, and you know that too. She's going to haggle at you, she's going to try to turn you into a different person altogether, and you're going to hate her—only there won't be any way out because she thinks she can change you. Not going to happen. Worms in the brain. Hence Abram's mythic appeal, the comfort of madness—and he was mad, wasn't he? Possibly he even deserved to be chased by men with dogs, blown up. How did you do it, Father? Yes, the way everyone does it. Have mercy, Lord of the Song Dogs, forgive. Wings beating in the branches, a great ungainly bird as if welded out of jagged, blue-black metal, long jointed legs, wedge-shaped head of the heron, a ghost of primeval times vaulting upward into empty air.

*

April.

They'd been kissing for some time, and the low sound as of some odd, peaceful music playing far away, sound of running water, his hands touching over the soft parts of her body, and she said, "I can't stand it any more, please, Isaac, do it now, do something...."

Then he understood, and they both climbed into the rear seat of the Buick and slowly, slowly he removed her clothing.

But Joanne said, "I don't see what Abram has to do with any of this. You're not even being coherent. You see connections where none exist. Let's just say that McCain—I mean Abram—did rape her and she died of a knock on the head, cerebral hemorrhage. That was years ago. You simply can't spend forever brooding about it. We have our own lives to live, Isaac, our own lives together."

And Abram said, "Ike, you see those two big salmon making their way upstream? Well, the entirety of a man's life is a matter of swimming upcurrent in search of identity, in search of an origin. Were it not for the counterforce, then life would have no meaning. It's the sharp current that mostly turns us into men."

*

The dormitory room in Berkeley, Oxford Hall, a ramshackle old pile of red bricks, student cooperative with undulating hallways the result of a condemned wall-bearing structure having been heaved many times by earthquakes minor and major: past midnight, and Isaac McCain and Mack Madison were in the process of consuming the last of a gallon jug of Mills Winery burgundy.

Dirty socks lying in a pile in the corner of Madison's side of the room, two desks heaped with books and papers, both young men smoking pipes.

"So you and your commie friend are actually going to have that book of poems printed?" Isaac mumbled, lifting the nearly empty bottle and taking a pull. "Wouldn't it be better to wait for a real publisher to come along?"

"You *academic* types are a genuine drag," Madison grinned. "You know what would be a good job for you? Digging up dandelions, that's what. Pass the wine. Dandelion wine, if we have any.... Because you just can't tolerate seeing dandelions in a lawn. Now me, I love weeds. That's why I write poems, Ike. It's the dandelion school of literature I belong to. Old Yeats, he just established his own publishing company, isn't that right? And Blake—and Whitman. Well, Petras and I, that's what we're doing. You think I ought to wait, ehh?"

"Good grief, Mack, I don't know. The angry young dandelion men? *Dent-de-lion*, tooth of the lion. Well, Dad, he published his own book...."

Isaac reached for the bottle, drank.

"Three years since it all happened," Mack continued, "and still doesn't seem real—or even possible. You think you would have married her? The way she used to jack you around, you and Burtie Bulldog? Truth, now. Eventually she'd have goaded the two of you into killing each other. Am I right or not?"

"Don't spoil the night, Madison. Here we are, half drunk, mellow, feeling no pain, and not even thinking about finals. Don't get serious on me, Words-words, old bean."

"Sure, sure. Okay, then, have it your way. What the hell? So you'll never go back to Diggins for the rest of your life. We had a damned good crew there at Crooked Pines, but I understand your reasons. You figure they need someone else up on the Plumas? That mineral survey thing sounds okay to me—just walk the hills and jot things down on maps. I told you, I already sent in an application. Two thieves like us, we ought to stick together during the summers. Maybe I'll even head up to Oregon with you to do grad work—good writing program there, from what I've heard...."

"Kill the jug, and let's hit the hay. Come on, Mackpoet, let me have the damned thing."

"Ain't sleepy yet. Let's rob a bank. Better yet, let's go slip into one of the girls' dorms. On nights like this, you know the little femlins are just lying there in the darkness, reading D.H. Lawrence and tickling their clits. Did I tell you about those twin redheads I saw when I was driving the pot run last week? Honest to God, Ike, they were wandering around the hallways in just their panties—no bras or anything!"

"I never believe anything a crazy, commie-symp poet tells me. You really don't expect me to buy that tale, do you?"

Madison re-lit his pipe, winked, puffed.

"Commie-symp, hell. I'm the token Republican at those cell meetings. Now look. Tuesday night, if you can pry yourself away from the damned books—you come with me. By the blood of St. Lucifer, I figure there'll be naked nymphets all over the place."

"What's the good of just looking?" Isaac demanded. "If I want that, I can go to the strip-joint in Oakland and watch Tempest Storm bounce her aging boobies."

"Plastic flowers, old and worn out," Madison replied. "Can't compare to genuine dandelions."

*

It was not difficult for him to find his way down the mountain, even without a flashlight—for the moon silvered everything. A long time, yes, but somehow he still knew the trail—this trail like many others the wild creatures used. It was the same as always, time's passage irrelevant.

Isaac waded the creek, his dog Doom sprawling in dark water, drinking, the wagging tail whipping shadows.

Once across, Isaac lurched up the grassy meadow, running clumsily. He passed behind the cabin, its windows glowing with lantern light, and made his way through the dark doorway of the printshop. He lit his own lantern and pulled off wet shoes.

Then a voice from outside:

"McCain—Isaac, are you decent? I've brought you some hot coffee."

*

"This cabin was a shambles when I moved in," Iphigenia said. "Some floor planking was ripped up, so I nailed the pieces in place. A lot of holes in the ground outside. Some guys down at the café told me there'd been a rumor your father had gold hidden, and people must have come looking for it over the years. None of the holes were recent—at least, I don't think they were."

Isaac nodded.

"A year after Dad's death, I hired a fellow named Tom Jennings to keep an eye on the place. Tom moved to Colorado five years ago, and after that I didn't know whom to get in touch with. The road at the top of the hill was supposed to be kept chained. I wasn't all that surprised the night I drove in, though. Deer hunters come equipped with bolt cutters."

"Did he have gold, Isaac? I've used the rifle to run a few people off, but I'm not here during afternoons."

"Know about that rifle," Isaac grinned. "You sure as hell looked like you meant business the other morning, Ginny. But then you'd no way of knowing who I was, I guess."

"I did, though, without knowing *why*. Your voice through the door.... Sometimes I'd imagine what it would be like if you did show up. Once I started living here, I naturally got curious. For the first year I kept asking people what happened, I mean the locals, but most wouldn't talk about it. I mean, they just refused. After that I did some research—actually went through the newspaper archives. But I want you to tell me. I want to know all about you— I mean, your father. About you too, of course."

Isaac stretched out his long legs, glanced at the Coleman lanterns.

"Oh, there was gold, all right," he said. "Dad had a mineshaft on the hill, an odd vein of black dirt in a fissure in the rocks. Gold's still there, for that matter, but the mine's blasted shut. That's where Abram...."

"What? Your eyes look wild, Isaac. Are you all right? Did I say something...?"

"No, no," he replied, shaking his head and running his fingers over his beard. "Silly to get emotional almost twenty years after the fact. I'll tell you later. If you went through the old newspapers, then you already know a good part of what happened. After nineteen years, it's time I got over it—but it's still difficult to talk about. If you want to hear, I'll tell the whole business. But I want to know about you too, Ginny. Like, for instance—you don't have a...boyfriend?"

She stared directly at him, tried not to smile.

"I'm not Lesbian, if that's what you're getting at, Dr. McCain."

*

One night of rain. After that the skies cleared, sun returned, and the earth baked dry in unseasonably late heat that lasted only a day or two. Great domes of cloud built over the mountains, and a brief downpour hit just after darkness, rattling whatever dry leaves remained on oaks and maples. Rain heaved against the printshop roof as Isaac sat reading, his dog lying on a rug by the wood stove, thumping his tail nervously on the floor as thunder ripped darkness.

"*Olelbis* is giving hell to Old Coyote Man for bungling creation, Doomer Dog. It's nothing to worry about. Sometimes the two of them shout at each other for hours. *Olelbis*, you see, is the Big Coyote. You hear his name in the *O-lel, Oleli*? You have powerful relatives, my man, and don't even know about it."

The storm broke, and Isaac rose to go next door to have coffee with Ginny.

They met halfway between the buildings, she with a pair of steaming mugs.

"Clearing," she laughed. "See how the stars start to pop out all along the west? A residue of fire, Isaac McCain. Just smell the air! It's like—it's like wine tonight."

"I don't think the argument's finished yet, Yellow Eyes."

"What argument?"

"Between the Dreamer Who Sits Above and his Premier Agent. You know the story by any chance?"

"Some Indian myth—or what?"

"I'm just a Halfbreed," McCain laughed, "so my pipeline to the Spirit World's only half-built. But it's no myth, my girl. The Big Dreamer, the Big Dog, he thought about how the world should be, and then he turned the job of building it over to Coyote Clown. *Oleli*, he was careless and had a few whims of his own, like us, for instance. It's the only way of reconciling the opposed concepts of a Perfect Creator and an imperfect creation. Your Christian theologians have wrestled with the problem for centuries, all to no avail. Locked in by a staunch refusal to see the world as it by-Gawd is. What Christian thinker has said even one comprehensible thing about the existence of the tapeworm, for instance? Augustine, Aquinas, friend Dante, Ponderous Johnny Milton? Herr Luther or Father Merton? Not likely. I tell you, it's false religion, false philosophy, that's what. Now the Native North Americans, they were realists of the first water—and that means they understood that trees and animals and stars and fish were all people, possibly of a higher order. Death? Nobody's ever been overly fond of the idea, but in the final analysis, one simply stepped off the top of *Estawm Yan* or *Wahgalu* or Shasta and headed across the sky-track to Upper Meadows, the Spirit World. The living grieved because they'd been left behind, momentarily deserted. At some level or another, the people comprehended that mountains and rivers are alive, and when a human dies, he simply becomes part of everything else. Call it Raven Man's tunnel. In the far north, one crawled through the hole and then crossed the Spirit River. After that, people lived in a land where there was no death—no boundaries—no limitations. And the good went on being good, while the evil continued to harvest the crops they continued to plant. Only it's simpler than anything I've said just now. The problem is, maybe, that I've been trained to think like a transplanted European, and I don't know whether that's good or bad."

Ginny smiled, nodded appreciatively at Isaac's discourse.

"You sound like you believe it, at least."

"Damned right. It's a medicine that Dr. McCain prescribes—a palliative, possibly, even a placebo, yet a cure for the world's ills nonetheless. On the other hand, The Lord watches over us all. After nearly twenty centuries, He looks down from the cross upon this pitiful, pitiable human mélange. But if we stand here much longer, we're subject to flash floods, I think."

"This is a fine night for walking in the woods, Isaac. I often do that. Will you come with me? I like to sit by the creek and listen to the water's sound. Isaac, come with me! You spend all your time reading, and you never pay any attention to...."

"To Ginny?" he asked, laughing.

"I meant no such thing, You know I didn't mean to say anything like that. But come with me. You're so stodgy. What if it does start raining again? Feel how warm the wind is, how fresh everything smells."

*

Wind, yes, soft wind—and the dripping of wet foliage, darkness along Deer Creek beneath a canopy of alders hung with rough ropes of grapevines upward to the top branches, freshly moist moss blanketing large boulders along the stream's edge, water still low in its black bed, despite the brief rain.

In dimness were two human forms, together but not close, at the edge of the pool, and a dog's white blur, nose down among wet leaves, hunting.

The young woman took her shoes off and sat down, dangling her feet in the water's margin. The flaring of a single match illuminated their faces a moment, a cupping of hands, ritual lighting of cigarettes.

Isaac and Iphigenia were silent a time, she moving one foot back and forth in the pool, he bent forward, smoking.

"Would you mind if I go swimming?" she asked suddenly. "The darkness is so perfect you can't see me. The pool's deep enough. You look the other way while I undress."

"Not allowed," he replied.

"Why not? You've seen naked women before anyway, I know you have. You're a man of the world. I'll bet your coed students took their clothes off for you.... That's true, isn't it?"

She stood up, withdrew a step.

"Unless I can swim too," he said.

A silence. They both drew on their cigarettes, a red glow hovering about their faces.

"All right, Isaac. I get the other side, and you get this one. It's dark."

"Haven't you ever seen a naked man before?" he asked, and they both laughed.

"You look the other way, Isaac McCain. I'll undress. Then you can come in. I don't think the water's too cold."

"No," he replied. "I believe I'll watch you. I didn't ask you to bring me that coffee, after all."

Iphigenia couldn't think of anything else to say, decided to ignore him. She turned away and undressed quickly—could feel his eyes on her through the darkness. But to herself: *The son of a bitch! I'll swim in my underthings....* Only then did she remember she wasn't wearing any.

She dived out from the bank into deep water, stayed beneath the surface despite a searing chill, disoriented momentarily, felt for stones along the bottom, and emerged on the other side. She was laughing and shivering at the same time.

"All right!" she shouted. "You come in then. Stay on your own side, though, and I'll stay here. I get to watch too."

Did.

The dim blur of McCain's big body, half in shadows, a sensation of strength to her, perhaps even of gentleness. How awkward he was! Wading into the water, losing his balance, splashing in. And she thought, *I wonder what he's like, how big he must...is. I wonder if I could....*

"Yellow-Eyes!" he shouted. "I've got you cut off—you'll never escape."

"I'm not afraid of you, Isaac McCain. You could never catch me anyhow. I'm used to being barefoot!"

"Going to fetch the rifle and shoot at me again?"

After a moment: "No, I wouldn't do that. I'd not miss twice."

But finally they dressed.

Night air seemed more chill than before, and they were grateful for the warmth of their clothing after immersion in the stinging water of the creek. They walked side by side toward the cabin, still careful not to touch each other, and they found it difficult to think of things to say.

Between the two buildings they paused, uncomfortably, and Isaac said, "I'm wide awake now. A nighttime creek's marvelous good at curing a case of the drowsiness. Think perhaps I'll read a while longer."

"You have enough gas for your Coleman lantern? I've got four full cans—one's just opened."

"I think so. Well, goodnight, Ginny. I enjoyed the...walk. Such a fine night! You don't work tomorrow. Perhaps we could take a jaunt up over Burlington Ridge if the sky's clear. You'd like that?"

"Yes," she said. "I would. I'd really like that."

*

He awoke to an insistent knocking on the door. Ginny was up early.

"Isaac McCain!" she sang. "Get out of bed and come have breakfast. Then it's time to gather mushrooms. They're up, just over night it seems like. They're in the meadow and out under the oaks, white ones and the small button kind. You've got to help me."

He'd fallen asleep in his chair.

Doom was motionless in the corner, thumping his tail.

Isaac stirred himself, rose, and half staggered toward the door.

"Yellow-Eyes," he said. "What the devil are you talking about? Of course there are mushrooms after the rain."

He opened the door. She was standing there in a blue work-shirt and Levis, her face flushed with excitement.

"Come eat," she ordered. "I've fixed breakfast—even a snack for your neurotic hound. Isaac, we're going to have mushrooms all winter. We'll get gunny sacks full of them and dry them on strings."

He put his hands on his hips and glared down at her, this slip of a girl with her odd eyes and a mane of near copper-colored hair.

"What in hell's gotten into you?"

She reached up and pulled at his beard.

"You're such a...rock, Isaac. I should let you fix your own damned breakfast. Did you sleep at all last night? I couldn't for hours, and then I dreamed until dawn. I won't tell you what I dreamed. Come on now, let's eat."

*

Later they scoured the meadow and worked on hands and knees under black oaks and manzanita bushes, feeling for small lumps beneath the leaves. By noon three burlap sacks were nearly full.

"That's enough," she said suddenly, standing up. "The deer have to eat too. By tomorrow we'll see just small wedge-shaped holes where the mushrooms have been pawed out. You've got to help me string them, Isaac. Do you suppose we could put them up in the printshop? You have more than enough room."

"Chicken-of-the-woods," he said. "I remember now. Have you ever seen them? They grow on oaks, on dead branches, almost like conks. Dad prized them most—we cut them into slices and fried them with venison. Not sure I could still tell which are the good ones. You've a handbook, haven't you?"

"Isaac and his books! All those crates you brought in last week—more books, right? What good are they? But no, I don't know what kind you're talking about. These woods are full of things. In spring I gather ladybugs when the snow melts and they swarm out—I sell them to the people at the feed store. And I made that blackberry jam we had this morning—from the vines downstream in the narrow meadow. Even gooseberries make jelly. You boil the stickery little globes for just a minute, then the skins and the spines peel right off. I get hellgrammites out of the creek in June and sell them at the bait and tackle stores. They turn into Dobsonflies, did you know that? I even dig up dogwood seedlings and wild mock orange with the fine double white flowers, sell to the nursery. Maidenhair ferns along the streambank too, among the rocks, if they're growing too thick. I think I could almost live from just what's within two or three miles of here—if I could plant a good garden and shoot deer. But I can't do that, or catch fish either. I wouldn't feel right about it somehow. Even fish have rights. I gathered pine nuts last month, right after you showed up. The forest is almost a garden, a huge wild garden. And grapes too, but I didn't pick any this year—they're small from the dry summer and not sweet at all. But last year I made ten gallons of wine in one of those big springwater bottles. It was good but a little strong, almost chewable. I've got some left. You'll try it? Great Heavens, I'm babbling like a schoolgirl, aren't I?"

"What about grapes. If fish have rights, then...."

"You're making fun of me."

"Iphigenia," he said, "you're amazing. My dad used to make wine. I remember the taste. But from everything you've told me— you'd be a fair Injun squaw, for certain. All that's missing are the *ootim hai*, acorn kernels. You need a mortar and a *bai* and a *booi*, a place for leaching the acorns. We could eat *oosaw* all winter long. That's Maidu for *acorn mush*. A bit of local trivia for you...."

"You liked your father's homemade wine?" Ginny asked, sitting down with her back against a small oak.

"Not as I recall, but I was just a kid. Dad didn't want me drinking, yet once my friend Pinello and I sneaked off with a quart or so of the stuff and took it down canyon and drank it. Neither of us felt very good afterward, as I recollect—like we wanted to throw up, but couldn't."

"Bad Isaac," Iphigenia said, drawing up her knees, locking her hands.

*

They strung mushrooms until late afternoon, and then they walked upstream, crossed the creek, and climbed the ridge. The air was clear after the rain, with only a dim hint of the usual autumn haze over the hills. To the east dark clouds had formed again, fading to light rose color in thin afternoon light.

"Subtropical moisture coming up the east side of the range," he said, "on a conveyer belt from the ocean off Baja. It'll rain again this evening, though maybe not as hard. The clouds aren't so thick this time, and the air's a tad chilly. We won't be able to swim tonight, and I'll bet there's going to be frost before morning. It's a wonder we haven't had it already. The oaks and maples should turn a fine yellow after all."

"Everything's coming late this year," Ginny nodded. "Look. Let's go back, and I'll fix dinner. I'll make spaghetti with mushrooms—it's awfully good that way. You know, Isaac, I really don't like having a job, even if it's only during the afternoons. The work doesn't bother me. No, it's just that I don't like the world out there, though the fellas who stop at the café are nice enough. People are building new houses along the highway...."

"Things are changing, all right," he agreed. "It's got so tight that a good Republican president can't even have his boys sneak into Democrat headquarters without subsequent witch-hunts and earthquakes in tandem. That, and the computers, and too damned many human beings. You and me, we're anachronisms, I guess—a malcontented Halfbreed and a runaway Greek goddess...."

"Be serious, damn it. I'm not complaining, not really. I manage easily enough on what I make. Not into food stamps and the like—no independence that way. Get to keep all my tips. It's mostly truckers who stop at the café—and woodcutters and campers, sometimes people driving up from town, though that's just on weekends. We're not open Mondays."

"You'll poison us both," he said. "I'll bet half our mushrooms are death angels. I remember Dad saying one could get sick just from eating something after handling one. The damned fungi used to come up on the north side of the cabin, where you've got flowers. A strange sort of evolutionary adaptation, when you get right down to it. Deer won't touch them."

As they got to their feet, Isaac started to embrace her, then hesitated.

I'm frightened. I'm frightened of her. She's ten years younger than I, that's not much. And it isn't the problem, either. It's like she wants me but keeps me at arm's length. Or maybe it's that I feel like a boy again, too scared to ask his girl for a kiss. She's playing with me? Why am I afraid of her?

They walked down from the ridge, under twilit pines and firs, she sauntering ahead, McCain trying not to notice the tempting female movements of her hips, trying not to notice the female smell of her, a faint warm odor mixed with damp fragrance of pine needles and oak leaves.

*

Isaac McCain sat reading by the light of his Coleman. Doom put his head on his master's lap, raised one paw tentatively, his tail slowly wagging.

"Doomer, you're too damned big to be a lap dog. How many times do we have to debate the issue? Oh hell, come on then."

The English setter scrambled up, rested his chin in the crook of Isaac's arm, sighed happily.

"For a dog," the master grumbled, "life's ridiculously simple. You only get excited when a bitch is in heat. Then you go mad for a time, and after that the issue's over with. But us folks, Doomer, we're different. We never get out of heat, not completely—and that goes for males and females both. Jesuits and Franciscans have been at the perverse joy of denial for centuries, but there are still lots of priests' kids. By the Big Coyote's whiskers, I've turned coward I believe. Here I am, thirty-eight years old and deathly afraid to make a good solid pass at a yellow-eyed female of the same species, even though she's living in my own house, just a few feet away from me—all this after my mind finally snapped and I left my professorship and the otherwise satisfactory life that went with it and came hightailing back to the very place I swore I'd never return to. I tell you sir, it doesn't make sense—no sense at all."

Isaac pushed the dog onto the rug in front of the chair, stood up, folded his book over the chair arm, and walked to one of the bookcases he'd recently set up. Then he turned, glanced at Abram's volumes on the other side of the room, lit a cigarette, stared vacantly at the old Colt's Armory press, walked to it, yanked at the flywheel. He thought about his friend Madison, made a brief comparative analysis of their lives, something the both of them had been doing for years, the outfall of the friendly competition that had existed between them since their senior year in high school. Madison had a solid job at the local community college and was presently on sabbatical. He, McCain, had quit his university post.

Madison wrote poems, while Isaac was a scholar with a growing reputation. Madison had gone through two fouled-up marriages, while McCain had never been married. Madison was now head over heels in love with a longhaired lanky rebel named Sandy Sorenson who'd just walked out on her old man and had left a hyperkinetic four-year-old daughter behind, at least temporarily.

That won't last. Mack's got two other kids of his own, and by the end of a year, he and Sandy will be saddled with all three of the heathens. That's my prediction. Serve them right, both of them. I detest seeing happy people....

He laughed, spun the flywheel of the press once more.

"What I want to know is—how does that spripèd skonch always seem to land on his feet? He runs across the tight-wire like Nietzsche's clown, while I'm forever falling off. Where the hell's he get that self-confidence of his? I'm bigger, probably smarter, and besides that, I've got a Ph.D.—he doesn't. What the devil's the matter with me anyway? By heaven, I'm going to do it. To hell with this dallying about."

Iphigenia's light was still on, and Isaac knocked at the door—at the same time feeling like a school boy on his way to a first date.

"It's McCain," he said. "May I come in?"

A brief silence before she answered.

"Yes. The door's not locked—you know that."

She was sitting by the wood stove, drinking a glass of red wine. As she rose, her blue silk bathrobe momentarily revealed the cleavage between her breasts.

"It's late," she half-smiled. "I was just going to bed."

"Iphigenia Singares," he blurted, "Ginny, damn it anyway, let's make love. I've been waiting for days. I can't even sleep for thinking about you. Don't you want it too? Tell me you don't want it as much as I do."

"No, Isaac," she replied. "I won't tell you that. How much do you want it?"

He studied her expression, then began to laugh. Slowly, as if the moment were rehearsed, Ginny untied the cord about her middle, so that the blue silk opened down the front. She shrugged her shoulders slightly, and the robe fell to the floor.

How lovely her body is, my God she's lovely! I knew it all along, but I couldn't tell, mostly she wears men's clothing....

He stood, feeling very foolish now, staring at her.

"Do you like me?" she asked. "I shaved my legs and under my arms—I shouldn't have done that, but I wanted you to like my body. I did it this morning, right after I woke up. Yes, I want you Isaac McCain, you great oaf."

*

Sunlight. The sunlight awoke him. In a moment the memory of the preceding night came to him—and he reached over to where the girl had lain, but he did not find her—found only latent heat from her body among the pile of blankets. The cabin was still chilly, but a faint odor of smoke was in the air. He could hear the sputtering of burning wood, cedar chunks certainiy, in the stove in the other room. He could hear the *plink-plink* of perking coffee, could smell the aroma. Isaac looked to where his clothing was folded over the back of a wooden chair. Then he was aware of singing.

Ginny.

Isaac closed his eyes and concentrated on the words of a ballad, a sad ballad about love and the passing of love. He tried momentarily to recall the image of Joanne Duboce's face, but what came was Iphigenia Singares standing before him, naked as a jaybird. He sprawled out on the bed, his arms reaching to either side in a cruciform. He luxuriated in the delicious moment of awareness of his own male body, strength of his hands clutching at bedboards, and he thought: *This is the same spot, and I am lying here in my father's bed....*

*

Just past noon Mack Madison's green GMC four-wheel-drive pickup came bouncing down the road, Mack and Sandy Sorenson in the cab, and skidded to a halt next to Isaac's Buick coupe and Ginny's banged up VW. Isaac looked out the window and shook his head.

"Polecat-the-Poet always picks the wrong time to come visiting," he growled.

"I'll get dressed," Ginny said, retreating to the bedroom. "Put the coffee onto the stove, will you, Isaac?"

He did so and then strode outside to meet his friend.

"Dr. Isaac McHamburger!" Madison called out as he gallantly opened the truck door for Sandy. "Big Mac! Last Bear, old friend! We've come to take you away from all this. University of Oregon's put out a warrant for your arrest...."

"President Madison Hisself," Isaac grinned, shaking his friend's hand and giving Sandy a polite hug. "What are you two thieves doing up here? I thought you'd left for the Sea of Cortez."

"Change of plans, change of plans, you ponderous old classicist. We're on our way to Tuscarora. You want to come with us? Hey, what's going on here? I just realized you walked out of the wrong building."

Isaac stared down over the tops of his glasses, winked.

"You folks want some coffee? Sandy, haven't you seen through this fraudulent poet yet?"

"I'm still hoping he won't see through me," she smiled.

"Blindness is the human condition," Mack said quickly. "I believe, sir, you mentioned something about coffee? I need coffee."

"Java it is. Come on in, you two."

Madison gave McCain a playful shove with his shoulder and whispered, "Does this child sense something afoot? You and Miss Singares? You bunking with her now? That's it, *nicht wahr?*"

Isaac shrugged.

"I knew it!" Madison laughed. "Sandy, what did I tell you on the way up? By God, we'll have a double wedding—do it Injun and White both, if that's what they want."

"Mack, how does your lady stand you? Come on, first things first. Let's investigate the coffee pot."

Mack gave Isaac another shove and pushed past him into the cabin, caught Ginny as she was coming out of the bedroom, and reached for her hand, kissed it.

"Congratulations, Madam," he said. "I see you've caught the big fish!"

*

Isaac walked the long ridges, hills gray-blue with November haze, The oak groves still singing gold against heavy green of pine and fir. His thirty-ought-six rested against the crook of his arm, a familiar feeling, taking him back years, years before when he and Abram had hunted together, had tramped these same pathways etched in his deepest being, changed though, changed in the long process of seasons and storms, rediscovered, voices of the woods whispering to him, lure of earth and overhang of forest, the waning note of a bluejay whimsically imitating a hawk: and he thought how once he and his father had been cutting oak wood for winter, up on Burlington, the gray-green truck half loaded.

He'd seen a rattler, its head just visible beneath a pine log—he'd taken a shovel and poked at the head, thinking to scare the snake out. In an instant the serpent was after him. He threw a shovel and ran, yelled to his father.

Abram cut the snake in half with an axe. *Ike, I think he was hungry. You were his dinner. That hide would have made a good belt, but now it's dog collars.*

An unspoken bond with the mountains, deep red soil, cold springs on the hillside, icy water for summer afternoons, the surge and flux of winter storms, heavy gray silence of falling snow, ripe flood of the creek at the time of spring runoff. Isaac stopped—a reflex preceding cognition. In the clearing below, two deer—a young buck and a doe. He lifted his rifle, peered through the scope.

Thinking: *Kill the female, and I cut into the breeding population—not only her but her offspring for the next several years. Males are expendable—one buck can impregnate as many does as are able and willing.... Perhaps it's that way with humans as well.*

He sighted down on the forkhorn, set himself for his shot.

Didn't fire.

Perspiration had come to his forehead, and it was only when the two animals had moved away, into a copse of young firs, that he realized he didn't want to shoot at all.

"Maybe later," he told the dog, "after I've been home a while longer. Right now I'm still a stranger to these woods, whether I like it or not. A damned flatlander, so to speak. No right to be killing the varmints, not yet...."

Doom stared up at his master, the brown eyes curious, and whimpered softly.

"Suppose I'd shot the deer and dressed it out," Isaac said. "If I gave you the heart, would you eat it? Not likely. You're a sissy hound—you've grown up on the canned stuff and a few slow, stupid rabbits. You like to run deer, but what in hell would you do if you caught one?"

The dog wagged his tail, growled softly.

"Now take the human race," Isaac said, sitting next to the dog and laying the rifle aside, looping one arm over the setter's back. "A few years down the road we're traveling, and the world's population is going to double, then double again. The problem is, there's not going to be enough food. We don't need nuclear

weapons to find doomsday—just plain love-humping will be sufficient.   Time was when a significant number of women died in
childbirth, one in four maybe, and a considerable percentage of the
newborns died of one thing or another within a year or two or
three. Nowadays most of us make it to child-getting time, even if
your master hasn't arrived there yet.   Who knows, maybe I'm
sterile? If not, it's been blind luck and my lady friends taking pills.
Wouldn't be so bad, though, to have a young one.   Doom, you'd
probably display a full set of classic symptoms of sibling jealousy—
am I right?"

The dog yawned, bit gently at Isaac's forearm.

"And that's the problem.   Most of us want to sculpt out our
own image in human clay.   What about you?   You're only interested in ladies when they come into heat.   Your ancestors got
civilized right along with mine, and *Malus caninus* lost interest in
having any family except a human one. I'm on to your game,
Doomer.   But with humans, it hasn't happened that way.   Might
have, I suppose, if we'd had dogs to feed us.   So now what we've
got is a problem with excessive numbers—we need either a planet
ten or twelve times the size of this one, or else we need to show a
bit of restraint.   The option's that of mass starvation and a hella-
cious population crash.   You guys will be chewing our bones before
too long, it's damned near a cinch.   After that you'll have to revert
to pulling down sick deer and catching rats and mice.   But your wild
brothers, the coyotes and wolves, they're better prepared for
survival in a world with not many human critters.   It looks to me
like you're going to have to rediscover some forgotten habits of
behavior, old friend."

"It's *Canis familiaris*," said Doom, and he bit at a flea.

The English setter slipped away, paced to a manzanita bush,
and lifted his leg.   Then he kicked at the duff with his hind feet.

*

Near sundown Isaac waded across Deer Creek at the upper end
of the meadow—dark by the streamside, and he whistled softly in
the failing light, emerged from the cover of creek alders, stopped.

Two men were standing at the door to the cabin, and one was
pounding with his fist.   The other shouted something, and Isaac
was able to catch the words: "Open the door, bitch, or I'll kick it
in!"

The second man said something as well, but the syllables were lost in the air. Isaac recognized the tone of the voice nonetheless—familiar, a sound known at some point in his past. But who was it? Mind and body came instantly and intensely alive. How far into the past?

A voice over the telephone, last heard there. Tumbled memories, distorted, unformed.

Isaac kneeled to the ground, reached for Doom's collar.

"Ginny's in trouble," he whispered. "Whoever they are, they aren't being friendly. Could be armed—and there's no sense in taking chances. Not expecting anyone else, they think she's alone in the cabin. They've been through here before, most likely. Well, the twilight's on my side."

Whose voice is that?

No conclusion drawn but anger, sudden rage and a hatred long contained, emergent now, like fire that's smoldered among punky roots all winter, incubation beneath snow, day by day inching through fibers, unhurried, inevitable as the spring melt—and dry, hot days to follow. The fire escapes and is fanned into flame....

Take them from behind. Send the dog one way, you go the other. They seem to be drunk.

Isaac grasped his rifle and said, "Doomer Dog, it looks like we've got a little business here."

He looped his belt through the dog's collar and began working his way along the edge of the woods, keeping to the shadows until he was near the cabin.

"Get them, Doom!" he said. "Put teeth in their legs if you want. Get them, damn it!"

He loosed the dog, then ran to the rear of the printshop, came around from the opposite side. Doom stood stiff-legged by the door, fangs bared, growling ferociously.

"Must be her mutt," the taller of the two men said. "Don't shoot it yet—it ain't going to attack. She'll come out now. Wait."

That voice, years back....

Isaac knew who they were—the memory trace flared in his skull, flared hatred. He lifted his rifle and stepped out of the shadows from behind Ginny's car.

"Touch my dog, and I'll kill the both of you. Throw the guns down, gents. Now, Gawddamn it, or I'll put slugs in you for the sheer damned pleasure of it. Malicious trespassing, I'd say. Do what I tell you!"

The two men turned slowly, too slowly. Isaac fired once, away from them.

"I won't miss again—put down the guns. Deer season's over. Bullardi and Abbot, old friends, you're on my property—you came to the wrong place. That's it. Leave the guns and get the hell out of here. I'll return your toys when I have a moment."

"Damn it to hell!" the shorter individual called out, "don't shoot no more, you crazy sonofabitch! We was just horsing around!"

And the other:

"Who are you—you know me? Isaac McCain—is that you, Ike? Hey, man, we were just joking a bit. Didn't mean no harm."

"There we go, lads," Isaac said. "Now just move on over this way, get clear of the door. Here, Doom, come here! My old friend Burt, how the devil are you? Still like to push at folks, ehh? I'll sure remember to come down, buy a car from you one of these days, a brand new red Chevy with a sunroof maybe. You'll make some money off me. Hell, I'm just a dumb Halfbreed, ain't that right? You park your rig up on the hill, Burt? I'd say you and Frank ought to be on your way home. It gets dark early up here, and I've got a habit of shooting at shadows. Next time you come kicking on someone's door, you sonofabitch, you'd best be certain the owner's not around. You gents might get yourselves blown away for nothing."

"I'll have the cops on you!" Bullardi yelled. "McCain, you're as freaking crazy as your old man was!"

Abbot grabbed hold of Bullardi's arm, cautioned his friend: "Come on, Burt, don't argue. That approach never worked with him. Let's get out. Ain't worth a hole in the head, you know?"

"Great idea," Isaac agreed. "Yeah, bring the law on up. We'll straighten this thing out, the whole damned business. You just do that. Dad used his dynamite the wrong way, I won't."

Rifle fire from the doorway of the cabin, two quick shots echoing into the forest.

Then Ginny's voice: "I've got a gun too. You're in a crossfire, you whores! If he doesn't shoot you, I sure as hell will!"

Isaac laughed, felt an immense sense of relief, and squeezed off another round himself, red-white fire from the point of the rifle streaking a few feet out into darkness.

"Guess you fellas had best be moving. You hear what the lady's saying? I'm going to follow along behind until you get into your vehicle and head for Diggins. You won't see me, but I'll be there. Give you a little escort service. I'll bring these guns of yours on down one of these days. That's it. Get moving. Good fellows. By God, maybe I will let you sell me a car, Burt. You have any decent used pickups on the lot? Nonetheless, hunting season's over. Goodnight, esteemed classmates."

Isaac whistled for Doom—then a second time. The setter, walking stiff-legged and still staring at the intruders, finally minded.

"Goodnight, sweet ladies, gooonight. Y'all don't bother to come back now, you hear? Understand me, I'll be right behind you. Even look this direction, and I swear to Christ I'll kill the both of you. You *done crossed over* into McCain country, as a matter of bleedin' fact."

***

Canto Five:
ТЬE BREAKING

THE BRUISE IS NOT THERE,
NOR THE BULLYING BOY,
NOR THE GIRL WHO GAVE HIM THE BITTER GIFT,
UNDER THE HAWS IN THE HOLLOW DARK AND
    THE WINDLESS AIR;
BUT THE RUE REMAINS,
THE RUE REMAINS IN THE DELICATE ECHO OF WHAT
    WAS DONE;
AND HE WHO LABORS ABOVE THE LINES
LEANS TO AN ACHE AS OLD ALMOST
AS THE HOWL THAT SHOOK HIM IN HIS OWN BIRTH,
AS THE HEAVY BLOW THAT BEAT HIM TO BREATH
WHEN THE WOMB HAD WIDENED.

                [WILLIAM EVERSON,
                "THE ANSWER"]

        *

JUNE 11, 1954:

The headlights of the 1940 Buick poured out into darkness along a highway that churned like motorboat swath behind them. Graduation night! High school was over, over! Isaac McCain and April Incendie, alone in the car together, driving somewhere impossible, like Bodega Bay. The old brick building in Grass Valley was a memory but too soon to think about, and the girl's parents presumed her to be at an all-night party at a friend's house.

Isaac and April savored freedom, escape from everything they had known, and stared up through the windshield toward a full silver moon that glided along above them. The headlights of the car sought out the endless road that seemed to flee before them in the rushing and singing night.

They pulled onto a graveled shoulder at the crest of a long hill and got out, illumined fog filling the valley below, and they breathed in the smell of salt ocean air. His arm was around her as they climbed a grassy hill toward a grove of eucalyptus. From the rise they could actually see the ocean itself, half-obscured by fog and hundreds of feet below where they stood.

A bell tolled, slowly and irregularly, out at sea somewhere, and fog drifted silver in moonlight.

They lay down in dry grass and kissed, his hands going over her, under her blouse, between her legs. She held tightly to him, desperately kissed him.

"No," she said. "Please, Isaac, not here."

He bit at her throat and unbuttoned her clothing.

Then two naked bodies moved together in the moonlight, a primitive, lonely rhythm punctuated by a distant bell and the ocean's hushed sound.

"Why are you crying?" he asked afterward. "This is no time to cry."

"You big dumbo. Because I'm happy, of course," she replied, clinging to him and running her fingers over the taut muscles of his back.

"Did it hurt this time?"

"No, no. You're shivering, Ike. Why are you shivering? It's not cold tonight."

"Yes, I'm cold," he lied. "Let's get dressed."

They did so and then ran down the hill. Isaac leaped over a sagging barbed wire fence, rolled in dry grass on the lower side.

"My gazelle!" she laughed. "You'll break your legs, both of them!"

He lay in the grass, moaning conspicuously as the moon burned down through drifting fog.

*

When the sun finally came up, however, the two were sitting on the beach at Bodega Bay, and Isaac had built a fire out of driftwood. They sat close together and waited for the Seaside Café to open.

"Clam chowder and toast and coffee—that will taste really great," April smiled.

"God, I'm hungry. I think I'll eat you alive, Miss Incendie. That's it—I'm going to have April for breakfast."

"Quit pawing at me Isaac. Aren't you ever satisfied?"

"I'm an octopus," he growled, wrestling her onto the sand and kissing her.

"Help!" she cried out. "Somebody help me—I'm being...attacked!"

And they lay together, her head on his chest, observed seagulls floating over gray-green waves. He rose then, took a step or two, and flung a fragment of sandstone out over the water, but the stone did not fly nearly as far as he'd hoped.

The bell was still ringing, its sound muted: and off to the south, somewhere in a heavy bank of fog that hovered half a mile offshore, white gulls came in a downward spiral of sunlight.

*

JUNE 18, 1954:

When the siren sounded, the members of Crooked Pines Fire Crew were sitting in their tent. They figured Old Lee was playing a trick. This was a new job for all six young men, and they hadn't actually; considered the possibility of a fire-call occurring after hours.

But reality had come calling. Then onto the tanker truck—Lugie, Barney, Mack, Isaac, Hyatt, and Smith—with Lee the Foreman driving and Pegelow in the cab and operating the radio.

"Structure fire, boys," Lee said. "Isaac, looks like it's down at your dad's place—any kerosene in that printshop?"

Isaac gestured futilely.

"You sure its our place?" he managed.

Images: Oliver the mule. Rabbit hutches. Printing presses.

Isaac thought: *Yes, and though no one knows it except me and Mack, Elizabeth Collingwood's there, our high school French teacher. She could lose her job if the story gets back to town....*

The pumper truck turned off the highway below the campground, dropped gears, and spun on down the rutted road that led over the canyon rim toward McCain Flat and Deer Creek—the cumbersome green Ford, complete with its reels of hose and racks of fire tools, moaning along beneath an overhang of pine and fir.

It wasn't the printshop. The house itself was ablaze. Flames lashed out of broken windows, and the roof burst through just as the tanker truck hissed to a halt. Immediately the young men were in motion, starting the pump engine, reeling out firehoses, each crewman desperately trying to remember bits and pieces of what he'd learned during the week's training Lee had been able to give them.

"Keep away!" the foreman shouted. "It's no use trying to save the house—douse that grass fire behind the shed! Madison! Grab a backpack and get over there!"

Isaac searched about for his father, didn't see him, and followed Mack toward the printshop. Abram was there, like the shadow behind an old rock wall in late afternoon—a stunned expression on his face and seeming smaller and more vulnerable than his son could ever remember.

"Ike? That you, boy? It's not possible. Hello, Mack. Put out that fire if you can—my mind's not right. Finished. It's finished. It's finished, Isaac...."

But the son knew, and was swallowed into horror—knew and at the same time resisted the knowledge, easing it into place, gently, soundlessly, like falling leaves.

"Dad, she's in town, isn't she? She's staying at her apartment for a few days?"

The elder McCain, there in the dry grass, was crumpled and childlike for all his great size. He dug his fingernails into his eyes and sobbed, his big muscular body convulsing and tremoring painfully.

Isaac reached down, touched his father's face that was illuminated in light and shadow.

"My God, Ike, Elizabeth was in the house when something...."

Isaac turned away. He was frantic, not ready to comprehend. It was too fast—things were forever coming too fast. He sprayed water on the leaping grass fire, and thinking, "Her fingers are like burning twigs in the dark."

He stared up the hill, caught sight of Oliver, whose two wide eyes reflected smears of light. The mule was pulling at his tie-rope and braying into the night and the smoke.

Twin smells of water and fire—and that other smell, of death, now etched indelibly into the darkness.

A hand on his shoulder.

Isaac turned, looked at Abram, standing there now like a pillar of limestone, gray and old in the flickering, a timeless grief and despair in the deep-set eyes, the face, though bearded, almost like that one he'd seen in a textbook, the face of Chief Joseph of the Nez Percé.

Mack Madison came up, a Pulaski tool in one hand and a now-empty five-gallon backpack pump strapped to his shoulders, stood by uneasily.

"Miss Collingwood," he asked, "she's all right?"

Abram said: "Son—Mack, you too—you boys have got to understand, you don't know. There are demons...."

He drew Isaac to his chest, held him.

*

JULY 10, 1954:

Cloudy during the day and a trace of rain—after dinner at the guard camp, the boys stood around outside the mess hall, pitching horseshoes.

"Good news, men," Lee called out. "HQ says the fire danger's down. McCain, you and Madison get your days off after all. Now then, who's champion out here? Let an old man show you fellows how to play this game. Not a one of you holds the durned shoe right. Look here now...."

Madison let out a whoop and headed for the tent to get his things together, Isaac following at a brisk walk.

"You coming down town later?" Mack asked, dumping some books and his dirty clothes into a Navy duffle bag his father had given him. "I've had a hell of a premonition all week, Isaac. Softball game at the park tonight—there's an absolutely gorgeous little blonde in short-shorts, just moved here from New Orleans, and tonight's the night I'm supposed to meet her."

"Last night you said you were going to convince Kara Switzer to go steady again. You're as two-faced as that damned Oppenheimer—no loyalty in you."

"Get serious, then. I promise not to join the Russian army when the war starts, if that makes you feel any better. Sheets, mon, Kara isn't interested in old Mack any more. You and me, we'll be off to Berkeley before too much longer, and make-out queen Kara, she's not going to want to put her social life on hold. So it's in my best interest to meet the blonde from New Orleans."

"Your blonde is nothing more than a dream, Mack. That's all you do is dream. It's bad enough we're both confirmed bookworms, but at least I keep my damned feet on the ground."

Mack Madison laughed and did a little jig-step.

"Sure you do," he said. "And you probably also think April Incendie isn't going to be going out with the Bulldog while we're in Berkeley, and you with your nose stuck in a book. Look, you come on down to the softball game. According to my faithful crystal ball, Miss New Orleans has a red-haired buddy from Los Angeles—locks down to her derrière, and that's the truth. The two of them are waiting for us, I tell you—both virgins, and both searching for a cure for the affliction."

Then Mack was in his Ford, rear wheels spurting gravel as he roared onto the highway.

Isaac started the Buick's straight-eight and followed, but turned down the road to McCain Flat, drove the winding, dusty trail home. He felt a need to be with his father now, the knowledge that Abram needed him. Fire and Miss Collingwood's death had been crushing blows. The Forest Service was good enough to give him a week off at that time, and he'd hardly let Abram out of his sight—being half convinced his father was contemplating suicide.

His mind isn't right. This thing has torn out his insides. Dying. Miss Collingwood's death is killing him as well. It's death that I don't understand, that sets earth's teeth on edge.

The funeral had been a chanting for about three pounds of charred bones.

On days with no fires, Lee gave permission for Isaac to drive home to make certain his father was all right, but after two weeks, Abram McCain began setting type again.

"My own book of poems," he'd told Isaac. "Don't wait this long to do yours."

Under gray afternoon sky, Oliver the mule was loose, grazing solemnly in sweet grass about fifty yards from where the cabin had been. Abram had cleared away and burned the remains of the cabin and had whitewashed the old foundation during the four days since Isaac was last home.

Isaac thought: *It looks like new, ready to take on the weight of another house.*

Then he heard noise of the hand-feed letter press, a slapping of the leather drive belt, purr of a gasoline motor, light thumping of the impresssion plate.

Isaac opened the door to the shop and stepped inside.

Abram McCain was behind the Colt's Armory press, surprisingly agile and even delicate in his movements, a red band tied about his forehead. He was bare to the waist, hairy arms glistening with sweat.

"Close the door, Ike, or that damned mule will be in here, trampling all over everything. Get me a stack of Kilmory text out of the big box, will you? By golly, this run's almost through, and I don't want to break my rhythm. You showed up just in time."

"Hi, Dad," Isaac said. "How's the book coming? You must be printing around the clock. How many sheets you need?"

Abram finished his run without missing an impression and shut down the press, its flywheel squealing against the pressure of the braking lever.

"This is the book I'll stand by. Son, I've worked as printer, off and on, for most of my life—and I've done some damned fine work, yet always for other men, their books. I've waited. Maybe too long. But Isaac, these poems string out behind me like stones. I wrote a couple of them last week, and I wrote some of them years ago, when your mother was still alive. We're all poets, Ike. Your friend Mack, I've seen him scribbling in that notebook of his. You'll catch the disease eventually. There's a bit of the poet in every human being alive—if it doesn't die young, of starvation. It's there, even in you, my boy. Well, no sense talking your ear off, is there? Ike, I'm going to start putting up the new cabin as soon as I've got my book done. Maybe you can give me a hand with the framing if the Federal fire department allows you any days off next week. But probably I'll be pounding boards, now and again, all fall long, while you're down at the university. You get home for Christmas at least, now, you hear? I'll have the thing finished by then. This'll be the third house on the same foundation—foundation's the most important part of any structure."

"You painted it white," Isaac grinned. "It looks all ready to go."

"Oliver!" Abram raged. "Curses upon your head, you square-toothed cow! Either come in here and help me run the press, or get the hell out!"

The mule was standing in the open doorway, his ears bent forward. He ruffled his nostrils slightly and turned his head to one side, sniffing at a galley of type on the composition stone, nuzzling the lead with his lips.

*

AUGUST 3-4, 1954:

"Yo-sem-it-ee!" Mack nodded. "*Uz-mati!* That's where we're going when we get off work this afternoon. Hell, yes. I promised my brother Tobe I'd take him fishing, and Yosemite's as good a place as any. In the meanwhile, McIsaac, you and old Mad Mack are going to climb a mountain. You up for it, or you going to spend your time mooning over Lady Incendie? Look, Kara's getting it on with her shot-putter friend, and April's stepping out with the Bulldog. There's nothing we can do about it, so let's go climb a damned mountain. Maybe Dirty Doug Cantrill would like to go along—hell, your Buick will hold ten or twelve of us, won't it?"

"My car?" Isaac asked. "You get heap crazy idea, and you want to go in my car?"

"Of course," Madison said.

"Doug's working at the auto parts place—he can't get away. You know that."

"What about me?" Red Lugie suggested. "I'm willing. Heck, I can outclimb the both of you. Besides, you two'll fall off the top and break your necks if I'm not there to keep watch."

Madison clapped Lugie on the shoulder.

"What do you say, McCain? You with us or not?"

"Do I have any choice in the matter?" Isaac complained.

The sky was gray, threatening rain, and at five o'clock the foreman announced that fire danger was way down—no one would be held on standby.

Isaac drove to the flat, told his father where he intended to go, and picked up his packsack and sleeping bag.

"Head up the Tioga road," Abram suggested. "It's dirt and rock, but your hot-rod'll make it. It's beautiful country, son. Wild varmints all over the place—at least there were last time I was down that way, about twenty years since. Watch out for the bears, though. Blackies, they won't be any problem as long as you don't get into a contest of wills over a slab of bacon. If a bear gets your grub, it's best not to try to make him return it. Those park bears can get mighty pushy. You be coming here Sunday, or you figure to get in late? I'll fix up some stew for you and Mack and Red if you want."

Then Isaac was in his car and on his way to the Madison berry farm. Red Lugie was already there, and after a short talk with Mack's mother and father, the boys, including young Toby Madison, piled into Isaac's coupe.

                              *

They traveled south, down Highway Forty-nine, through Auburn and Placerville and Jackson and on into the night.

It was past midnight when the reached the area just below Yosemite National Park. Here they pitched camp beneath some digger pines close by the Merced River, built a small campfire, and boiled water for coffee.

"You sure there's going to be a place for me to go fishing?" Toby Madison asked several times.

"Would your big brother lie to you, Tobe?" Mack replied.

"All the time," Toby said. "You sure there's a place to fish?"

"An excessively suspicious nature," Isaac noted, sipping at his coffee.

"He also doesn't trust us," Red Lugie grinned. "He knows us too well."

"I trust Red," Toby mumbled. "If he says so, then it's so."

"Have faith," Mack said. "Isaac, what are we going to do about the problem with our fickle girlfriends? Perhaps we could work out some sort of strategy. Mine's still in high school—my former girlfriend, I should say. But you—what you ought to do is convince April to come down to Berkeley for the spring semester. What you should have done months ago was talk her into going to Berkeley right off the bat. Her family's got money, and her grades were as good as ours, maybe better, I don't know. Okay, okay. You were valedictorian, I admit it. Maybe I'm a little jealous, but what the hell? One way or the other, April was eligible for admission, and...."

"She doesn't want to leave Diggins, Mack. Quite definite about it. She wants to live at home and go to Sierra College."

"Bullardi'll be there, playing Joe Jockstrap on the football team. Not so good, not so good. She could be Mrs. Bulldog by next spring. I'll tell you, Ike, I think she damned well enjoys pitting you two against one another. Just my theory, that's all."

Isaac shrugged and poured another cup of coffee.

"Mack's right," Red said. That's what she does, Isaac. She's been going back and forth with you guys for the past year and probably longer than that, before the high schools joined and we got to know you. You both ought to drop her. I think so. Hell, I don't know. I don't understand about girls with brains. You like her, and that's all that matters."

"Now Kara Switzer," Mack shrugged, "her problem is that she's still just a kid—the same age as Tobe here. So why do I keep busting my ass to get her to go steady? Maybe that fictitious blonde from New Orleans is down at Berkeley by now."

"If so," Isaac laughed, "she's probably studying French or German or Latin."

"Had to bring that up, didn't you, you malcontented mither? Okay, so I didn't take any foreign language. I'll have to eventually. Well, it doesn't make any difference. I'm fated to meet her, I tell you. We'll probably get married and have seven kids."

"You sure there's a place to fish?" Toby asked.

Isaac, Red, and Mack glanced at one another and shook their heads.

"Let's get some sleep," Isaac suggested.

"Right," Mack agreed. "Tomorrow we climb either Conness or Dana, the first men ever to ascend those hoary heights."

"Oh bullpucky," Red growled, setting his coffee cup down and unzipping his sleeping bag.

*

Toby was up before dawn, demanding his companions roll out and be on their way.

Mack insisted that he wished to sleep in, but Isaac and Red threatened to pour water on him, and at length he arose. The four, shivering above a re-kindled campfire, ate a cold breakfast, extinguished the small blaze, and piled into the Buick, once again on the road to Yosemite.

Three hours later they were close to Tioga Pass, the Buick not too greatly the worse for its passage over a long, twisting, unpaved road to the high country, and Mack let his brother off at a big creek, arranging to meet him about sundown.

Toby fussed for a few minutes, first deciding he wished to mountain-climb instead, and finally that he'd go fishing after all.

*

Isaac, Mack, and Red parked the car just at the summit. Wind was blowing, and the day was overcast, the temperature here near ten thousand feet just above freezing.

"Great weather for August," Isaac said.

"Great weather for freezing our tails off," Mack grumbled. "Whose idea was this, anyway?"

They pulled on double pairs of pants and double shirts, checked their gear, and set off up the trail toward the top of Mt. Dana, a large, relatively uninspiring red-gray rockpile listed as 13,060 feet.

*

At twelve thousand the wind was cold and fierce, numbing their hands and faces, and they crawled down into a space between lichened boulders. Mack struggled to get his little sterno burner going, cursed when the matches refused to stay lit. But at length the small canister of jellied gasoline began to flicker and give off heat. Red removed the liner from the forest service hard hat he was wearing and poured some water from a canteen.

"What the hell you doing, Loog?" Isaac asked.

"Coffee, of course. Tinfoil packets here somewhere. Swiped them out of the cookshack at Crooked Pines."

"How you going to explain to Lee what happened to your helmet? You'll never get the soot marks off," Mack said.

"Dumbass. Sterno don't leave soot. Besides, that's what a hard-hat's for."

"This damned wind," Isaac said. "We'll all become hypothermic and die here on the mountain."

"What's hypo...what's that crazy word supposed to mean?" Red demanded.

"We get cold, like a lizard at night," Mack said, taking the water-filled hardhat from Red and holding it in place over the burner.

"Ike, you always got some six-bit word or another," Red growled. "It don't take being smart to figure out that we're cold. Swear to Heaven!"

"That it doesn't," Isaac agreed. "Well, at least water boils quicker up here. The coffee's a good idea."

"Your dad," Mack asked, "how's he getting along? What I mean is, he seemed...different the last time I was down at the flat. My pa said your pa was over in the cemetery the other day, singing at the top of his lungs. Dad wasn't actually there—Hoagland, that Mormon guy who's got the orchard on the other side of Peardale Store, he and his wife were putting flowers on their daughter's grave. Anyhow, Hoagland told my dad about it...."

Isaac shrugged, watched as Red opened the packets of instant coffee and stirred them into the hardhat.

"He's printing a book of his own poems, and he's getting ready to rebuild the cabin. I think he's come through it all right. It's funny—how we never think of older people falling in love. At least I never did. When Dad and Miss Collingwood started seeing each other, I didn't think anything about it. I mean, I never guessed they were going to start sleeping together just like...."

Madison laughed.

"Just like we would with our girlfriends, if they'd go along with the idea? I used to think maybe Mom and Dad just had sex twice, and that's how Toby and I came into the world. Suppose we'll still be interested in making out when we get to be old men? No point in worrying about it, though, until after we actually get started screwing on a more or less regular basis...."

"Crude, crude. Anyhow, speak for yourself."

"I want to have at least ten kids," Red grinned. "That way they can support me."

"I don't want any kids," Mack said. "Kids must be a royal pain in the neck. What do you think, Ike?"

Isaac shook his head.

"I think, gentlemen, that we ought to drink this vile brew and then attack the rockpile again. We're never going to reach the north pole at this rate."

"Careful, Madison," Red cautioned. "You'll burn your mouth on the rim of the bluebastardly hardhat."

"Stop cussing so Goddamned much, my carrot-haired friend. No problem, no problem," Madison replied, taking a gulp of the coffee. "You didn't bring any sugar, perchance?"

They consumed the steaming liquid, and Red replaced the liner in his aluminum hat.

Mack put the lid on the sterno can and tucked the little stove into his pack.

"Let's have at it," Isaac suggested. "You guys with me?"

"What we should of done," Red grinned, "was go to one of the whorehouses over in Nevada. Either that or go fishing with Toby. Lord Almighty, it's cold!"

"Wouldn't have let you in anyhow," Madison said.

"What you talking about, Mack?" Lugie demanded as he put on his hard hat.

"They don't service redheads," Madison delcared.

Lugie looked puzzled for a moment and then grinned broadly.

"What I hear, that's all they do service. I mean, every man's got one...."

Isaac laughed into the cold wind that was running like an invisible river across the hump of Mt. Dana.

"Come along, you fools," he said. "I'll lead you into the promised land."

*

The trail along the upper saddle was easy enough, and the landscape, well above timberline, was composed of fractured red rock spattered in places with lichens. Wind howled among the crags, and the day continued to be decidedly unpleasant. Not even the usual assortment of spring flowers that appear in the Sierras in late summer....

"Probably a hundred rotten degrees down in Sacramento today!" Red shouted into the wind that nearly nulled his words.

"Be nice if part of it found its way up here," Isaac yelled, rubbing at his numb cheeks.

*

Then they were on the top of Dana, standing finally on the utmost crag, thirteen thousand feet above sea level. They gazed down to a small glacier, deep in its gouged cirque on the east flank of the mountain, looked southward toward the peaks of Ritter and Lyell, north to Conness, the latter mountain lumplike and seemingly close, so close it might almost have been touched.

Across a great trench eastward, they could see the blue-black surface of Mono Lake, and beyond that gray desert ranges that reached off into Nevada.

Nothing lives on these heights. This is no proper place for human beings....

"Damn the human race!" Isaac shouted.

But the echo he was hoping for never came—his words drowned in the wind.

"What the hell you talking about?" Red wanted to know.

"The madness has taken hold of him," Mack laughed. "Maybe you guys gave me *Mad Mack* for a nickname, but Isaac's the loony one."

"Joseph McCarthy eats commies!" Isaac shouted.

"I like Ike Eisenhower!" Madison joined in. "Don't know why I like the bald-headed old drill sergeant, but I do!"

"Crazy as two drunk hornytoads!" Red yelled. "Anyone asks me, I don't know either one. Give me the damned camera, and you guys pose up on the high rock. I'll take your picture. Then one of you take mine. Give us something to show our grandkids."

"Listen to him," Mack grinned. "You know what he's been doing after work, Ike? Stump-breaking deer, without question."

"I was wrong, I guess," Red said.

"About what?"

"Always figured you two was the smart ones. You're dumber than stumps."

"He's got a point," Isaac laughed, scrambling to the top of the highest crag. "A man could indeed go crazy from spending too much time up here. Nothing but rocks and gray sky and this wind. It's not human at all."

"Isn't supposed to be," Madison said, standing on one foot, arms out, and posing.

Isaac flexed his fingers, took the camera from Red, and snapped a few more pictures.

Then the three set off at an easy lope down the mountain's flank, cold air burning their lungs.

*

"Three hours up, and forty-five minutes down," Mack laughed when they d reached the Buick. "Come on, Ike, get that huge engine started and the heater on. We re all damned near froze to death!"

"Exercise and brisk air—both are good for the circulation," Isaac mumbled.

They met Toby at the appointed place. The younger Madison's face was red, and his lips nearly blue; but he had a string of trout.

All four were laughing and joking as they drove the rutted Tioga Road out of the high country and down to Merced River, where they found a likely campsite and cooked trout fish for dinner.

A pair of small black bears looked longingly from across the river but made no attempt to cross.

In the morning they drove to the southern end of the park, to Mariposa Grove, to see the Grizzly Giant first-hand, a tree that some believed older than the General Sherman. Isaac placed his hard-hat over his heart in silent and reverential prayer.

"This brochure says the big fellow may be four thousand years old," Mack Madison remarked. "By my calculations, that's older than...God."

"It would have been growing a good long while when the Israelites left Egypt, at least," Isaac agreed.

Mack was jotting down some notes—insisted he was going to write a novel about all this one day.

Then they were out of the national park and on their way toward Crooked Pines Campground.

Mack drove the Buick, and Isaac dozed, his mind pleasantly haunted by images of Sierran peaks and inhuman spaces.

*

SEPTEMBER 1, 1954:

The truck's headlights reached out under twin walls of pine and fir on either side of Highway 20.

Abram McCain crouched in a ditch beside the asphalt, hunkered down on the balls of his feet. He cradled a thirty-pound stone, moved slowly from side to side, singing to himself.

A truck was rapidly approaching.

"Hummmmmmm," he whispered. "It's time."

He rose from the ditch, stood on the blacktop's edge, his shoulders drawn forward. He waited there, completely naked in moonlight that was only beginning to find its way down through the heavy foliage about him.

"Swine!" he said slowly, precisely. "*Swinus castratus!*"

The truck's lights were on him now. The driver was hitting his brakes, the big rig weaving back and forth on the highway like some large, writhing snake.

McCain stepped forward, directly into the path of the on-coming vehicle. Growling, he raised the stone above his head and set it hurtling between the lights—could hear large tires hissing into an agonized scream on pavement as he leaped into the roadside ditch. He waited for the sound he knew was coming: rock as it bounded, skidding along the monster's hood, shattering the windshield, and disappearing into the cab itself.

"You bastards!" McCain shouted. "You filthy bastards, don't leave a man any room, you tree-murdering sons-a-bitches!"

Abram McCain's voice was drowned by the truck's passing roar.

He watched from where he stood as red brakelights flashed desperately—then the Peterbilt lurched to one side, hit a soft shoulder, and tilted slowly, almost ridiculously, logs ripping loose from their chain moorings, bouncing, skidding along the asphalt. The logging truck slid sideways, onto an embankment, trampling a small copse of firs before coming to rest.

Abram McCain ran madly through the forest, stumbling, rising to his feet, running again. He shouted at the top of his lungs: stopped, looked wildly about, rolled on his back in kitkitdizze and bracken.

"Bastards!" he sang. "I'll get all of you, you bastards! Acorn Girl and Ben McCain, I'm finishing the job you two started! I'll bring the Goddamned world to its knees, no question!"

He scrambled to his feet once more, pulled with both hands at his beard, rubbed at his eyes—stood tall, naked, and awkward in the moonlight.

"This is my world," he said, more quietly now. "Thousands of years my people lived here, brothers and sisters to the animal people. *Ishanahura*, Loon Woman, she lay with her brother, and maybe that caused.... No. Not that, and not the God-cursed gold, either. Ben looked for gold, found fire instead, fire and massacre under the snow-crown of *Wahgalu*, but already the disease was upon us, all of us. Too many, too many—and bil!:ons more waiting to be born, waiting in darkness for their moment of light. This race ends in annihilation...."

Then he disappeared, soundlessly, into the dark forest.

*

Perhaps half an hour later the Crooked Pines Crew arrived at the scene of the accident.

"Ten-twenty," Lee said into the mike. "Highway Patrol isn't here yet, where are they? Little fire out in the brush. My boys'll have it under control shortly. Ten-four, Mike, we'll stay on stand-by. The driver's okay, even if he ain't happy. Maybe dozed off, I don't know. He's jabbering. Yeah. Ten-four, ten-four."

A log lay at an angle in the middle of the roadway, and red flares spat on black pavement.

The foreman stepped down from the Mormon-Harrington and strode to where a dazed truck driver stood.

"Don't know, so help me God, I don't know what happened. I'm driving along, thinking about getting home and putting it to the wife and then some shuteye when all of a sudden this great big gorilla rares up out of nowhere, damnit, and lets fly with a bigass Goddamned rock right through my windshield.. . Maybe it was Bigfoot."

"You been drinking, have you?" Lee asked.

"Hell, no. I swear to the Blue Nun herself, I haven't even had a lousy beer. Didn't stop at Washington House—we been running late all day. It's just like I said, naked as a blarsted matinee Injun...."

"Headdress and all?" Lee asked.

"Listen, you bunghole fire-stomper, I'm telling the Goddamn truth, whether you like it or don't. Go look in the truck and see if there ain't a damned rock in the cab—come right in through the windshield. I'm telling you, the oversized ostrich was tryin' to kill me. Shee-it! This whole thing's like some kind of nightmare, only it's on both sides of bein' asleep."

"Figure that's it," Lee said. "You musta dozed off for a minute...."

Lee scratched his ear and turned to Red Lugie, motioned toward the smashed truck. Lugie jogged over, climbed up, peered inside, then returned to where his foreman was waiting.

"There's a rock, okay. Bigger'n a loaf of Wonder Bread. And the windshield's all caved in. Could of happened when he crashed, though...."

Lee rubbed his hand across his mouth. He turned to the truckdriver.

"You gonna tell the CHP what you're telling me?"

"What do you want me to say, Smokey the Bear? That's what happened. Shee-it, I'm goin' to lose my job over this, sure as hell. Of all the rotten luck...."

The driver sat down on the roadbank and lit a cigarette, his hands shaking badly.

"Sure you're all right?" Lee asked. "No blow to the head or anything like that?"

A red light appeared on the highway downgrade, and a moment later a patrol car pulled up, its service radio crackling with voices and static.

*

SEPTEMBER 16, 1954:

The night was not quite cold enough for the year's first frost, though two inches of snow had fallen at Donner Pass twenty-four hours earlier.

Isaac looked absently at April Incendie, surprised (not for the first time) at the luxuriance of long blond hair tied with a yellow ribbon and pulled tight behind her head. He wished desperately he were not heading off to the university in Berkeley—he considered scrapping the whole idea. It might have been better, he mused, if he'd gotten C grades through high school. Then nobody would have had any real expectations of him—and maybe nobody did anyway. Berkeley was all right for someone like Mack Madison, maybe, but what could college life hold for a Halfbreed kid who'd grown up at the end of a dirt trail, down in a fir forest?

True, he reflected, he was a certifiable genius. but so what?

He and April went to the high school football game, and afterward they drove and talked as always before, ended up on an old road behind LaBarr Meadows, south of town. The sky was completely, frighteningly clear now, with a shred of moon low in the west.

Isaac stopped the car at the edge of an irrigated meadow, and he and April held one another and kissed for a time.

"Look at that pile of hay, like a mountain out there, all shadows except at the top. Let's climb it."

They ran across the meadow, stumbling and falling once in rough-cut stubble.

"Sometimes," he said, "Dad used to mow our meadow—with a hand scythe. He piled up the hay and put a tarp over it. When I was a kid, I used to dig tunnels, burrow clear down to the bottom of the stack and curl up and just think."

"What does a little boy think about, Isaac?"

"Don't get sarcastic, Ape. Come on, oh golden-maned beauty of mine, don't spoil things. Let's climb to the top. We're scaling Shasta."

She laughed, but the laughter didn't sound quite sincere.

"Sometimes I'm afraid you'll never grow up, Isaac McCain. You'll always be a boy, just like that father of yours."

"That something you heard your pa say, right? He doesn't understand Dad—hardly knows him, in fact. You don't, either. Nobody does, not even me. Abram doesn't live in the same world as the rest of us. His mind's drifting—a century ago. Come on, woman, let's hit the hay...."

The image of the logging truck flashed through his mind. He knew full well who had thrown the big rock. *Only one person could have done that....*

They scrambled up, Isaac pulling April along by one hand.

Then they sat on top of the stack and stared at a sky full of blue flame. Isaac rolled over on April, but was surprised at her resistance. He kissed her and was vexed when he put his hand on her breast and she pushed him away.

"Isaac, I don't feel like it tonight. I'll get...grass seeds in my clothing."

"What's the matter, April? Surely you don't want to waste a perfectly good night like this?"

She turned away from him, said softly: "That's all we ever do, you know—we waste time."

"All right, be serious then. The demons will drive us off our mountain—you'll see, my girl. When they do, you'll cry and cry."

She relaxed after that, but she still wasn't with him.

"It's too cold," she said as he started to take off her sweater.

Isaac sat up, held her face between his hands, made note of a faint glow of moonlight in her hair—and her hair was all silver, like an old woman's. He felt her sadness, tried to move away from it.

She's unhappy because I'm going down to Berkeley. She loves me and doesn't want me to leave....

"Okay," he said. "Look, April. I'm not removing to the end of the earth, after all. I'll be home on weekends. I've already promised you that. We just have to be patient, take things one day at a time."

"Why is that, Isaac?"

He couldn't think of an appropriate answer.

"You know," he said, "Dad claims the world is full of spirits, like little stars of fire in the trees and in the rocks. This night's so beautiful I can almost believe...."

"He's just a crazy old Indian," April replied, her voice chill with resentment, "and you're too much like him. You can't see the most obvious things, Isaac. You're too busy worrying about demons that aren't even there."

Isaac drew back, looked away from her, off across dark hills.

"People think your father's crazy, Isaac, don't you know that? How long had our French teacher been living with him up there, anyway? Why didn't you tell me? It's a scandal all over town."

Isaac felt a surge of anger.

"Your parents, ehh? I'll tell you. I'm not like my father, but I think you ought to know this much. Abram's a very religious person, not like your folks. They go to church for show, and you know it. Rotary and Elks and all the rest of it—that's just so much elemental bearscat. I'm sorry, but it's true. Your dad's always talking about responsibility, but what's he mean? Abram doesn't give me that kind of bunk, and he's not trying to live my life for me, either. I think for myself, I make up my own mind about things. All right, I'm part Indian—so what? But that bothers you, doesn't it? Well, doesn't it? I'm proud to be who I am, April. And, yes, whatever kind of religion I've got, I guess it's part Indian, too. You have your God hung up on a cross, but He doesn't mean anything to you—and not to your folks, either. Well, Jesus isn't just *your* God. He's mine too. He belongs to everybody. The wild Indians are gone long ago, but some of our ideas remain—and that's where the demons, as you call them, come from."

"I don't want to listen to this stuff," April said. "You're not even Christian, are you?"

"I'm Christian, but maybe not in a way you comprehend. I understand Christ, I see him as God, I talk to Him in the forest at night."

"I don't want to hear it, Isaac. You can't change, and neither can I."

"You're going to listen, though. Call them what you like. The concepts aren't especially Indian, and I don't even know very much about Indian people, including my own relatives, I'm ashamed to say. To tell the truth, I read books, that's all, just like Mack. A damned bookworm. About my own family, I know only what Dad's told me—just like you or anybody else. But the spirits—they're out in the woods—and they were right here on this haystack until we started arguing and chased them off. They make things come alive, maybe even *are* life. Gilby, our physics teacher—you know how he was always talking about x-factors? That's what spirits are. They cause life, and we should love whatever it is that makes life."

"You're so smart that you're utterly stupid, Isaac. Even when we were in grade school, the other kids always called you the walking encyclopedia. Did you suppose that was because they admired you, or what? Sometimes I don't think you *really* know very much at all, not about anything that matters."

"Call names all you want, April. I'm just trying to tell you what I believe."

"You don't know enough to *believe* anything, and you're still just a kid, and your head's full of crazy ideas. Your father put them there."

"Luminous bull guano. Look, Barney Bandino and Red Lugie knocked a porcupine out of a cedar, then killed it with two-by-fours. I wouldn't talk to the miscreants for hours. Porcupines take a few trees, yeah, but mostly they just eat the tops out. And even that wouldn't be a problem if human beings hadn't trapped all the fishers. They were the porky's only natural enemy, and they kept the population under control. Things used to balance before there were so many people. Now the grizzlies are gone, and bounty hunters are trying to wipe out the last damned cougars. Oh, hell. I don't want to fight, April. I'm sorry—it's just that.... But like right now, if we're very still and just listen, we could hear spirits laughing."

"I don't hear anything except crickets."

"That's because you're not still enough—down inside. That's what my dad would say. Okay, I've hunted deer, and so has Abram. And I used to run a trapline until I got so I couldn't kill the critters anymore. I'm not innocent, but there was no reason for the guys to beat that poor dumb porcupine to death. That's when I got angry. What really bothered me was that they just killed, without ever thinking about why they were doing it. Ever since the Whites landed on this continent, they've been killing wild things for no damned reason. We keep on doing it, like shooting hawks. Does anyone really believe the big birds carry off little children? I don't know, maybe none of this makes sense."

"You talk about Whites like you weren't one of us. You and your father are only Indian because you like to think about things that way. Isaac, what's happened to us?"

He put his arm around her, and they sat together, close.

"I'm frightened," she said at last. "Everything's changing."

"But not between us."

"I don't know. All you ever seem to be interested in is sex, Isaac. Am I just a body to you, or something more?"

"Is it wrong to want to make love?"

"Yes...no. I don't know. Maybe I feel guilty because I ought to be happy, and I'm not."

"Tell me what's really wrong. You're not like yourself tonight. It's because I'm going to be away during the weeks, isn't it?"

He held her tightly and kissed her eyes. They were wet. She clung to him desperately, convulsing, as if with pain. Then she grew quiet, looked up at him.

"Isn't there something you want to ask me, Isaac?"

It was as though he heard her and yet also heard nothing. He tried to imagine what it was she wanted him to say, but his eyes burned in the stars.

"No," he replied. "I don't think so."

The words soaked into the hay like droplets of autumn rain. Silence lay between the boy and the girl, while a voice deep within Isaac's skull chanted, *Confused! Confused!*

April looked away from him finally, stared to where the Buick was hiding under shadows of oaks at the edge of this small world they'd entered.

"Please take me home, Isaac. I want to go home now."

When, at length, he pulled to the curb in front of her house, she said, "No. I don't want you to walk me in. I'm sorry—I'm very sorry, Isaac. I don't want to see you again."

She took off the little silver football he'd won and given to her because she was his girl, his steady girl. Then, before he had time to understand why, she was gone into the house.

But an hour later he realized what question it was she'd wanted him to ask her.

*

DECEMBER 20, 1954:
An oil heater hummed in one corner of the library in Diggins, California. The room, in fact, was uncomfortably warm. In the middle were three walnut-stained columns, on the right some glass-faced bookshelves, conspicuously locked. A bronze plaque hung above the center bookshelf, its metal discolored as if by finger marks.

A white-haired man read a newspaper, squinting, the sheets held out at arm's length in front of him, while to one side a small cluster of high school students, absorbed in their own concerns, laughed occasionally. A plump woman in a crisp nurse's uniform worked with pen and paper, apparently writing a letter, and at the far corner, both elbows on the surface of an oak table, a remarkably striking young woman with long, yellow hair—she was reading a book.

Outside: the sounds of rain and wind.

The library door opened, a breath of chill air with it, and Isaac McCain entered. He wore a University of California jacket. Wiping rain from his face, he compressed his lips and strode across the reading room toward April Incendie.

"Thought you might be here," he whispered.

"Isaac? You startled me...."

They walked out through the library door, got into the Buick, drove up the rainy highway, and turned down a rutted road that led to the McCain place.

They were not, however, very comfortable together.

No lights were on in either the printshop or the rebuilt cabin.

Isaac stepped out of his automobile and, as in slow motion, entered first the cabin and then the printshop before returning to the car.

"Damn! That rain's really coming down. I don't know where Dad is. But look, April, here's a copy of his book of poems. Didn't know he was a poet, did you? Abram's the one who got Madison started, in fact. Mack used to come up sometimes, and he and I would help Dad at the printing press. No kidding—and that's where Mack got the idea of being a poet, I think. I don't know where Dad's at, though. His pickup's here. You want to come in? Only take a minute to start up the generator."

"Was he expecting you home?"

"Yeah, but I didn't say when. My fault, I guess."

"Your father's so big and awkward," she said. "He wanders around town aimlessly, Isaac. I've always been afraid of him, that's the truth, but now he's just sort of pathetic. Perhaps you ought to enroll at the junior college this spring—so that...."

"I can take care of him?"

"That, yes, that too. There was an article about his book in the town newspaper—praising the poems. But...."

"But what?"

"People are saying he wanders around in the woods naked."

"The newspaper said that?"

"No, no, of course not. I mean, people in town are saying so. There's been talk about having him committed to a mental institution. Did you know that? I think you ought to come home, Ike."

"That would include your father, I suppose. What you don't understand, you lock up. Is that it? April, if the rednecks in town ever did anything to my father, I'd kill a few people. They can have both McCains behind bars. I mean it, April. I damn well mean it. Your father, the sheriff, whomever—I'll track them down and kill them."

"You're talking crazy. Don't be angry with me, please. It's been such a long time since we've seen each other. Let's not spoil it. I never said I felt that way, and I'd like to read the book. Maybe it's as you once said, I just never understood him. Anyway, I feel sorry for him now. You're different than he is, but you're so much alike, Isaac. I don't know what I think...."

"Dad doesn't need sympathy. Maybe he just needs people. I stopped over at Mack's place—he rode up from Berkeley with me. Mr. Madison says he hasn't seen Dad in months—they used to go prospecting together. He's isolated himself ever since that night when Miss Collingwood was killed."

"Yes."

"The fire—when Miss Collingwood was burned to death. I know. Dad writes me a letter occasionally. I should have gotten home for Thanksgiving, I guess, but I was behind in my studies."

"That's what your friend Mack told me. But he still manages to come home on weekends every so often. Why don't you? I saw Mack and Kara Switzer at the movies a couple of weeks ago. I think possibly they're getting together again. You know something, Isaac? I never really believed you when you told me your father had gone to Yale or wherever it was. The newspaper article mentioned that. Abram McCain is a well-known printer, I guess. It's just that here in Diggins no one pays any attention."

"Harvard, not that it makes any difference. Yes, Dad has a bunch of printer friends down in the Bay Area. He owned a printshop in Los Gatos for a number of years before he moved to the mountains—before I was born. In the university library one afternoon I actually came across a volume he'd printed—in the rare book collection, as a matter of fact."

"The paper called him *a fine craftsman.*"

"It's true. When I'm finished with school, I'm going to come home and work with him. That's what he wants, and I guess I want it too. Honest to God, Dad's the strongest and best person I've ever known. It's funny, April, but being away at college has made me realize how much I love that old man. He shouldn't keep working as hard as he does, but there's no stopping him. We're going to be partners. I'll build another house up under the oaks and...."

"Everything's changing around here, Isaac. They've closed down the North Star Mine, and it looks like the others are going to close too. My father says that an age has ended."

"Come on," Isaac replied, "let's talk about us. I've missed you, April, I swear to God. It's lonely down there, and I hate the city with a damned passion—maybe the university as well. Weekends I walk up into the hills, just to be alone. And I lost my boxing match, the last one. That's why I didn't write. I got beaten by an ex-marine, couldn't think straight for hours. Madison won his division, naturally, the sonofabitch. I'd hate Mack if he weren't my best friend. The beanpole bastard does everything so damned easily, while I have to work and struggle. Well, that's not important. Jesus, just listen to the rain come down—like fingers drumming on the car roof."

"I wish you'd quit boxing. You're going to get hurt eventually. I don't know why you want to fight people—you've always been that way, you and Mack—and Burt too. At least in high school it was just wrestling. Isaac, you didn't go down to Berkeley to...fight...did you?"

McCain declined to answer. He turned on the radio and scanned the dial to find some suitable music, discovered *You, You, You* in progress on one of the Sacramento stations. April turned her face away from him, seemed as though she might start crying.

"You don't understand how it is for a man," Isaac said. "I can't quit now. Next year maybe I'll win my match in the tournament, and then it will be time to think about quitting. A man doesn't quit when he's losing, though maybe I'll switch over to wrestling. It's more civilized, I have to admit. Mack talked me into it."

"A silly college tournament. Why's it important at all? But mostly it's because Mack won, isn't it?"

He put his arm around her and kissed her, began to unbutton her blouse.

"No, Ike. No, I'm not going to. You can't just come back like this and think you can make love to me. You made your decision when you left for Berkeley. I'm sorry. I hoped we could still be friends."

Isaac continued to unbutton the blouse.

She submitted in silence.

He removed her clothing and kissed her breasts, dropped his hands down and pulled off her skirt and panties.

"Lie down on the seat, April. I want you bad—I've wanted you for a Goddamned long time...."

She reached out to grasp the seat, clutching at the upholstery, at the same time furious with herself because she, too, was caught with desire. Yet even as he took her, she was thinking, *No, I'm not going to let you do it to me, Isaac McCain.*

The car's windows became clouded with mist. A few minutes passed. Then Isaac started the engine, wiped the windshield, turned the vehicle about, and drove back up the rivulet-striped road.

As red taillights disappeared under shadows of pine and fir, Abram McCain stepped out from behind some low brush. He was completely naked and shivering in the downpour. But he laughed loudly into darkness, and the rain continued.

*

DECEMBER 22, 1954:

The two McCains spent the day splitting firewood, sky clear now and winter sunlight a mellow presence over gray and green woods. They took down three big cedar snags at the east end of the property. Isaac watched intently as his father ran the chainsaw, red chips spurting from the gash.

Be a cold day in hell, before he'd take out any of the live trees—even oaks, though the forest service girdles them to make way for pines....

Then they worked side by side, a one-two rhythm of splitting mauls, clean, crackling scent of split cedar.

Oliver the mule was in harness, dragging carts full of wood downhill to the pickup, Long Ears visibly unhappy with having to work. But by early sundown, the wood was stacked neatly inside the printshop, and the two men had pancakes and eggs for dinner, Abram laughing at the novelty.

They stoked the outdoor boiler and lit it, then showered together when the water was steaming hot.

"Don't grow any more," Abram chuckled. "You're as tall as I am now. Put on some weight, by heavens, and another year will see you whipping your old man at arm-wrestling."

Isaac reached for a towel and dried off.

"Dad, I think I'll drive into town and visit April. I'm trying to get her back, I think. She's been going with Burt Bullardi since I left for college, you know, but I believe she still loves me."

"That car salesman's son—the one who beat you out of first-string center on the basketball team a year ago? Well, you boys have been around the block once or twice together, haven't you? It's good to be young. I remember that much."

"He's okay, I guess. It's just that he wants her, and I do too. I'll win, though. The Bulldog's not smart enough to hang onto that little lady."

"Intelligence doesn't have much to do with it, Son. But maybe you're right. The truth is, I've always had a doubt or two about your Miss Incendie. I think she enjoys having you boys at each other's throats. You probably don't want to hear this, but Sheriff Hutchings told me the other day that old man Bullardi's been telling people his kid and the girl are planning to get married. Well, that's just talk, most probably."

Isaac thought about his father's words for a moment and then laughed.

"Guess I'll have to turn on the Isaac charm, then."

*

The two of them in the Buick, parked on the road that crossed an earth-fill dam at Loma Rica: the night was clear and even warm for the last part of December.

"This is the shortest day of the year," Isaac said, "or else yesterday was. From now on the days'll get longer. It'll be summer soon, April, and I'll be with the guys at Crooked Pines Campground, fighting fires."

"I suppose you think we'll start dating again? That it makes no difference, your leaving me behind once. You will again, Isaac. And I can't live with that, I won't do it."

"Then why don't you come down to Berkeley with me? Good grief, your parents can afford it. I always hoped you'd attend the university. Why wait another year? We could see each other every day."

"So you can have me and all those other girls too?"

"What other girls? April, it's you I love—damn it, don't you know that by now? Haven't you always known it, ever since we were little kids together?"

"I've got a mind too, Isaac. I have to have my own private self—I can't just be an extension of you. Sometimes it seems to me you just want me physically, like last night, whenever you want me, that you're not interested in the rest of me. I'm weak, and I give in. But I'm still not just some panties you can get into whenever you want. I'll have my own career, and that's why I'm taking business courses at the junior college in Auburn. I'm not going to be dependent upon anyone."

"April, you'll end up taking orders all your life that way. Why not be a teacher, even teach at Nevada Union if you want?"

"One difference between us, Isaac, is that you want to come back here, and I want to get away. Diggins is a hole, literally. It's just what the name says it is—a worn-out hole. Grass Valley's no different. Yes, I want out. Sometimes I hate you, you know that? You're so damned self-certain. Why would you want to stay in Diggins? And why aren't you here now, instead of at Berkeley?"

"That's what I'm suggesting, then. Why don't you come to the university with me if you want out so damned much? April Incendie, you're not making the least bit of sense."

"You! You'll graduate and then go up and run your father's printshop and live down there in that other Godforsaken hole? You think that'd be a life for me? You think down there would be a good place to raise our...."

"Children? We don't have any, April. Right now it's just you and me—and the fact that we love each other."

Then a red light came on.

"Cops," Isaac shrugged. "On the necking patrol, I guess."

April turned quickly in her seat.

"The sound of that engine—Isaac, it's Burt! He's got some red cellophane over his spotlight, he was fooling around with it last week. Lock the doors, lock the doors—look, he's got someone with him. I should never have come tonight. I had to break a date with him. He heard you were home, I guess, and so he's been looking for us. We should never have come here...."

"Well I'll be damned," Isaac grinned. "My old pal the Bulldog."

Within moments Bullardi and Abbot were beside the car, Burt pounding on the side window.

"McCain, crazy-somebeech, you got guts to fight me, Isaac baby? You got guts to let April see what you really are?"

"He's got no guts," Abbot laughed. "Look at the big Breed...."

"Frankie, get my tire-iron out of the trunk. Tell you what—I'm going to bust in these Goddamned windows!"

"Ignore them, Isaac," April urged. "Start the car, and let's go. Please, ignore them—I don't want you fighting over me. Burt's mean when he gets drunk. He's drunk. I can tell. Let's leave, Isaac, please! Burt Bullardi, you go on now! I'll see you tomorrow. I just wanted to talk to Isaac, that's all...."

"Two inebriates? A little booze, and they think they'll smash up my car for playtime? Not very damned likely. I'll cave their Goddamn skulls for them. Let go of me, April—this thing's got to be settled, it's overdue."

"Isaac...."

But he was already out of the car, had used the door to push Burt off balance. Bullardi staggered, caught his balance, lunged at him.

A voice inside Isaac's head said *left hook*, and the body pivoted, the punch leaped out, muscles locked—a fierce, liberating joy of contact.

Mad Mack, where in hell are you when I need you? What are friends for?

Frank Abbot was coming at him from one side.

Knife. Frank carries a knife, always has....

Isaac stepped out of the headlights, away from a charging form in front of him. He braced himself, drove home the right hand, an easy, practiced movement. Blood spurted from lips over the teeth.

Where's Abbot? I don't see him....

He and Burt grappled with one another, then struggled prone on wet, hard-packed earth. They gouged at each other. Isaac brought his left elbow down onto Bullardi's cheekbone, hard, and took pleasure in the recoil of the blow.

Hitting Bullardi then, both fists into the face until the body of his antagonist went limp, suddenly motionless, unconscious.

Isaac rose, his mind a black fury, stepped aside to kick his fallen enemy in the face. But Abbot jumped him from behind, and the two fell forward across Burt.

The knife, the knife was tearing into the flesh of his leg.

He twisted and brought up his knee. Abbot screamed, and Isaac grabbed him by the shirt, pulled him to his feet, then put his full weight into a blow to the throat.

Abbot was whimpering now, struggling for breath, and McCain began to hit him again and again with the back of his hand, hurled his opponent away.

Slowly Isaac picked up the fallen knife, stared at it, stood over the two of them. His face contorted with hatred. He lifted the blade, crouched above Bullardi and Abbott—when he heard a voice, April's:

"Ike! No! For God's sake, don't do it, Isaac!"

He stood, confused, his terrible anger instantly quelling, the frenzy passing out of him. He turned and threw the blade far out into some manzanita and wild lilac brush.

Now in front of the headlights, he examined the knife wound in his leg—a three-inch gash, blood matting his pantsleg against the flesh.

"Peculiar," he said as he got into the car. "I've been cut, and I don't even feel it. Probably I will in a few minutes."

"You can't just leave them there...Isaac?"

"Hell, they'll wake up and think they've got hangovers, that's all. Maybe a black eye or two, but they'll live. But if I'm lucky, I mean if God's on my side, maybe they'll catch pneumonia."

*

He drove April home, and neither spoke again all the way. The night air rushed by them.

Would I have done it if...?

He tried to relax, to suppress the quivering of his limbs—concentrated on the numb half-pain now emanating from the knife wound.

It was well after midnight when Isaac parked his Buick in front of April's house. The windows were all dark, but a porch light was on, casting an almost surreal amber glow.

"Your folks must have gone to bed," he mumbled.

Nothing makes sense. The world is fraying apart.

***

Canto Six:
A PROGRESS OF SPRING

WE DO NOT TRIFLE WITH DIVINITY.
NO, WE ARE THE HEIRS OF CUSTOMS AND TRADITIONS
HALLOWED BY AGE AND HANDED DOWN TO US
BY OUR FATHERS. NO QUIBBLING LOGIC CAN TOPPLE
    THEM,
WHATEVER SUBTLETIES THIS CLEVER AGE INVENTS.
PEOPLE SAY: "AREN'T YOU ASHAMED? AT YOUR AGE,
GOING DANCING, WREATHING YOUR HEAD WITH
    IVY?"
WELL, I AM NOT ASHAMED. DID THE GOD DECLARE
THAT JUST THE YOUNG OR JUST THE OLD SHOULD
    DANCE?
NO, HE DESIRES HIS HONOR FROM ALL MANKIND.
HE WANTS NO ONE EXCLUDED FROM HIS WORSHIP.

[EURIPIDES, *THE BACCHAE*]

*

MARCH 3, 1955:

Abram McCain!

Shirt off, bare-chested to the rich spring sun, silver bracelets set with turquoise on either wrist, a red headband with a hawk's feather, his hands like vises: he crouched on a hillside and watched a flock of sheep in the meadow below. Soft wind rushed about him, and he stroked his beard.

You're crazy as an outhouse rat, Abram McCain!

He set out at a slow run, angling down through pines and oaks, then along the edge of a tangle of wild lilac, to where the sheep were grazing. He slowed to a walk so as not to frighten the animals, moved among them.

A ram looked up, lowered its head, then came toward him at a slow trot. Began to charge. Abram waited for the animal, knife in hand. He braced himself for the butt, took it, and threw himself across the ram's shoulders, knife searching for the throat, finding it, slicing in to cartilage and bone. Blood. Blood spurting out over his hands.

You're a lunatic, Abram McCain! Goddamned Halfbreed.

The other sheep watched sullenly, became more tentative in their grazing. Some began to bleat. McCain laughed, approached another animal.

*

"Of course I'm certain who it was. Do you think I could make a mistake about that? Twelve of my sheep, I tell you, he hacked them to pieces with a knife. I watched from the barn, I sure as hell wasn't going out there. The man's mad, I tell you, and dressed up like a wild Indian he was. It'll be people next. But right now somebody's going to pay for them sheep. I'll sue the sonofabitch. I'm going to see that big crazy lunatic incarcerated. They say he's got money, damn it!"

*

"Hum, fiddle, hum! The stupid, stupid animals, not even enough sense to run. Sheep, be my metaphor! Ha! One good owl could have killed the lot of them and the master too. I'm covered with blood."

They're going to lock you up. You pretending to be Ishi, or what?

"No, that's not likely."

The badge boys will set dogs on you.

"Christ, Lucy, you should have heard them bleat! It would have done your heart good. It had been so long. That's why I asked Elizabeth to come live with me. Acorn Girl, she blew up a whole camp full of Gringo miners, she and Ben. Goddamn it, I should have been allowed to stumble out of this darkness sooner. Ah, well, it's good for a man's digestion. Red and white, red and white, the blood doesn't mix so well. It generates madness maybe. I'm not blaming you, Ben, you understand me now. And not True Bear or Fire Woman either. Damn it, I've created my own fate, and neither grandparents nor parents nor the United States Government's responsible."

Abram McCain! Do you hear the wind coming down over Burlington Ridge? Do you hear sounds of woodcutters' saws? Or the ring of splitting mauls? Sounds of bulldozers? The roar of traffic? Or the light in the water at the foot of the falls? How it wavers in the depths? How it loses itself in spray by the big rock where an ouzel quivers and pulses and the hellgrammites crawl?

Do you hear all the richness and green of spring? Oh, you are not Aikat, the god-like one who killed Thunder and married his daughter, you are Hunchup, the witch doctor who kills Half-white girls with poison air. Maatim-tsaa, the acorn flour-break tree, its pollen drifts in the wind, settling, sticking in your beard. Kneel down and make Toomwey, your prayer. Set up an Ustu pole and hang it with woven baskets, build a fire at the base, make your mourning, Abram McCain!

"My book is written now: they'll listen, they'll hear my voice. You can't go on killing a man forever—and the coyotes are smirking, what buzzing songs! Your brothers and sisters, Oleli the Clown. My loins are hungry too—I'll out-hump them all. Do you hear me, Oliver? You silly gray fool, don't you know me? Don't be afraid now, I can't take that. Yes, I'll turn you loose for a while. No mule or man can spend his whole life on a tie-rope. Bellowing brute! We're two of a kind, Ollie McCain."

                                        *

"There was a witness. The sheep farmer over in Willow Valley. I ought to take you in. You know, maybe you need a padded cell. But in this case, I think he'll settle for payment and something for damages. Why in hell did you do it? I don't think you're crazy, of course, but some people do, Abram. I've known you for twenty years. You don't live like other men, but I think you're as sane as I am, which ain't saying much. Don't go playing Geronimo anymore, Goddamn it, and don't kill no more sheep. I mean it, Abram. I got to uphold the law, and it applies to all of us, red, white, yellow, green, whatever. Hell, I'm ready to pack 'er in right now. Go fishing. That's what the two of us ought to do—you recall that great little hole over on the Walker River? Jesus, all we had to do was throw our lines in...."

                                        *

Thinking: I guess it was the spring weather. The equation no longer balances. The thing makes little sense now, after the fact. But if you think about it long enough, maybe you'll see why I did it. You'll go looking for some sheep yourself, it's a damned good cathartic. I'll pay that farmer his price, without saying.

I'm Abram McCain, and I'm tougher than hell. I can whip any man on the earth. I can twist down oak trees. My name is Abram McCain!

Thinking: Is that you, Isaac? Son, I don't know. My mind isn't right sometimes. Yes, I'm pleased with what some of them have said about my book, but their motives aren't good. I waited too long. Don't you do that. Keep with your studies. I'm proud of you, I want you to respect me. Well, we have peculiar bloodlines. That's no excuse. I think I've got hold of myself now. You know, sometimes when the light spills down into this meadow in the mornings, it's like I can hear the voice of Old Man Coyote himself saying things to me. Only—I can't ever quite make out what he's getting at. It calms me, all the same. Yes, going to be all right now. I don't know: maybe I've still another book to write. I was up on the north coast a week ago—walked along the beaches all day long, and I kept thinking that the sea rocks stick up like rotten teeth, eroded by perpetual lashings, and high tide flings up bodies of broken sea birds, to be eaten by crows and ranging dogs. I'll do right by you, Isaac. I promise you, son. You're going to be a better man than I've been. You work for me this summer if you want to. I've got a contract to print a book of etchings by a college professor back East. Maybe you'd rather go on fighting fire for the Forest Service, and that's all right. You need to be with the young men, you needed more friends while you were growing up, and I knew it. Mostly there was just you and the Paanak boys and the kid who was killed in the car wreck, Mack too, but he lived too far away, otherwise you'd have spent all your time wandering, a couple of thieves if there ever were such. Between the pair of you boys, I'll bet there wasn't a gully or a deer trail in the county you didn't know about. There were good times, too, but it's ungodly lonely along Deer Creek. Well, you think about it, anyway. What have your professors got you reading now? Tell me about it. My God, Ike, the time's gone quickly.

*

She was on the path, certain now of her directions. She knew what she would do. She would run to the park and across the graveled roadway and pound on the door of one of the houses if anyone where still following. If not, she'd simply walk on home. She started to her feet and began to run. Someone was close: she tried to turn. Concussion: pressure: noise. She continued to churn her legs, but her balance was gone. The brackens, wet, rank, were in her mouth.

*

MARCH 4, 1955:

Abram McCain, sitting amidst kitkitdizze, watching. Damp warmth of air suggests early morning. Thunderheads heaped the intense blue sky, sunlight pouring down in yellow bands. Hundreds of angels took wing from the peak of a mountain and disappeared into an ambiance. Music, incredibly sweet, issued from gray, bare stones and died away into infinite stillness. A cross appeared, took substance, became real. Christ clung to the cross, but his thighs were shaggy, his feet cloven hooves, and his head was that of a coyote. The nails slowly dissolved from his hands and feet, and he descended from the cross—the rood, too, dissolving to nothingness—and yet remained visible, sensation of light..

Christ sprawled casually upon the utmost peak of the mountain and began to play a flute. Within moments the entire summit area turned green with vegetation, burst into bloom. Delicate, silkenclad women appeared, holding hands. They formed a circle and sat at the feet of the Master.

The sound of reed pipes.

Three women, completely naked and chewing on pieces of *mat-meni,* acorn bread, discovered Abram among the brackens.

"Look! Look who's here!" laughed the first woman. "It's Pano, the grizzly bear man."

"No. His name's Burning Man," said the second.

"We knew he would come," said the third.

"Of course he'd show up," echoed the first.

"All right, I'll leave, then," McCain shrugged. "Didn't mean to intrude, damn it. No point in staying where I'm not welcome."

"Silly man, big *tsamyempi!*"

Two of the women entwined themselves about him, stroking, caressing. The third began to nurse. McCain lay supine in the brackens and howled with pleasure.

"Not yet!" the first woman cried. "Oh, not yet! Bring him with us. Don't let him get away!"

The second, her hair jet black and her skin a coppery brown, took Abram by the hand—he rose, went with them to the circle, and sat down again.

First woman: "Listen!"

Second woman: "Listen!"

Third woman: "Listen!"

Coyote-Head, his skin a luminescent green, began to speak: "Sexuality is the great and final mystery, folks. No woman is truly a woman who doesn't worship the ding-dong. And no man is truly a man who doesn't worship the vulva, whether or not he secretly believes it has teeth. Sensual pleasure's the ultimate answer to the human predicament, whatever that is. A coon has got to answer the question, *Am I afraid of my own sexual nature?* A woman must be able to answer the question, *Am I afraid of the pleasure my body creates?* Go ahead, say it. I'm a total sexist—but by damn, all of nature actively pursues sweet orgasm. Tingle, tingle, tingle. What do you think these oak trees are up to? Mankind alone, cursed by consciousness, has learned to fear such pleasure. The green burst of spring's a consummate rush toward orgasm. Even three-century-old pines shudder with the drifting of pollen."

"I'm itching to say something, all right," McCain whispered.

He looked about, uncertain whether to violate the proceedings, noted a huge-headed man, his arms painted with daubed pigments and wearing a cape, sitting stiffly against a boulder—*Kuksu*, First Man, at least by appearance.

But McCain stared resolutely at the Master.

The green light faded, and now Coyote-Head was wearing a horned helmet of bronze. Two ravens flew down, squawking, and one alit on either of the Master's shoulders. Coyote-Head began to speak once more, but now his voice was deeper and slower:

"First off, leave the young ones alone. I'm talking to men and women both. You raise the those that are your own, but you don't start diddling with them. In Other Side Camp we have special tortures for adults who touch the children. And Cain: we have places for his ilk, too. The curse of Cain is nothing more than man's inbred impulse toward violence and the use of weapons, and yet this curse is man's greatest blessing if he can but learn to control it. Cain is the specter of man's brutal past and even more brutal present. He lurks deep in the bones, in the marrow, he's a cunning sonofabitch. He bears weapons. It's not enough to banish Cain, for we cannot do that. Let's tame him, then. The arm which flings the spear of war may also wield the hammer of peace, by cracky."

McCain rose, pushed the three women away from him.

"No! You strippèd-ass bandit, you're talking nonsense, and you know it damned well. If you've got some plan to cut the earth's population in half, let's say, then I'll sit here and listen awhile."

"The chair recognizes Abram McCain the Halfbreed. What do you wish to tell us, Burning Man?"

Abram looked about to see if he had any support among the various listeners. A whispered tittering. The second woman attempted to pull at Abram's hand, but he resisted her embrace.

"I want to hear about Abel. The way I see it, you stayed at a distance, Oleli, and howled at the moon while Gringo invaders massacred my people...."

"Objection sustained," Coyote-Head replied. "Mr. McCain's point is well taken, though I'm not certain who these people are that he claims as his own. Well, no matter. Perhaps I was a bit careless a century ago, and these past few years my little cousins have had to eat poison. All right, Cain and Abel live within the same skin, but the old feud has to be resolved. Passive and active principles must learn to accept each other and to form a partnership, for otherwise there's no damned future at all. I don't like what's happened either. Cain is Abel guarding his boundaries, while Abel is Cain conversing with a friend or a beloved. War is the ultimate denial of Abel—yes, and of Cain as well. Actually, I suppose wars are all right, but not the kind the *Walems* are capable of now. They've taken all the damned fun out of it. So let's say wars are consummately wrong. Those who fight in spite of their consciences are criminals, and those who fight willingly are dupes and fools. Let presidents and prime ministers go at each other with clubs if they want to. The monsters, Hitler and Stalin, they're dead now, but that Mao Zedong, he'll still butcher millions. As for Eisenhower, it's true he whipped the Germans for us, but what's he done for coyotes? Answer me that!"

"Hear! Hear!" Abram shouted. "Yet what about the warpath? Haven't you yourself always loved the war-path? The Crows and Blackfoots had some good ones, and even the Maidu could get riled at times. I've done my homework. And you—you're the one who made us the way we are. You put the brains in our skulls long ago, when Estawm Yan was still surrounded by water, and the *Ootimtsaa* tree was no more than a sprout, so to speak—yes, a brain just like your own."

"So I made a minor mistake, what the hell? It's permissible for Crows to kill Blackfoots, and vice versa. That's not war, it's fun— good, clean fun. Keeps the population in check, though even that would go better if women did the fighting. You want to cut down on a breeding population, that's how you do it. Kill half the ladies."

A round of applause spread instantly among the listeners. Out of the corner of his eye, McCain noticed a pair of women in the back of the group. They were kissing and fondling one another. *Damned female boy-humpery, that's what....*

Coyote-Head smiled patiently and then began to speak once more.

"From the dawn not only of civilization but also of human time, mankind has survived because it's been able to find convenient enemies. Cain sought out Cain, but of course he was a farmer instead of a nomad. Well, now it's time for Abel to search out Abel and embrace him. The greatest enemy has always been inside. Cain can be a sonofabitch, I admit it. Set a man to planting things, and pretty soon he wants a big house and a new Chrysler. I never thought my experiment would get out of hand this way, honest to God. Let the great dams crack, the cities be silver and quiet beneath a passionless moon. When people are living in small villages again, things will quiet down, and no one'll be putting out poisoned bait or steel leg traps. You dumb warthogs ought to take care of the coyotes I've given you. We think just like people, only better. Tell you what: there's another enemy, and that's Frenzy. Get enough people on the planet, and you'll see. There's trouble ahead, I tell you. I mean *real* trouble. Not going to be enough room left to lift a leg against a bush."

"No! May it never happen!" the Listeners cried out.

Coyote-Head shrugged.

"One day the food will all be gone, and then everyone will start killing and eating everyone else. Big cats may not like the taste of you, but they'll grit their teeth. Dumb asses! You want to get it down to the point where you're the only animals left alive? Just keep screwing, folks. I don't need to tell you that, I know. But you've got brains, damn it, use them! For Christ's sake, put something into your drinking water. Or do you want me to take care of that too? Slope-heads, bumble-bunnies, surely you're capable of thinking past lunch."

In raw disbelief, Abram tugged at his beard. As he watched, Coyote-Head's bronze helmet dissolved into the fabric of the air, and the ravens flew away. McCain stared intensely into Coyote-Head's deep, sad, timeless eyes. A red-haired woman crouched at the god's feet, which she kissed in adoration, running her tongue over the blunt, black claws.

"We need more buffaloes and whales and eagles," Coyote-Head continued. "Yes, the human herd needs to be thinned, and I suppose it'll be up to me to do it. I haven't decided how as yet, but in another fifty years or so, it'll have to be taken care of. You folks did the job for the buffalo—why can't you take care of your own problem? But enough of parables, enough of war as well. Doesn't work anyway. Enough of destroying the dream of Olelbis. You people are imperfect because I created you, and I got tired and wasn't paying close attention. But you're my creatures, all of you, and I've given you the tool of intellect. One of these days I'll write up a list of things I want you to do—I'll wait until my stomach's good and full, and I don't have other matters on my mind. In the meanwhile, maybe you all ought to try thinking...."

Again McCain rose to his feet. Nearly a third of the Listeners fixed their attention upon him, looking away from Coyote-Head.

"I've got a question, *Canis homo latrans.*"

"All right. What did you think of my speech, McCain? The chair recognizes you. Out with it."

"Why am I haunted by demons? Why have I lived this long and worked so hard for it all to come to nothing? What would you have me do?"

"Die, of course. If it weren't for death, the young people wouldn't be able to go to funerals. I like funerals, I really do."

"I don't understand...."

"Come here, Abram McCain. Come to me."

Abram looked about, profoundly uncertain. All the Listeners turned their eyes toward the ground.

Utter silence.

McCain moved slowly forward, walked to the Master, stood beside him. He was much taller than Coyote-Head, who smiled and twitched his whiskers, then touched at Abram's eyes and returned to the Listeners, began to speak:

"Let there be light. That worked once before. Let there be time and space and an earth and a universe to explore. Some universities might be good. The cities are too big already. Let there be forests and mountains and oceans and deserts, places where men and women can be alone to worship the wonders of creation and the infinite patience which has brought them up from the tide pools. Let ancient pines tingle to the drifting of pollen. Go ye unto the bristlecone pines and converse with them, for in that way ye will by God get some sense of perspective. I didn't put you on earth so you could screw up the planet—you're not the only

ones around, you know. Use your heads, damn it. I'm the Lord of
Becoming and the Lord of Was, the final substance from which
mankind was formed—and the animal and fish and bird people too,
insects and shelled varmints and trees and bushes and even mi-
crobes and such like. Give reverence to the Four Sacred Directions, and don't take yourselves so damned seriously. A few billion
years, and the sun's going to go black, after all. Might make a nice
nova. Amen."

A silence followed.

Abram McCain turned about to discover the mists dissolving
into morning sunlight. On every side he saw revealed lush valleys
wound through by clear rivers. Countless birds shrieked through
the transparent air. Immense herds of animals moved over the
land, bears and cats and wolves and antelopes and buffalo and
elephants and oxen and camels and yaks and reindeer and a
thousand other kinds.

Coyote-Head turned away, followed by a crowd of women, and
began to descend the mountain. Music swelled once more to
crescendo, broke into nothingness. The vision faded completely,
and so McCain sat down among the brackens and stared in simple
disbelief.

"Great balls of bat dung!" he sputtered. "Is that the best he
can come up with? I've heard it all before, and it isn't going to do
a damned bit of good. Eat each other when the food runs out?
Isn't that what we've been doing all along?"

"Hello, Abram. I've returned because...I wanted to."

It was the second Woman—brown eyes, copper face, trailing
black hair. For a moment he supposed it might be Lucy Septien,
whom long ago he'd loved and courted and married, but no—only a
specter, only a phantom out of his distempered imagination....

"What do you want, girl?"

"I didn't get a chance to pleasure you before. Don't you
remember me?"

"You're a figment, like all the rest."

"My mouth and tongue aren't figments."

"Go away. Disappear, damn it."

"I want *you* first."

In an instant Abram McCain's loins were afire, his body beyond
restriction, quite without his willing it or being able to control it, as
though *glamourized* by some unseen force. Soft music. Occasional
peals of thunder in the background.

*

MARCH 8, 1955:

Burt Bullardi and April Incendie drove to Auburn, to a restaurant for dinner. A light rain was falling. Darkness.

"All right," April said, "what happened this time? You're always late, Burt."

"You'll never believe me," he laughed.

"Probably not, but tell the lie anyway."

"Well, it's true. I'll swear on a *Bible.*"

"Don't say that."

"Come on now, Miss Priss. Listen. I was driving over through the park about an hour ago, maybe an hour and a half ago. Just getting dark, and I heard this kind of wailing noise. At first I wasn't sure where the sound was coming from. I stopped the car and beamed my damned spotlight around, then I saw something up in the big cedar tree next to the benches. Just guess."

"No contest."

"Huh?"

"I mean I can't guess. So tell me."

"Okay. Well, it was old Abraham in the tree, Ike's daddy."

"McCain?"

"Right you are, honey girl. About sixty feet up, more or less, and singing!"

"The devil will get you for telling lies."

"Hey, I'm not blowin' smoke. Excuse me. But I tell you Abraham was up in the tree, singing like a sick Indian—which he is, of course. And get this, April. He's naked as a big jaybird."

For a moment she laughed hysterically and then stopped.

"Oh my God! Is this true? Isaac's father up in a tree, naked? I can't believe it."

"Well, it's true, all right. See how much better off you are with me than with Ike? Just a matter of time—he's like his father, it's in the blood. That son of a bitch, I've got a score to settle with him. If we're lucky, though, he'll stay wherever the hell he's at."

"Let's not talk about Isaac."

"Because you're still stuck on him, right? You think I don't know it?"

"No, that's not true. I'm not, Burt."

"Bullcrap. Excuse me, but I get angry just thinking about him. Anyway, let me tell you about Abraham. Just too perfect for words, see? So I drove real quick over to get Frank, and Lukins was there too. We took Abbot's shotgun just in case, because the old man might want to come down out of that tree. He was still there, singing his lungs out—we couldn't even understand the words. Injun lingo, probably. *Get the hell out of here!* we yelled, and then we put the red light on him. Lukins shouted, *We're gonna sic dogs on you, you crazy old freak!* But Abraham just kept on singing, kinda slow and soft now, like a church chant. We couldn't tell what he was singing, the words I mean, like I said before. That animal ought to be locked up, I swear to God."

"Or put in a hospital."

"Yeah. Well, we used the white light then and tried to blind him. Guess we wanted to see him fall down or something. Maybe even kill himself—and we'd all be rid of a damned pest. One guy over at the OK Pool Hall says Abraham's got a couple of mountain lions trained to kill sheep, but that don't sound likely. Anyhow, then he started swearing at us: *Go away, go away and leave me be. May the coyotes chew out your livers!* Swear to God, that's what he said. Maybe it's coyotes he's got trained. So we shouted at him some more, and then Abbot let fly with a blast from the twelve-gauge."

"Burt, he's human!"

"Maybe. But Abbot just fired into the air. We figured it would bring the cops if nothing else, the noise I mean. Then they could take care of him, only there's some who say Abraham and Sheriff Hutchings have got something queer going between them, if you know what I mean, and that's why old man McCain ain't already been locked up. So he roared like a damned bear, like thunder even. Luke had already jumped into the car, just from Abraham's voice. Then he yelled down out of the tree that he was going to bust our backs, and Abbot let fly with another blast from the shotgun, a little closer this time. Might even have caught him with the edge of the pattern, for all I know. Well, down he came, busting branches all the way."

"He fell?"

"Nope. Just climbed like a great big monkey. I don't really think Abbot hit him, but some of the branches wouldn't hold. Anyway, we got into the car quick. Luke already had the motor running. I took the shotgun and pointed it out the window, and Abbot put the spot right on him—he looked like a damned gorilla. Injuns are all crazy, you know that? They are, just like the one that gets drunk every day and sleeps in the alley next to the bank. Old man McCain started toward us then. I told him to stay where he was, or I was going to fill him full of birdshot. He stopped in his damned tracks and looked kind of puzzled for a moment, like maybe he was coming to his senses or something. After that he started running for the woods, and we drove down the road after him. Cops never did show up, of course. If anything ever really happened in Diggins, I don't know what the hell we'd do. So anyway, we went on over to Abbot's place, and then I came to pick you up."

April Incendie shook her head and fussed with her gold-colored hair before she spoke.

"His name isn't Abraham, it's Abram. And that's about the cruelest thing I ever heard of. Burt, what you did was terrible!"

"Aww, come off it, Incendie. We figured someone had to chase him out of town. I mean, you just can't have big naked apes singing in the trees. Jesus Christ! God knows what he might of done if we hadn't chased him out."

Then April broke into a spasm of laughter, and Burt began laughing too.

They drove on into the town of Auburn, parked the car, walked quietly down a wet sidewalk to the restaurant, entered. The hostess showed them to a table in one corner of the dining area. After a few minutes a peroxide waitress came to take their order.

They talked in low tones.

The meal was served.

Burt said, "Hey, I got a surprise. Dad's taking me into the business. I'll be the new parts manager for awhile, but Dad says eventually he's going to change the sign to *Bullardi & Son Chevrolet-Pontiac*. That won't be for a couple of years, naturally. He says I've gotta learn the business inside-out first—I'll start just as soon as school's over. Of course, I could get drafted, too, and that would put things off for awhile."

"Not if you stay in school. But what about your studies, Burt? You're going to finish college, aren't you?"

"Okay, now listen up. College ain't my bucket of stumpwater, I've already come to that conclusion. Hell, I'm subject to flunk bonehead English a second time, for criminy sakes. Besides, what good will it do me? What kind of job would it get me? I could be a coach, maybe. But I've already played enough basketball and football, and like I say, my grades aren't worth a damn. Incendie, you like studying, I don't. It's just not for me—I'm not like your precious Isaac or his pal Madison either one. Isaac's got his own tree to climb, and I'm damned glad he's down where he is. Maybe that university of his is my best ally."

"You promised not to talk...."

"Abbot says he saw you downtown with Mack Madison Sunday afternoon—is that right? What is it with you, anyway? I suppose now I've got both of those jackasses as rivals, ehh? Sometimes you piss me off, Incendie. Truth is, you play me and Ike both like God-damned harmonicas. If I was gonna hate somebody, I oughta hate you. Truth is, I don't really hate old Ike at all. I taught the big blowhard how to put up a decent hook shot. But what's with you and Madison? One university boy ain't enough?"

"He was home for the weekend—we were just talking; that's the truth. He took Kara Switzer to the dance Saturday night and was on his way back to Berkeley. Don't be so insanely jealous—you don't own me, Burt Bullardi. But I admit it. The fight up at Loma Rica, that was my fault. I had no business being with Ike that night, none at all."

"His fault too. Sometimes that son of a bitch does grate on me. I could forget everything, though, if I was just sure it's me you love, not him."

"It's you, Burt. I swear to God."

"Anyway, I need a good steady job to keep me out of trouble. You mean that, April? You really mean it? I don't know why I'm stuck on you—I could have damned near any female I want, and you gotta admit it."

"I do, Burt. And I really mean it."

"They won't draft me if.... Look, Dad's always given me everything, even my car. It'll be good making it on my own."

"Working for your father, is that really making it on your own? I mean, taking a ready-made job?"

Burt sipped at his coffee, put the cup down, turned it around two or three times. Then he drank from his water glass.

"Why the hell not?" he demanded. "Dad's getting older. He's not going to want to run the place forever—that's what he said himself. He'd either have to sell out or let me take it over. And I'll do a good job for him. I always do a good job at anything I set my mind to. I'm not stupid, you know that, April? Hey, this really is good steak, you think so? I like this little place."

"You so seldom set your mind to anything...."

"You mean like high school? What about football, Incendie? I was all-league, wasn't I? And all-league for the junior college this fall? Not too shabby, I'd say."

"With half the little floozies at school running after you. Yes, and you love it that way, Burt Bullardi."

"So you started going out with Ike again at Christmas—is that what it was, you were jealous? Getting even?"

April said nothing, instead pretended to study a landscape painting that hung on the wall above their table.

Bullardi finished his coffee and stared at April, smiling as he did so.

She's a good bitch, one of the best, come down to it. She'll forget about Ike. Strange how knowing he wants her makes me want her even more. Besides, I can have whatever other women I want, whenever I want them. Nobody pushes Burt Bullardi around and gets away with it. There'll be a payback for that night at Loma Rica, yeah, for both of them. Truth is, she's the best looking female at the college, just like she was the best looker in high school. Marry her and get her knocked up, not even the draft is going to touch this good old boy. Having a kid won't be all that bad. I like kids. April's going to be mine, my wife, I can tell that right now....

"What are you thinking of, Burt? You're a thousand miles away."

"Not that far, Kiddo. Dreaming, I guess. Thinking about you. Hell, I know this isn't probably the right place, but I've got a little surprise for you, and all of a sudden it seems like maybe this is the right place and the right time."

From the pocket of his letterman's sweater, Burt withdrew a small, rounded compact finished in black velvet. He opened the container and extended it toward April Incendie.

"The one with the diamond," he said, "that's yours right now, if you want it. The other comes later. What do you say, April? Will you by-God marry me?"

Her face registered surprise, even bewilderment, although she had been expecting something of the sort. The fact that he'd already purchased rings, however, was somewhat unexpected. The cynical portion of her nature debated as to what he would do with them in the event she declined his offer. That red-haired cheerleader with freckles and the great mop of hair, would she be next in line? All bones and no meat, that one, and small in the breasts besides.

April's reflections, at this moment, amused her—and indeed she felt very far away, almost completely detached from whatever thing *love* was. A choice had been offered, a proposition tendered—and she recalled standing by, listening as Burt's father cinched up the sale of a new Chevrolet pickup to one of the cattle ranchers from Penn Valley.

"Burt," she said, "my Burt. This is something of a shock. I always supposed that after I finished college we might...."

"Don't have to get hitched right away, not until I have some dough behind me and a house and stuff. But what do you think?"

"Do you truly love me, Mr. Bullardi?" she smiled.

"Damn it, you know I do, Incendie."

"What will you do with the rings if I say no?"

"Hell with the rings. I'll commit suicide, that's what."

"No you won't."

"Probably not. Like you say, I've got all them others running after me."

"I hate you, Burt Bullardi."

"Now we're getting someplace. The truth is, you're crazy about me—crazy enough to be jealous."

"Yes."

"Be careful, now. What are you saying *yes* to? That you'll marry me?"

Through April's mind Panic ran rampant. He leaped up on old stone walls and kicked the rocks loose. He shouted, laughed, wept. His eyes were red, and he had a blue tongue. He made filthy gestures and signed himself with the cross. He threw stones through store windows. He even climbed up into a tree, naked, and began to chant Indian medicine songs.

Go away, Panic. You aren't helping a bit....

"April," Burt said, "I need a definite answer, one way or the other. I know it's traditional to give a gal a few hours to think things over, or even a few days. But I'm not buying that. April, Goddamn it, you know right now what your answer's going to be. I can see it in your eyes. So tell me. Will you marry me?"

"Maybe."

"No damned *maybe*. I need to know one way or the other, like I said. I've got plans to make, you know. Say *Yes*."

One little bit of sound, a single syllable, and yet it decides so much and so completely and defines my life....

She considered Isaac, then put the thought away—momentarily regretful.

"Yes."

"Yes? I love you, April Incendie. I love you a hell of a lot."

"I love you too. My Burt. Yes, I'll marry you."

"You already said that."

"I'll marry you."

"By God, then I'll marry you too, what the hell? The man ought to have the right to answer just as much as the girl. So all right. I'll marry your ass."

"Burt!"

"Sorry, that just sort of slipped out. Anyhow, I'll marry you."

"It's a deal, then."

Now they were laughing hysterically.

The waitress came to their table, proffering a pot.

"You kids like some more coffee?"

"We'll marry you!" Burt sputtered, "if you'll give us some more of that terrible coffee."

Burt and April broke out into new wails of laughter, nearly upsetting the freshly poured cups.

"You two kids trying to sober up or something?" the platinum blond waitress asked.

*

APRIL 1, 1955:

He'd been hiding in a willow thicket for nearly three hours, waiting for darkness to pour up out of the earth and cover things. He observed as the boy called in the hens for evening's feeding, a ration of scratch most likely, chuckled at the scurrying of chickens into the coop, watched as the boy latched the door and walked off whistling toward a small farmhouse, pleased with himself. Lights came on in a south window, yellow squares pasted against waning twilight.

"Nip of frost in the air tonight," Abram whispered. "Be a good time to go coon hunting, if I were of a mind. Used to do that, a long while ago. Hardly seems real now, though."

He lay on the earth and stared up through interlaced willow branches, their catkins out, leaves ready to explode to a mist of small green spears. Damp earth soaked through his jacket but felt good along his shoulder blades. He turned over and began to crawl the two hundred yards or so through meadow grass to the hen house.

The earth is rich. The earth is rich with smells. I am crawling over decomposed bodies, the remains of my own people and of a billion other things that have lived, I have known this brief interval between two walls of darkness. The Great Compost continues its work, the cold is only apparent, there's fire in the soil—there's fever in the earth itself and in me and in the mud I crawl on. It's all coming down to a vast explosion, the heat will not be denied much longer. This Compost rages toward the east, O it is beautiful, beautiful. I'm a cougar, a catamount, and I slink on my belly in search of food—my own inner fire must be sustained, the fever borne. Is my madness more than that? I shall have chicken and dumplings. Lucy Septien, why did you leave me? I was never strong enough to stand alone, and now I've been untrue to you and bear the guilt of another woman's death. Her name was Elizabeth, Lucy. Now I can't even remember why I went to her bed—or invited her into mine. It was our bed, I had no right....

McCain reached the frail shadows of the chicken house, paused, reached up for the latch. A nervous clatter of noise from within.

He slid inside, pulled the door closed. A rustling of hen sounds. Silence. Slowly, on all fours, he crawled to the roosting area.

A squawk.

He did not move.

Then a hand reached up, fingers spread around a hen's neck, pressed tight, closed the fist. He pulled the flapping chicken to his chest, smothered its motion. Once more he reached up, and again the big fist closed.

Then the rooster crowed.

Chickens cackled with fear, movements of wings—McCain huddled behind some bales of straw, the two dead chickens under one arm. He knew what would come. The entryway, a flashlight. He could sense, not see, the figures standing there.

"Benny, damn it, you done left the door unlatched! How many times I have to tell you?"

"But I locked it, Pa, I know I locked it."

"Son, you gotta *think*. A damned coyote's going to pry that gate open, and we'll have dead chickens."

The flashlight played about the coop, the eyes of the hens pale yellow in the beam.

"All right, biddies," the father said. "It's all right, girls. Settle down now."

The door closed.

McCain heard the latch fall into place. Waited. Hens buzzed on the roost, quieted. Abram crawled toward the entryway, thinking: *I'd best wait five minutes....*

After a time he leaned his shoulder against the makeshift door, drove his weight against dusty pine boards, and the latch pulled loose.

Noise from the chickens, and then the rooster crowed once more.

He was running across the meadow when he heard the rifle fire, and he rolled in high grass, sprang to his feet, moved zigzag toward low shadows of the willow copse. The rifle snapped again, and then he was under cover. He ran with great, long strides up the creek trail. By thin moonlight he could see perfectly. At length he slowed to a fast walk, sucking for breath now, and kept the pace for perhaps a mile.

He sat down, took out his knife, and slit the hens' throats. Blood came slowly, dribbling, still warm.

"They'll be just fine," he said. "A good pair of stewing hens, Lucy. Elizabeth is dead, just like you, and I'm an old fool. You're both part of the earth and the air."

Abram smeared the warm blood on his face.

Far down Deer Creek Canyon a dog was baying. Coyotes on the black ridge above screamed at the night and then went silent once again.

*

APRIL 2, 1955:

Thinking: Why did I come in, Oliver? Why did I come in out of the sunflower forest? Only shadows now. Once there were villages called *Taisida, Tsekankan, Kulkumish, Tonimbutuk, Yokolimdu, Pan-pakan*, and *Yamaku*—those and many more, so many.... *Oidoing-koyo*, close by the ranch at Upper Eden, just under Lassen's Peak, where I grew up. Mom and Dad, your bully-boy's got troubles, he doesn't think right. McCains have bad luck with fire. But it's more than that—I've taken upon myself the curse of man. There's such a thing as too much rationality, by God! We cover the earth with asphalt, and we foul our nest. Seeds refuse to sprout, even though it's springtime. Demeter yet withholds her gifts. Another Fimbull winter? Nidhogg, coiled about the Yggdrasil's base, desires the Mimir. What are we to do, Ollie? It's not your curse, so I suspect you know. You feel the ancient tides that no longer come to wash me clean, to lave me with their currents. Oliver, I sought out these woods long ago, yes, to cleanse my mind. My father, True Bear, he wanted me home at Upper Eden, but I was too proud, too pigheaded stubborn. So I came here, and what I presumed was simple creek water turned to fire. Is it fire that purifies? Is that my one salvation? Could that be the only God? The fire? Green-fire, as I've always supposed, or the hunger inside me? Sweet Oliver, shall we eat the world? No cessation? A mouth, an anus, and that which twists within? I render unto the soil. Ha, ha! I hear so many voices lately, and most of them are not familiar to me. Even deep in the mine—hard rock of this planet disgorges gold and something far more precious than gold. I'm Abram McCain, and I've come to repossess the primitive past of my people. I'm Pano the Grizzly, and my life is *Tukung Kayaw*, the fast-moving clouds. Yuba Sue Skillman was my aunt, and from her and True Bear I bring to mind a few pitiful phrases of a vanished language—and from *Auna Yi*, my mother, a few words from yet another vanished language. But the world is haunted with images, fear forms impregnate the dark. No escape, Oliver? Onward then, it's time for a spring planting. I'll make the little white seeds flame into flesh. Crazy, crazy. Forgive me, Lucy, we dreamed together once, and you gave me a son. Is it Isaac? Yes, that's his name. Will he hate me too at last, will he say, *This man was cruel, insane?* Dear God of these mountains and the blue ridges and haze-filled autumn afternoons when warmth and chill compete for total possession, dear God, deliver me again. Coyote-Head, old Numunana, Old Man Who Does Everything—you've got many names, Dog-Headed-God. I am grown old. The strength you gave me, such strength as plays the tendons of few men, has begun to bate. This curse, this gift has been mine for more than sixty years, but perhaps now marks the final cipher. For I have known the earth, few men in this corrupt age have known it more. It comes to me, Oliver. It sings in my ears, and all the secrets of creation lie about me. I feel the harmonic, I feel the total purpose of it all. We will reach the stars, but the cost is so terribly, so terrifically great—this consciousness, this deep-burning fire inside. Even now there are few men alive I could not crush with these hands, or is that also one of my illusions? You've been good to me, Lord of Creation, old Muzzle-Twitcher. You find the dung I leave in the woods, and you roll in it. That's your way. You have given me bodily strength and intellect as well. Have I misused those gifts? And hence am punished? I'll set up *Ustu* poles then and tie baskets to them, I'll light the fires of sacrifice and mourning. So many dead. *Usto-ma* village, the massacre that Ben and *Ooti* and the others revenged, the corpses of miners lying on the ground

beside Steephollow Creek, the children of the Grizzly striking out—
but to no avail, to no avail.... I reflect upon the story, True Bear,
my father. You too, brother Axel. You spoke well, both of you.
Why, then, did I never pass the words on to my own son? I told
him some things, but I didn't repeat the exact words as I should
have done. I gave him books instead, my White blood gave my son
books, just as they were given to me.... I failed to bear fruit. Or is
it just that you and I don't always see things eye-to-eye, Old God
Dog? And I take the whole matter personally. These are your
whims? Other men, men with lesser gifts, they have brought
forth—then why not I? One frail and brittle volume of verses for all
these endless trampings through the wonder of things. Loneliness.
Fire. Oliver, you ignore the yellow-beaked magpies that come to
your feed bin by day. I should be more like you. Wild grapes lace
through cedars by the creek, long tendrils reach through the air,
find, grasp, move upward toward immortal light, the greatest light.
I've watered those vines during dry summers, but I did so
needlessly. They're thicker than my arms at their bases, and now
with spring the leaves and coils of green begin once more their
perpetual searching, clinging, driving upward toward God. Perhaps
I could climb them and step off into *Hipining Kawyaw*, the Upper
Meadow, Valley Above. In September purple clusters will hang
pendant in the air, unless coons get them, or the sweeping birds.
No man has such wisdom as your fine fat raccoon! I can see them
now by the stream, dipping out trout by moonlight, pawing at fish
flopping on the bank, curious eyes gleaming a fire more controlled
and more at ease than mine. Even wash the fish before they'll eat.
They wash everything! The sugar lumps I leave them—I spy
through my rifle scope. They dip the sugar, and it dissolves. They
never learn, philosophers though they be. Oh, the brightest learn
to dip quickly, very quickly, or else the sweet is gone. Possibly,
Oliver, it would be well if men could figure out as much. Perhaps
even with sugar the ringtail's got us beat—or me, at least. I'm not
including mules, you understand. You've got your own problems, I
guess. Like me, you're looking for a Jenny. Isaac. Can you learn
from a crazy old man? You do not have my strength, not yet. But
your mind is clear. For God's sake, keep it that way. What a
blessing, what a blessing! Maybe your gift is greater. But you're
young, Isaac my boy. I pray that God saves you: there's still plenty
of time for mad McCain fever.

***

Canto Seven:
The yellow dancer

AH, ALL THIS HAS NO BEARING ON MY GRIEF;
BUT I DO NOT BELIEVE THE GODS COMMIT
ADULTERY, OR BIND EACH OTHER IN CHAINS.
I NEVER DID BELIEVE IT; I NEVER SHALL;
NOR THAT ONE GOD IS TYRANT OF THE REST.
IF GOD IS TRULY GOOD, HE IS PERFECT,
LACKING NOTHING. THESE ARE POETS' WRETCHED
LIES.

[EURIPIDES, *HERACLES*]

*

JUNE 9, 1955:

No one was home.

Isaac lit a fire in the stove and walked across the room. Through the west window he watched the giant red flaring of sunset, color boiling up through high clouds far to the northwest. He started the Coleman and then went out to his Buick to bring in luggage.

The mule was loose, came down to greet him.

"Hello, Ollie, you haven't forgotten the prodigal scholar? How are you, Hard-Head? Hey, look what I've got—half a loaf of bread. You'd like it? It's a present from Mack, I guess."

He pulled the mule's ears and gave the animal a hug.

"Damn! It's good to be home again—but where's Dad? You send him to town for carrots?"

Isaac brought in his two battered suitcases, set them by his bed, walked over to the stove, put on some coffee. He was suddenly aware of a strange smell—like dog odor. He turned around just in time to see a nose disappear behind a chair.

"What in hell?" he mumbled, moving cautiously across the room. Then the young coyote bolted, knocking over a tall ashtray, into the back room.

"A song dog! For Christ's sake, Dad's got a wild one, a *coytl* in the house."

But the half-tame brush wolf was under the bed now, would not be tempted out. Isaac laughed, poured coffee, and sat down in the rocking chair.

"I don't suppose the damned thing's eaten Father, so I guess it's all right."

He sipped coffee, leaned back in the overstuffed rocker, tired, his eyes heavy, his mind dull and drifting. He slid from being fully awake into a hypnogogic mélange of images, out of sequence, distorted.

April—they were children, swimming together naked in the creek, just above town. She dived and did not come up, he shouted for her, plunged into the water to find her, and became disoriented—couldn't hold his breath any longer, knew he would drown. He breathed, waiting for death, but death didn't come.

Then older, he was sixteen. April and Betty Sue and Tommy Pinello—one, two, three, four, he couldn't count them, white lines on the highway, Pinello's forty-six Ford, almost like Madison's but a different color, the vee-eight cackling madly, they were drinking beer.... Pinello swerved the white lines, speedometer at ninety-five on the downgrade. Headlights ahead of them, coming at them.... Off the pavement, the car jerking back on itself. He stood over April as she regained consciousness. Betty Sue was on the ground beside her friend, blood clotted in the wavy brown hair. The Ford was smashed against a tree, its front end tilted up, a wheel still spinning, and April said, "Isaac, what happened? Am I going to die?"

"No, you're all right, just don't move." He couldn't seem to help laughing, a smile slashed across his face.

"Isaac, what's wrong?"

And April was laughing too, couldn't stop—or was she genuinely amused, had she in fact not caused the accident? Betty Sue sobbed, whimpered, but he, Isaac McCain, stood tall in the darkness and beauty and horror of it all.

"Tommy, where's Tommy?"

"He's in the car," Isaac said. "Pinello didn't make it—he's dead. The steering wheel broke, and the post went right through him. I tried to get him out, but he was dead—dead and grinning. Don't go look, either of you...."

He bit at his tongue and cheeks to keep from laughing again, he was dizzy, his sides hurt. An attendant in a Halloween costume tried to help, but Isaac pushed him away. The man had no eyes, blood was trickling from the sockets. Other costumed men were using crowbars to work at the wreckage, trying to free the shattered remains of a human form from twisted metal.

A funeral then, Tommy's face made partly from flaming wicks protruding from the cheekbones, the lips red-purple.

"That's not Tommy," April said. "That's someone who looks like him."

"Yes," Isaac replied, understanding the masquerade, knowing the real Tommy Pinello was standing behind them somewhere, would momentarily come forward, bantering as always, would say: "Looks just like me, don't it? Well, don't it?" Isaac turned to see if he could indeed detect Pinello somewhere among the crowd of mourners, but instead he saw Mack Madison standing there naked, his silly instrument not only fully erect but at least two feet long. As a matter of fact, Kara Switzer was actually sitting on it, her feet swinging in rhythm. She was wearing a white dress adorned with roses and poppies, and she was smiling. Afternoon sun flashed from behind clouds, and many, many birds sang.

*

"Isaac!" a big voice said. "Ike, wake up. You didn't let Horse out? I wasn't expecting you until tomorrow, son."

Isaac shook his head, got up.

"Dad? Abram, what time is it? What horse? Have you got a horse too? There's a coyote under the bed—where'd he come from?"

"Son," Abram said, his hands on the boy's shoulders, "damn I'm glad you're home. My coyote friend—that's Horse, Horse the hound. You're a stranger, you scared him. Horse! You come out here, you little bush-tailed coward."

A pointed nose emerged from behind the door, cautious. A moment later a full canine face came into view, amber eyes staring first at Abram and then at Isaac.

"Come out here, wild brother," Abram said. "We've got company. Some family's come to visit for a spell."

*

White lines, flowing.
Seeing her again, it was not the way he had imagined.
Things are not going to be all right, then.

Rain spattered against the Buick's windshield. He stopped at the spring where the Forest Service got water for Crooked Pines Camp.

"Only the initiated are allowed to come here," Isaac said. "You should feel honored."

"You're bitter, aren't you?" April asked. "You're different, Isaac."

The smell of rain. The air. Thunder. No stars.

Isaac leaned over the wooden tank to drink, while April reached down and cupped her hands.

Distinctive cry of a horned owl....

The night was cloud-torn, thunder-shattered. rain was waiting, waiting to spill down.

"Some new level of reality is about to make itself known to us," Isaac proclaimed, "a new level of reality only dimly perceived until this moment, forms beginning to emerge, voices ready to communicate. I can even hear the sound of my wristwatch, its spring singing away inside the metal case. Goddamn it, I love you, April Incendie."

"Is it something from Nietzsche or someone like that? You didn't just make it up?"

"You actually heard what I said?"

"Yes, I heard. But are you certain, Isaac? You've said it before, and...."

"That noise—pigeons flying. Listen to the wind, it's whispering in the pines. You smell so good. I'd almost forgotten how you smell. The darkness."

April laughed.

"You sound like Mack Madison—the time when we all got drunk together at Yuba River. That's what comes of studying poetry in English classes. Listen, Ike. Sometimes I've wondered if you could love anybody. Or maybe it's me. Maybe people like us shouldn't ever try to love."

"Stuff and nonsense."

Down the hill, under big trees. Still that waiting for rain. Even the trees could feel it coming on and knew it and wanted it, rain from thunderheads over the hump-backed Sierra, a baptism of violence, a drowning.

"I shouldn't be with you tonight," April said, crying softly now. "It's all so foolish, so pathetic. But I had to see you, Isaac. Maybe I want to believe you understand. I'm not deserting you, it's that you don't need me, Burt does. You have to go away, and I have to stay here."

Her reserve was gone, and she wept openly, bitterly.

He knew then and was positive of it as he had never been positive of anything until that moment—he loved her, his life without her would be a nightmare because he loved her, and she didn't even know it and maybe even worse because he was so strangled by his own egotism and self-interest and by his insecurity about being a Halfbreed and different than she was that he had in fact never been able to make her see that he loved her.

The wind was dark and charged with electricity.

Isaac grabbed April hard, twisted her sideways, and kissed her.

*

Rain droplets stung at their naked bodies, and he nearly cried out with the ache of wanting her. He clung to her, like a man drowning, aware of the heat of her flesh and of his own, aware of perspiration that enveloped them—the desperate, sinking rhythms of their bodies together.

Afterward he kissed her eyelids, her hair. Blood was raging in his face, and he could feel the heavy come-and-go of his own heart. He wanted to tell her, to tell her something, to find the correct words.

Then she was moving from him, ebb tide, separation, the finality of withdrawal—away from him, away.

"I'm cold," April said. "It's raining. We'd better go, Isaac. This is crazy, and I can't help myself. I'm here with you, making love, but I've promised to marry Burt. And I won't even let him...."

Too late. In the wind. Too late....

"I told you Burt asked me to marry him."

"Yes. You said that."

"He asked me again just this afternoon."

"Well, he's persistent I guess. And?"

"And I said *yes* again. I have his ring in my purse. I couldn't wear it with you."

"April, Goddamn it, why did you come with me tonight? I thought...."

"To ask permission, Ike. I think I have to have your permission to marry him."

Isaac stood up, pulled on his shorts and trousers.

"You don't believe that bull-honk, do you?"

"Yes, I do. It's been...please, don't be angry with me. You know it would never work out for us. You know you have to be left alone."

He pulled on his shirt, buttoned it.

"Why do I have to be alone? What the hell kind of an idea is that?"

"I don't know," she said, standing up, fastening her bra.

"Where the hell are my shoes?" he asked—and then, after a moment's silence, "All right. You have my damned permission."

                         *

JUNE 11, 1955:

The following night they were together once more.

It made no sense, and April knew it—knew further that she was risking the very solid, tangible thing that she had with Burt Bullardi. At the same time, there was something about Isaac that she couldn't seem to stay away from, could not resist. Senseless and irresistible.

"It's peaceful here after dark," Isaac said. "The glow of the burner and a few sparks flying up and dying that way."

"Like us? I think you might have picked a better spot. Why do you always look for these little places at the end of the world?"

"We could drive down to Marysville and go to a motel," he grinned. "Besides, this is actually close to town. Would you rather be somewhere else?"

"No. Let's get it over with. What do you want to tell me?"

"Not tell, ask. The question is—why?"

"Why am I going to marry Burt?"

"Precisely. Why do you want to marry Burt when you're in love with me?"

She shrugged.

"He's kind and gentle," she said. "And besides, he wants to marry me. You don't."

"Kind and gentle, my ass."

"Please don't be vulgar. Maybe we'd best go."

"You don't love that sonofabitch, April. You love me. Damn it, isn't that so?"

"I don't think love is enough. You take me for granted—yes, you do. You always have. It's like you're so interested in Isaac McCain that you don't even see anyone else. I'm sorry I had to say that, but it's true. You don't even see anyone else."

"Me cigar-store Injun," he said. "Heap dumb."

"That's just part of your defense. If it were nothing more, then I...."

"April! My God, I love you, you know that."

"But I'm afraid of your kind of love, Isaac. You swallow me up. You don't leave me anything of myself. I have to have myself—I can't hero-worship you. I want my own life, and I don't want to be anybody's plaything. It's not going to be that way, do you understand? Find an Indian girl down at your precious university—maybe a Chinese girl—someone who'll smile and say *yes* all the time. I don't want to belong to a man, and that's the way it would be with you. I won't be a doormat. You want me, but you don't love me. You want me sexually whenever you choose. What I want doesn't really matter. I'm sorry, my mind's made up. Please take me home, Ike. I shouldn't even be here. It was all over between us last summer."

"What's happened to you, April? I don't understand what's happened to you at all. You're not like other girls...."

"You son of a bitch, Isaac, you chewed me up and then spit me out. It hurts me even to say these things. Yes, I love you, but it's not enough. You've never grown up. You're the only one I've ever had sex with—I told Burt, not until we're married. I'm a hypocrite, and it's terribly wrong of me. But I can't yet. I will. Oh, Isaac...I don't want to start crying now. Please take me home."

At that moment an automobile pulled onto the sawmill landing from the entrance way, and Isaac and April both recognized immediately who it was.

"Oh my God," she whimpered, "Burt! My damned mother must have told him I'd gone somewhere with you, and he started looking.... Please let me go. I've got to be with him...I'm so sorry about all this...I should never have come with you...please, if you ever cared anything about me, don't fight.   Just go away, please...."

Isaac laughed.

"I'll kill that sonofabitch Bulldog. This time I'm going to break off one of his arms and beat him to death with it."

Then Burt and Isaac were standing in the space between their cars. Both sets of headlights were on. Burt grabbed a couple short sections of two-by-four from a pile beside the burner: he tossed one chunk of mill-end onto the ground in front of Isaac.

"This time it's for keeps, Ike baby. You just can't stay away from my woman, can you? All right, pick it up. Ain't nobody going to interfere...."

April was screaming.

Like sparks from the burner. We are like sparks from the burner.

Isaac stared at the two-by-four in front of him, then glanced at Burt.

Isaac, thinking: *My dumbass enemy. We were friends once, more or less, but now we're a pair of fighting cocks—the cowboy and the Indian, straight out of one of those movies we both watched when we were kids....*

He reached over, slowly, and picked up the section of green lumber.

"Burt," he said, "I don't want to fight you any more. We've gone through it before, and nothing's been solved. The girl—she's yours. It's all over with April and me. Take her and leave me alone. I won't bother her any more, I give you my bleedin' word on it. Yours, you hear me?"

A strange sense of calm. The anger was gone. Smoke. I don't care any more, April Incendie....

A soft wind, headlights, a young woman, two young men. The moment of confrontation—inevitable, inevitable, and Isaac knew it. Words weren't going to solve anything.

Burt Bullardi's eyes were animal-like: those of a raccoon Isaac had clubbed to death once, the animal in a trap. Isaac realized Burt was afraid. It had never before occurred to him that Burt Bullardi was capable of fear.

He has always been as much afraid of me as I have been of him, I never knew that, why did I never know that before?

"You filthy yellow Halfbreed! It's different now, hey? I'm going to beat your brains out, McCain!"

April bolted between them, turned from one to the other. She moved toward Burt, put her hands on his upraised arm.

"Please, no! I don't want you to do this! No, Burt, for God's sake. It's like he said, it's over with us. Take me home, take me anywhere. I'll do whatever you want, Burt."

"Get out of the way, Incendie. So help me Christ, get out of my way. Me and Ike have got to settle things."

April turned, ran to Isaac, threw her arms around him.

"Please, Isaac, Isaac, please!"

"Sorry, girl. You hear what the Bulldog's saying."

He flung her away from him, hard, so that she fell in front of the headlights of Burt's car.

"Yellow son-of-a-bitch! I'll kill you, McCain!"

"Have at it, then, Burt-the-Bulldog."

They circled each other in the area illumined by headlights. They did not speak again: there were only the lights and the clubs and the dark presence of a sawmill burner throwing up sparks behind them. Burt swung suddenly, caught Isaac a glancing blow, the arm going numb.

Isaac stalked his enemy, lashed out, slipped to his knees. He leaped up, stumbled away, avoiding a blow that nearly smashed his face. The two circled again, and Isaac was dimly aware of headlights coming down the mill road above them.

He spun into spill-off sawdust from the conveyor belt, blood in his eyes from a gash in his forehead. Long seconds passed before he fully realized he'd been struck.

He must have thrown the thing at me. Yes, and he's going to hit me again, he's going to kill me, just the way I'd kill him if it were the other way around.

Isaac was unable to focus his eyes. He searched for Bullardi but couldn't see him.

My face is in the sawdust....

He turned over, could hear April's screams.

Stupid girl, stupid girl....

He saw her then, her arms wrapped around Burt, struggling with him for possession of the club. He searched for his own two-by-four, found it, twisted about sideways and swung at Burt's shins. Bullardi screamed and lurched sideways. Isaac got to his knees, still unable to see clearly, and raised the two-by-four over his head. But there were new headlights—those from the mill road above?

And a red light.

A voice, a form in the darkness, the nose of a pistol directed at him.

Isaac lowered his club, dropped it to the dust at his feet.

*

JUNE 17, 1955:

Why is everything haloed in amber? Another fire, I imagine. I want to go back to where it happened. Will you take me there? I walked through the woods in dark yellow sunlight, I call to mind the forest was quiet, waiting. Deer Creek was slow, sluggish in the heat, and black pebbles stared up out of the streambed, a hot blast of wind Stirred the bristly pine tops, waved through cedars. Butterflies danced above blackberry tangles, and thick heat settled over everything—yellow and thick, I could smell the smoke. Sun was the color of brick.

It wasn't Deer Creek at all—no, the ocean, Point Sur not far away, where they built that lighthouse, its gleam coming round over the waves at night.

Lucy Septien, my raven-haired beauty. True Bear owns Eden, but we can't go back there—we'll have to find our own. We'll do it, too. Your lips touch the side of my face, and I go mad for you. Spanish blood in you, Spanish and Indian, my flower of the Salinas Valley, *Mi alma, venusto, venusto, I want you Lucinda Septien!*

We walked together for some time, and then I put my hands around her from behind and pressed them over her breasts—she did not object. It began then. I was trying to see it all again.

You look over there.

What can I say? She took my hand, and we walked together among sand dunes and through blooming copses of yellow bush lupines, and from there up through an arroyo and into the amber woods. Flowing water and a grove of magnificent redwoods. A porcupine bristled across our path and scuttled off into the chaparral.

Smoke.

Death.

Death has a beautiful smell, Oliver. Men with tools and water, fighting the fire and breathing the smoke, sweating, exhausted, sixteen straight hours on the lines, mouths covered with handkerchiefs, wet and blackened, they eat rapidly and sleep shivering under olive-drab blankets, while half a mile away the cancerous thing releases gigantic heat, crowns through timber, roars up hillsides. It will scorch the sides of the Ventana Cones, it will burn clear to *Nuestra Señora de la Soledad....*

Dense smoke settling over the hills, heavy, like fog until a man's eyes water and he coughs constantly, sun glaring down a dull lifeless orange. Everything wilts before the heat, but by late afternoon a cool breeze from over the ocean begins to disperse the smoke.

God you've got a nice little quaintness. I'm swimming in a tight, warm pool of fire....

Fire.

It's eaten in on itself until there's nothing left for it to con-
sume, ashes settle like snow over the Coast Range, tongues of
flame lick out of stumps and fallen logs, playing over my face like
green music.

Far away, a long time ago.

This is Deer Creek, Oliver. It's our creek. We came here, she
and I. Lucinda Dolores Septien McCain! I will die whole because I
had her with me for a time, oh, too short a time.

Our new world. The earth steaming without moisture.

La Veta Madre....

The west slope of the Sierra, eighty miles south of Wahgalu,
long parallel ridges, conifers, deciduous, slashes of Yuba, Bear,
American, Rubicon, Screwauger, Greenhorn, Steephollow where
my grandmother took revenge upon those who had slain her little
ones and raped her and left her for dead, Pano the Grizzly gave her
medicine, but it was poison to the Walems, Lucy. Yes, I showed
you where that must have happened. True Bear told me, but how
could he have known? Pock-marks of old hydraulic days, Yellow
scars where earth was eaten for gold, Malakoff, You Bet, Spanish,
Alpha, Omega—peaceful country, now that the gold fever has
gone, but no longer the land of Ooti's people, their sun has died in
the sky, the people have vanished—slain by the Walems or diseases
the Walems brought here with them or by greed the Walems also
brought, melded with the whole, their bloodlines forgotten, their
oral traditions, religion, diet changed—who still gathers the acorns
and fills the *daw* with *ootim hai?* The *booi* is unused, the *bai* lies
buried beneath a century of pine and oak compost. Only *Panaak*
the woodpecker, he still gathers sacred fruit, secrets it away in
tsoon holes in standing cedar snags. You saw it before it was all
changed, Ben McCain, how beautiful it must have been—to turn a
rock and find those oblong flakes of gold in the sand, *worthless
metal,* Ooti would have called it, your Maidu wife, my grandmother.... *Toomwey,* now I make my prayer. The myth! The
myth! These long green restless hills, gold fever still endemic,
lingering, waiting, bitch-goddess, old Earth-Whore, smiling and
beckoning and breasts all virginal but dripping with milk and dew,
simpering and sidling and reeking it out to every young male alive,
*Come touch my body, I will not resist you, I have something for
you, you know what.*

As down from the high white granite and old red cap rock of
the California Sierra the rivers flow, gouging, twisting, falling, racing—swift and coursing westward to a joining with *Nem Seyoo,* the

Sacramento River. *Why not make love by the water?* Yes. Sometimes the canyons are thick with fir or studded by jack pines and
buckeye and oak and redbud and mock orange—what if the rivers
have all been dredged for gold? The best gold remains, though
rocks have been piled and covered with earth to form levees to
contain spring floods. Ask the people in Marysville about that
damned Yuba, watch out for the tricky Yuba.

John Muir's spirit drifts in the wind, Caleb Greenwood's, Jim
Beckwourth's, Joaquin Miller's, Acorn Girl's, and Ben's. I would
like to shake hands with all of them. How did I know it would be so
damned lonely? How could I have known the madness was so close
inside? Time has washed over me—an exile, I've lived my life in
the wrong century, and now female demons crowd about me and
touch me and make me want....

Isaac. Ike, it's all yours now. The madness, the vague discon-
tents that plague us, the burning, the touching at God these
summer mornings, yes, even that, let the fires burn through your
being. Prod every hole in the earth, Coyote did, what do you think
caused the *koolem aw?* I think there's still a kind of gold hidden
away, something that neither Ben's people nor Ooti's people
found. You'll see, my son, you'll see. Hell, I've worked myself to
death. Lucy Septien, are you calling me? Elizabeth Collingwood
too? Liz, you knew French when you were alive—what do all these
words mean? Look there in the oak, find them in wild honeysuckle
vines, they become little red berries in autumn.

Lucy? You want to know how Isaac is? *Forgive, forgive.*

I'd hoped to work with you this summer, Isaac, to teach you
the presses. But I knew, I knew you'd have to find your own way—
no one can teach us. So I've been at it days and nights, the man's
etchings are all printed, and there's nothing left to do. My years
have run, and I'm tired—but I still want time to walk the woods.
That remains.

Isaac, do you feel the air in the mornings, just after sunrise?
You'll find that—and so much more. Every man does whose guts
are real, who's risen out of red clay, as we are. I swear, it's been
good. The myth! These mountains of ours will be here long after
Homo sapiens sapiens has vanished, featherless biped, big-brained
ape who's fond of torture and who'll eat his own kind before going
down into final darkness.

These mountains, from Shasta and Lassen to the high granite
of the south, they've suckled me in fair and foul, prodded and
nursed me again and again from the edge of blackness. Come to

me once more! Smiling and beckoning, bare-breasted and dripping milk and dew just as always, siren voices and ghost voices down from the human past, from the human beginnings: *come touch my body, I will not resist you, resist you....* Are you listening out there?

Who says a man's old in his sixties? No, that's not it. But my time has run—it was short, I capture it all in a moment's remembrance.

They're yours now, Isaac, the madness, the wonder, the miracle, and the horror.

*

JUNE 18, 1955:

Sheriff Ed Hutchings stared down at four dead sheep. The throats had been cut.

"You actually see him doing it?"

"No, but you know damned well it was him. This is the second time. I tell you, that big Indian has got to be locked up. I want to file a criminal complaint this time. I hear he's an old friend of yours—a hunting buddy or some such?"

Hutchings spat tobacco juice, shrugged.

"If it was McCain, he'll pay you for them, of course."

"Not a matter of paying for livestock any more. I'd never know again that when I come out here in the morning there might not be a bunch of my sheep dead. I swear to God, Hutchings, if you don't do something, I'll shoot the man myself. I'll get some of the fellas together, and we'll take things into our own hands. How far is it from mutilated woolies to mutilated human beings?"

Hutchings nodded, then walked to the stream bank and knelt.

"We don't even have foot tracks," he said. "Look, I'll head on up there right now. You can't file a damned charge without some evidence, my friend. You didn't see what happened, and there's no other witness. Fact is, I've got the same suspicion you have, but let me handle it. Get that out of your head about shooting somebody. Four dead sheep ain't worth committing a murder, Mr. Eldrickson. You'd spend the rest of you life in the jug—seven, eight years, anyhow—gas chamber if they went hard on you. It could have been kids, after all, or it could have been someone who hasn't any love for you or McCain either one. You've been talking around town a lot lately, so I've heard, and by this time there are probably a couple hundred people who know how you feel regards McCain. One thing I've learned about Diggins: *word spreads.* It's good pasture he's got, and your critters wander up that way at times—no, I tell you I've seen them on McCain's land. A fella could mend fences once in awhile if he were of a mind to. You ain't grazing government land after all, but that's neither here nor there. Calm down and let the law handle it. Looks to me like the man needs help, if it *was* him. But like I say, we can't prove it wasn't dumbass kids who figured McCain would be blamed and hoped he would be. Or maybe dumbass kids who didn't have any reason at all."

"You weren't elected for life, Hutchings. You're aware of that?"

"Long as we agree to the fact that I *was elected*, Tom Eldrickson, that's all I'm concerned with. In this country we have elections every so often. You just let me handle it. Like I said, I'm going to take a drive up there directly. Can't blame you for being angry as hell, but until I know a good bit more than I do presently, you're just going to have to be patient. Incidentally, your neighbors downstream phoned me last week. One of their dogs died of strychnine, and they figure you been putting out bait for coyotes. Thought you'd like to know. Anyway, I'll be back."

"...Shoot that son of a bitch," Eldrickson was saying as Hutchings drove off.

                                        *

The sheriff parked in the clearing above McCain's cabin, sat in his county car, stared across at the cabin and printshop. He clutched the steering wheel, breathed deeply, and then got out. He pressed the revolver against his leg and walked toward the cabin.

No one was home. The old green Dodge pickup was gone.

Hutchings was thinking, "I'll talk with that boy of his up at fire camp," when he noticed an envelope thumbtacked to the door, his own name lettered on it.

Hutch, I imagine you'll be up today, but I've got to drive some stuff to San Francisco and probably won't return until late tonight. I know what you're going to say, and I haven't got any explanation. If the thing has to go to court, why there's nothing I can do about it. If he's willing to settle it like last time, why fine. I'm sorry— honest to God I am. I swear it won't happen again. Don't know what the hell got into me. Maybe I do need help, just like you suggested. I'm up here by myself too damned much. You've known me for twenty years or so, and you know I always pay my bills. If Eldrickson wants more, it can be worked out.

A sheaf of ten one-hundred dollar bills in the envelope....

Hutchings scratched his head and re-read the note.

"Good Aching Christ, Abe's blown his fuse. He needs help all right, help down at state mental hospital, just like half the damned town's been saying for the last year."

The sheriff walked over to his car: little streams of red dust marked down the sides of his black Chevrolet, outlined a big star painted on the door.

He flipped the long antenna on the rear fender, watched a small explosion of reddish particles settle through the air.

"The man's mind has disintegrated, no question," he said aloud as he got into his vehicle.

*

It was hot.

A wind had been blowing, and from the top of the long grade, they could see a blue-gray smoke plume several miles ahead.

"Whoo-eee!" Mack Madison sang. "She's crowning through bear clover!"

"The pumper won't work when we get there," Isaac McCain laughed, "and there'll be foxes with burning tails setting spotfires all over hell."

"Seems like they'd get around to watering these roads once in a while," Red Lugie mumbled. "We're subject to die of dust poisoning before we even get there."

"Ike's in love with fire," Barney Bandino declared. "Just look at his damned eyes!"

"You love fires, Ike?" Red asked. "Damn, I don't. We'll end up losing our days off again."

"It's not McCain," Madison said. "I'm the tomcat that invented fire. I was two years old at the time. God wasn't even born yet."

"The truth," Bandino said, "is that Madison's as ugly as a bucketful of assholes, and McCain's even uglier. This isn't a game— don't you Berkeley clowns know that? No more kerosene in the back pumps."

"The way that smoke is," Red muttered, "it looks like an A-bomb or something."

"And getting worse by the minute," Madison agreed. "Bandino, why don't you write your weight down on a piece of paper. I'll stick it in my wallet just in case."

"In case of what—what the hell you talking about?"

"In case you fall into the crapper when we get back to Crooked Pines, if we ever do. That way Ike and I will know how much to shovel out."

*

No way to get the Mormon-Harrington close to the flames. The crew waited along a logging trail that angled down a hillside, could hear fire below—sharp, exploding sounds of trees bursting with heat, smoke pluming upward like something alive.

Other crews were coming in: Shady Creek, Big Bend, Iron Mine, Camptonville.

Sparks in the air. Spot fires starting.

It's spreading like some kind of crazy cancer, it's eating the earth alive....

Backpack pumps. McCloud tools. Pulaskis. Axes.

The fire popped and hissed downhill from them, and the fire crew members had handkerchiefs around their mouths. Their eyes stung. A hot wind drove the inferno, urging it onward, pushing it up in long tongues of flame.

Isaac glanced at Mack, who was hacking away at the duff with a McCloud tool, shook his head.

It feels good. It's a living organism.

Assistant Ranger McClean arrived and immediately took Barney Bandino with him, his announced intention that of backfiring down the slope.

"We're going to get fried if they aren't careful!" Isaac yelled at Mack. "It's the wrong thing to do—It's not going to work. The damned fool, it isn't going to work at all, and it's going to get hotter than hell around here. Look—spotfires up the ridge, three of them...."

"A good day to die!" Mack yelled. "Isn't that what you *Native Am-ar-kins* are supposed to say before battle? You ain't the only one what reads Goddamned *friction* books, McCain."

"Use the fine spray, boys!" Lee the Foreman hollered. "Conserve water!"

Isaac realized the soles of his boots stank from hot coals underfoot.

*

An hour after dark the fire was completely out of control, partly because the assistant ranger's backfire had worked its way downhill to meet the mother blaze, and the two came together like rivers joining. Flames coiled, crowned through big trees as though fed by gasoline, a perfect spiral of yellow leaping through pines above the crew, boiling into the dark sky, shooting off comet tails of sparks.

"Pull in the hoses!" Lee shouted. "We gotta move out!"

It came toward them, noise below, down the road, and fire in a red wall over their heads, sucking oxygen with it, drawing in cool air at its base. Smoke streams trailed lengthwise, sucked along the blackened ground.

"Ike, where's Barney?" Lee asked.

"Still with the junior brass—I don't know...."

But fire was around them, over their heads now, leaping, jumping across low brush and not even burning it. Isaac stood motionless, watching, no longer aware of danger but obsessed with fire itself, hypnotic beauty.

"Wake up, Isaac!" Mack Madison yelled. "Lee's pulling out...."

Then they were walking behind the Mormon-Harrington, carrying hose lines because there was no time to reel them in, the truck crawling ahead as a curtain of fire spread through the trees above, hissing and flaring. Broken limbs fell.

They were going out under it.

"Red!" Isaac yelled. "Mack! There's not much oxygen—the fire's using it up. Breathe deep."

Trees, black skeletons, stood hissing and steaming in the night.

*

Fire camp at Snow Tent Spring. Men in olive-drab, men wearing brass badges pored over maps, and unidentified voices rattled on the radio, alternating with static-filled pauses.

Three thousand acres. Jumped the river, heading up the other side.

Isaac clasped Mack's shoulder and gestured in the direction from which they'd come. A series of glowing clouds worked their way upward against a screen of darkness.

Lee was talking to some of the brass, talking about Barney.

Nobody knew where Assistant Ranger Hugh McClean or Barney Bandino were.

They couldn't have been burned up. It couldn't have happened.

"Barney's out in the Goddamned fire, ain't he?" Red Lugie asked.

"Don't sell old cow-pie short," Mack said. "Italians are naturally fire-resistant."

But the words rang hollow, and even Madison lapsed into thin-lipped silence.

Word came up from headquarters: get some sleep, on the firelines again at four in the morning.

Isaac thought: *It's changing. I'm being washed here and there in an absurdity. April. Me. Barney. Mack. The damned backfire. A pillar of fire off to the north, and it wants us to worship it. We must fall down and worship it because it is beautiful and terrible and the agent of God. Fire has controlled things all along—it brought us here because it was hungry and because it wanted us to know. But know what? Even the trees, they've waited patiently for fire to come to them, they wish to be burned, they desire it. The process of change, of change, and the forest lusts for it. Maybe we want to be burned too, maybe we're also thirsty for the flames. Only I am so Goddamned tired that I don't even care, but I'll worship the sonofabitch tomorrow if it insists....*

"You guess he's burned up, Isaac?" Mack asked.

"He's safe, damn it. Don't say that, Madison."

"Take it easy, Ichabod. You're right, we got to keep hoping. We found a way out, didn't we?"

"Barney's smart," Red agreed. "He'll be all right."

"One way or the other," Mack shrugged, "We're going to be out on the lines before sunrise. It's beyond our control—out of human control. We're nothing but pissants on the planet's back, when you get right down to it. Jesus, Ike, Berkeley seems so damned far away right now, doesn't it? It's like last year never happened at all."

The fire crew members crawled into some camp-issue paper sleeping bags thrown out under young Douglas firs and listened to the sound of a portable generator, inhaled odor of smoke. Without further talk, they fell into exhausted sleep.

*

Some time after midnight: strange lights flared in the sky, and the air was saturated with a thin, acrid smell. Shadowed forms of men in sleeping bags.

"McCain, you conscious?" Madison asked.

"Yeah."

"I woke up—can't drift off to sleep. Not with old Barney out there."

"Me either," Lugie said.

"Let's take one of the pickups and go find him," Mack suggested. "We can't just lie here and do nothing."

Isaac was silent a moment and then asked, "Where in hell would we look? You guys figure we could get back in there?"

"I don't know, but we ought to try. Red, what do you think?"

"Mack's right."

"We'd have to go past all the brass down at the radio setup. They'll stop us, I imagine."

"We got to try," Red whispered. "We can't leave him out there."

The colloquy was cut short by the sound of footsteps in the brush below. The snapping of a limb. Someone cursed.

"Sonofabitch!" Isaac said. "It's Bandino, sure as hell."

Voice from downhill: "Where the Christ are you guys?"

Voice from uphill: "Can the talk, you Crooked-Piners! We're tryin' to get some freakin' sleep!"

Isaac, Mack, and Red scrambled out of their bags, grabbed Barney almost at once, hugged him, clapped him on the back.

"Bandino," Lugie demanded, "you okay?"

"We thought you were out in the burn somewhere," Mack added.

"Am I ever glad to see you whores," Barney laughed, "even if it's so dark I can't see you at all. Move off me, McCain, you queer or something? Fellas, tell this overgrown Injun to put me down, Goddamn it, he's busting my ribs. Ain't it enough that I had to put out the damned forest fire all by myself?"

"We were hoping you were dead," Isaac laughed.

"You guys' ugly faces look good, even if I can't see 'em! Me and the fuzz-faced assistant ranger got cut off—we had to lie out in the burn for two hours or so. I damned near strangled to death, swear to St. Jerome...."

Voice from uphill: "Knock off the Goddamned noise!"

They found their way over to the rest of the crew. After waking up everyone there, Barney Bandino was asleep within minutes. He snored quite loudly.

"You boys had to bring him along, didn't you?" Lee the Foreman complained. "Now none of us will get any more shuteye."

*

But they did, and even the rough ground was comfortable beneath them. Sleep, but not enough. Camp's bell went off at five after four. Men crowded around the spring trough, splashed water on their faces, and trudged over to long, makeshift tables for a breakfast of eggs, greasy bread, bacon, and coffee.

Then the camp emptied, men in the backs of trucks, headlamps searching out into smoky darkness, dust swirling from spinning tires, the morning air amazingly chill.

The fire had ran to the top of the ridge where the Crooked Pines crew had attempted to hold it, and there it stopped. Two caterpillars had burned during the night, and a ninety-year-old miner was dead, known only as Zack, whose hovel stood on a bluff above the Middle Fork of the Yuba. In addition, a convict working on the far side of the fireline had been crushed beneath a burning snag.

Killer fire.

But it had stopped moving.

Smoke hung heavy and low in the woods, against a brighter white-gray of false dawn.

The Mormon-Harrington jerked forward, whining in low range.

*

JUNE 30, 1955:

A week, then more. Eleven days.

Large pockets of fire inside the lines.

The firefighters worked in a world of ashes, with extensive areas half a foot deep in powdery grayness that blew in small whirlwinds among tall black skeletons.

But there were steaks to eat at night, steaks too large to fit on a plate, while daytime menu consisted of "C" rations and fruit juice in cans.

Forest service professionals, shanghaied loggers, short-term convicts, college boys working at summer employment: they moved alike in slow motion, talked, worked, ate deliberately, conserving strength, hardly aware of the passing of time.

They'd even quit rubbing their eyes.

"How long have we been here?" Mack asked.

"Two months and three days," Bandino replied.

"Shame you weren't burned up at that," Isaac growled.

"Yeah, a crying shame."

But the foreman had good news: "Last shift, men. Home to Crooked Pines tonight—leave the rest of 'er for the Iron Mine crew. Let's get in as early as we can."

"A shower's going to be good, Lee," Lugie said. "Damned if it isn't."

Then they were wading through gray snow, and swirls of air twisted up plumes of ash.

"It's like an A-bomb, Mack," Isaac said. "It really is. Just like an A-bomb had hit—those films we saw in Air Force ROTC...."

"Hell, an A-bomb would have done a much better job. Look down there...."

In the draw below, fire had left an oasis, a dense green scar across an otherwise gray and steaming landscape. Isaac and Mack moved downhill and under verdant covering to where a spring issued from beneath large bending ferns, and azaleas bloomed, oblivious to fire, untouched, pristine, silent, and seemingly unaware of the devastation around them. Numerous deer stood about, stunned, and stared with blank, uncomprehending, fearless eyes. The creatures moved a step or two, as if contemplating flight, then turned, stared once again.

"Fire," Isaac said. "The danger of fire is greater than the danger of men. It's created a sense of communion."

In the streambed they found a dead bear, burned to death—and strange-shaped charred patterns in the rough, dark fur.

Odor of death, almost sweet, overpowering—or is it azaleas?

The black bear's teeth were showing, the face caught still, petrified, filmed eyes open, flies swarming the mouth—and where flames had eaten through fur and flesh, the undercoat still smoking and giving off an odor that was both unpleasant and at the same time neutral. When wind blew, softly, gently along the stream, the profusion of azaleas nodded and exhaled a fragrance of wild honey.

Live coals: orange in the undercoat, stench of burning hair, even fleas darting across unburned fur.

"Found its way to the glade too late," Mack shrugged.

A porcupine scuttled from under some ferns, crossed the creek without hesitation, and rustled up the far bank.

Burned flesh and the odor of azaleas.

Water skippers moved about on the stream's mottled surface that undulated in irregular sunlight—creek maples above, green leaves trembling in a yellow stillness.

"It'll burn again," Isaac said. "A hundred years, a thousand. Fire sweeps everything clean. It's not really the enemy at all, and the woods have time on their side. Things will grow again—this spot will seed itself out into the burn, and next spring there'll be little green shoots everywhere."

"Well, right now it's like a Goddamned desert, except for here. Jesus, McCain, that bear must have been scared—can you imagine what it'd be like? Fire in his fur, and he came running for the stream but got here too late. I'll bet it wasn't fire that killed El Bruin—a heart attack, I'll bet, or a burst aorta. Bears have weak aortas."

"Know that for a fact, do you?"

"Read it somewhere. Ernest Thompson Seton, maybe."

"Let's get out of here," Isaac said. "Let's return to the real world. I can't stand the smell of these azaleas—let us have the good healthy essence of smoke. My lungs yearn for it. On to the river, friend Madison!"

"You dumb sonofabitch," Mack said. "Teach you everything I know, and you're still as ignorant as the day you crawled out from under a rock."

"On to the river!" McCain insisted. "We shall scoop up dead fish and fling them into the sky!"

But the canyon bottom, too, was untouched by fire, only a few old stumps smoking on the rim of the bluff of the north bank. More deer, some alive and wary, others dead. All along the Yuba a thin green line divided the blackened canyonsides from growth of willow and mock orange and bunchgrass.

The two young men swam and dived for a time, leaped down from high rocks into bluegreen water, their naked bodies wet and alive in midday air.

"Poor old Red's dying for a shower," Mack laughed, "but we got ours first. You ready to head up country, Ike?"

Traversing the steep canyon on their way out, they found a huge rattlesnake looped around a red rock, dozing, unaware of them. But then the eyes gleamed, and a black tongue darted as the reptile assessed possible danger.

"Maybe we ought to kill him," Mack said.

"What for?"

"As big as he is, I'd guess he's been around since the days of Adam and Eve. Get rid of him now, and there'll be no more evil in the world. Might be worth a try. It might be Nidhogg himself, Old Scratch."

"Eden's west of here," Ike laughed. "That's what Dad says— my Eden, not yours, Madison. Yuba Buttes, where Coyote created the human race."

"One myth's as good as another, I suppose. My people, on the other hand, were Vikings—much given to pillage and rapine. We had ice-monsters and trees that grew up from the center of the earth. My forebears could have whipped yours easy, and don't you forget it."

"I think they did, in fact. I guess one half of my ancestors whipped the other half, and that's why I've got a split personality."

"Always wondered about it."

"You think maybe the snake's dying, Mack? Doesn't seem in a mood to move. Hey, look at the rattles on him—must have a dozen or so."

"He's not moving because he's a damned philosopher. Philosophers like to sit around and think about things."

"Vultures," Isaac said, pointing. "Must be twenty, maybe more. Looking for roast beef sandwiches."

"Come on, McCain. Maybe the US-Fuss'll let us go see our lady friends tonight, or is April still wearing that bigass ring the Bulldog laid on her?"

"Unfortunately, yes."

*

The dark green Mormon-Harrington rumbled down a dusty road to the little town of Washington, to pavement, then up the canyon road to the highway and west to Crooked Pines.

Hot showers, the first in nearly two weeks.

The crew shaved, relaxed, played ping-pong after dinner, and pitched horseshoes until darkness came. Lee won every game, and most of his shoes were ringers. He chuckled and pretended he was old and blind, couldn't even see the peg—insisted the ringers were going on accidentally. The foreman puffed his perpetual cigarette and tossed spinning steel through waning twilight.

Unfortunately, all days off were canceled for as long as the fire danger remained high.

At ten o'clock Lee shut down the gasoline generator, and the crew sacked out.

They were in the tents, still talking, when the siren began to whoop.

"Son-of-a-rotten-dirty-bitch!" Barney Bandino howled. "That damned Lee's faking us out, a practical joke. Can't he let us get some shuteye?"

"Probably wants to play horseshoes again," Lugie suggested.

But they reached for their pants and shirts and boots and hardhats and ran for the pumper truck.

"In the canyon," Lee explained. "This one's down in the hole, below Skillman Flat. Fitzweiller log landing, or close by."

The engine revved, and big tires sang against asphalt—then off the paved road and along Burlington ridge and down toward Deer Creek. They could see a red crescent of flame in the darkness below. It ran through the trees, low to the ground, eating into heavy duff, its source apparent. Heavy equipment, logging equipment—two bulldozers and a company pickup, a hoist, a cache of tools, jagged remnants of fuel drums scattered about. Fire was up high in two or three near-standing pines.

The Mormon-Harrington pulled to a stop, and immediately the boys were spinning out the two main hoses. Lee started the pump motor, and the lengths of canvas came hard, charged with water.

They got a line around the burn quickly, Bandino and Madison operating nozzles, and Lee and Whitey Pegelow the TTO sitting atop the vehicle. Isaac and Red cut fireline and mumbled at the luck of the draw.

"We was lucky," Whitey said. "Lucky to get here as soon as we did. This one might have been trouble...."

"A real fine job, men, a real fine job," Lee said. "Two or three more Snow Tents, and you'll begin to look like a *gen-u-wine* fire crew."

"Shee-it, Uncle Lee, we're the best damned fire crew on the Tahoe National Forest right now," Mack Madison insisted.

"Gasoline exploded," Lee nodded. "Equipment's all shot, and that water truck's ruined—and the pickup as well. Wouldn't be surprised if she were started on purpose—an insurance fire, most likely. Could have been sparks, though the tree butchers ain't supposed to be working up here until fire danger's dropped down. No telling. But the Fitzweillers have lost them a bunch of stuff."

"Bandino," Isaac said. "Look at this."

Barney directed his head lamp toward the company pickup. An axe was buried in the door, obviously driven through the metal with a great deal of force.

Then they discovered the gasoline tank on one cat had been ripped open, as with an axe.

Lee walked over to where his crew members were standing, nodded.

"No question," he said. "Them Fitzweillers are going to be real agitated. Probably fifty thousand worth of damage here, maybe more. Must be somebody don't like them much."

"The dozers ain't ruined, anyhow," Whitey said.

But Isaac was thinking:

Dad. Abram. Two bulldozers, a utility truck, a pickup, and the barrels of fuel. He took an axe and went to work, first on the pickup, smashing the windshield and lights and then under the hood and into the motor and radiator and even the fenders and doors. Next came the cats—gauges, hoses, fuel tanks. He must have rolled those full gasoline drums over to the cats and poured the stuff all over everything. Yes, he's probably strong enough to do it if he were angry. He pitched the tools up onto the dozers and got off good way and took some oil-sopped rags and lit them afire and threw them on top. The flames would have knocked even him off his feet. Could even have killed him. And the whole business went up in a big sucking noise like it was thirsty. Then he must have watched and laughed and laughed as flames chased up into the night like fast yellow dogs. When a gas tank exploded, fire rained all over the place. It's only a couple of miles down to our place from here. Abram. No. I'm wrong. Dad wouldn't do that, not even if the loggers did cut all the big trees....

***

Canto Eight:
SUMMER RAINSTORM

*

JULY 4, 1955:

The Copland Music: *Appalachian Spring.*

Swallows darted the air behind the house, stinging flight, mad spirals.

Come thunder, rain, caress the vulnerable earth.

Dogs baying.

Queen of the Fourth of July.

Burt drove, while April sat atop the rear seat of Burt's new '55 Chevrolet convertible, fire-engine red and cream two-tone, smiled, glittered in a gold-sequined bathing suit.

Mouth, breasts, buttocks, legs.

Clapping, whistling.

Burt in a light suit and an old-fashioned stovepipe hat.

Did Isaac come? she wondered, basking in this moment of glory. *He'll not approve, no matter. Angry. He'll be angry with me, but that doesn't make any difference, does it?*

The sun. It had never been so bright before.

Men stared at her, desired her—young men and older men alike—their coyote eyes.

Why do I keep thinking of Isaac? He doesn't understand me and my needs, and that's why I'm going to marry Burt, even though he doesn't excite me and I don't really love him, whatever love is. Burt's the victim in this, but he doesn't know it. I'll be a

*bitch for him, I'll be his whore. I've trapped him, and I'll make him
enjoy being trapped. I'll make him growl with lust, and then I'll
satisfy him because I know how to do that, yes, thank you, Isaac.
Today I'm a woman, almost a goddess—that's what they think,
look at them out there! I'm the very root of the mystery. Poor
Isaac, Isaac the dreamer.*

She touched fingers to her lips, blew kisses to the throng.

The crowded street smelled of beer and mustard.

Burt was honking the horn.

Abram McCain stepped into the roadway, lurched out from the
curb where he'd been standing alone. People moved away from
him—infection of fear, April's fear too.

Abram. The others. The hunger.

Disgusting.

Would they drink her blood when this was over? She'd read
about that in anthropology, the idiot darkness of the human past.
Perhaps her glowing body, that of a sun goddess, would be torn
apart and the gobbets of flesh burned so that pear and apple
orchards might bear.

Old fool!

"Father and son," she whispered. "In forty years, that's Isaac."

A man in a blue uniform pushed his way through the crowd,
but McCain was gone. As April turned, she could see him disappear into an alley beyond the hotel. For a moment she actually
doubted her own perceptions—had Isaac's father been present at
all? The expression on his face—wistful, sad, and making some
sort of judgment upon her and what she was doing?

Burt turned to her.

"We ought to lock that animal up, I'm telling you. Or shoot it,
maybe."

But she thought: *He's seen the most secret part of me, so that
now, as a plant in delicate flower, I will wither in the burning and
blinding and wonderful heat of this day. I am Aphrodite of the
beautiful buttocks, Phryne of Athens, Aphrodite Porn—just as in
the old Greek stories we read in world lit.... Disgusting. Some
tribes fear contagion and will not go near a menstrual woman, who
retires to a moon lodge. My period's starting, it reminds me that
this is an illusion, a dream, a fantasy. A swarm of bees trailing out
from the hollow of a liveoak. I hear the sounds of chainsaws, and
in a flaming circle the wolves have become snakes that wind perfectly into a living rope. I touch at it, and the spark, always the
spark. It comes, and I am thrown into the mist and pale blue light*

and I am searching...no...in the flaming circle, and the wolves have become.... Fish in a deep river, blood on boulders, and snakes lambent and writhing...let this be over...I am sick...I am....

*

Evening.

The sun was huge, elliptical and the color of oaken embers pulsing but with no visible flames. April Incendie watched through the window of Burt's car for a moment as he talked to Old Sammy, who ran the Exxon service station. She wondered if her headache would ever stop. She'd taken some pills her mother used for the migraine, but her eyes continued to throb. Burt kept talking to Sammy for what seemed like a long time, and then he got into the car, started the engine, swung out onto the paved street, sped through the gears, smirked.

"You like the way the '55 purrs?" he asked.

"Nice," April said. "But it's loud now—have you done something to it?"

"Dual glass-packs," he grinned. "Incendie, that ring looks damned good on you."

"It's lonely, though," she smiled. "It needs another to keep it company."

"Lady, you took the words right out of my mouth. What was Ike's crazy freak of a father doing, anyway? I keep saying it—he needs shooting. In the old days we'd have strung him up, if we could of found a thick enough rope. He'll get it, too, only the shame is he's subject to kill somebody first. And that's the truth."

Perhaps I'm still that homely little towhead of a girl who used to play down at the creek...with Isaac.

*

Skyrockets in the night above Diggins. People milled in the dark, children ran wildly, sparklers, shouting, laughing, and the sharp yelp of cannonade as the fireworks were catapulted upward into the night. Firecrackers snapped below, while above the park bright, momentary trails leaped outward from intense centers, like exotic flowers, their imprints glowing. Gashes of light. Then concussion. Clouds beyond, moonlit thunderheads piled high to the east. Distant thunder growled, and silver strings of lightning played over the Sierra.

"God's putting on his own fireworks display," April said.

"Bet you we get some rain. This is one hell of a crazy summer, when you think about it."

"I can smell the air—yes, I can smell it coming."

"Hey, Incendie, let's head on over to the street dance. It's getting kind of boring around here."

*

Loggers were down from the hills, drunk, noisy, all of them trying to make contact with the wives and daughters of the town. Even at the Plaza, an occasional firecracker barked, and the teen-agers yelled and whooped.

Later April stood in front of the large window of the Bullardi residence and looked out over the lights of town.

"Mom and Dad are up at Tahoe for the holiday, gambling," Burt explained. "The place is ours, honey doll."

"Wonderful."

But she was thinking: *I can see the pattern of my life, I have made this choice. Is it possible that until now the nature of what I've done hasn't been clear? Ike and Burt, they're different in most ways, but that doesn't matter. The common point is that they have such anger in them, and maybe I've caused it. I like playing with fire. I've stood between them, desperately weighing one against the other, really wanting them to be friends and knowing it's not possible. Did I make the wrong choice? No, I don't think so. Isaac, you and your Goddamned dream—what dream is it? Will you grow into your father's lunacy? Yes, probably. You can't share your vision, whatever it is. Burt's more practical, more direct, probably more honest, and no dreamer. He's not all that bright, but he'll succeed. And he can share; he's a better person. I don't trust you, Isaac McCain, I never have—no, and it doesn't have anything to do with your being part Indian, whatever lie you may tell yourself. Besides, I shouldn't have to wait forever; there was no reason why I should have waited. Burt, you're the victim because.... I'm sorry, Isaac.*

"Here, it's champagne," Burt laughed. "We're celebrating. It's good. You ever tried this stuff before? No, don't tell me."

"Does it make sense, Burt? I mean, really? Life? I feel small tonight, I feel like nothing I've ever done makes sense. Burt?"

"Hey, girl, what are you talking about? We make sense, don't we?"

"Yes, I suppose so. Will you be a good father to our children, Burt?"

"What's this *father* baloney? You've never even let me...April? Let's make—love. Isn't it about time, for Christ's sake? I bet I could give you twins, I've waited so long. We're engaged, damn it. I should have forced you, that's what you want. You always put me off, but you used to make it with Ike, didn't you? Damn it, I don't want to know that either. Look. The house is empty, we've got it all to ourselves. You ain't easy, like the other girls."

She raised one eyebrow.

"Have there been many...other girls?"

"A few, you know that. Don't go asking questions, and I won't either."

"Damn you, Burt Bullardi."

"Come on, Incendie, we're celebrating. I'm going to show you what it's all about, then you'll see what a real man's like."

He wrestled her down to the floor. She didn't resist, but her mind said, *You don't want this, April, and you know it.*

Burt lay on top of her, kissed her, bit at her neck, reached down and put his hand between her legs.

Stopped.

Sat up.

"You on the rag? For Christ's sake, why didn't you say so?"

"I'm sorry, I really am. I forgot, I swear."

"For Goddamn Christ's sake, Incendie. Don't tell me you've got lockjaw too?"

"You crude male," she said, half laughing.

He got up and walked quickly into the other room, slammed the door behind him.

April lay there, frightened, stunned. She watched for him to come back, not sure what to expect when he did, and she imagined his strong, powerful male form moving smoothly, angrily, distant, almost cat-like.

After a long minute or two he still hadn't returned. April picked up the keys from the table, slipped out the front door, and ran, wildly hoping the Chevrolet would start without difficulty, was relieved when it did. She pulled out, rear tires screeching, and drove toward the Plaza. On a side street she parked the red convertible, a nearly new car Burt's father had repossessed, paid off at the going rate, and then given his son. She left the key in the ignition.

He doesn't have another vehicle. He'll have to call a taxi or walk if he wants to follow me—or phone Frank Abbot. Yes, and he will. He'll find the Chevy. What am I doing? Isaac? Please be here, Isaac. I need you. This time I have to find you.

She started to walk toward the dance, stopped. She removed the engagement ring from her finger, returned to the car, and slipped the ring into the glove compartment.

Ran.

Crying.

She was moving through the crowd of people when she heard her name spoken.

"April!"

She stopped, trembling, and turned about.

"Jesus, April," Isaac said. "It's good to see you! What's the matter? You're white as a sheet. You're pissed at the Bulldog, aren't you—need a bit of premarital counseling? Well, you want to go somewhere? My car's up by the courthouse."

"I've left him," she said. "I took his Chevy. I don't want to marry him, Isaac. I want you. Please...."

"I'm supposed to buy that? Come on, April, this dumb Injun wasn't born yesterday. Heap smart, by Gawd."

"Stop that, Isaac! Listen to me! Look. I returned his ring."

"Okay, okay. Just now? He's following, I take it, and so the two of us will get to have another minor altercation."

"No. Not yet. He will, though. Poor Burt."

"Poor Burt, hell. You two just had a fight, huh? But tomorrow you'll be back together—You just want us to go at it again? It's fun, watching us?"

"Please! I love you, Ike."

"I've got nothing for you, April, not like he has. I'm a dreamer, remember? You said so. But Burt, he's your solid citizen—he'll provide for you."

"Never mind, you mean bastard! I don't want either one of you, then. You're both savages!"

"Okay, Ape...Miss Incendie, okay. Look, I'm sorry. You need help, so you turn to me, good old Isaac. Let's go talk. If you're mine in some way or another, then I guess I have to bail you out. Trouble, and you run to me."

April was crying.

"Please, Ike, please...."

"Let's go, then."

"Yes."

*

They drove to Wolf Mountain and sat in the Buick, said very little to each other, and gazed down at the lights of Sacramento valley, the distant lights that looked so close, no more than arm's length away.

"All those people," Isaac remarked. "Some are dying, some are frightened, and some are making love. It's beautiful from here, even if it is like a damned disease. All the world out there, the great comedy, and we've known so little of it, April. Let's take it together, wherever it leads? The last two weeks are a blur. Our crew's been on a big fire and on standby ever since, until tonight. Gawd, I'm tired of fires. It's time to get civilized, maybe."

"Yes," she answered. "I want that."

The Aaron Copland music was playing: Appalachian Spring. Voices—what voices? They shrieked in the night. Music poured out of the summer earth and enveloped them.

They kissed once more, held each other, believing their personal storm was past. They were grateful for the warmth and the closeness, for the dark. Silent lightning forked over moon-shadowed mountains far eastward.

On the way down to Diggins, Isaac said, "We nearly lost Barney. It was like a desert, and then Mack and I came to a glade where no fire had burned. Not even the wild animals were afraid of us...."

"Let me out here, Isaac. I want to walk home. It's all right. Everything is going to be all right now. I love you, Ike McCain."

"No way. I'll take you on home. You think Burt's waiting there, don't you?"

"Yes, probably. He deserves an explanation, I owe him that much."

"April, Goddamn it, you're either with me or you aren't. I don't want you around Burt—for explanation or for any other reason. You said you'd made your choice."

"You don't own me, Isaac."

"Not if you don't want me to."

"Ike, let's don't fight about this. Trust me, please. I'll tell him one more time, it's over. No goodbye kisses, I promise you. I ran away with his '55 Chevy...."

"So it's back to playing us off, one against the other? That's what it really is?"

"No, I swear it. I wouldn't do that—not ever again."

"You've already done it, and we both ought to drop you like poison."

"Don't say that, you're being cruel. Isaac, Isaac! Please, you say you love me. Then don't do this. I've been wrong, I was so confused. But I'm through with Burt, I promise that."

"April Incendie, Goddamn it. I wish I didn't love you. Okay, your way. Go ahead. I'll phone you tomorrow after work. You'll be home about six? Make up your mind, now. I'll be down again in a week...."

He watched her walk away. Then he began whistling, inventing the tune. He revved the straight-eight and drove up the grade toward Crooked Pines Camp. If Madison were back from his date with Kara, maybe the two of them would talk. Mack liked to analyze things, and analysis was clearly in order.

*

JULY 5, 1955:

The street dance was still in full swing, even though the time was now a few minutes after midnight. Some people were beginning to leave as the air became heavier with impending summer rain. Bands of colored light played over the musicians.

April Incendie ran down the street and into the Plaza. Only when she'd joined the throng did it occur to her that Burt might be there. He would have found the two-tone Chevy by now, and he might well be waiting for her. She didn't want to see him— suddenly she wanted desperately to be with Isaac again.

But the car was parked on the side street, just where she'd left it.

She crossed the wide lawn where a few hours earlier fireworks had been set off. Rain began to fall, a thin, light rain. Her hair would get wet.

The uncertain coursings of years, of thousands of thousands of years, were not more insistent: the rains came and passed, and earth became dry. New creatures roamed in grasslands that had once been impenetrable forests, and the ape that had learned how to hunt when there was no need came into its own. Hunters. Wielders of hand-hewn bones. They would have the white goddess at last, would bring her to bay, would atone for all the impotence, all the frustration and vexation and despair. Circe. You like the young lord from Troy? He violated even his own daughters. Let

*the men do the shooting, Helen, spare yourself. Killing's against
your nature, it would hurt with unhappy thought some later time....*

"Isaac...."

Close lightning was swallowed by ensuing thunder. April ran
toward the edge of the woods so as to be under the protection of a
big cedar's branches. She would wait for the rain to stop.

A downpour hit.

April sprinted to the outward-reaching folds of the great cedar
where she had played as a child. She'd been climbing that tree the
day of her first period and could see bloodstains on the denim of
her bluejeans.

Cool rain poured down through intense darkness, and thunder
rattled and boomed over the Sierra.

Then she heard the sound of hurried footsteps in the gravel of
the park roadway. She peered out from behind cedar boughs:
could see nothing. Darkness, and the odor of something like
turpentine.

She ran, suddenly terrified.

"It's Burt? I don't dare...."

Rain drenched her, stung at her eyes as she proceeded along a
path which led into the woods.

*I'm going the wrong way, the wrong way. Why did I come this
way?*

Footsteps behind her.

She stumbled over a root or vine, fell, bruised her arm and
ripped her dress. Then she was on her feet once more, running.

Hid in a tangle of wild grapevines which hung like drapery from
poplars along the creek, she worked herself into a small dry hollow,
afraid to breathe lest the dry leaves beneath her might rustle and
give away her hiding place. Through dense foliage she could
discern the dim shape of her pursuer. *It* was walking slowly now,
groping its way after her. She waited. She could see or hear
nothing more. Rain demons drummed at the earth, and thunder
sent waves of sound washing across the night.

*Miss Incendie, are you quite certain you've not imagined all of
this? There's no one out there.*

April worked her way from her hiding place and moved cautiously along the path which led toward the park's edge.

A hand touched at her face.

She screamed and ran, her lungs burning with cold, wet air.
Then, when no steps seemed to be following, she stopped to

breathe. She closed her eyes and fought away a sensation of utter numbness.

Footfalls again, still behind her, pursuing. She raced away once more, leaving the path and turning inexplicably toward thick woods, as a deer might flee toward the deepest fastness, blind that even hunting dogs can find their way into the black heart of the forest.

Twice she fell and struggled to her feet, plunged onward, hid among some boulders.

You must think! Think!

"All I've done is to get farther from safety...I must find the park...screaming will do no good, not out here...I've got to catch my breath. Damn this rain anyway! Why aren't I more frightened? It's as though all this has happened before, long ago, so long ago I can't even bring it to mind...."

Cunning and a primitive kind of instinct had supplanted fear, even as she comprehended that it was all a game, however deadly the consequences. She was the hunted, the quarry, the prey. She laughed.

She thought: *I'm going to be raped. Unless I am very crafty and very quick, I'm going to be raped. Who in God's name is it? Burt? He's strong, but I can kick. Wouldn't he call my name—has he gone crazy? Better that I don't know...and he hasn't caught me yet. This fox can still run.*

She crept from her hiding place and started once again in the direction of the park. She could imagine a line of white Victorian houses beyond the ball diamond. There lay safety. Then she heard the footsteps, bolted forward, splashed through the shallow creek, turned her ankle among loose stones, fell, rose, ran once more— aware of but not feeling berry vines that tore at her clothing, thorns biting at legs and arms. And as she ran, words formed slowly: *Your blue dress will be absolutely ruined....* But she ran without emotion, gaining confidence, yet with no idea of the right direction. It no longer mattered.

Once she hid, threw herself flat in tall, pungent brackens, muffled her breath with her hands. She could hear nothing, but she did not move, had to fight an urge to laugh.

It's only a game, only a game, only a stupid game....

She rose to her knees and peered into darkness: dim forms, shapes, degrees of blackness. She crawled through wet brackens and at length discovered the path, became certain of her directions. She knew what she would do. She'd sprint to the park and across the graveled roadway to those houses, would pound on a door where lights were still burning—yes, if the *footsteps* were still behind her. If not, she'd simply walk on home.

She started to her feet and began to run.

Someone was close, and she tried to veer.

Concussion.

Pressure and noise.

She continued to move, but her balance was gone. Brackens, wet and rank, were in her mouth. She'd bite, kick. Kick hard. Darkness caressed her face. She lay very still among brackens. Perhaps darkness itself would save her. She closed her eyes, listened to trampling feet, waited.

It was quiet once more, and she started to move, then thought better of it.

So long as I'm still, it can't find me.

Rain fell. She could feel blood running down over her eyes, and she knew that her mind was blurred. She tried to concentrate on Isaac, then on Burt. Had she done the right thing? Had she been fair to Isaac? He loved her, she knew that.

Burt, is it you? You've hit me with something, damn you. I'm bleeding. Is it my fault, I owe you this?

And she thought: *My period, I'm bleeding twice. It's hilarious, it's beautiful!*

She bit at her hand until the sensation of pain managed to work its way in through a haze and a numbness.

The footsteps are near. It will be all right. My period. I'm going to be raped, hold still and enjoy it. You filthy barbarian, I'll kick, kick hard. You want pleasure, but you're not going to get it the way you want it. If I were a man, I'd kill you....

She couldn't think. She felt rain on her hair.

Then she cried out, "Burt, help me! I'll do whatever you want! You've hurt me, I can't see!"

Hot breath on her face. Hands searching at her body, ripping her clothes. Rain on her flesh, on her legs, cold, hot, her arms bound to her sides, the dress pulled up over her head.

Briars. All right, relax. Let it be over with, it's nothing I haven't done before. No, wait, I'm not ready yet, please!

Into her.

Jamming into her.

She could hardly breathe because of the weight upon her.

In the clearing, under manzanita blossoms, she and Betty Sue lying in the sunlight, *He is hurting me*, and childhood and womanhood and death and butterflies and men whistling and Isaac hitting the home run that day in the ball game against Marysville, and the pained expression in Burt's eyes when she said, "No, I'm going to be Ike's girl now." *He is hurting me so much, I didn't know.* Her own fault then? She'd played one against the other, everyone said so, and now this? Isaac and old Abram at the parade. *He is hurting me hurting hurting.* Just walking out there and the sun so bright....

April realized she was being turned over, something forced onto her finger, the ring? What? Tantalizing, the cold rain on the backs of her legs and buttocks, *No, please not that, you filthy beast!* But he was forcing himself into her and she bit hard on her tongue and tried to wrench herself away but she could not move and she screamed again and again but no sounds came....

Drowning into darkness and *harder harder* and the images poured up from sheer black, came alive and leaped out at her to devour her, she was searching for the light *hurting me* but there was no light, she could not find any switch on the wall in the dark room, black waves, pounding, roaring, roaring, *I can't stand it! For God's sake, please stop please please, you're tearing me open!* In the distance, the hundreds, the hands, hunger bruising at her breasts *please* and she was trying to reach out once again toward the light, trying to understand, trying, her being, her body, dragged down, and the sea, the waves, *someone's voice, oh whose voice?* But the sounds were all scrambled.

Then he was gone.

It was gone.

Rain fell. Her arms were free once more. She was aware of death nearby, a silent presence, grinning in darkness. She knew she couldn't just lie there, she had to move, had to find her way home. There was yet hope. She was still alive. She would heal and forget all this, everything that had happened.

Lightning flashed, and there were faces about her, faces she knew she should have recognized but didn't, mouths that seemed to be speaking, voices she couldn't hear even though she heard them.

She pulled the torn clothing about her and tried to stand up, wondered if she would be able to order another blue dress to replace the ruined garment. But it was no good: she lacked strength. A lash of pain flowed down out of her eyes and covered her entire body.

Goddamn you both. I love. I hate you....

*

JULY 5, 1955:

"Did she say it was McCain? That's the first thing I need to know."

"The girl was babbling, for God's sake," Andrew Incendie replied. "Yes, she said it was him—or as much as said it was him. She came crawling home early this morning, the most pitiful thing I've ever seen. I tell you, I'm going to kill that son of a bitch of a crazy Indian myself. Her face was puffed up, blood smeared all over her, clothing in shreds."

"She say specifically it was Abram McCain?" Hutchings asked again.

"She was in pain. Goddamn it, man, you've got to understand that. No, she didn't say *specifically*. It happened out in the woods beyond the park, apparently, after the dance last night, I guess. Who in hell else could it have been? Yesterday at the parade...."

"Mind if I smoke, Andy?" Sheriff Hutchings asked, lighting a cigarette. "Only about two or three thousand fellas, actually, including those two boyfriends of hers. Your daughter's been playing with fire all along, in my opinion. Everyone in town knows those two hate each other, young Bullardi and McCain's kid. Wasn't she with Bullardi Last night? Saw them together about nine o'clock, as it turns out. Later one of my deputies saw her with Isaac McCain. Positive identification. Ike works at Crooked Pines, as I guess you know. The foreman said young Mr. McCain pulled in last night just after midnight. Your daughter was at the dance right about then...."

"You're not suggesting it was Burt, are you?" Incendie demanded. He was incredulous. "April and Burt are going to get married—if she lives through this ordeal. His father owns half of this town—you're talking nonsense, Hutchings. Who says she was with Isaac McCain last night? I don't understand her, Ed, but I guess parents never do. Burt said she got angry at him, some damned thing or another, so he let her go—she took his car. If you'd seen the boy this morning, you'd know better than to be thinking that sort of thing. What the hell's the matter with you, Hutchings? Burt loves April—they're engaged to be married, for God's sake. I wouldn't blame Burt if he took a shotgun to that madman, and if you don't do something quick, I imagine that's just what's going to happen—if I don't beat him to it myself. That crazy Indian raped my daughter, and I've got a gun too, a double-barreled twelve gauge...."

Hutchings shook his head.

"Andy, I'm not suggesting anything about young Burt Bullardi. But I have to talk to your daughter first. Yeah, I've got to talk to her and to Burt and to the other one, Abram's kid."

"Isaac McCain," Carolyn Incendie said. "He's been the trouble-maker in this affair all along."

"Yep, Isaac," Hutchings nodded. "The notorious McCains. But when two young bucks are fighting over a girl, damned near anything can happen. The Highway Patrol boys broke up a little to-do over at the Yuba Lumber Company burner about three weeks ago. Should have brought them in and locked them up, all three of them, in my opinion. That includes your daughter. Overnight in the county jail might have shaken some sense into them. Oh yes, your girl was there, right in the thick of things, didn't you know that? Goading the boys on, as I figure it. Young McCain was down and bleeding, according to report, and Bullardi was standing over him with a two-by-four club. Incendie, with you and Burt's father both local businessmen, the officers made a judgment call, I guess you'd say, to hush things up. First you've heard of the matter, is it?"

"Isaac McCain is bad for April," Mrs. Incendie said. "I've al-ways believed that to be true."

"Goddamn it, Hutchings, you're out of your mind! All right, so both boys are in love with our daughter. Young Ike's all right, Indian or not. I've nothing against him. He's enrolled at the university in Berkeley and is likely to make something of himself, a lawyer or even a doctor. He's not the problem—it's that crazy son-of-a-bitch of a father of his. The man's out of his mind, running around in the woods naked and bellowing and God knows what all...."

"Well, Andy," Hutchings shrugged, "I got to talk to some people first. Maybe you're right about Abram, but a lot of mistakes have been made by men who went off half-cocked, and I've got no intention of picking up anybody without some solid evidence. A good legal-beagle from Sacramento would get a change of venue, the way this town's riled up, and anywhere but in Diggins, a judge would throw the thing out of court. I want the guilty one, and I want my charges to stick. When April comes around, then hope-fully we'll have a good part of what we need. After that I'll have to verify the man's whereabouts. Suppose McCain just happened to be sitting in on a poker game with Big Chief Louis Kelly, down at the Washington House last night—twenty miles away and half a dozen witnesses? You see what I mean? But if she says it was

him, then that's another matter.   Even so, McCain will have a
lawyer, like I say, probably someone from Sacramento or the Bay
Area—he's got friends down there. They'll plead him a *diminished
capacity*, or something of the sort. Eccentric old buzzard that he is,
Abram McCain's got money and friends, though not many around
here. Jesus Christ, what a mess—I shouldn't even be talking about
it. Hell, half the logging crews on the Tahoe Forest were in town
yesterday, and most of them drinking by dance time. Who knows
what happened, anyway?"

"What in God's name are you talking about, Hutchings?
You're aware what people around town are saying? *McCain owns
you, otherwise he'd have been in jail or a nut farm long since.*
Evidence? For Christ's sake, my girl's been raped! Can't you get
that through your thick skull? April's been raped—damned near
clubbed to death.   And who the hell is it that goes wandering
around in the middle of the night? We all know about it—we all
know the man's crazy as a stripèd-neck loon. There's nobody in
Diggins who's safe with that kind of thing prowling about. Carolyn
and me, we were up all night worrying, and then this morning April
came home half-crawling...and...Jesus! We need an old-fashioned
lynch party. What's the damned law for, anyhow? Rights for the
criminals, not for the victims?"

Hutchings took a deep breath and stared first at Incendie and
then at the wife.

"Where's young Bullardi right now?"

"How in hell would I know? Well, at home, maybe. He's been
trying to get hold of his folks—they're up at Tahoe, from what he
said."

*

Sheriff Ed Hutchings walked up and down the creek, searching.
But there were no footprints, nothing. It occurred to him that he
might well have passed over the exact spot and not have known it.
The previous night's downpour hadn't helped a bit. April Incendie
herself, he reflected, might not be able to find the place again—if
she pulled through at all. There was a good chance she wouldn't.
Comas, he knew from experience, were tricky things. Sometimes a
little pressure to the human brain was enough to scramble the
matrix....

He kept wondering—what in hell was she doing out in the
woods? Had she accompanied someone? A gun, and whoever it

was forced her? Some punk from the city, possibly, up to celebrate
the Fourth of July?

"The town wants Abram, wants him bad. It don't even matter
who raped the Incendie girl. This whole thing is crazy, no sense to
it. Raining like hell last night, and maybe the rapist figured she was
dead and carried her out here and dumped the body and it came
back to life?"

McCain's guilty, he's the one....

The story was burning through Diggins like a grass fire. The
town listened and said to itself: *We waited too long.*

*

Doc Carner nodded.

"You may speak with her for a few minutes. She's conscious
now, but take it easy on her, Sheriff."

Then Hutchings was at April's bedside.

"I think it might have been him," the girl said slowly, having to
concentrate in order to make the syllables form. "No, nothing
was...very clear. It was dark, but I've got my ring back. Terribly
strong. I couldn't do anything after I was hit...."

Hutchings sat by the side of the bed, the doctor behind him.
The sheriff felt clumsy, out of place, as though he were intruding,
but he was obliged to press on. In truth, he wished desperately that
he had a female deputy to do the questioning—three rape cases
within the past two years, and each time he found himself choked
up, embarrassed both for himself and for the young women who'd
been the victims. Nevertheless, justice itself was at stake, and
possibly even the life of a man he'd known and liked for a number
of years. For a moment Hutchings almost felt that he, himself,
were on trial, a single, stubborn, solitary holdout against an overwhelming voice of communal logic. Sixty years earlier, a *posse
comitatus* would have formed spontaneously—and the presumed
guilty party would have been hunted down and lynched. But times
had changed, the world had changed utterly, what with two world
wars, a stock market crash, prohibition, and a *police action* in
Korea. Even the big gold mines of the region were almost certainly
on their last legs. Yes, but had human nature been in any way
improved? All day Hutchings had felt an almost tangible hatred
running through the town, *his own towns*, both of them, even
among his own county deputies. He was not even certain of his
capacity to control the deputies themselves.

"April, what do you mean? *Nothing was very clear?*"

"Dark," she said, struggling with her words. "He hit me. I don't know what...happened. I...."

The doctor tapped Hutchings on the shoulder, shook his head.

"You get a look at the man's face, April? You'd know if it was McCain, wouldn't you?"

"Isaac wouldn't...."

"Ike McCain? What about his father?"

"Nothing...makes sense. I'm afraid. I keep thinking strange things, I couldn't see. Dreams, crazy dreams. Then the rain stopped and morning...sun shining in the trees like it didn't care. Is Isaac here yet? Isaac...."

"Was it Isaac, then?"

"Raining. Who are you? Where's my father?"

"She can't see you, Sheriff," the doctor whispered. "Her vision's blurred. A severe trauma to the brain can cause massive distortions of perception, usually does."

Hutchings ignored the words.

"Was it anyone you know, April?"

"He kept...hurting me. He wouldn't stop. I told him...."

"Told him what?"

"I think we'd better let it go for now, Sheriff," Doctor Carner said. "She needs rest."

He motioned to the door.

Hutchings was about to ask another question, but instead he stood up and whistled through his teeth. Then he walked slowly out of the room, shaking his head, the doctor behind him.

"She has a concussion, and there's the possibility of a cerebral hematoma—you know, a blood clot. I'm waiting on the X-rays right now. Skull fracture—these things are tricky, highly unpredictable in terms of their effect. A specialist is driving up from Sacramento—I'm a general practitioner, not a brain surgeon. He's one of the best. Yes, we may have to operate in order to relieve pressure on the brain itself. It's bad, but her condition's stable at the moment...."

"Poor little gal—and such a pretty thing, too," Hutchings said, lighting a cigarette. "Truth is, I need a female officer for problems like this, someone who's had training. I haven't got enough nerve for asking the questions that need to be asked. That Yuba River rape case last year—I nearly flubbed the whole thing. If it hadn't been for your testimony, Doc, I'd have lost the case. At least we got a conviction...."

Carner nodded.

"Man has a good deal of the savage left in him, I'm afraid, if *savage* is even the right word. *Sexual insanity,* that would come closer. It's much worse in the cities, though, and that's why I left my practice in Cleveland and came out here. But I don't suppose I have to tell you about the shortcomings in human nature, do I? Over the years, you've seen it all."

"More shortcomings in some than in others," Hutchings remarked. "There's violence down inside all of us, like the human race has got no business driving around in automobiles or carrying guns or building bombs. Things have gotten out of hand, maybe always were. A couple of big wars now, and we haven't learned a damned thing from them. And the Korean business, it was just round one—won't be over until we've sent our boys straight into Moscow and Beijing, so probably there's going to be A-bombs flying before too long. Well, maybe we was all right before we got so damned smart. Couldn't hurt each other as much then, at least not all at once. But this sort of thing, with the Incendie girl—I suspect that's been going on since we were all living in the trees or the caves or whatever. Or don't you hold with that?"

Carner nodded noncommittally.

"Damned banty roosters are always chasing the hens," Hutchings said. "Well, hell, I ain't paid for being a cracker-barrel philosopher. I draw my paycheck for catching people, poachers, thieves, and murderers, only I have to know first who it is I'm trying to fetch up...."

*

Isaac McCain was lying on his bunk at Crooked Pines Camp, reading. At the table, in the center of the wooden-frame tent, Bandino, Lugie, and Madison were playing cards. The Coleman lantern had begun to pulse and flicker.

"McCain," Madison said, "how's about getting off your ass and putting some white gas into the lantern? Lee'll be turning off the generator any minute now, and I need lumens if I'm going to take these guys to the cleaners. *Let there be light,* that's the university's motto. Us Berkeley bums have to stick together."

"Screw you, Mack," Isaac said without looking up. "Get it yourself."

"Hey, come on now, for the love of the Bandit," Barney said. "I got a big hand going here."

"*Band-Aid* is closer to the truth," Mack winked.

"I just about got the both of them," Red laughed. "Juice up the lantern, Ichabod Crane."

Madison was staring down into his cards when Lee appeared in the doorway of the tent.

"Good to see you men improving your minds," he chuckled. "Ike, there's a telephone call for you over at the office."

Mack looked up.

"I'll bet it's April Incendie," he said, "or is she Burt's girl this week? I lose track of you guys sometimes."

Isaac put his book aside.

"Who is it, Lee?"

The foreman shrugged.

"Somethin' going on, I guess. Ike, I didn't tell you, but the sheriff's office phoned this morning, wanted to know what time you pulled into camp last night. Seemed satisfied when I told 'em. Anyhow, this one says he's a friend of yours—didn't catch the name. The rest of you feel like taking some money from an old man? Maybe I'll sit up with you for a spell tonight."

Isaac walked across the open area to the office and knocked on the door. He felt something of a premonition, but had no idea of what.

"Hi, Alice," he said to the foreman's wife. "Lee says I've got a call."

Alice Bousfield smiled and motioned for Isaac to enter. He picked up the earpiece of the old-fashioned hand-crank Forest Service phone, hesitated for an instant, and then spoke into the mouthpiece.

"This is Isaac McCain," he said.

The voice on the other end of the line belonged to Burt Bullardi.

"What do you want, you sonofabitch?" Isaac asked, forgetting momentarily that Alice might still be in the room. He looked around to see if she'd heard him, but she'd stepped into the kitchen.

"What are you talking about?" Isaac asked, feeling Burt's words penetrate like lead, knowing he'd been hit and yet not feeling the pain that should be there. Without being told, he knew what Burt was saying—yet his mind rebelled. The stammered words went through him and passed away.

"Who's dead? You're not making any sense, Bulldog."

He didn't want to know. He already knew. He asked, but he
didn't want Burt to answer.

"No," he said. "I don't understand what the hell you're talking
about! How do you know? What...?"

But the voice on the other end of the line no longer even
sounded like Burt Bullardi—instead it was a series of blurted syllables interspersed with sobs. For a moment Isaac was not certain
there had been a voice.

"April...?"

Bullardi was still trying to speak when Isaac replaced the
telephone on its hook.

"Goodnight, Ike," Alice said as he walked toward the door. "Is
something the matter?"

"Goodnight," he heard himself answer, his own voice distant,
strange.

He didn't return to the tent. He wandered over to the improvement yard and stood at its rim, overlooking the deep black
canyon of Deer Creek. The night was very clear after the previous
day's thunderstorms, and he could see quite distinctly the lights of
Sacramento some seventy miles to the southwest.

He waited for pain to come. It hadn't as yet.

*Everything is changed. Everything will have to be defined all
over again....*

He lay down in thick dust that spurted from beneath the rain
crust, like egg shell, hardened by mountain sun since the showers
of the previous night, dust eddying about him like cement powder.
He could feel it in his hair. He stared up at the stars, white
millions, and the waning moon. It was different now. Earth had
tilted on its axis.

He waited for the pain he knew was coming.

Like gutshot.

He writhed about in the powdery dust, felt it in his eyes. He
was not certain how long he'd been lying there when he became
aware of voices close by. They were calling his name.

"Come on, Ichabod," Mack Madison said. "Let's get over to
the tent. Jonathan H. Christmas, you're covered with dirt, Ike."

"We got some coffee cooking on the stove," Lugie said.

Bandino grasped Isaac's hand and pulled him to his feet.

"Thanks, thanks fellas. April's gone, she's gone....It's all just
dust like here in the improvement yard, everything human is made
out of dust."

"Come on, Ike," Madison said. "It can't be helped now. We just heard on the damned radio. Bad news travels fast. Grab hold of him, Red."

At the same instant Isaac broke into a spasm of uncontrolled sobbing.

"Help me, fellas, will you? I can't see a damned thing.... There's burned flesh in my eyes."

"Think you're going to need a shower and clean duds first," Lugie said. "You can't hit the hay all covered with yard dirt."

"We could just scrape out a couple holes for his eyes," Bandino said, playing his lantern up and down Isaac's form. "At least his hardhat won't have to be washed up."

"Where *is* the hardhat?" Lugie demanded.

"It's in the tent, under his bunk. Mack, you going to steer him over to the showers? I'll fetch a clean uniform, double pronto. If Lee sees him this way, he'll swear McCain's gone gopher-loco."

*

Coyote-Head sat on a stump at the edge of the improvement yard and began to chant, softly, in words that could not have been understood even if there had been anyone to hear them. An intense green light seemed to illumine his ancient and yet perpetually youthful canine features—pointed ears, long snout, secret yellow eyes that revealed both pain and also delight in pain. He moved about in a circle, gesturing to the earth and to the sky. Voices, as of wailing. Sound of a huge heartbeat.

*

JULY 6-9, 1955:

Abram watched them from the ridgeside above his cabin.

Oliver was bellowing.

About twenty men, he guessed. He could see them entering the cabin, and some had rifles.

"Well, I can imagine what this is all about. Don't suppose it would do much good to go down there, either. The boys don't look all that friendly. I hope Horse the Hound is hidden behind his woodbox."

Abram watched intently as the men entered his unlocked cabin, then the printshop. Finally they stood around in a circle, talking.

"They know I'm not far away. My truck's down there."

The men were setting dogs loose, were holding items of his clothing for them to smell.

"Looks like trouble. Here I am with no gun or nothing, stuck like a coon up a tree. Guess I'd best start moving. Come along, old hulk of a body, it looks as though we've got a job to do."

The mine won't be any good. There's no way out. Your smell's all over the place. It'll take them a while to find a trail they can follow.

Abram strode out along a faint path that would take him over the ridge—out of Deer Creek's drainage and down into Steephollow on the other side.

From the ridge crest, he could hear dogs baying. He began to run downhill.

"About an hour to sundown. I can make the creek by then."

He could still hear the sounds of dogs, but the animals were far off to the north. He moved easily, jogging, surprised even at his own endurance. Then he was at the stream, wading his way downcanyon, careful always to stay in the water, cautious lest any part of him should rub against branches. He tried not to touch anything at all.

It's that girl. They're after you about that girl, Isaac's girlfriend. Stupid bastardos don't know the difference between sheep and people, only maybe there isn't any real difference.

*

Sometime after dark he came to a waterfall and a bridge: there was no way down. He'd have to climb, cross the road, and descend on the other side. Across the way, at the margin of some gravel flats, a single fire burned, two figures close about it—a man and a woman, the two of them apparently camped out.

Abram paused, stared at the flickering light.

This was the place, as he'd surmised years earlier, where Acorn Girl and Ben Goffe McCain had led the Maidu warriors against a company of White miners in the year 1850—if old True Bear McCain had gotten the story straight, at least.

"Grandfather Ben," Abram whispered to the night, "that must have been some little party—a regular grizzly bear dance. And you, riding a huge plough horse, according to the tale. You were an overgrown oaf too, like the lot of us—but what in God's name brought you here, a Connecticut Yankee in exile? If you were looking for a new life, a new identity, you found them, by God.

And here I am, your descendent a century later, on foot and chased by dogs, some guy's coon hounds, most likely. That battle you and Acorn Girl fought—long forgotten. The miners are all gone, and there's only a young couple camped out under scrub pines—them and an educated Halfbreed lunatic who's being chased...."

Then he was out into the gravel flats, keeping distance between himself and the campers until he was beyond them, around a bend in the creek canyon, and finally to Steephollow's confluence with Bear River. The larger stream was swift, meandering from one side of its gravel flat to the other, the current augmented by water diverted from Milton and Bowman and Spaulding, lakes up in the glacier-worn granite of the high country, water that would eventually find its way to low foothills, to plum and pear orchards and towns like Auburn and Loomis and Roseville.

He splashed ahead, let the current take him. He swam like a salamander. His limbs were dead tired, and he was nearly numb with cold, but he hadn't heard any dogs for three hours or so.

I'll float down to Greenhorn, then walk up the creek to that abandoned mine.... I've lost them, sure. For the moment, at least, they're not going to tree this overweight coon.

*

McCain went in through a broken window and curled up on the floor, shivering uncontrollably.

"I don't really believe any of this—it's a dream," he said to the darkness. "I'm too old to be horsing around this way. I'm past sixty, for bloody hell's sake—no sixty-year-old man could do what I've just done. I've covered damned near twenty miles. But the body's tired, tired and hungry and cold. I could eat rocks if I weren't so tired. A big, fat, wet toad—that's me. Old Man Coyote's written himself a hell of a script—black humor, that's what it is. Not funny at all, if you ask me. Somehow those boys have decided I'm the one who did in the Incendie girl, so they're chasing me. The murderer might even be with them, for all I know. Guess I make a hell of a scapegoat, when you get right down to it. And my own fault, too...."

He slept.

Afternoon sun awakened him. He sat up quickly, still wrestling against a virtual flood of dreams—bits and pieces of illusion, a sequence without coherence.

Yet the image of Lucinda Septien was clear in his mind, Lucy as she'd been in her early twenties—raven-haired and dark-skinned and beautiful, a stunner.

"Guess it's been a good life after all," he muttered, shaking his head.

His joints ached with first movement. Hunger burned through him.

He rose, walked slowly to a makeshift cupboard, its door hanging from one brittle leather hinge. There he found a rusty can of tomatoes and a half-full box of crackers, limp with moisture but not moldy. As a can opener, he used an iron hinge that was lying on the broken floor.

He ate.

"Not enough, but it's something."

Did you enjoy your meal, Abram McCain?

"Not bad, considering."

You've not many meals left.

"I ain't so sure about that. Why are you pestering me now, Dog-face?"

I've always had a special interest in you.

"Well, let's talk, then. What the hell? I don't feel like doing much else, truth to say."

How was she?

"What are you jabbering about? You know damned well I didn't have anything to do with.... You been rolling in fermented cow-dung, or what? That's what you smell like, at least."

Don't change the subject, Abram. Are you certain? The way you've been acting lately....

"My mind's all right, I tell you. I've passed through that. No sir, you're not going to get me now."

I've always had you, Abram McCain, and you've always known it.

"Not any more, you don't. There was a time, that much I'll admit. But my mind's clear at the moment. My mind has never been clearer than it is right now."

Then why am I here?

"I didn't call you, *Oleli* Piss-on-the-Stump. You came of your own volition."

But you're talking to me. Do you deny it?

"Nobody else around, that's all."

You've got a point there, I'll give you that much.

"Damned rights. And I could get rid of you if I wanted to."

Pride, Abram. Do not indulge yourself in pride. It's hardly worthy of you. Better men than yourself have tried to put me away. I recollect once when I had a little argument with White Bear....

"Another story? Well, in any case, I'm not going to worry about you."

Pano tried to pretend that he'd created himself, and so I took away his voice and made him go on all fours. Abe, I've been in your bones since I planted the Ootimtsaa tree.

"So you keep saying."

I was harbored in your great grandmother's womb and also in your grandfather's seed and your father's. There's no escaping.

"You're not the only Master, Peheipe. I've been at your rituals—you're just a portion of the mystery."

I live in the grapevines. I live in your own erect manhood—that is, when you can get it up. You old bulls, you bellow a lot and are generally pathetic.

"And hence you're the source of all my problems."

No more than you're the source of mine. I'm Clown-dog the Great. Did I ever tell you about the time I convinced the people it was better for them to die so the young folks could dress up for funerals? The problem is, no one celebrates the Ustu time any more. It was grand—tall poles hung with baskets of food and woven things, shell money and woodpeckers' scalps. And all of it set on fire! The people used to weep and chant and dance until dawn, and then they'd run back to their villages to find more things to burn in my honor, yes, and to honor all those who'd gone on to Upper Meadows since the beginning of time....

"So now time had a beginning, ehh? Well, half of one, six dozen of the other. My mind's clear, at least."

I'll stay close in case I'm needed for anything.

"Sure you don't want to tell me about the time you and Turtle and World-Maker went floating on a raft? I don't take none of your brag seriously any more. So do what you're best at—provide some real entertainment."

Flute music. Rhythmic pulsations of drums. Three young women, a blonde, a redhead, and a brunette, all quite naked—like Old Man Oleli, their bodies brilliantly green. They danced across the littered floor of the deserted cabin. They gyrated in unison. Coyote-Head turned to watch the girls, and his muzzle whiskers twitched. After a few moments, he joined their dance—as the music and chanting grew louder and louder. Jack Wilson, Wovoka himself, stood in one corner, his eyes glazed over, and muttered incoherent phrases. A long line of Indian dead passed through the room—Karok and Shasta and Wintun, Yana and Miwok and Maidu, Ohlone and Yurok, Klamat and Modoc. Men and women. Children. Old people. Kuksu, First-Man, his head several times normal size. The eyes of all were gouged out, the bodies frail, withered. Wovoka reached up and took into his hands a globe of incandescent fire. As the music and chanting reached intolerable intensity, Old Man Coyote grasped the blonde about the waist and wrestled her to the floor. She screamed wordlessly. Coyote-Head grinned, rubbed at his private parts. The other two girls assisted in subduing their unfortunate sister, laughing hysterically as they did so. Coyote was poised above his victim, who screamed again, wordlessly, and writhed beneath the god's plunging haunches. Then she began to move with him, in frenzied unison.

*

"I've got to find Isaac," he blurted. "My son has to know."

Abram had eaten only some blackberries that day, but late in the afternoon a porcupine scrambled across his path. He used a club to kill the creature, ripped the gut open with a rusted hatchet blade he'd found in the gravel along Greenhorn Creek. He had matches now: these he'd found in a jar in the cabin where he'd spent the preceding two nights.

He cooked and ate the meat that tasted oddly like pork.

All I need is a bit of salt and a bottle of wine. Wonder if they're still looking for the Injun who went to Harvard? Truth to say, this might be a good time to be drinking beer out on a Cape Cod beach somewhere—or tramping around up in the Maine woods. Anywhere but here, I guess. Well, I've got to get down to Diggins, to Hutchings' house, at night. The man will give me a fair shake. Those other miscreants will shoot me sure as God raises green apples in hell. But first I've got to reach Isaac. Going to have to keep on walking, tired or not. There'll be somebody posted at home, that's certain. But if there's no more than a couple of lads, I've got a good chance of taking care of the situation. Then I can get my truck and head on down to Diggins. If I have to stay on shank's mare, though, it'll be another thirty miles. Not sure I'm up to it, but who knows? The body's got kinks in it, it wants to let me down. All these years I've had strength, and now it's starting to leave me—now when I need it the most....

Abram put out the small fire, using mouthfuls of water from a nearby spring. Then he dozed for a while, was aware of the cries of bluejays.

Something was near.

"*Indawkaw-yi,*" he said, "bottoms up, it's boiling...."

They've come for you now.

Coyote Man stepped out from behind a tree. Flames issued from his eyes and genitals.

"Get the hell out of here, Old Fellow. Haven't got time for you just now. Visit again when I've a bit more leisure, won't you?"

No, you don't have much time.

McCain could hear the dogs. They were close—they were running close—they were running wild.

The men would have to be far behind.

"Come to tree the big coon, have they?"

Abram gazed desperately about, made note of an outcropping of boulders up a gullyside. He scrambled for it, waited there. He watched the first of them, a large black hound, sniffing the remains of the porcupine, backing off. Three other dogs were close behind.

Mean-looking hounds, aren't they, Abram? Jackal blood, that's the problem. Not even wolves act that way. Well, now, they seem to be coming to visit.

Abram held his club in one hand and the rusted hatchet blade in the other as the black hound wailed and leaped, its mouth open. McCain brought down the segment of limbwood, and the dog flipped to one side, whimpered, and lay still.

Here come some more. Six of them. Damn it, I do like excitement!

A blow from the club killed one, and a well-placed kick to the rib cage sent another howling away in pain.

Four dogs remained, running in a frenzy beneath the boulders, baying furiously.

You're trapped, my friend. The men are up on the ridge in a Jeep. They'll come down, though.

McCain ran at the dogs, flailing about with his club. A speckled hound leaped for his arm, and he slashed with his hatchet blade, tore open a throat. But the animals were chewing at his legs. He crushed a skull with the club, breaking the limb in half. He dropped the hatchet blade and caught yet another dog about the throat, bracing himself to the impact. He pressed with his thumbs, felt bones snap. He screamed and hurled the gasping animal at its fellows.

The remaining two drew away, waited. Abram rushed at them, hurling rocks.   Then they were gone, all that remained alive, slinking away into the cover of brush and trees.

"Vicious brutes !" he said, and he began to laugh. His laughter filled the afternoon woods.

Didn't think you had it in you. All right, so I was wrong for once.

Old Man Coyote closed his eyes, wrinkled his nose, and gaped at the sunlight. Abram shook his head and began to run up the gully.

Bluejays were screaming once more, and one was intent upon imitating the cry of a hawk. A doe and two fawns broke cover and bounded away from him.

His legs were nearly numb with puncture wounds.

***

Canto Nine:
AGAINST THE CURRENT

PASS THEN THROUGH THIS LITTLE SPACE OF TIME
CONFORMABLY TO NATURE, AND END THY JOURNEY
IN CONTENT, JUST AS AN OLIVE FALLS OFF WHEN IT IS
RIPE, BLESSING NATURE WHO PRODUCED IT, AND
THANKING THE TREE ON WHICH IT GREW.

[MARCUS AURELIUS,
THE MEDITATIONS]

*

JULY 10, 1955:

Isaac stood apart, listening.

Burt Bullardi and his father accompanied Mr. and Mrs. Incendie. It was a large gathering—family and friends and curious strangers. But the son of Abram McCain was not welcome. He was ignored, avoided. He knew what they were thinking, all of them.

The murderer's kid, offspring of the crazed Indian....

He knew this, was oblivious to it.

A sensation of dull pain without specific location, a stunned roaring in his eyes, wounds without laceration, an agony like jagged stones.

Earlier Isaac had stood by April's coffin in the chapel and looked down upon the cold, still beauty, her perfectly combed blond hair, the fragility of her body. He'd never thought of her that way before: slim wrists and hands, delicate features, hands themselves folded beneath her bodice, a diamond engagement ring visible.

He stared at the ring—had she lied to him after all? Put the ring on after they'd parted? Or had the morticians done it, as out of some insane feeling for appearance, propriety?

It didn't matter.

Yet it did. What was the meaning? He would never know, he supposed. Whom, after all, would he ask?

April Incendie's love: it was like her name, a spring blaze. Or it was quicksilver, the very substance miners used to extract gold from pulverized quartz, to draw the precious stuff into amalgam. Crushed, the mercury beaded again. But not this time.

"Goodbye, loved one. Sleep in the earth. Sleep well. If there's anything afterward, perhaps we'll meet. Is that possible? You're Catholic, and I'm...what? What do I believe? Or only quietness, darkness, the elements, and the processes of disintegration? No meaning to that. And my father? Is he the one who did this to you...in some spasm of rage and insanity? How will I be able to live now—why have you left me, both of you?"

Mack Madison and Red Lugie walked over to where Isaac was standing, and Mack, straight-faced and serious for once, placed a hand on his friend's shoulder.

A priest's words drifted above the heads of those assembled, syllables dissipating in the air.

"The final rite of passage," Isaac said, half whispering. "I don't want to stay any longer, fellas. You stay for me. Will you do that, Mack, Red?"

Madison nodded, glanced at Lugie.

Isaac turned and walked down the small grassy hill and up the street to where his Buick was parked.

Numbness.

To live now—to drive to Crooked Pines. And to wonder, the red beak of fire in his brain.

"The madman, my father—did he do this? They say so. Abram's running now, and they'll never catch him. He knows every trail in the forest for twenty miles around, most likely. Steal a car and head for Canada—then disappear into the tundra. A new name, a new identity. Goddamn it, nothing makes sense. She loved me, it was over with Burt—I should have taken her home, should have insisted. I wasn't strong enough. I should have mastered her, and I should have broken that miserable Bulldog in half. Yes, I should have forced the issue, and now it's too late, too late. April Incendie! We should have been married, and now you're sleeping with that jackass' ring on your finger...."

Midday sun, hot, bored down out of liquid cerulean blue, and a pair of hawks high up over Harmony Ridge scratched their wingtips along currents of sky. For a moment the two big birds were motionless.

Then they glided off toward the north.

*

July 10, 1955:

Late that afternoon Isaac told Alice Bousfield he was going to walk down to the improvement yard. Lee and the crew had gone to Washington campground to put in concrete forms for cookstoves, and the foreman had allowed Isaac to remain in camp and take it easy—handling the office, writing out fire permits, and the like. But it was five o'clock, and the crew hadn't as yet returned.

Isaac locked the office and strolled through the campground, speaking briefly with one of the *flatland touristers* and assuring him that Crooked Pines' water was indeed fit to drink. Once the camper's fears were allayed, Ike continued to the big improvement landing below the station. He sat on a pile of telephone poles that were heaped on the edge of the bank, and he looked out over bluegreen hills to the south, beyond the canyon of Deer Creek. A squirrel chattered, apparently in some kind of territorial dispute with a bluejay.

He heard no other sound, and yet he had the feeling someone was near. He stood up, turned slowly.

His father was standing directly behind him. How long had Abram been there?

"I had to see you, Ike," McCain said in a voice that was hardly more than a whisper.

The elder McCain's beard was singed with dust, eyes sunken with exhaustion.

Isaac's urge to embrace his father was counteracted by a flaring of rage.

"You did this to me?" he blurted. "You raped April? She's dead, you sonofabitch!"

"Son, don't listen to them. Death, and it's over."

Isaac stared at his father, sensed uneasiness. Then blind anger controlled him, a force beyond rationality. He flung himself desperately at the older man, throwing punches wildly, could not even at that moment believe what was happening. His hands and wrists were going numb, and there was blood on Abram's face.

Isaac stopped suddenly, stood there gasping for breath and trembling.

His father was a rock in front of him, hands at his sides, not protecting himself.

Isaac moved to one side, drove a fist full into Abram's face. The father stumbled back slightly, stood.

"Ike—son—don't. Don't make me whip on you. You've got a hell of a punch, boy. I didn't do it—I didn't do what they're saying.

Don't listen to them. I'm your daddy—you know who I am. Goddamn it, I'm sorry what's happened, but I'm innocent. Catch hold of yourself, Ike—I think you've loosened some of my old teeth...."

Isaac flung himself into McCain's arms and cried brokenly. Abram's arms were around him, the huge strength, and Isaac felt like a child, the time he'd burned his foot in the ashes of a brushfire and his father carried him uphill to the cabin and dressed the wound. Aunt Jessie, had she been there as well? Yes, and a radio was playing, Walter Winchell and news of a bombing raid over London. He had been what? Perhaps six years old, then....

"Dad, Dad," Isaac stammered, "I'm sorry...she's gone, Abram...she's... gone. Forgive me. I'll kill whoever it was...."

"Matters have gotten a tad *complicated*," Abram replied. "I have to go turn myself in. The sonsabitches'll shoot me if I don't. Some kind of posse, they've hunted me. It's going to be all right, we'll have a good lawyer, Ike. An old friend of mine, down in San Jose. If things go bad, he'll be in touch with you—Marlette's his name, Dan Marlette. He came to visit once when you were just a tadpole, but you probably don't recall. I've got three, four savings accounts and some stocks and the ranch at Upper Eden, Ike. Well, no point in wasting time with that stuff now. Son, you're too quick with those fists of yours—you lose your temper, just like your old man. I'll be okay. Got some business to take care of. Damn it, keep hold of yourself. You've got a long way to go yet, *miles to go before you sleep.* Don't shorten the journey...."

Isaac could feel Abram's fingers running over his hair, hesitantly, gently. Then Ike broke away from his father's embrace and ran blindly, without direction. Branches lashed at his face. He fell, headlong, twisted sideways against a dead log. He rose, plunged on down the hill, and finally threw himself full-length into the small stream at the bottom of the ravine. The water was sharp and cold, and its soft flames burned at the roots of his eyes.

*

Coyote-Head watched, a smile flickering about the muzzle. He pulled his slouch hat forward and nodded to the young, dark-skinned woman with him. He held up a finger as if in a signal for silence and then unbuttoned his denim trousers. The woman began to nurse at him as a dozen or more eagles and hawks dropped down into the trees about him and sat fanning their big wings and screaming.   The woman suckled like a newborn calf, ravenous for milk.

*

July 11, 1955:

Abram McCain watched from the hillside as morning sunlight spilled over the eastward ridge and slanted into the meadow where his cabin and printshop stood.

"McCain's Flat," he said aloud, savoring the sound.

He could see the Jeep. One man was hunched over a camp-fire, apparently drinking coffee—maybe coffee laced with whiskey. A second was sleeping.

"No friends of mine, but I guess I'll go visit 'em anyway."

He angled across the hillside and beneath a stand of firs.

Quietly.   Quietly.   Move like the snow.

Ten yards between him and the two men. The sleeper turned in his bag. A rifle slanted against the Jeep's fender, and the deputy with the coffee mug wore a pistol in a side holster.

McCain crawled through brush, kept low behind a storm-downed pine he'd been intending to cut up for firewood.

Twenty feet, more or less.

Then he rose, bellowed at the top of his lungs, and rushed them.

It'll hit you now if it's coming at all.

He rammed the deputy with one shoulder, sent the man sprawling into the grass, and leaped upon him, grasped a forearm, and twisted brutally. The deputy screamed in pain.

Abram had the pistol.

He held his man around the throat from behind, lifted him off the ground, and leveled the weapon at the individual struggling to extricate himself from a blue sleeping bag.

"That'll do," Abram said. "You move again, Mr. Man, and I'll ventilate you good."

Abram tied the two with a coil of hemp rope from inside the Jeep.

"You're Injun McCain, ehh? What you going to do with us? We got no quarrel with you...."

"And you're Hutch's boys, I take it, but I don't see any badges. Maybe you just came up here on your own, then. Well, what I ought to do is throw the pair of you to the bottom of a deep hole. Plenty of those around. Anyhow, I guess it wouldn't be fitting. I figure you're in prime and blatant violation of the laws of stupidity, so I'm arresting you on those grounds. Call it malicious trespass, then. That sounds official enough."

Abram picked up the rifle, a Winchester thirty-thirty, and checked to see if the weapon were loaded. Then he sighted down on a tree across the meadow.

Oliver began to bray.

"No!" one of the men pleaded. "For Christ's sake, don't shoot us. We haven't done anything to you. Please, Goddamn it! You're going to get yourself in deeper and deeper."

"Well, now. Just what were you fellows planning? Come to visit, did you? Hell, gents, it's not even my birthday."

"Hutchings wanted us to bring you in."

"With dogs, ehh? Damned dogs."

"We didn't have nothing to do with that—honest to God, McCain."

"You mean, they weren't *your* dogs?"

"We was against that idea from the beginning—weren't we, Al?"

The other man nodded. He was having difficulty breathing.

"You lads just sit here and cool your heels a bit," Abram said. "I'll be back directly. Don't go away, now."

McCain walked to his cabin, noted that someone had put a padlock on the door—Hutchings, maybe. He used the rifle barrel to pry off the lock.

"Horse, dog! Where the hell are you?"

The puppy was immediately leaping at his leg. Abram lifted the coyote and stroked its fur. The half-grown animal whimpered and licked wildly at McCain's face, then gaped at the air, eyes closed.

"Starving a bit, are you? You're all ribs, man! You and me, Horse, we're both hungry."

He mixed some powdered milk and then laughed as Horse virtually inhaled it from the bowl.

"Easy, old hound. Not too fast. We'll eat in just a few minutes—as soon as we take care of those two fellers outside. Can't let them just sit there—they're probably a mite uncomfortable. Your purebred *Walems,* they don't have our kind of patience. Why do you suppose that is, *Tio Coyote?* Well, possibly I tied them a bit too tight...."

With the pup at his heels, McCain walked to the Jeep, pistol in hand.

"I been thinking about it," he said. "Guess I'll turn you two loose. You tell Ed Hutchings to come up here by himself, and I'll go in with him. Hutch knows I'll keep my word. But if there's anyone else along, I'm going to kill a few men. You understand me, gents?"

McCain watched dust spew up from the tires of the departing Jeep, nodded.

He fed Oliver, talked to the mule for a few minutes, and took the tie-rope off him. Then, with his young coyote racing in mad circles about him, Abram returned to the cabin.

"Let's see what this guy's got to eat," he said. "I think I could stand a snack myself. Truth to say, Horse, my legs are bothering me. Stone bruises on my feet, and a minor case of proud flesh. Your domestic brothers don't brush their teeth, as it turns out. Moldy bread poultices, that's what my sister Jessie would have prescribed. You never met her—she's planted at Upper Eden, along with the rest of my clan—most of them, anyway. Six years ago, Horse. Isaac and I, we're the only ones left—and we still don't know whether the play's a goat-song or a laughing orgy."

*

Old Man Coyote sat on a stump on the far bank of Deer Creek.

I don't know, Abram. I doubt you can move that one.

McCain had carried some heavy stones from the heap and placed them in shallow water, just where the current picked up, below the pool. He was staring at a large gray rock when he heard Coyote-Head's voice.

"I do believe I can manage all right, thank you kindly. Why don't you be about your business?"

You are my business, but our dealings are almost through. I'm waiting for a Kuksu-hesi, the most sacred ritual. Did I ever tell you about the first one, when all the animal people met in conclave at Onolaitotl? That's when I created you humans.

"You don't say? Look, no reason for you to stick around on my account."

I've got plenty of time, plenty of that. But perhaps you should be thinking about Estawm Yan, the Upper Meadows. Things are better there. That's what everyone decides at last.

"If I can get that big rock down here and put it into this hole, the creek'll back up, and the little pond should be just about deep enough to swim in."

You want to go swimming?   Your strength's playing out, Abram. Those dogs....

"I'll get it, I tell you."

Late afternoon sunlight filtered through the trees, yellow-green. Strands of spider web trailed in the wind.   Bands of shadow undulated on the surface of the water.

That rock's joined to the granite core of the world. McCain, your strength's an illusion. It runs to the sea. I piss on a rock, and it's gone.

Abram heaved. Again. Finally he tipped the boulder on edge. Sweat ran off his naked chest. He wiped at forehead and beard and then wrapped his arms about the stone and lifted it, hugging the weight to his chest, staggered to the edge of the stream.

The stone is becoming heavier.

McCain tilted slowly sideways and fell, even as he did so heaving the boulder toward its intended spot. He lay there in shallow water, vaguely aware his insides hurt. He did not move for several minutes.

You want me to help you up, Big Guy?

"I'll make it, thank you anyway. Didn't think I could move the damned thing, did you?   Shouldn't underestimate a man, Dog-face."

I'm impressed. You always surprise me.

McCain lifted himself to one elbow, still lying in the creek.

"Let it be a lesson, then. There's nothing a man can't do if he puts his mind to it."

Pride, Abram. You'll never learn. But it's over now.   The Whitemen from Diggins will come for you. Hutchings may be your friend, but he'll bring at least thirty men. He'll have them hidden up in the woods. The truth of the matter is that you'll never live to get to jail, and you wouldn't like it much if you did. Your vaunted Indian blood—that's not the problem at all.

"Pshaw. Go pound on your drums, Peheipe. Find some dancers and priests to make fun of."

All gone, all gone. You and your clan—you're as responsible as anyone else. The lure of worthless yellow metal. It's been at you, and it'll get to your son as well, given a few years. Well, you like to wrestle with insanity.

"Come on down here, Mad Dog. I'll be happy to give it a try right now, if you don't mind taking advantage of an old man who's lost his strength. We'll see what kind of blood's in that hide of yours."

Humans get old quickly. Me, I've been around for thousands of years. I'll tell you about blood, though. It's yours, Abram. Haven't you known that all along?

"I've had suspicions, friend."

                               *

Abram McCain walked slowly uphill to his mineshaft, took the carbide lamp from its hook, lit a flame, and entered. He walked on into darkness, stepping between thin rails of track that in earlier times had been kept shiny by constant wear of the ore cart wheels. At the end of the shaft, he sat down, was silent for a time, listening to dripping water. He turned off the acetylene flame and leaned against a hanging wall, stared at nothingness.

"Beautiful in here," he said aloud. "The blackness is near perfect. What's afoot? Methinks this old codger detects a certain nefarious, jest-playing, luminous green light. Well, you shouldn't have come in here, Stump-pisser. You're out of your proper element."

Not so, not so. I like burrows. Besides, son of True Bear and Auna-yi, I had to come with you. Thought maybe we could take a jaunt to Upper Meadows together—though whether the Chief of the Dead will let you in without a gen-u-wine Maidu name, I can only surmise.

"You know damned well I've got a name. I just don't use it much."

Possibly you had one once, but you've long since forgotten....

"You're a crafty Old Dog, I'll give you that much. *Burning Man.* You want the Maidu words, friend? *Kakini Busda, the spirit is within.* At the old *Ustu* ceremonies, images of the dead were sometimes constructed out of stuffed wildcat skins—all fancied up. At the end of the *Burning,* they were walked into the fire. My mother told me the story—she got it from Grandmother Ooti, who may have been the last *Kuksu* shaman, for all I know. You satisfied?"

Abram—Burning Man—you continue to surprise me. Your mind's more complex than I supposed.

"Well, since that's settled, sit and listen, then. I'm going to compose a poem—call it a *death chant*, if you like. It'll never go into my book, but that's no great matter. This will be profound stuff, *Oleli*, Old Dog of the Mountains—the kind of cognition that ultimately brings all the world's philosophers to their knees. Well, I went to Harvard once, and us Harvards have got this strange compulsion to set the world right. So listen—forget about mice and squirrels for a moment, if you're able. You see, if you give a man a dream, and if you let him think there's a chance, then you're inviting trouble to your table. Pay attention. Keep those pointed ears open. Now, here I am, more than sixty years old and yet more ignorant, more alone, more foolish than when I started. Brother Axel, he wandered hither and yon and didn't worry about the problems of humanity, but I was different. I puzzled over things and looked for answers in books. Between ink-daubed pages and living my life, I've found out that a man sells his soul, sometimes, for what he supposes a great treasure. There's none, that's certain. Try love. Love begets violence. Love begets hatred. Isaac, he's learning now. Try ambition. Ambition toward what? And the world's filling up with machines and strange little men who run them. A few more years, and this human race is going to be rocketing off to find new planets to desecrate, I predict it. In fact, there's only one goal, and that's darkness—like here in the mine. We come out of darkness and pass through a little light and then lurch ahead into the inkpot. Home to the mother—that's what the poet down in Carmel says. Wish the old scribbler were here—we could discuss one or two things. He drinks too much since his wife died, but that's something I understand pretty well. A man should guard his precious dollar and two-bits worth of clay—keep it happy, fed, satisfied. He should comprehend that dissatisfaction breeds violence. That's your real Cain. It's always there and needs but a little frustration to set it off. So I killed some sheep—I'm not blaming you, Dog-face. I was feeling restless at the time. And somehow I got a whole damned town afraid of me. I wonder who did in the Incendie girl? I won't say she had it coming, but she'd been tempting fate. I was half afraid my own son had.... Fire's in all our natures. But Ike busted me in the teeth, so I guess he's clear. Fact: we manure ourselves into the Great Compost, and only in that do we possess nobility. No wonder most of the animal people are afraid of us. But death gives us stature: and the memory of death and the awareness of death. Old Mother Ocean, Outspinner of Life, mad weaver of time—why have you cast this creation of yours, half-formed, upon the dry land? Why have you given him hunger for which there's no food? Why have you inflicted the insanity of physical desire upon him, these coyote songs of wild laughter? Why have you made him the half-wit that he is?"

I gave you the mind you have. Is it my fault you don't know how to use it? You can think as well as I can, McCain, if you choose. Brother Elk, he wanted to give you antlers.

"It's true. You've finally said something that makes sense."

You haven't. I'm not on my knees yet.

"And you're not a philosopher, either. Consider the vile beauty of the human creature, the mad clarity, all of us mentally unbalanced. One hand kills, and the other caresses. Is it any wonder we fight wars, torture one another to death, scheme, plot, sacrifice anything for power, grub for money, and dream about sticking our dongs into volcanoes? The ladies, on the other hand, they dream of bearing the children of God—they want the volcano to stick its dong into them. I know. They want you again, *Oleli.* Ah, we're noble beings—and that's why we need a crazy God-Dog like you to urge us on."

Get to the point, McCain.

"A luminous green must, *Oleli.* That's what it's all about. The simple persistent urging of life, not individual, and not even any one species, but every bug and bird and fish of us. A strange and dreaming bit of chemistry, but determined. Sanity's not important, but feeling is. Let them throw their fire-bombs, it won't change a thing. I'll put my money on frogs for the next go-around, or maybe the praying mantis—a hell of a little animal, and damned smart, too. Mother Ocean, mindless green flux, unconscious, insensible, utter beauty, twisting out the continents, ebbing, gnawing at upthrust flanks of the land, swarmed over by gulls and herons and hawks and vultures and lashing up seaweed and shells. Whales wrestling with giant squids. I haven't forgotten: I haven't forgotten the waves, the primal rhythms. Accept, then. The Great Compost. Another thousand years, another million, a few hundreds of millions? Perhaps. The Ocean regenerates, and the Sierra regenerate. We cannot burn them down. That fire up at Snow Tent? Ike's first real taste of flame—hell, the woods are growing back already. The living ooze does not expire—one cell or billions of cells together, it lives forever, slime mold or human brain. Think on it, friend. It promises nothing, but we have faith in it, you and I. The current of time is not to be resisted. Once I tried to swim against Yuba River's current, where the water was boiling with bubbles. I was carried, buoyed, went further, was caught, drawn downward, sucked under the rocks and believed I would drown, couldn't fight against that current, the whole weight of the Sierra snowpack pushing down on me. Then I considered, this water finds its own way out. Let it carry you. Let it bear you. And I came again into sunlight."

Old Man Coyote laughed.

I remember the day. Did you know I was sitting up on a rock, watching? That was a long time ago, but it might have been Upper Meadows day. I was amused when you popped up like a big toad. Well said, Abram McCain, Burning Man. Hey, I particularly like the part about the luminous green must.

"Imagined you would."

But you still haven't come to any conclusion. That's the end of it? I feel the chant should continue. You're just getting to the important part.

"That's what I think, too. But I doubt that it's safe to let you hear such stuff. So you'd best be going now, Dog-face. Be seeing you later, I suppose?"

Oh, yes. The path from Estawm Yan to Hipining Kawyaw, it's not as distinct as it once was. The Whitemen, they don't use it.

McCain watched as the green glow faded from before his eyes. He lay there, listened to perpetual dripping of water. Then he lit the carbide lamp once more, fit a cap to a stick of dynamite, attached a short length of fuse, and touched the end to the flame of his lantern. He extinguished the lamp and stared intently as a little, spitting flame worked its exasperating way toward its destination.

"It's yours now, Isaac—the madness, the madness. Have at it, boy."

Abram hugged the stick of dynamite to his chest.

Wildcat skins, stitched and stuffed into human form, lurching toward flames that swirled upward at midnight, translating mortal clay into the Grand Otherness.

*

July 12, 1955:

Hutchings read the note.

If you sons of bitches want me, I am in the mine.

The deputies were quiet, subdued as they walked up the trail. Seven men—armed, scowling.

Voice: "He could be there in those rocks—bastard's probably got a rifle."

Voice: "Of course he does. Shee-it, we're sitting ducks."

They fanned out around the entrance to the mineshaft. Hutchings stood to one side of the opening, moved cautiously.

"Abram!" the sheriff yelled. "This is Ed Hutchings here. I've got some men with me—we have to take you in. I know about the dog chase—it wasn't my doing. Everything's under control now. Abram? You in there, McCain?"

A slight echo from the mine's interior. The men with guns were ready, but Hutchings waved them back. He drew his service revolver and motioned to a uniformed deputy.

"Jim, let me have that hardhat with the lantern on it. I'm going in."

"Don't think that's such a good idea, Hutch. The Injun'll get hungry after a time. Let's just wait him out."

"Who the hell's in charge here? Give me the tin hat. I don't want any dead men on my hands. What I want is a prisoner, a live one. You hear that—all of you? This business is going down by the books—any of you boys get trigger happy, you'll be on trial for murder."

Voice: "You're taking a hell of a chance, Sheriff."

"He knows me. We've known each other for years. McCain ain't guilty yet, and I want you to hold that thought. If he's going to come out at all, he'll come out because he trusts me."

Voice: "Crazy damn Injun!"

Voice: "Or maybe he'll come out *with* you. Then what the hell we going to do next?"

Voice: "Let's get that kid of his down here. Maybe McCain will listen to his own son."

Voice: "Or we could tell him we was going to arrest the kid."

Voice: "And maybe he can hear every damned word we're saying...."

Voice: "If he ain't up in those rocks over there, sighting in on us...."

"Jim," Hutchings said, "could be we should send these hotheads down the hill? Look, all of you! I don't want young McCain involved in this. If we ain't got law, we ain't got a damned thing. It's my job, and I'm going to do it. Ike McCain's probably living through six kinds of hell right now as it is—Abram and his son have been as close as a boy and his father can be. Problem is, you're scared—the bunch of you. You didn't want to hear that, ehh? It's not McCain you're afraid of, it's something else, I don't know what. But if we don't get the man in alive, so he can have his trial, that young fellow's going to end up murdering a couple of us. What the hell would you boys do in the same situation? Think of it. Now just stay back, and hold a cool head. I'm going in there."

Voice: "Keep your pistol ready, Ed! The man's crazy and bull strong."

Hutchings shrugged and stepped into the mouth of the adit.

"McCain! This is Ed again. I'm coming in...."

The sheriff walked slowly, uncertainly, into the darkness of the mineshaft, while his deputies formed into a semicircle outside the entrance, their weapons in hand. They waited.

After what seemed like a long while, Ed Hutchings emerged from the blackness, his service revolver holstered.

"He's in there, all right. Jesus Christ!"

"He going to come out, or...?" Jim asked.

"Yep," the sheriff said. "I guess he's going to come out, all right."

Voice: "When? What's he want?"

"Abram McCain don't want nothing now. He'll come out as soon as we can get someone up from Diggins to collect the pieces."

Voice: "What do you mean? What you talkin' about, Hutch?"

"What's the situation, then?" Jim asked, studying his boss' strained features.

"Dynamite," the sheriff said. "McCain blew himself up. He's scattered all over the damned place. Light me a cigarette, will you, Jim? Jesus, I'm shaking like hell. It wasn't exactly the kind of meeting I was expecting."

*

September 16, 1955:

End of summer.

Already faint touches of yellow flecked the oak leaves, already there was an evening chill.

Mack Madison stood in the meadow below the cabin. He held out a bunch of carrots, greens first, and Oliver the mule nibbled, ruffled his lips, bared his big, square teeth, and pawed three times at the ground.

Madison gave him a carrot, and the mule chewed contentedly.

Isaac climbed the hill alone and at length stood at the entrance to the mineshaft—stood watching long bands of cloud burning westward, immense flarings in towered cumulus, dark crimson edged in silver-gold, while light orange spume higher up trailed to yellow-green.

"A great cleanness," Isaac whispered, "the ovoid torch of the sun dropping now into night."

He breathed chill air deep into his lungs and knew suddenly an intense freedom, an intense release. He withdrew a short-barreled twenty-two pistol from the inside pocket of his wool jacket, raised the gun, and put his mouth about the muzzle. He closed his eyes, took a deep breath, waited.

Then he opened his eyes once more.

Cloud colors were fading, the sun gone, reds deepening to violet.

"No," he said. "It isn't time yet. This is cowardice. Abram, you don't want me to do it? No dramatics. I learned strength from you, and I guess it's not time to short the circuits. That damned Madison insisted on coming along with me. Well, I have to live, then. That's my sentence. I have to live out my life first—I have something to do. What? Either that or I simply lack sufficient nerve."

You must live. The beauty is yours for a time, the sheer and simple gift of the beauty of things. Go on, Ike. Leave me be. I like it here on the mountainside. Don't forget to visit the clan at Upper Eden once in awhile. Not necessary to go often—time's irrelevant to the dead.

Isaac fired the pistol eight times, emptied the cylinder, and then returned the weapon to his coat pocket.

Madison's voice echoed from below, the cabin in long shadows now:

"What the hell are you doing, Ike?"

Isaac walked slowly back down. He heard the quaver and trill of a single screech owl.

"What in Christ's name were you shooting at?" Mack demanded.

"A ghost—my own, probably. Let's put some food out for the coyote, in case he's of a mind to return...."

They did, although the last mound didn't appear to have been touched, except by birds. Then Isaac filled Oliver's tray with grain. The mule nuzzled the buttons on the sleeve of the wool jacket, and Isaac hugged him and scratched his ears.

"Ollie," he said, "I've hired someone to drive down twice a week. Don't know what to do beyond that. You're still waiting for

Dad to come home, aren't you? Me, too, but we've got a long wait ahead of us. You're going to be lonely, Long Ears. I'd give you to someone, but who'd want you? No, you're better off here. I think that's what Dad would have wanted. It's your meadow, now. What do you think, Mack? Maybe I ought to say to hell with college, stay here?"

"For two or three months," Madison replied. "Then Uncle Whiskers would draft your ass, and you'd have to leave anyway."

"A good point," Isaac shrugged. "This is a hell of a *free* country we've got. Slavery's illegal, but I guess military slavery isn't. I know, I know...."

Isaac gave the mule a slap on the rump and then walked over to the buildings, Madison a step behind. Flashlight in hand, Isaac made a final perfunctory inspection of the inside of the house and then set the bolts and padlocks. He and Mack got into the '40 Buick, and Isaac started the engine.

"I've always said so," Madison grinned. "This beast of yours will pass anything on the highway—except a gas station. Start the motor, and the fuel gauge automatically drops a quarter of a tank—maybe a tad more, a sconch down."

Isaac breathed deeply as he moved the transmission lever into first gear.

"This is it, Books old bean," he said. "I'm not coming back. I'm not coming back to Diggins, California, for a hell of a long time. And maybe not at all."

"No more summers with the forest service? Things will look different to you by next spring, Friend Ichabod."

"Not for me. Not on the Tahoe Forest, anyway."

"How's Lee going to get along without us? You want to go somewhere else, you overgrown scholarly dumbass *poseur*, I'll go with you. It'd be a drag for me, then, if you're gone. No one to argue with. Worry about it tomorrow. Lugie says he's joining the Army—he tell you that? Lee will have to train a whole new crew."

Isaac grinned in spite of himself.

"Barney'll be there. He can help the old man."

"Cow-pie Bandino. Sometimes I even like the sonofabitch. Says he wants to get on with the helicopter jockeys next summer, though. Not much reason for me to Crooked Pine either, I guess, now that I'm over the Switzer disease. Kara's a senior next year, and I guess the little make-out queen wants her freedom. A boyfriend in Berkeley and a dime...."

"Will get you a cup of coffee," Isaac nodded, "coffee and a doughnut both at that place in West Sacramento."

They drove up the hill under shadowed overhang of pine and fir. The forest breathed softly, was still. At the highway Isaac stopped, and Mack strode over to his Ford, got in, and started the vee-eight. The engine cackled, and twin puffs of blue smoke emerged from dual exhaust pipes. Madison pulled out ahead, flipped on the headlights, and roared down the grade toward Diggins. Isaac followed his friend, resisted the temptation to glance into the rearview mirror.

***

Canto Ten:
NUMUNANA LIVES
IN THE INYO

(HARK CLOSE AND STILL WHAT I NOW WHISPER
    TO YOU,
I LOVE YOU, O YOU ENTIRELY POSSESS ME,
O THAT YOU AND I ESCAPE FROM THE REST AND GO
    UTTERLY OFF, FREE AND LAWLESS,
TWO HAWKS IN THE AIR, TWO FISHES SWIMMING
    IN THE SEA NOT MORE LAWLESS THAN WE;)
THE FURIOUS STORM THROUGH ME CAREERING,
    I PASSIONATELY TREMBLING,
THE OATH OF INSEPARABLENESS OF TWO TOGETHER,
    OF THE WOMAN THAT LOVES ME AND WHOM I
LOVE MORE THAN MY LIFE, THAT OATH SWEARING,
(O I WILLINGLY STAKE ALL FOR YOU,
O LET ME BE LOST IF IT MUST BE SO!
O YOU AND I! WHAT IS IT TO US WHAT THE REST
    DO OR THINK?
WHAT IS ALL ELSE TO US? ONLY THAT WE ENJOY EACH
    OTHER AND EXHAUST EACH OTHER IF IT MUST
    BE SO....)

                        [WALT WHITMAN,
                        "PENT-UP ACHING RIVERS"]

        *

DECEMBER 21, 1974

Night was a net of crows' wings, fog a coiling in darkness.

He groped through dense stands of fir to the crest of a boulder-strewn ridge where cold lights burned yellow and red and blue-green, of indeterminate source in the shattered air and exploding through silence and fog. He stumbled among frozen bunch grass, confused, his feet numb—until the fog cleared, and stars pulsed above.

A gigantic tree rose before him, titanic and leafless in this dark of the winter solstice, roarings and twistings of blue flame about a huge black bole that thrust to myriad branches and climbed night to the stars.

Three slender white-garbed women moved through a texture of shadow and gyrated to bursts of string music amidst volleys of wind-blown hail, while out of the flames came muted screams of creatures in horrible torment, chill flowers of pain.

The dance stilled to ice. No music, no cries—and the women consumed in fierce light, flames in their hair, eyes gushing fire, flesh falling off in hissing heat until skeletons stood for a moment to dissolve in an inward rush of dark, forms etched to air, visible in the way that meteors fade.

The clotted voice surged from his throat.

*

DECEMBER 22, 1974:

Isaac Last Bear McCain emerged from the dark of his past, just as the sun, at that moment suspended, curled northward to climb the midday sky and bring the rains and the snows of winter. Even as surely the days would grow longer, living things sensed it. Cold was residual and flew after: for the year had turned, the pivot screamed, and the ice-grip broke.

"Rivers," he said, "will flow high, the melt of snowbanks under trees—resurrection of the Lord, the green of new vegetation proceeds from the Great Valley of Nem Seyoo and the first low risings, upward to high granite, mysterious Inyo, still the Range of Light despite all the human pismires that crawl upon its back. Ferns along streambanks, black oaks, pale leaves unfolding in longer days that will come as melting ice draws up into cirques of basalt and granite. I feel magma beginning to rise from down deep. Yes, I emerge from the dark of my past even as the days will now grow longer, trailing storms. We point to the new birth, we seek a resurgence, an awakening of meristem, red swarms of ladybugs covering the duff, quick spring air reeking its feral presence, quaver of coyotes on moonlit nights, exquisite wails of loneliness, desire and joy."

Numunana! Numunana! He is the Great One, Olelbis the Dreamer! In the Inyo, in the high granite places—He lives forever! The dwelling place of a great spirit, potent spirit of air and thunder and lightning, fecund spirit of earth....

"I am...*Ishi-Pano*, Last Bear, son of Burning-Man. I am Isaac McCain, and I have come home to myself; I have been gone a long while. It's not just that I've returned to Deer Creek, to the canyon where I was raised—but something deeper than that. I don't know what it is, but I can feel it, am certain. Perhaps it was necessary for me to lose myself and to wander endlessly in a world of books, to know it and to succeed in it, before I could find what I'd lost or maybe never even had. It's not just that—hell, I'm as much White as Indian, the great grandson of old Benjamin Goffe turned Ben McCain—it isn't a function of blood, then. The human creature wandered down from Eden, cast out according to myth, and set about changing things to his own desire throughout the realm of non-Eden. What God placed so insane a commandment? Adam, thou shalt go! *Kuksu*, First Man, get thee from Estawm Yan! The peregrinations of the mind are endless and universally without conclusion, while our fate is that of seeing much and understanding little. But so what? I've come home to myself, and I know it. I was always an alien in that other land. Where's Eden? Not in the Near East, and not on the Yuba Buttes either. Right here, per-haps—or maybe on Ben's land below Lassen, old Wahgalu, Waga-nupa....

"I sense male and female presences, and these interpenetrate in joy until the air and earth alike flush with something mysterious. There are tremorings deep in the granite core, shudderings of sky. Time for a big earthquake or some mountain to blow its top. But the human race is well capable of creating its own mass disasters, and it will. What made the dinosaurs grow tired of this planet? Not answerable. But beneath the snow that lies on these moun-tains, a Great Compost breeds, and it will itch out greenness when the cold has passed. I love the streams flooding milky green and the ouzel diving, emerging, I love the woods wrenched to a green sweetness. *Wildness*, that's what we've lost, all of us. We've for-gotten how to converse with salamanders and owls...."

*

JANUARY 1, 1975:

Isaac spent the day driving in the Diggins area and then wasted an hour or more walking the streets of his former hometown. The whole experience was unsatisfying—deeply troubling.

Much, much was changed. It wasn't just the new freeway that looped its way through town. Two decades, more or less, had passed since he'd taken such a tour of his home terrain. Only his automobile was the same. Yes, the weekend following his father's funeral, he'd driven all about, aimlessly then, not really looking for anything in particular, sunk in his own misery and deadening loneliness.

But now!

Everything was changed or changing. Expensive new houses grew everywhere, like exotic flowers with redwood petals. The abandoned airport at Loma Rica was now a bustling operation, a center of communication and commerce—nerve endings that reached out to Sacramento, San Francisco, Los Angeles, serving the needs of growing high technology operations that had located in the county. Huge tracts were carved out for housing developments, and real estate had apparently replaced mining, logging, and agriculture as the basis for the region's economy. The town itself, brightly lit at nights, was a mélange of antique stores, art galleries, restaurants, and novelty shops—all operating from behind a façade of pseudo-Gold Rush. Grass Valley, four miles distant and the larger of the "twin cities," had apparently caught the disease as well and would doubtless transform itself also.

During his school years, the towns were dominated by *Wops* and *Cousin Jacks*—strutting *guappo* Italian orchardists and Cornish hard rock miners with their attendant household gods, the *Tommyknockers*—these were the old families, the ones who possessed power. But at that time, a word such as *Wop* or *Jack*, bandied about, had been sufficient to start a bar fight. Now, however, *The Wops & the Cousin Jacks, working together,* were a community service organization—the "natives" having joined forces against a flood of newcomers. Okies, still regarded as "immigrants" when Isaac was a boy, many living in mining shacks and former company housing, the first Okies (whether or not from Oklahoma) having found their way to the Mother Lode country in the wake of the Dust Bowl disaster of the thirties, had been drawn to the logging woods. Many of these families, too, were now established "old timers," land owners, mill owners, some of them real estate speculators—their children working as school teachers, doctors, lawyers, building contractors....

Even Mack and his brother Toby, their father from Connecticut and their mother from Laguna Beach in Southern California, those boys had been seen as Okies as well. A scattering of Orientals remained, still involved in small businesses and the like. Isaac made note there were a few more Blacks and Hispanics. And the local Indian people were, if anything, less visible than had been the case during the forties and fifties. At that time, those Maidu families who lived in the area kept away from town, slowly deserting the *rancheria* near Diggins, some squatting on government land, but others acquired title to property of their own. The latter, Isaac assumed, had probably sold and moved elsewhere—sold out at what they'd probably seen as a fair profit. Even Abram's friend Louis Kelly, claimant to the title of the last of the head chiefs of the Maidu of Nevada County, was dead, a quiet death in a state hospital, a few of his stories recorded in a master's thesis and shelved in a university library.

Now expensive homes flourished in the back country, and many of the old graded one-lane roads had been paved and even citified, with names like *Beneficent Land, Sequoia Court, Golden Circle,* and *Deer Creek Park Estates.*

In short, the *Flatlanders* had taken over—yes, and with a significant population of counterculture people in the behind the scenes, many of whom were rumored to make their livings through the cultivation of marijuana plants. There were, in any case, numerous spacy-eyed, bearded individuals driving shiny new four-wheel-drive pickups about town—and many smaller businesses were seemingly geared to holding the dopers as regular *clientèle.*

Often, Isaac observed, it was impossible to tell hippies from rednecks—and, indeed, a generalized alliance of sorts seemed to have formed between the two groups.

Population within the area had tripled—more people living in the hills than at any time since the Gold Rush itself. In past years there had been celebrities in residence such as Mark Twain and Bret Harte, Josiah Royce, later George Mathis the artist, and now Gary Snyder the poet living "north of the river," where Ginsberg also had a cabin, and Stegner the novelist was in Grass Valley. A drama company had opened, and various artists plied their trades and had shows both locally and in the big cities of Sacramento and the Bay Area.

No man can step into the same river twice, McCain mused, rehearsing the words of Heraclitus. Everywhere forested areas were subdivided, laved with recent lanes of blacktop, sprinkled with houses. Names like *Boise-Cascade* and *Occidental Petroleum* and *Southern Pacific* were on signs, in small print, everywhere.

One quite considerable real estate development, consisting of three or four square miles total, lay up creek from Diggins itself and included the old Eldrickson place, close about the upper end of a big new Scott's Flat Reservoir on Deer Creek—not all that far downcanyon from the McCain land, uncomfortably close, in fact.

Isaac made particular note of one sign: *Deer Creek Park Estates, A Division of Bullardi Enterprises.*

Burt had done well, quite well, with Chevy dealerships in Marysville and Auburn and Diggins—now he was neck-deep in a big land scam as well—with probably a real estate office or two to boot, him pulling the strings from behind the scene, and a construction company and maybe some shares in the large mill south of town—in league with some corporation, more than likely. Well, Burt had always been ambitious. But how did he get hold of the Eldrickson Ranch?

Isaac dropped his Buick into first gear and proceeded along a new-cut road through the woods, ungraveled as yet but wide, drainage ditches along its edges, a thoroughfare designed for pavement.

A doe and two fawns bounded away, and Doom growled, nose pressed against the side window, tail wagging.

"A three-legged dog like you, you'd never catch them," Isaac assured the English setter. "You'll be ten soon. It's time to get philosophical. Leave deer chasing to the young ones."

Doom, spinning about and leaping into the rear seat for a trailing glimpse of the deer, was apparently not convinced.

                                   *

Cold.

A full moon hung above the Sierra, and broken winter grass in the meadow below McCain's cabin burned frost in the still night. A screech owl chittered, and wind rustled the few pale leaves clinging stubbornly to the uppermost limbs of black oaks.

Iphigenia Singares heard the noise of an engine, a car coming down the road. She rose from the chair where she'd been reading, took her rifle from its pegs, opened the door, and stared out as a three-legged white dog bounded from the car, in sudden pursuit of an imagined rabbit.

The man's voice: "Doom, wretched cur, get up here!"

"Ike," Ginny called, "I'm glad you're home. I thought I heard something down by the creek. How did it turn out?"

"Hell with that idiot dog. Let's get inside. The temperature will hit zero tonight, sure as hell. Doom's sore about having to stay in the car so long. We went on a little mid-county survey, you might say. That's why I'm late. I satisfied my curiosity, but now I'm depressed as hell. Coffee for Isaac? Then I'll tell you about my telephone conference with the university."

"Make your own coffee if that's how it is."

Half an hour later Isaac and Ginny were playing chess. Doom was lying on a braided rug by the wood stove, sleeping, occasionally growling softly.

"They'll have you back, then?" Ginny asked.

"That's what the Dean said. The university wants to call this a *medical leave of absence*. I gather the official departmental interpretation of my actions is that I've suffered a temporary psychological lapse. A nervous breakdown. The Dean was in good spirits. I half expected him to be hungover and grouchy in the aftermath of New Year's Eve, but maybe he stayed home, sipped liquor, and read Milton—I don't know. In any case, he says the department's doing its best to make allowances. It's very decent of the lot of them, to put it mildly. Possibly something good was said about my book at the MLA conference, so they've decided to allow their prodigal son to return."

Ginny felt tense.

"You're returning to Oregon, then? There's no reason...why you should stay here, I suppose."

"Didn't commit myself, Yellow-Eyes. I wouldn't mind returning to the classroom. Hell, I haven't known anything except the life of the university, not since I was a boy...."

Ginny stared at the chessboard. She didn't look up. Her hand trembled slightly as she made her move.

"Check."

"Guessed you just might do that," Isaac grinned. "Let's see.... Doom, I believe she wants to trade queens. No, I didn't commit myself. If I returned, would you come with me, Ms. Singares? You need to get on with your own education, and that's not possible from here. Think I want a lady who's never been *eddy-cated?*"

"Do you want me?"

"Yes. I want you very much. You don't need to ask."

"Really?"

"Is a bear Catholic?"

She raised one eyebrow.

"What's that supposed to mean, Isaac?"

"Variation on the old saw—here's the whole thing. Is a bear Catholic? Does the Pope shit in the woods?"

"You and your execrable jokes. Be serious. Ike. Yes, sometimes I need to ask. I'm too dependent on you now, and that frightens me."

"Eugene's not a bad place. Or do I intuit that you're not fond of the thought of leaving Deer Creek Canyon?"

"I don't want to live in a city," Ginny replied, "not in any city. Oh, I know, the mountains are close by, and all that. You've got that place on the McKenzie River. It's beautiful there. I'll come along if you want me, Isaac. I'll try, but it might not work out. Sometimes I'm not certain I even exist except when I'm here. When I think about things, the house gets full of dreams—you know, everything's blurred, nothing has weight. If it's strong inside you that you have to return, then I'll tag along. You big, homely sonofabitch, I...."

"Now, now. The McKenzie River place won't work. I also talked to my real estate agent this morning. The place is sold, and I said I'd sign the papers. We can always rent an apartment downtown. There. That blocks your check for awhile."

"I refuse to live in the city, you perverse pandering pirate!"

"Gin, my reason tells me I ought to go return to the classroom—I won't have another chance. If I don't, I'm throwing away a whole career. But I think I'd be throwing away something a hell of a lot more valuable if I went back to being the Big Professor, Isaac the Whale. I've come alive these past few months—I was a dead man before that. My scar—I think I was born with the scar, or else I got it twenty years ago, when.... The night in Tex's Bar just made it visible. It's the metaphor of my life, but if I shave the beard now, I'm thinking the scar's gone. You brought me to life again, Yellow-Eyes, and these woods helped too. The original Half-breed Lazarus. All the years I was gone, this place was a presence in the dark of my mind. I could hear something calling me, but I wasn't sure what it was. Or I refused to listen.... Now that I'm here, the university seems an illusion to me, a *house full of dreams*, as you put it."

Ginny glanced at the chessboard, made a move, and looked up once more.

"Check again," she said. "It's official, Isaac? You've sold your place on the McKenzie? You think it's fun, stringing me along this way?"

"Damn, you're persistent. Notice the bishop, though, how he angles across and gathers in the unwary rook. You didn't see that, did you? Want to take the move over?"

"Not fair. I was listening to you and not paying attention to the board. No, he's yours. I'm not beaten yet."

"We could come here for summers—and you'd have a chance to go to school."

"But would we?"

"Certainly, certainly."

"Play the whole middle-class trip? We'd get married, and I could have five children and belong to some faculty wives' association. A big color television and a gas furnace.... You wouldn't have to split firewood any more, and we'd probably stop loving each other and start hating instead."

"There's a check I don't think Last Bear can get out of."

"I haven't even moved yet. What check?"

"Not having to split firewood."

"Why can't we just stay here? You've often said you don't need any more money, and I never did. You've sold the house up there—invest in something and live off the interest. What good's more money, anyway? If you're teaching, you won't have time to read or write. Those are your words, not mine."

"Not sure we can stay here in any case," Isaac replied. "The tide of the Goddamned late-twentieth-century is *a-cumin' in*. There's a *For Sale* sign everywhere you look. My old friend, that jerk we ran off last fall, he's the one who's behind the big land development down canyon, *Bullardi Enterprises*. Everyone who's got property is cutting the woods up into little squares and oblongs, and people from the city are buying it for five or ten thousand an acre, a great deal more than that sometimes, even without water or power. It's a disease, a damned disease. I stopped in at Deer Creek Park Estates, looked around. Everything's cut and graded, fire hydrants sticking up out of red dirt, some of the roads already paved. When spring hits, the building of houses will start. Diggins is a tourist trap—restoration of old buildings, phony new buildings—you know. Even the counterculture people have gone commercial. North of the Yuba, the marijuana farms have apparently become a regular agribusiness thing. The locals are saying it's good for the economy, and even some of them are doing a little growing of their own. Money's changing hands, lots of it."

"Maybe so," Iphigenia said, "but that doesn't have to affect us, does it? There's national forest behind us."

"Doesn't have to, not for a time, perhaps, but this area is doomed—that's what I've concluded. Diggins isn't the same town anymore. Maybe it's better in some obscure *human* way, and maybe it's worse. In any case, it's different. An age has ended, Ginny, and it's probably just as well that my dad didn't live to see it.

He'd no doubt have waited his time, a good hot day in August and a wind blowing, and then he'd have set the forest on fire. True, we've got a little island here, safe for a time, safe after a fashion. There's forest service land, but the logging has speeded up. The government's forgotten all about its old sustained-yield concept, now that there's a huge market in Japan and elsewhere. They've turned perfectly good *wilderness* into tree farms, for God's sake! Clear-cutting and a coniferous monoculture comes next, mark my words."

"Somewhere else, then? Canada? Hundreds of thousands of square miles up there, all of it empty. I've studied the maps. We could go to the Yukon?"

Isaac lit a cigarette, blew smoke into the air.

"My roots are here," he said. "I don't know. That's what pulled me home. Maybe it's time for us to take a drive to Upper Eden, the old McCain place north of Chester. The area's far less populated, and most of my clan's buried there. That's another matter. I think I've made a decision, Gin. I didn't commit myself to the Dean—said I'd get back to him. What worries me is that *The Martian Chronicles, Brave New World,* and *Nineteen Eighty-Four* are already too damned close, and there's no sense trying to give the nightmare greater proximity. I'm half expecting Spock and Kirk to come beaming down to take a look at the mess. You've read Ed Abbey. Maybe out in Nevada someplace there's actually land so utterly worthless to all civilized purposes.... The entire ethos of the West is based on the idea, no the *reality*, of wild land. A university isn't a place for someone like me. I sit around dreaming of Lewis and Clark and Bridger and Clyman, of Ishi and Worrotetot and Great-grandmother Ooti, I've written a book about the terrific impact of the vastness of landscape upon the literature of the American West, I transcribe Native-American legends and muse upon the significance of my own cultural and blood lineage—and to what purpose? That which remains is going fast. I think the Coleman's low on fuel—no, I'll get it. You sure take a long time moving, Ms. Singares. I'm not returning, not ever—though maybe a time will come when you'll wish I had. A teaching job's the illusion of security, but there's no security in a world gone utterly mad."

*

FEBRUARY 9, 1975:

Wind started before noon, grew more violent under a slate sky. By supper time the last of the dead leaves had been stripped from the oaks. Coyotes wailed on Burlington Ridge just after darkness and then went silent. The printshop's metal roofing clattered with each gust of wind, and dead pine needles and willow leaves streamed like showers of sand. Isaac brought in great armfuls of firewood, heaped it in the bin as Ginny put meat, soup, and potatoes on the table. A loose windowpane rattled in its wooden frame, and the door, not firmly latched, flew open and banged against the wall.

Isaac set the lock.

"No rain yet," he said. "That wind's as dry as the breath of hell—if it keeps on, it'll take down some of the trees above the printshop. No real danger unless it changes direction though. Dinner's ready?"

Ginny stared out the window.

"Isaac, someone's here. I think it's your friend Madison—a guy with a GMC pickup, at least. Don't go out there without your pistol...."

Doctor Hamburger!

The booming voice was audible even above the whining of the wind, and Isaac shook his head.

"Madison's always had a great sense of timing," he said, striding to the door, opening it, and stepping outside.

"Mad Mack the Dancing Master!" he shouted. "Is that you?"

"Who else? Sandy and Mack, come to visit the bearded hermit of Deer Creek Canyon...."

The headlights went out, a pickup door slammed, and Mack and Sandy came running toward the house.

"No night for man nor beast!" Madison laughed. "Where the hell's my coffee? Had to fight off grizzly bears and catamounts just to get here...."

Grinning, he held up a gallon jug of red wine.

"Mills' special, a buck and a half a throw?" Isaac asked. "No wonder you've been writing free verse these last few years. You're still with this lunatic, Sandy? Come on in, you two. We were just sitting down to dinner."

Madison and Sandy Sorenson entered the cabin. Isaac latched the door behind them.

Iphigenia smiled, held out her arms to receive Mack's embrace, and then turned to Sandy.

"We seem to have arrived in a whirlwind and a storm," Sandy laughed. "You guys go ahead and eat. No, that's all right. Mack and I stopped at a fast food place downtown. We can't stay long, really. Since we were as far as Diggins, my friend here insisted we had to come say hello."

"Ginny looks wholesome and domestic with that apron on," Mack laughed. "Got to hand it to you, Ike. You have a way of training 'em. On the other hand, SS here has got me trained. She'll have me writing cookbooks instead of poetry before long."

"I suppose you've brought along two or three hundred pages of verse," Isaac grinned, "and will read the whole thing to us if we insist."

"Naturally. Just happen to have a sheaf right here in my jacket pocket. Drink wine with your meal, and I'll read while you eat. Where are the glasses? I'll pour. Sit down, sit down, Brother Isaac."

"The trouble with poets," Isaac said, winking at Ginny, "is that they're forever hanging onto one's sleeve. All right, Mackus, let's hear some of your incomprehensible *verbiage*. Really...we want to hear what the inveterate incult has to say for himself."

"*Incult* is an adjective, not a noun. I teach you everything I know, and you still don't know anything. All right, then, since you insist," Madison agreed, shuffling through a wad of folded pages and then taking a long drink from his water glass full of wine. "Now here's a Pulitzer Prize offering—I call it 'Abandoned Homestead,' in honor of our place down in Newcastle."

Old house with fig trees
Growing close, and dying
Pear trees all about, I
Wonder—whose hands
Fit in hewn chunks of granite, drove
Nail to beam, cut shingles,
Placed them so? Time

Has undone those labors—
Except the fig trees grow,
Search dark into the earth
For moisture, upward
To the chemistry of light.

And do not care if shingles

Weather, if floors break through.

Madison looked up, awaiting some comment.

"Shows promise," Isaac nodded. "It really does. Another twenty years or so, and perhaps you'll write something decent. Have more wine, Mack old friend. That's *promise*, a noun, from the Latin *prōmissum*, I believe."

"Blackguard fool! The wretched doctoral program warped your judgment years ago. You probably even still like 'Lycidas,' don't you? Hell with the poetry. The real reason I came up here tonight was to ask you to be my best man...."

Madison let the words trail off, glanced from Isaac to Iphigenia, and then back again.

"That's right," he continued. "Miss Sorenson and I have decided to tie the proverbial knot, next month maybe. Would you two be willing to drive over to Reno with us to stand as witness to the solemn occasion?"

Isaac burst out laughing.

"Ah, Sandy," he said, "you're making a terrible mistake, lass. But congratulations to the both of you. What do you think, Ginny? Up for a trip to the capital city of sin and illusion? Well, it couldn't happen to two nicer people. We'll do it, by Gawd!"

*

After Madison's pickup disappeared into windy darkness, Isaac and Iphigenia sat next to the wood stove and drank another glass of wine. The storm was growing more violent, and gusts sent small tremors through the house. Doom was nervous, sitting next to the table, his sad brown eyes expectant, tail drumming on the board floor.

Isaac rubbed his fingers across his mouth.

"Dry as it's been," he said, "this wind could run fire on the ridges, even in winter. Maybe that's what we need—a fire. What do you think about Mack and Sandy?"

"They seem very happy. How long have they known each other, Ike?"

"Not much longer than we have, truth to tell. Yeah, as happy as if they had good sense. Maybe we ought to make it a four-way thing—two marriages, I mean, as long as we're going up there."

Iphigenia did not respond. She smiled slightly and sipped at her glass of wine.

"But right now," he continued, "what we need is a good fire. The fire would bring rain—reverse sympathetic magic. We'll violate the order of nature, douse that big pile of brush I cleared from the lower meadow. Kerosene, set it off. It'll work, I tell you. Besides, Gin, the fire couldn't go anywhere—the brush is up against those rocks. You want to do it? Hell of a fine night for a bonfire. God won't even see the rocks, and so the old gentleman will send rain to quench our flames."

"You're being whimsical. You sure it's safe? All right, let's do it, then. We'll see if your magic works. Let's go out into the wind and howl. We can put the coyotes to shame. I'll bet they're holed up to keep out of the wind. Let's proceed with the plan, Isaac McCain."

"Get married, you mean?"

"I didn't say that. Put on your coat."

*

They wore double clothing, carried flashlights and the can of kerosene down the path to the big brush pile, Doom with them—staying close this time, not running madly off into the woods, even whimpering at times.

Isaac poured kerosene at the base of the pile, and wind turned the thin oil to a spray.

"Get away, Ginny!" he shouted, "way back—over there! This thing may go off like a bomb."

"Hurry, Isaac, or it won't do any good. I felt rain—God's going to beat you to the punch. You see—He knows!"

"You mean *She!*" Isaac laughed. "This whole damned Cosmos is a grand matriarchy. Old Man Coyote just does her bidding. Watch out, now!"

Five matches and the fire refused to ignite, trickles of flame sucked up by gusting air. Then a rest between bursts, and flames leaped, suddenly, concussion-like, a yellow cone dancing twenty feet downwind, a long trail of sparks streaming upward.

"Jesus," he said, "it better start raining at that. There's no way to put the thing out now. Just look at the sonofabitch!"

"I can't hear you," Ginny said, coming nearer, Doom hanging close at her heels.

The rain began.

First it was a thin dampness in the air, turning suddenly into a downpour. Isaac and Iphigenia ran for a rocky overhang by the creek. They stood up against sheer stone and held each other and laughed between kisses, Doom pressing in against his master's legs.

"We've done it!" Isaac shouted. "We've broken the drought—I told you!"

"No," she insisted. "He's playing a trick on you. He put the idea into your head in order to make you come out in the middle of a windstorm because He wanted that pile of brush burned. The entire storm's for that reason alone."

Isaac cupped his hands on her buttocks and lifted her to his own height.

"Such, my red-haired, yellow-eyed love, is precisely the sort of manipulation no man, mortal or divine, could ever comprehend—but which every woman who ever lived understands most perfectly. I rest my case: the Divinity is clearly *female*."

"Put me down, you great oaf, or I'll turn you into an oak tree."

For an hour the rain pounded in. Isaac built another fire, a small one from twigs and dry leaves under the stony rim, and man and woman stood with their hands over the flames. Then a cessation, and fog moved along the creek and through the long meadow.

They started toward the cabin, Doom close behind them, when Ginny noticed a light high on Burlington Ridge—a thin, pale green light among trees.

"Isaac, what's that? Look, look, up on the hill!"

McCain took his pistol from its holster, and they climbed the ridge, up a steep trail unused for nearly twenty years except by hunters or deer, past the caved-in mouth of Abram's mine, angling toward ridgecrest. Their flashlights cast small tunnels of whiteness into the fog.

"Near the big oak in the saddle—whatever it was," Isaac said.

"Could our fire have thrown sparks, another fire started?"

"I don't see how, not in that rain. Nothing could ignite without kerosene or white gas or something of the sort. We're close. You stay behind me, Gin—I think someone's up there. It's a hell of a wretched night to be camping out. Where's Doom? The sonofabitch has run off, hasn't he?"

The trail reversed angle, and they came to a clearing. The light was still visible, the great oak illuminated in a dim suffusion of greenness. Isaac and Ginny stood as if mesmerized, stared. Nothing: just light, the glow beginning to dim.

A noise behind them, and Isaac spun about. leveling his new Smith & Wesson thirty-eight.

"Doom!" he said, relieved. "He's been running a deer, Gin, or something—a three-legged stalker."

The dog stopped by his master, then sensed tension. He snuffled at the air and growled.

"Who's there?" McCain bellowed. "What the hell are you doing on my land? Who are you?"

The dim glow faded, was gone, extinguished. Only two flashlights played through fog now.

"What's that noise, Isaac?" Ginny asked in a whisper. "Do you hear it?"

Doom growled once more, the fur stiff on his neck.

"No. Hear what?"

"Laughing. Someone's laughing. Over there, Isaac, beyond the tree. Don't you hear it?"

"Just wind in the brush," he said. "That's what it is."

"Now it's stopped. And the wind's still blowing. I'm frightened. Let's go home. Could it be a mountain lion?"

They didn't speak on the trail down. When they came to the creek and crossed the old log bridge, Isaac said, "I saw that light once before—when I was a boy. It was just after sundown, shadows, but things were still visible. I went to the creek to get Dad. Abram was sitting on the creekbank, and the light was in the rocks up above. It lasted just a few seconds then. When it faded, Dad stood, nodded, as if he'd been speaking to someone, and came walking toward me. I asked what it was—and he smiled and said, "Son, you read too many books, you've got too much imagination. Human critters aren't supposed to see things like that. Let's go Have us some dinner, boy." I never asked again, but I never forgot, either. There has to be some explanation—electricity from the storm, perhaps. But there was no storm that other time, and even then I supposed Dad was putting me off. It's the damnedest puzzle—you recall before Christmas, when I told you about having a strange dream, those ghostly women in flames? The big tree? I've got the same feeling now as when I awoke from that dream.... Maybe the fat oak in the saddle's the Ootimtsaa tree, and the Maidu blood in me's doing strange things. Or maybe the world's ending—dreams and real things beginning to come together, to fuse, the boundaries breaking through. A very strange feeling...."

"Could we both have imagined it, Isaac? That's not possible, and you know it isn't. Even Doom sensed something."

Isaac raised his Smith & Wesson and fired three shots into the dark, then returned the pistol to its holster.

"Whatever it was, Gin, I guess it's not dangerous. Here comes the rain again—we'd best run for it. Come on, we'll get a soaking...."

They reached the cabin and entered, the dog right at their heels. Isaac stoked up the fire and drank wine from the jug.

"New theory," he grinned. "Mack's poem got loose and is prowling around up on the ridge."

Iphigenia frowned, then laughed.

About midnight Isaac went out for more wood, and when he returned, his hair was covered with snow.

"The stuff's sticking," he said, "and piling up fast. If it keeps on, we'll be snowed in by morning."

*

FEBRUARY 10, 1975:

They awoke late. The wind had subsided, but snow continued to fall. Isaac rose first, shivered in the cold as he pulled on his clothing, sharp air tingling his bare flesh. He stuffed wood into the stove, splashed a small amount of white gas on the split chunks, stood back, and tossed a match inside the door. The stove jolted, flame leaped, and then flames evened out.

Soon the metal was red in places, and the cabin warmed quickly. Isaac stood at the window, looked out, could see only a few feet into downward swirling whiteness.

"We've got nearly two feet," he announced, "and there's no sign of a let-up. It may be a month before we get out of here."

Ginny rose from bed, stood naked beside the stove.

"Careful, Yellow-Eyes," Isaac grinned. "You'll catch a welt on that beautiful backside of yours. Well, we've got food and wine, plenty of that. We'll drink the rest of Mack's stuff first, though. What'll we do to amuse ourselves? Read books, I guess. Can't think of anything else."

"I've an idea," Ginny said, coming up behind him, reaching around, putting her hands over the front of his trousers, squeezing. "Unless you'd rather read, of course...."

"All you're interested in is sex. Don't women ever think of anything else?"

He pretended to struggle free, but she leaped on his back, her legs clamped about his middle, her hands on his beard.

"Bear me into the bedroom, faithful horse," she said. "You'll not get away this time! I'm going to be Calypso, and you're my Odysseus. Come into my cave—see, I've read some good books too. I'll pull out your beard if you don't make love to me, Isaac McCain!"

Isaac took three steps toward the bed, then lurched sideways, yanked open the door, and dived headlong into deep snow beyond the stoop. He roared, and she screamed, her naked body floundering in cold powdery snow as he rolled over and bit at her neck.

*

FEBRUARY 14, 1975:

Snow on St. Valentine's Day.

Three days it had fallen out of a grayness, and then the wind shifted and the clouds broke. Dawn came with a clear sky, bright burning cold blue. Icicles hung like a fringe from cabin eaves, snow up to the windowsills, frozen hard.

Isaac awoke early, raised himself to one elbow, and stared at Ginny. A cloud of auburn hair half covered her face, and the slim body beneath a mound of blankets revealed smooth, regular breathing. A slight twitching of facial muscles. He kissed her forehead, licked at the strands of hair. Her hand reached instincttively toward him, touched his shoulder. She continued to sleep, but Isaac rose and dressed.

Doom was thumping his tail on the board floor.

Man and dog went outside together, McCain testing his weight on the crusted snow. It held him. He shielded his eyes against unaccustomed brightness and walked down the easy slope toward Deer Creek, the stream making a dark slash against whiteness, a lacework of ice at its edges. To one side of the little falls hung a delicate crystalline curtain. He crossed the log bridge, worked his way slowly up the hillside, past the mine entrance, and on to the ridgecrest and the big oak, its black bark lined in white, snow beginning to loosen and fall in sunlight.

He stood at the base of the great tree, rehearsed climbing it often as a boy, brought to mind the view from its high branches.

"What the hell—why not?"

He climbed, moving carefully, pulling himself up from the main crotch, slowly recalling movements, translated twenty years and more, easing himself to a high fork where branches swirled and made a stairway. Isaac scuffed away snow and pulled himself finally to a double fork at the tree's height, feeling the certain spring of limbs, black-barked strength.

Eastward loomed the sprawl of the Sierra Nevada, high peaks visible from where he perched, glittering white against a mostly blue sky. To the south and north ran interbranching ridges, these hiding canyons of the Yubas, the Bear, Steephollow, Greenhorn—and westward rose the rounded white top of Banner Mountain with its steel-frame forestry lookout tower—yes, and now a building development or two clutching at the prominent hill's tree-covered flanks. Further west were greens and browns of lower hills where no snow had fallen, and beyond them the great valley of the Sacramento, Nem Seyoo as the Maidu had once called the arterial river of the California heartland. From the valley floor, dreamlike, rose conspicuously ragged spires of Estawm Yan, the sacred Middle Hills, otherwise known as Sutter Buttes or Yuba Buttes. All about the peaks spread lush farmland, glittering green with new grass this time of year, farmland speckled with small cities and towns. Further yet rose the Coast Range and the Yolla Bolly peaks, these also edged with white against a line of blue.

Isaac shouted, a long peal of sound. But there was no echo, his voice lost in a snow-drenched forest. He shouted again, but still no answering peal. He laughed, glanced downward. Eighty or a hundred feet below him was the black-ticked, white form of his dog, nearly indistinguishable against the snow. Doom, forefeet up against the tree's trunk, howled mournfully.

*

When Isaac returned to the cabin, Ginny was sulking. It was nearly noon. He'd let time slip past him. She poured hot coffee and pretended to read. Finally she spoke.

"Couldn't you have left a note, for God's sake? I didn't know where you were. I don't think you love me, Isaac, not enough. You shouldn't have done that."

"I'm sorry, Yellow-Eyes. I intended to walk just down to the creek, but then the woods caught me. You know. So I went up to the big oak and climbed it—haven't done that since I was a kid, needless to say."

"You what?"

"Climbed the big oak. Just curious if I still could, is all. Ginny, the whole world's a blazing white. God but it's lovely. Let's go back up there—we'll both climb. I'll show you how—I mean, there's a knack to this particular tree. Well, it's not all that difficult."

Iphigenia rubbed at her eyes, looked away from him, out the window.

"I love you," she said at last, "and I wanted to tell you something today. I feel very foolish, but it seemed right to wait. Isaac, I'm—pregnant. Do you want a child?"

*

FEBRUARY 17, 1975:

Cold now, a wind blowing all night. But the wood stove hummed until its updraft glowed a soft orange color, and the little cabin was warm and dark. The hour was late, wine glasses stood empty on a bedside stand, and Isaac and Iphigenia lay naked together.

She crouched above him, musky smell of the pubis, the womb-opening, his tongue on the bud of desire, slow, fast, slow again, plunging as well into the life-opening. Oh, patiently, patiently, the changing of tempo, reaching forward to squeeze her breasts, then his fingers gently clawing along her sides.

Her mouth drew away from him. Her breathing was animal-like, the entire body drawn rigid, he could feel it coming, her voice a gurgle, a whine, rising in gasps to a wail in the darkness, in the thin flicker of candlelight. Her hips convulsed, her entire body was writhing.

He clutched her legs, his tongue oblivious and aching and governed by its own knowledge, separate from him, belonging to her now. She screamed and lurched forward, gasping, twitching, moans forcing out the syllables: *No more....*

He turned her over then, mounted from the rear, sliding into her, abeyance of consciousness, buttocks arched to receive him, her face buried in the pillow, her gasps muffled with each forward stroke. His hand gripped her hair. His mind was in suspension, or off in some distant, wild place, aware only of the movements, pulsations, dark forces of male and female bodies, slowly, slowly, then faster, time speeding, receding, their bodies slippery with sweat—in the darkness a dual movement of bodies, the in-thrust-

ing, the arched haunches, faster, her wails, her groans, his own
voice unlocking his lips in an ancient, wordless language, straining
upward, his body convulsing, her body convulsing, intermingled
wails, everything twined, gasping and crying, and the sweat, movements, mindless, male and female, opening, prodding, instants
turned hours, unendurable, thirsted-for, wrenching last moment and
white fire of release....

*

FEBRUARY 21, 1975:

Isaac thought: *This human life is a little madness turned in at
either end with darkness—and the streams, Steephollow, Woodpecker Ravine and Mad Mack's cabin that I haven't even seen yet,
Greenhorn, Deer Creek, the American Rivers and Ko-lo-ma village
where gold was discovered and where the Maidu were massacred
long ago, Acorn Girl's first husband and her children, Screwauger
Canyon, Shirttail Canyon, the Bear, the Yubas, Susan River, the
Feather (Río de las Plumas), Cosumnes, the American River
(Yalesumnes).... I hear water among the stones, the ouzel where it
dives beneath the surface, out again, perches pulsing on a shaded
rock, nodding in a green and overwhelming mystery of light—and a
blue heron stands one-legged in shallows, eyes clouded with passing
time. Snow vanishes, red bugs are swarming alongside remaining
snowbanks, the woods reek with odor of deer, nights shot through
with coyote wails. After all this time, am I not innocent? Will the
Great Compost have not only my flesh but my soul as well? Wind
in the pines across the creek has a restful sound—it doesn't care.
A man can forget what the wind sounds like. But one can walk
into the wind and know peace, genuine peace. It is almost time for
ootim yaawn, the flowers of the acorns—ootim yaawn ye-koonai,
ye-koonai, ye-koonal, acorn flower, soon it be mush that already be
cool and hard, only it wiggle.... Yes, Ginny is pregnant, a sperm
has penetrated an egg, the cells divide rapidly, a miracle's in progress. There's fate in this. My life constellates from a missed
offramp, reverses, transforms itself, becomes a stranger to itself,
grows giddy from its own image in moving water. Well, Old Man
Coyote takes care of all of us, ministers to us as the whim moves
him.*

Coyote Man said, *You know why you missed that turn: you
came home to love the woman, to father her child. No family is
more dear to me than yours—the line must be continued.*

Isaac McCain laughed.

"You're my father's madness," he said. "There's no reason I should listen to you."

You will listen, just as your father did.

"It was you by the big oak the other night? I knew it, *Oleli* Man, yet I didn't believe it. Even Ginny saw lights in the fog and shadow."

Earth itself must shudder to its base, for what are we but raw emotion laced with cunning intellect, and that so slight our fingers trickle fire? I created the mountains and plains, the birds and the fish and the animals. I did all this for the Great One, the Dreamer. Now I'm like a man, and yet I neither live nor die, but am instead the sap that eats the earth, roots that claw between the grains, leaves that pierce the sky. I live here in the forest—these woods have always been my home. Oh, I've wandered about for ages awaiting this time, Isaac. My blood is red as yours, my heart is tuned to that same metronome. My other name is Fire, and when turned loose, I'll burn the cities down. Genocide against my people, ehh? Well, I take revenge as best I can. My victories are small but constant. Let's kill some Walems and burn their houses....

"With you to lead the people, it's no wonder what happened. You twitched a memory trace, and I drove south, a man made captive to a past he thought he'd escaped. The wind hinted at winter, a year at its breaking point. Aspen leaves sailed on the air, and my life revolved about a certain point in time."

Isaac, can you feel the short, fast bursts of wind? Do you remember thunderheads looming over these mountains in summer? From here one can see bands of rain over the far ridges—and Sierra Buttes, those jagged old spires that thrust up so lonely, unbelievable solitude. Your place is beyond them, not here—your place is below Wahgalu, the spot Benjamin and Ooti called Upper Eden, where True Bear and Fire Woman lived, Axel and Jessie. Don't forget that I told you. Too damned many Whitemen around here. Even Abram dreamed about going home. Ah, there are bloodstains all over the place.... Blood on the rocks, blood in the earth....

"Did he do it, Dog-face? My father? Is he the one who raped April Incendie and left her for dead? He murdered her? And you caused it?"

Why should I answer your questions? Humans ought to be able to figure things out for themselves. I gave you a brain like my own so you could invent as many answers as you wished. But no, Isaac, it wasn't your father. All your degrees, and you cannot comprehend even so simple a thing? Be honest now—don't you know the murderer? Your father's assassin as well, get right down to it. Only a great fool could have failed to understand—someone who never learned how to flake an arrowhead or who never collected boxes of woodpecker scalps. Ah! You were afraid to find out.

"The old rage festers within me, *Oleli.* But murder's a terrible act. How do I know you're not controlling my mind?"

What's murder? You civilized people are pitiful, and that's the truth. I read your newspapers. Sometimes I even have breakfast at one of the cafés in Diggins. Infiltration, that's the answer. I make note the most terrible crimes go unavenged—rapists and murderers let loose to repeat their acts. Did Acorn Girl turn the other cheek? That's a weakling's code, disgusting to my mind. I tell you, a revenge-taking's in order. Ben McCain, he learned from his woman. True Bear and Auna-yi, they left their enemy wounded, to perish in flame. You White weaklings and your laws! There's deeper law.... Okay, Isaac, I know the thing that bothers you. Consult your dreams. The ring, the ring. Isn't it clear yet? Are you a doctor unable to heal yourself?

"You're not making sense, Coyote-Clown."

I'll tell you about sense. You need a vision. I'll give you one. See him, Abram McCain, shirtless. He walked through the forest that morning, his ragged canvas shoes sloughing along, step after step, striding through the ten or so miles between the printshop and Diggins. On the brow of a hill, he sat down to rest beneath a small madrone. With a large, bony-strong-hand he fished Bull Durham out of a pocket and rolled a cigarette, paper between forefinger and thumb, cupping the yellow-brown flecks of burley tobacco....

"I can see all that. Let's get on with it, shall we? At this rate, we'll sit here ten years."

All right. Abram could visualize the entire length of trail he'd come to know so well, twists and turns, dog-backs, now along the creek bottom, now angling down a ridge, sometimes all but invisible to any eye but his own, the trail leading him now toward his desire....

"Toward April Incendie? My April. You sonofabitch, you're playing with my mind, tormenting me, aren't you?"

Be patient. Abram hoped you'd marry, would give him grandchildren. It was the Fourth of July that day, the day of the big

*Walem celebration. Abram walked into town to find a prostitute—
things get so complicated in the Whiteman's world. He paid her
fifty dollars, god only knows what for.*

"If that were true, then...."

*It's true. You have no reason to doubt my word, the word of
Old Coyote Man Who Does Everything. I also see everything, at
least when I bother to look. I've lived about you all your life, am as
close as your blood.*

"Perhaps it was someone who never even lived in these hills, a
stranger who came to town...."

*You know better than that—it was no stranger. You'll think of
it presently. The answer will ring in your mind.*

"Why don't you just tell me? I've wrestled this matter through
a thousand times or more. If it wasn't Abram...."

*No need to worry that further, your father was innocent. I
hereby by God pronounce him innocent of all charges. Isaac, if you
walk the woods softly, and put other thoughts away from you so
that you can see and know the trees and rocks and the moss, and if
your eye is keen, you may see the ouzel ahead of you, perhaps
near where green water spills, small beads of moisture fresh upon
its sand-gray feathers. And if you're very still, it will not fly away or
plunge into the spume, and you may watch it perched there, frail
body pulsing, twitching rhythmically every second or third moment.
Ouzel he's a loner, she is too. In springtime they find each other
and mate. You've heard the music? Transparent, exquisite,
wonderfully sweet—better than a mockingbird's. Your father knew.
He walked through the forest as though he wished to disturb no
single thing about him, lest he violate some secret harmony his
human senses wouldn't allow him to perceive. Too gentle, to my
way of thinking. Truth to say, I liked him, but I never quite
understood him.*

"He killed Eldrickson's sheep, didn't he? And blew up the
Fitzweiller log landing?"

*Sheep need killing, domestic ones at least. I'd have wool
between my teeth all the time, if I had my way. But the fuzz-bellies
kick and....*

"Burt Bullardi?"

*My brave philosopher! The secret lies buried in your father's
gold mine.*

"What are you talking about now? That makes no damned
sense at all."

You consult oracles, you get riddles. What did you expect? But I have the matter on good authority. Well, Deer Creek runs in the north of the Inyo, where the mountains are not so high as above Yosemite or the Evolution Basin. A great place, Isaac. You ever been to Mt. Dana? But it was here, along the American and the Yuba, that the Walems found gold a century and a quarter ago. Not many years, when you think about it. Time for massacres and a lot of digging, that's all. Mother Lode, ehh? Towns came with the gold, and some are long since deserted, forest and the elements working together to ingest decayed wooden buildings. For a time small glass vials of chemicals stood upon the shelves of the little assay office in You Bet, though a portion of the roof was blown away and the door hung absurdly—a dozen years ago heavy January snows crushed the thing. One house remains in You Bet, and Sandy Bar sleeps beneath the green flood of a reservoir. Where's my brother, Pano the grizzly? He'd be pleased to see it happen, but he's gone to Upper Meadows. You call yourself Last Bear, but Last Grizzly's more accurate. Are you worthy of that name?

Some of the towns didn't die, though, acquired the veneer of a new age, continued to live because of the forest, because of timber and red, orchard-sustaining earth—and because people from the great cities drive up to the hills on weekends, build houses, retire, cluster like insects. Still the heat of the first gold lingers—and deeper than that, deep in rocks or hidden in pitchy cores of stumps and leaching into red soil, that other fever, primal, and the beating of hearts. I cannot die, and I can't be controlled. I'm wrought into the tiny threads of life. I swell in the wind, in the rain, in milky-white seed.

"Song-Dog, you also get carried away on the wings of your own yawp—as bad as that fellow Mercutio in *Romeo and Juliet.* Do you know what it got him? You wear a slouch hat and a denim shirt. You have a coyote face, and your silly ding-a-ling's sticking out half the time. I know who you are."

I'm on your side, Isaac, do you realize that?

"Yes, yes. No one seems to recall much about him, *Oleli.* The forgetting occurred quickly, as I gather. Yet sometimes people talk, even now. A couple of old-timers downtown the other day, I overheard them arguing about what happened. Memory. But mostly they don't think about it at all, for they've chosen to forget—made that decision right away. The thing happened, and then it was over."

*Many deaths go unmourned. I always liked the Ustu cere-
monies, did I tell you that? I'd come around after the people
returned to their villages, and there was always something to eat—a
basketful of deer meat, or what not.*

"Yeah, you mentioned it."

*A generation has died Isaac—one of many. Your father's
heyday is gone, he was the last of them. Don't presume to take his
place, you can't do it. Abram was born too late, I guess. Burning-
Man's spirit was in the mountains, even though he got sent off to
school and learned to play games with that machine of his. Some
earlier time, and he'd have trapped beaver and hunted buffalo.
Might even have gone helling around with O'Bragh or one of those
boys—might even have helped Ben Goffe on his way to California,
a guide for his own grandfather. He'd probably not have been so
worried about a few trees, wouldn't have been able to envision the
limits of things, the ending. Well, now, you've tormented yourself
for nearly twenty years, that's probably long enough.*

"Abram, they drove you to suicide. I still don't know myself
and maybe never will—what happened, I mean. But I am your son.
You continue to live in me, and I'll have my revenge."

*You're coming around. To hell with these armchair liberals and
their bleeding hearts. It's time for some good, wholesome, bone-
splitting fun. Because it is fun, damn it. Angry fun, and necessary.
Even when the monitors and longtoms ceased to blast with gushing
water into white and yellow gravels of the ridges, some men
couldn't give up the search for worthless yellow metal—men of a
different and dwindling race, little concerned that the larger towns
were changing, that parking meters now grew by the main streets.
White blood, Red blood, it made no difference. The sun died in the
skies for my people, and now these others became my people.
Their sun has died as well. I suggest you consider fire.*

"Father, you searched for gold you didn't need. Even you were
driven to bore back into the earth. What were you looking for,
Abram McCain? What did you find there in the darkness?"

*Mother Lode, the source, the ancient richness from which all
the river gold came. Men searched for it, but if it ever existed, the
forest hid it and refused to reveal its secret. Old Greenwood said
he knew, and he led the damned fools on a goose chase. Jim
Marshall didn't know, but a pack stayed at his heels just the same.
Hell, if the thing existed only in the imaginations of those who
sought it, that hardly matters. Still men searched. Abram McCain*

*searched as well, though he knew better. And his son.... There's
fever in the earth, I tell you.*

"Why include me, *Peheipe Oleli?* I left these hills and didn't
return for nineteen years. I've been spared the insanity."

*Ha! Ha! I laugh at you! You haven't been spared. It's the
curse of your White blood. Open the mine, Isaac, you'll find a
certain treasure there. Think of the sun—you walked through the
woods in dark yellow light, you and that poetry-slinging friend of
yours. A Scot is he, a babbling, blaspheming Scot? Azaleas
bloomed, and a dead bear lay in the water of a stream. That big
rattlesnake by the rock? It was me, in disguise, Nidhogg the Dog.
Fire in the trees, and your eyes stinging. Spot fires north of the
Yuba, tongues of flame bursting the night, tall pines flaring an
incandescent seed.*

"You've got the sequence reversed. Why should I listen to you?
I tell you, I've been spared this madness."

*Isaac, Isaac. It was I who pulled the trigger that night in Tex's
Tavern, I left you scarred. Did this never occur to you?*

"Oh, hell. A little thing. My beard hides the disfigurement."

*

FEBRUARY 26, 1975:

Shortly before noon, Mack Madison and Sandy Sorenson
showed up. They were on their way to Reno to get married, just as
they'd said they would.

Isaac and Iphigenia put things in order while Mack was drinking
a beer and talking about a novel he fancied he might write, and
then the four of them and Doom as well piled into Isaac's Buick
and headed up Highway 20 toward Donner Summit and Truckee
and on into Nevada. The high peaks were glistening with snow,
and brilliant sunlight produced moments of intense glare.

The green waters of Truckee River foamed along through the
gorge, and Mack and Ike engaged in a long discussion of the merits
of a welfare government, the sexual folly of Wilbur Mills, the
growing national deficit, the victory of the Menominee Indians in
Wisconsin in having occupied a Catholic novitiate house for more
than a month and having received assurance the unused facility
would be transferred to their tribe, to be used as a hospital, as well
as some talk of a soon-to-be-announced Supreme Court decision
concerning mineral deposits on the continental shelf beyond the

three-mile limit—whether to be governed by state or federal authority.

"Damn it, Mack, this is my wedding day!" Sandy protested.
"Knock off the hypothetical malarkey. Solve the nation's problems
some other time. Ginny, why'd we have to bring along these two
contentious men, anyway?"

"Females of our species have always had poor judgment,"
Iphigenia replied. "Look—we're almost there. Perhaps we'll be
able to find a couple of superior *animals* in one of the casinos."

Reno City Limits.

"You hear what your lady's saying, Madison?" Isaac laughed.
"I knew she'd see through you before it was too late."

"Ginny," Mack growled, "you mind repeating that? This big
lug didn't hear you—he never listens to anyone but himself."

*

The marriage was performed by a justice of the peace—in an
anteroom in the county courthouse. The marriage-maker even
offered an extra—wedding vows of the Washoe Indians, the words
claimed to provide reinforcement to the traditional Christian for-
mat. Isaac winked at Iphigenia, who pressed her tongue against
her cheek.

Then they were outside, on the street, and Mack insisted they
visit Harrah's Club—for good luck. Twenty or thirty dollars' worth
of nickels, dimes, and quarters later, a buzzer went off on the slot
machine Sandy was playing, and the tray filled with silver. A short-
skirted attendant came with a brown paper bag full of coins, handed it to Sandy, and said in a practiced voice, "Play it off, please."

"I'm getting claustrophobia in this damned place," Ginny complained. "How long are we have to stay here? Let's go shoot a
few cowboys or blow up a dam."

"Time to be off, then!" Mad Mack laughed. "What about it,
Ichabod Crane? I've got a great idea. Let's head up to Quincy,
then on to your grandpa's old place. We haven't been that way in
half a lifetime. You have renters staying in the ranch house? Well,
we can get motel rooms at Lake Almanor...."

Isaac shrugged. He was on the verge of insisting the party
drive straight back to Deer Creek, but the idea of setting foot on
the old place once again took hold of him.

"House is empty, if the roof hasn't caved in," he said. "But wood-rats for company probably isn't Sandy's idea of what a wedding night should be. I wouldn't mind, but...."

"Let's go, then!" Sandy laughed. "It sounds like fun. Pack rats, aren't they? We'll buy a couple of gallons of wine and build a big fire. I can get into Mack's pants whenever I want to, after all, but a girl doesn't have many opportunities to visit the Garden of Eden—isn't that what it's called, Isaac?"

"Upper Eden," he replied. "Yes, that's what it used to be called, at least."

"How long will it take us to get there?"

"Oh, three, four hours, I suppose. Eleven o'clock, and then there's no way of knowing what we'll find. If the place is still more or less intact, there'll be bedding and the like. Mack Madison, it's a crazy idea. You want to head up to Chester, though, okay. We can go on to the ranch tomorrow. At least give Sandy a nice motel for her wedding night, you wretched heathen Scot barbarian. He's Grendel himself, I tell you."

"We can buy whatever we need at the Thrifty Drugstore," Sandy said. "If there are rats, they've eaten all the blankets. But so what? Ginny, this big hermit of yours is a born-again conservative—no sense of adventure. We'll buy sleeping bags, camping equipment. Mack's got five hundred dollars in his pocket. He was just going to blow it on gambling...."

"Ginny?" Mack asked.

Iphigenia grinned, nodded.

"You've been outvoted, Doctor Hamburger. Let's head for the Gawd-forsaken, *incult* wilds of Upper Eden."

"An adjective, you say?" Isaac shrugged.

*

FEBRUARY 27, 1975:

The hour was close to midnight when they arrived. The doors of the old board-and-batten ranch house were securely locked, and a cursory examination by flashlight suggested, remarkably enough, that the place had not been vandalized.

Isaac found a rusty skeleton key in its appointed place on a nail behind the doorframe of the horse barn, and after a few moments of working the lock mechanism of the front door, managed to gain entry to the main building.

Aside from some accumulated dust and cobwebs, the old McCain house appeared to be in good order. Even the woodbox was full—from Isaac's last visit, several years earlier.

"Fire in the fireplace—let's get 'er going," Mack said. The girls can bring in our outfit—squaws' work, ain't that so, Isaac?"

"Haul in your own outfit, you son of a bitch!" Sandy laughed. "Come on, Ginny, let's drink some wine. Let the resident males do whatever work needs to be done. Does Isaac know how to light a fire?"

"Yes, yes, he does. That's one thing he most definitely knows how to do."

"I always get stuck with the heavy work," Madison grumbled as he headed out to the Buick.

Soon a blaze was roaring in the big fireplace constructed of chunks of lava and plagioclase andesite, and a brand-new Coleman lantern was pulsing white light. The main room grew warm, and first one, and then the second jug of red wine disappeared.

The two couples retired to opposite sides of the fireplace and crawled into their sleeping bags.

Isaac lay beside Ginny, stroking her hair and staring up at the beam ceiling.

"I like this place," she murmured. "Maybe we could come live here part of the time. Would you object to that, Isaac?"

"An interesting thought," he whispered. "Ghosts here too, but a different kind. Not nearly as many people. Diggins is right at the edge of the human madness, but up here things are different. About a thousand acres go with the ranch, and the closest neighbors are down at Childe's Meadows. If we want to be hermits, Ginny, this would be the place, all right. I was nervous on the way up, for some reason or another, but right now I feel very...calm."

Ginny murmured something incomprehensible. Isaac realized she had dozed off, her sleeping bag pressed close against his.

Very calm and very drunk. Must be three in the morning, maybe later. Tomorrow I'll go out and say hello to Grandpa True Bear and Grandma Fanny and Aunt Jessie and the others....

"Not tonight, Mack, not here...," Isaac heard Sandy whisper.

Then he slept, Doom growling contentedly against his legs.

***

Canto Eleven:
I AM MY FATHER

ODYSSEUS SAT DOWN, BUT TELEMACHUS, SOFTENED AT LAST, FLUNG HIS ARMS ROUND HIS NOBLE FATHER'S NECK AND BURST INTO TEARS. AND NOW THEY BOTH BROKE DOWN AND SOBBED ALOUD WITHOUT PAUSE LIKE BIRDS BEREAVED, LIKE THE SEA-EAGLE OR THE TALONED VULTURE WHEN VILLAGERS HAVE ROBBED THE NEST OF THEIR UNFLEDGED YOUNG. SO DID THESE TWO LET THE PITEOUS TEARS RUN STREAMING FROM THEIR EYES. AND SUNSET WOULD HAVE FOUND THEM STILL IN TENDER MOOD, IF TELEMACHUS HAD NOT SUDDENLY THOUGHT OF ASKING HIS FATHER A QUESTION.

[HOMER, *THE ODYSSEY*]

*

MARCH 2, 1975:

The snow was gone from the meadow, and buds on the apple tree were ready to burst—new grass was already up. Isaac worked through the pleasant morning. Then Ginny came up the hill with lunch.

He'd dug open the entrance to the mine.

Doom, dripping wet, ran from the creek and shook water on them as they ate sandwiches, then rolled on his back in the kitkitdizze.

"Gets around all right for a three-legged old mutt, doesn't he, Gin? *The Power of Positive Growling*, by English S. Doomerdog."

"Isaac, it's not safe. I don't want you to go in there."

But he laughed at her and fastened on the headlamp.

"I won't go far. I've no intention of allowing the mountain to swallow me. You hang onto the Doomer. I don't want him falling into a winze or.... God knows what's there. I've got to reveal the mystery, Ginny Yellow-Eyes."

"Then I'm coming too. It's better if we both get buried—you go, Isaac, I'm also going in. You won't stop me."

"All right then, stubborn person. Stay behind me. This candle will tell us if the air's good. Probably an old wives' tale, or something that pertains to coal mines or marshland tunnels—though if it were methane gas, a candle would blow us to hell. Well, there's a vent halfway in. We'll see light if it's still open—I should have climbed up the rockpile to look, I guess. If the shaft's not open, we'll turn around."

They moved into cool darkness, the dog behind them, and heard a slow dripping of water, echoed sounds of their footsteps. The shaft turned to the left, and they perceived a dim glow from above.

"Won't need that candle anymore," Isaac said.

"How far does the shaft go? Haven't you seen enough yet?"

"No. It's not much farther. I want to look at the end of the tunnel. The auriferous vein's a maverick, Dad said, black sand that carries gold. Most adits follow a quartz seam. Let's see what it looks like—we'll dig some sand and pan it in the creek. Abram insisted he could make his living out of the hole if he had to, and that was when gold was thirty-two dollars to the ounce. He died here instead—blew himself up with dynamite at the end of the tunnel, according to what the sheriff told me. I think his spirit's still in here, Gin."

"Doom's whining, Isaac. Let's go back now."

At the shaft's terminus, Isaac studied the ledge, then dug with a rock hammer. He took samples and put them into a burlap sack.

"All right, let's depart—see what we have here."

"I hope there's nothing," she said. "You ought to blast the entrance closed again. This is dangerous. I don't want you up here anymore."

They walked out silently. Ginny was angry. He knew it, knew she had reason.

"Aren't you even a little bit curious, Yellow-Eyes?"

"No, not at all. Not even if it's pure gold—better it stays in the ground. Our child needs a father, and I need you, Isaac."

But the waters of Deer Creek swirled fine-grained sand away and left what Isaac McCain had sought: little lumps of heavy metal, a handful in the iron pan.

*

MARCH 10, 1975:

Isaac stopped at the old wooden bridge across Steephollow, locked his Buick, and walked downstream, Doom with him, past the beginnings of the gravel flats. Once a mill had stood nearby and a mining encampment—yes, in all likelihood this was the very place where Benjamin Goffe McCain and Acorn Girl and her Maidu made their attack, seeking and taking revenge upon the Whitemen who'd massacred an Indian village up the hollow.

He proceeded into the dim, overgrown canyon itself, the woods sprawling hushed under thin warmth of a spring afternoon. He stripped and swam briefly in the chill waters of a shallow pool, emerged, and petted the dog.

Thought.

He drew his Smith & Wesson from its holster and fired five times. The dog whimpered, nudged nervously closer to his master, tail wagging.

"For all this, Doomer Dog, it could very well have been my father. It could have been Abram. His mind was not his own those last few months. Well, it happened a long time ago, a lot of water down the flume. Whatever the case, I've forgiven him, and so the matter should rest. But it doesn't. By returning to these hills, I've brought forth the hell of memory. April Incendie, you little twit, forgive me. I loved you deeply, and that's a fact. You're part of the earth now. Time has jolted me forward, but I'm not alone. Old Mad Mack, he's still around, and so's the damned Bulldog. But it's more than that, April. I've found my mate. You would have found yours, eventually, but I wasn't the one. It's easy for me to say that now. The problem, our problem, it wasn't just you—it was Ichabod McCain as well. I was a clumsy, ego-drunk fool—eighteen years old and imagined I knew it all. The big fish swims upstream to die—but no, not yet. These woods cover me, and I move more deeply into a new life, its full dimensions as yet unknown. *Former Professor McCain.* I like the sound of that. And yes, I'm the son of Abram McCain, I'm Isaac the son of Abram, *Ishi-Pano*, the son of Burning-Man, two ghosts from an old moss-covered book written by desert nomads, runaway slaves, and the like—not even written, perhaps no more than a few hieroglyphics at best, perhaps no more than a story caught up in oral tradition, and two thousand years later it was copied down, a nameless scribe working with ink on parchment or sheepskin. Well, I know your lunacy, Father, it also lives in my skull, and I lust for revenge. I go out wandering and spend my time talking to an illusion, a Dog-headed God who led various Native tribes astray for thousands of years, since the days of the ice. Green lights in the forest at night—hawgwash."

Burt Bullardi killed her.

"I'm not thinking clearly, White Brother. I must think clearly—this is serious business. Burt loved her, just as I did, would not have...."

Burt Bullardi killed her, you damned fool, and you're going to kill him. You've waited far too long. I'm patient, Isaac, but my patience has limits. I want a revenge-taking. You must rip him open and laugh to watch hot blood drench the earth, for you are bound. You turned away from a duty which was yours, and a great sorrow froze your being, nulled you. You were a boy then, and your anger and your violence were checked. You left your home, thinking never to return. The method found madness for Swellfoot, why should it work for you? Okay, so your world got dented a bit. The entire human cosmos is on a downhill run. Let's speed it up. You've come home in quest of your birthright and a need for revenge, something restored to memory after long forgetting. I told you, Isaac....

"It's true. Somehow I suppose I've always known it had to be the Bulldog, no one else, for isn't he pretty much the other half of my own nature? The hatred was set between us as we grew up. He tracked her down, she who was torn between us as though on Procrustes' bed, and he violated her in the dark of a summer rainstorm. She died from that. My father, my great mad father, they blamed you—hunted you with dogs, *crazy Injun hermit of Deer Creek*, but you killed the dogs and returned to the darkness by your own hand, a rending blast in the mine. Doom, are you listening? April—she was a beautiful girl, and I see her vividly, just the way she was—how her buttocks trembled when she walked—as if in anticipation—movement of her breasts as she breathed, the odor of her body—that alone might have driven any man to violence. A pool of gasoline, and matches flaring about her. All right, I've always known who it was, had to be, and yet I listened to the conventional wisdom of Diggins, the townsfolk who never liked Dad or me either one, *damned Halfbreed McCains*. The people about town, they said it was my father, and I was a coward—or simply too stunned to know what to do. If I'm right in all this, then Bullardi's bound to die at my hands. Otherwise the pattern will never be completed."

Doom looked up at his master, tugged at Isaac's coat sleeve.

I have waited long for this moment, I have waited for you, Isaac McCain, just as I waited for your father. I live in the roots and tendrils, my voice the laughter of the little coyotes at night. I tell you, earth is full of boneyards. The time lies ahead when no fur-

ther human spirits will trouble the wildness. I made a mistake in giving you the kind of mind you have.

Isaac rose, laughed.

"Doom, don't you start being *Oleli*-Man's mouthpiece, you hear me? Come on, Mr. Mutt, let's head for the car."

Close by the bridge, Isaac made note of a real estate sign—land for sale along the creek, five-acre parcels, so-called recreational sites.

Deer Creek Park Realty, a Division of Bullardi Enterprises, Inc.

*

March 11, 1975:

Ginny slept, but Isaac awoke, rose, dressed, shouldered a new cardboard crate of dynamite, and climbed to the mineshaft.

Half an hour later a small charge went off. Isaac stood outside the shaft, morning sunlight filtering the fir woods, stood in shadows away from the entrance. He laughed at the concussion and then disappeared into the tunnel, whistling.

He worked in darkness, his acetylene headlamp guttering, loaded the ancient ore cart, pushed it down rusty tracks the length of the shaft, toward a bright circle of light.

Ginny came up with lunch, Doom followed, tail whipping as he chased a squirrel through tangles of wild lilac. Then the man and the woman worked together, setting a new charge beneath the black vein, lighting a long fuse, scrambling out of the tunnel.

A fourth blast by late afternoon. In the glow of their lamps they could see only gray rock against the hanging wall.

"Pinched off," Isaac said. "That's the end of it, I guess, or else it's faulted downward or up. We'll blast more tomorrow. The treasure of the Sierra Madre, it's hidden in this mountain, I tell you."

"Maybe that's all there is, Isaac. You've used up the vein. We don't need gold, for pity's sake. You're letting this mine become an obsession."

He sat down on the pile of ore. She stood apart from him, her eyes amber in the lamp's halo, her hair clouding out from beneath the aluminum hardhat she wore.

"Ginny, my beautiful Ginny—you look like a salamander in that get-up. Okay, you're right. I don't want to be a miner. But I think we've got us a *pile* of the yellow stuff when I wash out the sand. It's all over the damned place. Dad spent nearly twenty years dig-

ging at the mountainside—all those stories, maybe he did stash a
fortune away somewhere, buried it again, possibly.   Isn't that
something?   Or maybe these last few rounds opened up the richest
part of it.   If I take the gold to a jeweler in D:ggins, there'll be
rumors all over hell about a new strike.   Old ways of thinking die
hard.   By 1850 or 51, half the men digging holes in the area were
Indians—did you know that?   Forgot all about their villages, their
families, the traditional ways of living—caught the Whiteman's disease.   There's more Indian blood around than you'd think, passing
for White, just as I've done for most of my life.   Since the laws,
enacted in haste, said Indians couldn't own land, couldn't have
guns, a great many Maidu just stopped being Indian, as simple as
that.   At first they worked for Whites, acquired White clothing and
equipment and lingo.   Presto, they were Spanish-Mexicans, nothing
to it.   Indian women took White husbands, and that's the story of
my family, as well.   Ben McCain got land, and he sent True Bear
McCain back East to be educated—later True Bear made sure his
son Abram did the same, since Uncle Axe apparently refused, and
then Abram sent me off to Berkeley.   So here I am, neither one
thing nor the other.   Look, Gin, you can see gold in the sand—
richer than hell.   Dad always said there'd be a pocket where the
vein pinched off.   Said he'd have to muck around to find it again
after that.   Well, we found gold today, all right.   Abram almost had
it, was almost there when the world turned on him.   Wonder how
much of the stuff he might have buried?"

   "You spend too much time worrying about your genetic code,"
Iphigenia said.   "America's the place where racial identity got lost,
if it ever existed in the first place.   When we first met, I told you I
was a Halfbreed—just not Indian, that's all.   Isaac, you believe the
human race is headed for extinction, and I guess I agree.   See, I
know about Malthus.   More important, I can see what's happening.
Someone's projected six billion of us on the planet by the year two
thousand, and a few years further down the line there'll be six or
seven billion more.   We'll go crazy if we don't just starve to death
or push the big red buttons.   Now you and I, we're bringing
another one into the world.   It's as Pogo says, we're the enemy, he
is us.   But right now it's just you and me and our child on the way.
We have to find sanity for the three of us and let the future fend for
itself.   Isn't that right?   Humans are clever, and if there's a possible
survival path, they'll find it—some of them will, at least."

   Isaac nodded.

"Well put," he said. "That's about the way I see it, all right.
But for now, let's wash out this sand and see what our stash is. I
feel like a kid again—the first time I ever saw ladybugs swarm in the
spring."

*

March 14, 1975:
A late snowstorm hit, not unusual, with half a foot of whiteness
falling from branches of pine and fir, dripping in sunlight when the
clouds had passed over and drifted away eastward into Nevada.

Isaac and Ginny made love after breakfast, lay together then,
her head against his chest, her hair touching his beard. They dozed
fitfully into sleep, awoke later, and lit cigarettes, but Ginny stubbed
hers out—in deference to the new life within her body: they lay
together, touching one another, and talked.

"Can't we just keep it?" she asked.

"The gold? Sure. It looks good in the big jar, a hell of a conversation piece for when Mack and Sandy come to visit. I understand now, it's like fire in a darkness. I know damned well there's
more gold in the mountain. Another round or two and we'd likely
find the vein again—maybe another pocket there, right there. It's
pinched on both sides, after all, wherever the other side is...."

"I don't want to mine any more, Isaac. We're going to be
printers now, you promised. We'll do Mack's new collection.
That's much more exciting, if you ask me."

"Salamander! You looked like a salamander In your mining
togs! I couldn't be more pleased if Old Man Gawd paid us a special
visit. Almost a hundred and seven ounces—Jesus! I'd never have
believed it. Now that gold's on a free market, the price is rising
constantly, for a while, at least—no way of knowing how high it'll
go. It was a hundred and eight dollars to the ounce last week and
moving up fast. What if it goes to three hundred, maybe four
hundred or higher? I heard a guy on the radio predict eight or nine
hundred an ounce—and what's it really worth? Makes jewelry and
it doesn't rust, and it's sure a way of getting humans to dig holes.
Well, it's part of the speculation madness now, just like stocks and
real estate. But let's call it a hundred and eight an ounce, just for
the fun of it. I did some mental arithmetic before I fell asleep last
night. Actually, I fell asleep and then woke up again. Say we've
got a hundred and five ounces clean—that's eleven thousand three
hundred and forty dollars. We gained our stake in just two days of

work—nobody in the time of the Rush ever made anything like that, Gin! We're by-God world record holders, I think. We ought to contact Guinness. As for Mack's poetry, we'd go broke trying to sell that, no matter how beautiful the print job."

"No more, damn you. I'll bite, I swear it. You know where. Why are you getting up? Isaac, come lie down with me!"

*

MARCH 29, 1975:

The snow melted out, and Easter day dawned glorious blue. The woods quickened, and overnight the great black oaks opened their leaf buds.

In praise of the one whose feral yellow eyes burn ancient fire, whose touch has rendered the whole of the macrocosm, an existence that gave him birth as well, self-creating, self-sustaining creator, spirit of mountain and prairie and river and lake, of rutilant sundowns foudroyant, like lightning, the one whose screams of joy shatter the night and echo the high still places in the granite mountains, nascent and then tabescent.

Coyote Man, Mantic Awareness, Numen, Old Man Gawd.

The Daughters of Earth nursed this one, the ear-splitting one, son of lightning and all vegetation, they nursed him in limestone caves in the Inyo. He grew as dripping waters join stone at the middle—until he ran singing, and the snows drew back to the big ridges and frozen lakes of the high country. The women followed. He led them through forests, and they shrieked and made dog-like barkings, they vied for his favors. Gray-red tentacles of wild grape, knotted veins that draw upward the sweetness of earth, vitis the vine, to high branches and sunlight, buds , burgeoning efflor-escence, open outward, new green leaves uncoiling, yellow of pollen like a fine spray of wine in the air: the fruit set but would not purple until autumn. Reborn Oleli! Dog-head and God-Head, you bring this happy season, you join with the Daughters of Earth!

*

APRIL 4, 1975:

Iphigenia Singares and Isaac McCain sat by the creek, thin bands of grapevine rising above them, leaves beginning, air rank with a warm moistness and insects and birds all about. The two humans rose to their feet, kissed, and Isaac held her at arm's length, his gaze fixed upon her belly.

She nodded, smiled.

"New life is growing within me, too. I think it's a girl, Isaac, you won't be disappointed? If you want a son to carry that name of yours into the next generation, we'll have to try again later."

"I can see it now," he replied. "I'll be surrounded by yellow-eyed women, coyote pups. You'll have half a dozen daughters before we're through, all yellow-eyed. The color's got to be dominant over *anything* else."

"My eyes aren't yellow. Why do you insist they are? Look, we'll have sons too, I promise."

"Coyote Woman," he said. "*Oleli-du*, that's your Maidu name. I've heard you baying at night. I've borne witness. Grandmother Moon transforms you to your true being, and you run the ridges and howl, catch jackrabbits and mice and slow quail."

"It's true—I love the wild brothers."

"And the wild sisters? You are one, Gin. That's why your eyes are yellow—daylight transforms all of you but your eyes. You're a metamorphosis, a coyotess."

He called to Doom then. The English setter hesitated, gazed off to the woods, and spun toward a stand of firs.

"Damn you, Doomer, why won't you mind?"

"He always comes home. Why worry about it? Let's go up and lay out the garden we're going to plant."

Isaac called again, but the only response was the echoing wail of a three-legged dog running deer.

"Ginny, that sonofabitch has got to learn some manners. You head on up to the house. I'm going to chase him."

"Isaac, for heaven's sake! Grown men don't chase dogs!"

*

Into the woods.

He could hear the dog far off, screaming in the afternoon air. Isaac hurled himself down the ravine, willow brush lashing his face. He ran without thinking, only sensing chase, a sensation of lightness as he moved under the firs and leaped a barbed wire fence near the stream.

The dog, baying.

His footsteps were certain, accustomed. Bluejays shouted, and he breathed deeply of the forest smells. He jogged down a long pine-covered crest, then downslope toward Deer Creek.

"Over the brink," he said. "I'm plunging over the brink."

Welcome home, Ike.

Out of control. He spun through emptiness, skidded along the wet, loose bark of a fallen snag. Blood. Stunned. He looked down at the jagged cut in his leg, an irregular gash in the flesh of his thigh. There was no pain, but a numbness.

Hello, Isaac. I've waited for you.

Imagination.

I'm always here—you know that.

Figment.

No more than you yourself. I am yours by birthright, just as I was your father's before you. You cannot resist me.

"You keep telling me that, Coyote-Head," Isaac mumbled. "You'll go away as soon as my senses clear. Where the hell are you, anyway?"

No, Isaac. You're wrong. I have no place to go. You yourself create me, create my voice, even as you ache for fulfillment. Don't you want that sweetness? Bullardi's hide hanging over some farmer's barbed wire fence? You've driven yourself down this ravine as surely as you live. We must come to terms with one another, or you'll end up just as your father ended. I offer strong wine, wine to be drunk immoderately. Even buffalo skulls must obey me at last, even my old friend Pano, the grizzly.

"There's no Pano in California."

You're here, Isaac, and your namesake will be back soon—just a matter of time.

"Where's my father?"

Have you forgotten everything? He's here, he's all around you. Your job's to find him. Welcome home, Isaac McCain.

"Have to catch that dog of mine. He's running deer."

You're not chasing your dog. Let's get that much straight. It's Ike McCain you so madly pursue.

"Coyote-faced green shadow, I see no reason to listen. You think you can play word games with me, you ignorant sonofabitch? Hell, man, you don't have a damned doctorate. Never even started graduate school."

Plunge on through the woods, dumbass. Hurl stones at passing trucks, you anomic misfit.

"Abram was innocent—said so yourself."

Yes, he was innocent.

"All right, all right. What is it you want me to do? Go look for the Grail?"

You know the answer to that.

"I've been wondering—what—I mean, with no fire hydrants to piss on? Rock piles and tree trunks I suppose? Okay, okay. So I'm supposed to murder my old pal Bullardi, even though there's no evidence he's guilty of anything in particular? I'm to be prosecuting attorney, judge, and jury all at once. Pistols at high noon on Main Street, ehh?"

That wasn't a bad movie, was it? Do not forsake me. Look, you miserable, miscreant human—the girl wears his ring in her grave.

"The girl, April, she's long since dead. But so what? Why vex me with that? Ancient history, ancient history."

Why's she wearing the damned ring?

"Burt probably asked them to bury it with her. The Bulldog loved her too—he might have done that. He's thick-headed and mush-brained at the same time."

Or he might have forced it onto her finger in his drunken rage, right after he raped her—a final and desperate assertion of his rights. Talk about pissing on a stump.... Whitemen have peculiar ideas about territory. Territorial imperative, is it?

"After all this time, how can I know? You want me to dig her up and ask her?"

Aren't there some records in the county courthouse? Your Yan-gees, the Walems, they keep records of everything. Besides, that doctor's still alive and pushing pills.

"I know, *Oleli.* I thought of him. I considered the matter."

Of course you did, Isaac. But you lack conviction.

"Why in hell can't I just live my life now? Ginny loves me, and we've got a little one on the way. Some bones are better left buried—they turn rotten after a time."

Isaac....

"Carner wouldn't know—who'd recollect such a thing? That pretty blond girl who was raped twenty years ago, was she wearing a ring when you first examined her, Doc? Not even that would prove anything. April told me she left the ring in Burt's car—she'd run off and taken his Chevy and driven into town. That's where I met her. She showed me, made a point of it, no ring on her finger, but she might have returned to the car, put the trinket back on. She danced from me to Burt like a little tarantula on summer pavement, one to the other. I loved her, but I wouldn't have put anything past her. Well, I was a kid then—none of it matters anymore, I tell you. *Isakawuate,* that's your Crow name, right?"

So I understand. But what happened to your father matters. Are you certain she left the ring in the car?

"Well, I didn't check her purse, for Gawd's sake. How would I know? She might have had it in her pocket all along. Or she might have returned the gewgaw bauble before she made off with his car. Only that doesn't make sense either, damn it. None of it makes sense, not now, not then. Burt wouldn't have.... It was someone else. Perhaps the coroner's report? But even then.... April, April, for Christ's sake, you worthless little bitch, I...."

Thou shalt not take the name of the Lord, thy God, in vain. You cuss too much. You need to become more precise with your words.

"So Doom keeps telling me. Have you two been comparing notes?"

Except that you know.

"Yes, yes, I know. The time draws near, but how do I do it without ruining Ginny's life in the process? The Bulldog problem's sleeping—maybe I'd best let it lie."

The businessman will give you all the help you need—if you just ask him.

Isaac pulled at his beard, turned.

From behind a copse of greasewood, a group of young women appeared, dancing wildly. Some were bare-breasted and wore tule aprons, others were dressed in gingham dresses and bonnets, others in skirts and sweaters. A dwarf with the face of a vulture sat on a stump, his hands rhythmically moving over the stretched hide of a drum. The women formed a circle about Coyote-Head, and, with screams of laughter, closed in upon him. He threw out his arms in cruciform, lay supine, submitted.

One female crouched over his face. Two others vied for the right to fellate the god. The women tore off their clothing as if the matter were choreographed, screamed in ecstasy, and swarmed over the prone Oleli-Man, their long hair swirling about him. Butterflies emerged from their mouths, spiraling upward and then disintegrating in the air.

The vulture-faced dwarf put aside his drum, spasmed with laughter, and furiously began to masturbate. One young woman made note, turned to the dwarf, kneeled before him. There were tears in her large, wide eyes.

Sensation of greenness, intense.

Coyotes swarming about the clearing, coyotes dancing through tall grass, hundreds of animals, coyotes howling, coyotes....

Then fading.
The clearing was empty.

*

Isaac pressed the torn flesh of his leg together. The bleeding had stopped. He rose, began to run once more, down through manzanita brush, hurling himself forward, oblivious to stinging lashes of leaf and twig, into an open meadow. He leaped a small stream and threw himself up the other side.

The dog was close.

Isaac was aware of a deer thrashing through brush. He stumbled uphill, hardly able to breathe, thinking, *He hears me, he knows I'm below him, is nonetheless coming this way....*

A young doe, its mouth foamed, bounded a fallen log past Isaac, paid no attention to the human, intent only upon the dog in pursuit.

He knows I'm here, but he can't turn now, he'll follow his prey, it's nearly exhausted, he won't turn aside even though he knows I'm here.

Drawing in great, painful breaths, Isaac waited beside the fallen log. Then a white blur in the air at shoulder height, he lunged for its middle, falling backward with Doom in his arms. Isaac wrestled him to the earth, the dog's eyes wild with excitement of the chase, and Isaac hit him again and again, knew very well the dog could not even feel the blows. He held Doom in his arms—suddenly, violently began to cry, cried in such a way as had not happened since childhood.

"You sonofabitch, Doom, you come when I call, damn it, you don't go off chasing deer when I tell you to come or by Odin himself, I'll chase you down every time and I'll beat the living hell out of you, you cantankerous deer-running English setter, don't you know you've got only three good legs?"

The dog's wide brown eyes stared up, apologetic, ashamed, as if to say, *I couldn't help it, master. Don't you understand? I had to run, just as you had to run too. I'm sorry....*

Isaac looped his belt through the dog's collar, and they began the long walk home to the cabin.

Isaac kept saying, "Heel, Doom, heel you sonofabitch!"

All the way, with only one or two exceptions—a sudden, darting squirrel, an old skunk waddling off into cover of manzanita—man and dog both pretended Last Bear McCain was the master.

*

Ike and Mack walked up to the mineshaft. Isaac had shown his friend the big bottle full of nuggets and fines, and Mack was most impressed—had immediately begun to envision *The McCain Mining Corporation,* with offices in London and Hong Kong.

Then he laughed and said, "Ike, don't let the fever get hold of you. My dad's got the disease, and it might be fatal. Another year of this, and you'll be drooling to get into bed with some university or another. Hell, you could take my job down at the community college, and you and Ginny could raise my new stepdaughter. She's going to end up living with us, sure as rotten apples in January. There goes freedom. Still gold deep in the mountain, lots of it, apparently? Save it for your old age, Ike. There's too much to do out in the sunlight."

They sat down on the edge of the tailings pile and stared off across the canyon toward Crooked Pines Campground.

"Good times, most of them," Isaac said finally. "A bunch of years ago now. We're not eighteen anymore, Mack."

"Would you want to be?"

"Nope. There's no way I'd want to go through all that hell again."

"Me, either," Mack said. "What's on your mind? You didn't bring me up here to show me a hole in the ground that I've seen once or twice before. Would you prefer that Sandy and I didn't use the Upper Eden place for a retreat? It's a great spot to go while I work on this crazy novel of mine, but there are other places as well, and...."

"No, that's not it. You guys use the ranch as long as you want. I'll proofread the manuscript when you're finished, though. Someone has to watch out for your abominable comma splices and such."

"Big Injun don't heap know nothing about style, even if he's got heap Ph.D. Okay, so what's on your mind, Ike? Something is. It's written all over your face."

"You're right, of course. Should have been a psychiatrist, Herr Sigmund Madison. Okay. Ever since I came here, I've been going over and over the thing with April Incendie and my Dad, how none of it's ever made sense to me."

"Keep the past buried, Isaac. You've got a whole new life in front of you. Don't screw it up."

"Hear me out, now. I've got this voice that keeps talking to me, and it tells me our old friend Burt was the rapist. I've gone over every inch of the bastardly trail, and that's the place I keep coming to."

"Voice inside the skull, ehh? The ghost of Yvor Winters, more likely than not. Well, I told you as much twenty years ago, if you'll think about it. As a thesis, it seems reasonable enough—Burt had motive and so forth, but evidence is another matter. And that's gone, if it ever existed at all. Bullardi was never my friend—in truth, I barely knew him. But it's a long time ago, Ike. You're thinking about going after the Bulldog, are you? Looks to me like he owns about half the county now. We made the mistake of attending college. He didn't. Anyhow, if you were of a mind, you should have put some lead into him when he was trying to tear the door off your cabin that day. Vandalism in progress, and.... Ike, forget about it. Time wounds all heels, and I figure Burt's about due for the heart attack that'll take him under. He's the type, I'd say. I saw him down in Auburn not long ago, prowling around in his bigass Caddy—probably on the trail of some deal or another. You know, with that development of his downstream from here, he may be toying with the idea of making you a good offer on your dad's homestead. You have close to a section, don't you? Your pop was intent on buying all the land around him as a means of keeping the world out. As is, you're sitting on the only considerable private property left on the creek, and Bullardi already holds the Eldrickson ranch. You could come out of a deal like that with close to a million dollars, my friend—move to Upper Eden and build a mansion for you and Ginny."

"Poets make poor real estate agents," Isaac growled. "If I'm right, I sure as hell don't want Burt's money. It's blood money, not so?"

"You want his scalp."

"Correct."

"What if he's innocent? If he's guilty and you can prove it, there's no statute of limitations on murder. Tom Bridger, the guy who played tennis and chess when we were in school together, he's county D.A. now. Did you know that? Go talk to him. But Ike, you don't have any evidence—*no damned evidence*. You'd be saying, "*You see, Tom, the Bulldog killed April Incendie and was indirectly responsible for my father's death as well—except, of course, that I can't prove any of this."*

Isaac nodded, lit a cigarette.

"Just this one thing," he replied. "When April was buried, she was wearing Burt's ring. That night, when she was with me, she didn't have it on. She told me she and Burt had split up—she'd left the rock in the glove compartment of his car. So why was it on her finger when she was buried?"

"Easy, Ichabod. Try this scenario. She went to the car, and Burt was there. Ergo, she made up with him, just as she'd done fifty times before. They kissed and made up, and she put his ring on and promised to be faithful to him forever thereafter."

"Then what in God's name was she doing out in the woods in the middle of a thunderstorm? It was raining like hell when I got back to Crooked Pines that night—isn't that right?"

Mack nodded.

"Lightning lit up the whole campground," he said. "And our damned tent leaked. You were talking about dropping out of the university and getting a job and marrying the girl. Yep, I remember quite clearly. Isaac, my friend, let it go—that's my advice. You know I'm infallible."

*

APRIL 5, 1975:

In the green glow of mid-afternoon and thin shade of new-leafed buckeye and soft insurgence of lush early grass and delicate odor of peach blossom and lupine, they lay together in each other's arms, she ripe with his seed and the inextricable windings of life and the cries of woodpeckers and jays, even shrill hiss of a near-flying hawk that discovered them and drifted sideways in sunlight and glittered silver.

She turned upon him and devoured him, shivers of pleasure stunned him. He lay fully in the grass and held her head with both hands, his eyes closed. He whimpered in the soft wind that held them, then opened his eyes, watched her as she pushed her mouth down upon him and withdrew, faster now, faster. His body convulsed in the green fire of her touch, and she took his seed, voraciously, milked him shudderingly dry and collapsed upon his loins.

He was covered by the outward wave of her hair, and the earth reached up with dark, moist hands and drew the two of them down through a fierce and yet strangely peaceful vortex.

*

APRIL 23, 1975:

"Dr. Carner," Isaac said, "you don't recall me, I'm sure. But I came to you once when I was in high school. My football coach sent me in with a badly sprained ankle, and you X-rayed to see if anything were broken. I'm Isaac McCain. I need some information."

"As a matter of fact," Carner said, winking, "I do recall, Dr. McCain. You were tight end on the team with Bandino, LeDuc, Reynolds, and Bullardi. A hell of a bunch: you fellows should have won the championship, '54 wasn't it? I was there that night in Oroville, in the rain. Always followed the local athletes. And you won a trophy at the Yuba Invitational that spring, right? I ran track myself when I was young, and I'm still a confirmed jogger. You're Abram McCain's son? Well, that was a terrible thing, what the townspeople did. Seems like yesterday. I'd never have recognized you, though. Age changes us."

Isaac grinned, shrugged.

"My friend Mack Madison won the Yuba trophy," he said. "Me, I played baseball, not track. Dr. Carner, you were April Incendie's attending physician, according to the records."

"Why yes, I was. She's the one your father.... Forgive me, Isaac. That remark slipped out while I wasn't watching. Nothing was ever proven."

Isaac nodded.

"This is a stupid question, Doc, but I have to ask it. You probably won't remember. Let me explain. I was in love with April. I was with her a couple of hours the night it happened, before she was raped. I think she loved me too, and I wanted to marry her. What I'm going to ask is trivial, but it's bothered me for twenty years, and you're the only one alive who might be able to help me out. Was April Incendie wearing an engagement ring when you first looked at her? It's probably not important and not something you'd be likely to recall after so long, but I have to ask...."

"As a matter of fact, I do, yes, clearly," Doc Carner replied. "That day was burned into my memory, you might say, just as it was for many of us. I recall thinking it peculiar."

"What's that?"

"The ring finger was badly damaged—broken at the knuckle. She must have fallen, perhaps she wrenched her hand backward. Yes, Isaac McCain, I do recollect. At that time, I believe Miss Incendie was engaged to our local entrepreneur, Burt Bullardi, the same who was on that football team. You say you were with her the night in question?"

"Yes. It's all in the police report, I'm sure, probably stored away in a box in the basement of the courthouse somewhere. Sheriff Hutchings took a deposition a couple of days later. I was working with the Forest Service up at Crooked Pines."

Carner scratched his chin, nodded.

"Hutchings is dead, you know. A heart attack, about five years ago. A good man. Have you moved to Diggins, Dr. McCain? Seems to me I heard you were a college teacher someplace in the Northwest—had written a book...."

"Yes," Isaac replied. "I'm living at Dad's old place. I've been in the county since last fall. Well, I couldn't handle the rat race any more. Thanks, Doc. Sorry to take up your time—I know you're busy. I'll be happy to pay for the visit."

"Not unless you need another X-ray on that ankle. Isaac, let me give you some advice. I'm an old man now, and sometimes an old man's advice is worth five or ten bucks. You'd like to clear your father's name—that's it, isn't it? No changing people's minds, but those of us that were here at the time know what happened wasn't right. Guilty or innocent, I should say your father was the victim of abiding racial mistrust. Those who know don't need to be convinced, not after twenty years. So you might set your own mind at ease. All in all, however, it's better to let the thing lie. I gather you've got some notion who killed the girl? Well, a lot of water has passed under the bridge, a lot of water's gone down Deer Creek, to use the cliché. In the final analysis, what do you hope to accomplish? In any case, your father died by his own hand, Isaac. I made out that report myself."

"Thank you, Doc. You're right, of course."

*

APRIL 24, 1975:

A full moon cast a gray-blue shimmer over stands of pine and fir. Isaac was hardly aware of the uneven ground beneath his bare feet. He and the dog were two white blurs, moving from shadow to shadow, noiseless in motion, millions of years of predatory impulses gleaming in their eyes.

Lupus, homo lupus. Ahh, there's an owl, silent, a shadow in shadows. And Doom and I, a man and a dog, hunters, not hungry, but challenged, the fine pursuit of our natures....

They came to the highway, crouched together behind some brush, watched, listened. Isaac held his dog by the collar, whispered, "That's the enemy. We must wait. We must think. We must work out a plan to destroy it."

Doom growled happily, his tail rattling in loose oak leaves.

No traffic for some time—then sound of a truck coming up the grade.

"You stay here, Mr. Mutt. I don't want you getting run over."

He's not going to do it. He's never minded you once in his life. He's not going to do it now.

"Damn you! You sit, you hear me? Don't move your ass."

Isaac lifted a large rock, joyed in the strength of his body, scrambled down the bank, stone hugged to his chest, his body naked in moonlight, and squatted by the roadway, waiting.

"Old scar-face, wounded one, I've passed beyond death, others have failed, have failed greatly, but I'll not fail. It isn't humanity we break away from. It's the age, the final age of mankind. The lemmings are running, countless jackrabbits lie dead along the highways, elephants and tigers vanish, the whales vanish—and what cause? Is it not the simple impact of humanity upon the planet? Ah, soon there'll be room enough. We've reached the end of our tether, and after a short time it won't be jackrabbits dead. Millions, perhaps even billions under the sentence of death by starvation and frenzy. Is that what Jeffers meant? Cannibalism's the limiting factor when nothing else remains to be eaten. We must lurch timeward and cast off this deadening shell, find the old strength in our actions, fire in the sinew, fever in the earth. We'll tap that. I am now as I came into being, a hunter...."

The lights of the truck were before him. He stood upright, body set, naked, his brain seething the clearest, cleanest fever it had ever known. Isaac laughed at the blast of an air horn, waited, could hear brakes screaming, the dog's frenzied barking from above. He put his full weight behind the twenty-pound stone and slung it toward those attacking lights.... The rock leaped outward to a shattering of glass, a thumping against metal....

He was running. Doom was with him.

Pistol shots, two of them. Willow whips stung him. He ran without effort through a timeless and destined night, leaped down a loose bank, shouldered his way through a tangle of grapevines, plunged into the rushing creek, steadied against the current, scooped gravel from the streambed and flung it high into the air.

"They supposed I was dead!" he shouted. "By God, they thought wrong. I was wounded in the face, disfigured, but my beard covers that. I am my father—I'll walk these hills forever!"

He stood in the stream, immersed to the waist, held out his arms, and threw back his head. He roared at a still, full moon.

You don't suppose the fellows with silicon chips and tricky electronic circuits will be able to figure a way of producing food from the oceans? They've been to the moon, after all, and they're thinking of technology for living on airless worlds. Oxygen and water out of the stones, energy from unstable elements and compounds. Hell, there's room for at least twenty billion humans on this planet alone, if all things are properly managed. How much space does a man need? They'll make minor adjustments in humanity's genetic spindles, move a few molecules of protein about. Human beings ten inches tall—think of it, Isaac. Ha! Ha! Presto, there's room for another twenty or thirty billion. Or simply put birth-control substance in the drinking water. Sterilize half the females at birth, actually reduce the population—you're clever creatures. After all, I gave you that brain....

Isaac McCain grinned.

"I'm only acting crazy—a bad Richard Burton, you might say. Coyote *Oleli*, you truly are insane—crazy as your basic hog at humping time, that's what. The moon's full. Go howl at it. I'm tired."

Then he climbed up the bank, covered himself with pine needles and oak leaves, shivered, and slept.

*

APRIL 25, 1975:

"It's past time to return those rifles," he told Ginny. "Doom stays home."

"Isaac, are you all right? You've ignored me all morning. Have I done something? Why are you acting this way, damn you?"

"No, it's nothing—well, a little thing, but not with us. Look, I'll see you later. Yes, there's something bothering me, and I've got to take care of it. The poet up on the San Juan Ridge, Snyder, he says we ought to cut the earth's population to one half its present level. A modest proposal, but how do we get rid of two billion people, Gin? We're impotent—we stand armed with bow and arrow against the combined missiles of the United States and Russia, against the combined populations of India and China. Well, those will take care of themselves, that's what I think. And you and I have created another soul, but someone has to go on. I wonder why that is? The life-force, relentless, eating itself."

"A woman?" she asked. "You're going off to meet someone, aren't you? Where were you last night, Isaac McCain?"

"Ginny, I swear to you, I've no interest in other females. Please trust me—I've got an old debt to pay, I owe a rooster to someone or another, possibly a cock to Aesclepius. I'll explain everything when I return. If you knew now, you'd try to stop me. No, it's a debt Abram didn't get a chance to take care of. The man's probably forgotten what's owed him by now, but honor's involved. It's not a large debt in the whole scheme of things, and one that we all owe at last. Damned if you don't have the eyes of a coyote! Tell Doom I'll bring him a good bone. Our life's ahead of us, Ginny, but first this errand...."

Iphigenia watched as the '40 Buick disappeared under the trees.

"That son of a bitch!" she said to herself. "There's someone all right. I'm leaving. I don't have to stay where I'm not wanted. What the hell's the matter with Isaac, anyway?"

She pressed both hands to her belly. For a moment she thought she detected movement. She sat down by the window and stared across the green meadow, made note of a coyote apparently hunting mice.

Doom sat by her feet, nose pressed to her knee, brown canine eyes staring up at her.

*

"Is Mr. Bullardi in?" Isaac asked a salesman.

The man glanced at the two rifles Isaac held in the crook of his arm, frowned.

"Those things loaded? No, Burt's not here. I think he's over at the real estate office this morning, or else out with one of the construction crews. Is there something I can help you with, sir?"

Isaac nodded.

"Well, you give him these. They're his. I borrowed them, so to speak. You give them to him. Look, I'd like to buy that car, the red one. How much is it?"

"The Monza? You're in the market for a new car, then? Five hundred dollar factory rebates—that applies to everything on the floor. How much are you thinking to put down, Mr. ...?

"McCain. Isaac McCain. I've known Burt ever since we were kids. A hell of a guy."

"You don't say? We've got quite a few models—trying to move them out ahead of the seventy-sixes, you know. You been in before? Okay, let's take a look at the Monza. Mr. McCain, why don't you let me have the artillery? I'll put the weapons in the boss's office. How much did you say you've got to work with?"

"Didn't say. I want this little buggy. I like red, as it turns out."

Isaac waited none too patiently as the salesman filled out papers, phoned the bank, wrote up insurance forms, accepted McCain's check, studied it, and phoned the bank once again.

"I have to verify the draft—you understand? Most of our sales are via credit, GMAC, and.... On the other hand, I've had quite a few pay cash for new rigs the last couple of months—four-wheel drives, mostly. You live up North San Juan way, do you?"

"No," Isaac laughed. "I'm not a pot farmer. The bank says I've got enough to cover a new car, I gather? Check's been double-checked? To tell you the truth, I'm a reformed English teacher, you might say. When's Bullardi going to be here? I do need to make contact with the gentleman. Only proper."

The salesman pushed his glasses down on his nose, squinted.

"Mr. Bullardi's a very busy man. He doesn't always keep me informed of his whereabouts, you understand? Technically, I'm just an employee—an associate, you might say. An old friend of his, are you? Well, Mr. McCain, I'd suggest giving him a phone call this evening some time—better yet, leave him a note. I'll see he gets it."

"Tried to phone a couple of days ago," Isaac replied. "Just a recorded message, no Burt."

"I'll see that Mr. Bullardi gets the guns. Here are your keys, Mr. McCain. By God, this is one of the easiest selling jobs I've ever had. Wish all our customers were like you—see a car, want it, and buy it with no haggling. A salesman's life would be a hell of a lot simpler, for sure. When a man sees what he wants and goes for it, I like that."

"I thank you, sir," Isaac grinned. "And old Burt will thank you too."

The salesman slid open a large glass door separating the showroom from the car yard and motioned to Isaac, who started the Monza's engine, revved it to screaming, and let out the clutch. The little red Chevy leaped forward, smashing through a thin partition into Bullardi's office.

"You damned fool!" the salesman shouted over and over, "you damned fool! You did that on purpose!"

Another salesman and two white-uniformed individuals from the service department rushed into the showroom to see what had happened.

Isaac wrenched open the door of the car and got out.

"You tell Bullardi—Ike McCain will be down in a day or two. I'm going to buy me another car, maybe two or three more. Tell him I promise to be careful—Chevrolets have always had a problem with the steering. You've got your money, and insurance will cover the damage. Hell, I probably won't even sue."

"Phone the cops?" the parts manager asked the salesman.

"An accident, I assure you. Ease off, gents, or I'll bust a few jaws. Aw hell, you're good fellows. I wouldn't do that. Tell you what. See if insurance will get my new car repaired—doesn't look all that bad, actually. Maybe I won't need to buy another. You tell Burt. We go a long way back. He'll do what's right."

Isaac stood there, surveying the wreck of the Chevrolet.

"I like red cars," he said. "I really do."

***

Canto Twelve:
The Hunt

IT IS UNLIKELY, HOWEVER, IN OUR PRESENT
COMFORTABLE CIRCUMSTANCES, THAT THE PACE OF
HUMAN CHANGE WILL EVER AGAIN SPEED AT THE
ACCELERATED RATE IT KNEW WHEN MAN STROVE
AGAINST EXTINCTION.   THE STORY OF EDEN IS A
GREATER ALLEGORY THAN MAN HAS EVER GUESSED.
FOR IT WAS TRULY MAN WHO, WALKING MEMORYLESS
THROUGH BARS OF SUNLIGHT AND SHADE IN THE
MORNING OF THE WORLD, SAT DOWN AND PASSED A
WONDERING HAND ACROSS HIS HEAVY FOREHEAD.
TIME AND DARKNESS, KNOWLEDGE OF GOOD AND
EVIL, HAVE WALKED WITH HIM EVER SINCE.

[LOREN EISELEY,
THE IMMENSE JOURNEY]

*

APRIL 26, 1975:
"You want me to leave, Isaac? It's over, then."

"Only if you think best, Gin. That isn't what I desire, for
damned sure. This is simply something that has to be done, an old
score to settle, an old debt to be paid—a kind of categorical moral
imperative, one might say."

"Why won't you explain to me? What has to be done? You're
not making sense, Isaac McCain. You said we were partners, and I
believed you."

Iphigenia Singares, I love you very much. You know that, and
besides, you have our child in your body. You're my mate, and
coyotes mate for life. But I need to be by myself for the next two
weeks—as I say, some unfinished business I have to take care of.
Should have done it twenty years ago. No, Goddamn it, there's no
one else. I'm not lying to you, for Christ's sake. After this is over,
we'll go wherever we want. Too damned many ghosts around
here—Deer Creek's famous for ghosts. Look, I'll meet you on May
10th at the ranch at Upper Eden. Mack and Sandy are up there,
and Madison can probably explain all this a great deal more
coherently than I can. Poets have always understood about divine

madness. I don't want Mack down here, though. You tell him that. The incompetent jabbering pontificator's always trying to look out for me. Probably thinks he can whip me at arm-wrestling, for that matter. No, what I've got to do has to be done alone. Even Mack ought to be able to understand that. Tell him I said he's been splitting too many infinitives in that novel of his. Well, I'll proof the manuscript for him when I get there. May 10th. Maybe I'll arrive ahead of time, who knows? I love you, Yellow-Eyes, but you do what I say. I can't explain any further."

"This is all so crazy! Isaac, where did you put those two deer rifles? They're not in the closet."

"I returned the guns. Figured my old friend Burt might want to go hunting again. It's crazy, but nonetheless necessary. Trust me, Ginny. I know this is hard, but you've got to trust me."

"Okay, you son-of-a-bitch, let's say I agree. I don't know why I should, but let's say I do—*just for purposes of argument*, to use your words. How am I supposed to get to Upper Eden or anywhere else, Isaac? I've got no money since I quit my job at the café—and I'm pregnant, damn it. The Volkswagen's had a dead battery for the past month. You want me to hitchhike, or what? Don't you understand anything, you oversized gorilla? You're talking madness. I think you need an appointment with a shrink—or a witch doctor."

"The whole human race needs that," he grinned. "But I don't suppose it would do any good, do you? Therapists are part of the problem, right along with the Watergate hullabaloo, a bankrupt railroad system, poisons in the food chain, nuclear reactors, scientific experimentation on animals, and our stumblebum of a president. A new and improved variety of *soma*, that's what we need. If I had some, I'd eat it or drink it or whatever one does. No, I'm not going to let you go hitchhiking around the country like some wandering representative of the counterculture. That's what we are, both of us, only there's more *counter* than *culture*. I want you to take the Buick—it's dependable. and look, here are some certified checks, a wad of them. A hundred and fifty thousand dollars worth, more or less. Buy a new Bug if you wish. Truth is, I've cashed out most everything else, had it transferred to an account in your name—Bank of America in Quincy. It's all been handled properly. No, you take these damned bank drafts—they're yours. Think of the kid's college education, will you? No arguments."

"Ike...."

"Now look. You take the money and the car. The checks are in your name. Ginny, you don't have to go to Upper Eden if you don't want to. You're free to find someone who's sane, if that's what you decide. But I'll be there on the tenth or sooner, if it's humanly possible. I love you, Iphigenia, and I want to be a father to that child of ours. You think it's a girl, don't you? Yellow-eyed women all over the place, Coyote women. Look. We'll meet at Upper Eden. Don't forget to tell Madison what I said about the split infinitives. Maybe I'll get the VW running and drive that."

"What are you going to do? It's about your father—something of that sort, isn't it? What's happened to you? I'm not even sure I know you any more."

"I'll be myself in two weeks, whoever I am. You've got to give me that much time. Do you love me?"

"I shouldn't, you great oaf. I really shouldn't. This is all so utterly insane.... What am I supposed to do with this wretched money?"

"Oh, buy a jug of wine, I guess. And believe in insanity. It may be the human race's only hope. Nothing's as crazy as love, Gin, and you know it too. I've got an obligation. The world's changing, it's always done that. It's doing it now. But not us, Ginny, do you understand what I'm saying?"

"Goddamn you, Isaac McCain!"

                              *

APRIL 28, 1975:
Isaac walked down to the cabin just before sunset. He taped together four sticks of dynamite, capped and fused the charge, and then cooked some beans and hamburger for dinner. Doom sat beside the table and begged.

"Tell you what, Mr. Dog. There's another pound or so of ground meat in the ice box. You'll settle for that—and let me eat my supper in peace?"

The dog thumped his tail on the wooden floor.

With equity restored to Doom's satisfaction, dog and master consumed their meals.

After dark they set out on foot, Isaac carrying a lantern.

"Long walk ahead of us," he informed the dog. "A long hike and a long hike home. We'll cut through Mr. Bullardi's new housing development—that road of his'll speed things up a bit."

The cry of a horned owl.

Two coyotes yelled happily at each other from opposite ridge crests, and a light rain began to fall, misting down through pine and oak.

Running water.

*

You are scarred. You are wounded. You cannot love. You've been emancipated from emotion. You merely want that girl in bed, it's nothing more than that. Hell, Isaac, one time when I was out wandering around....

"You're babbling, *Peheipe-Oleli.* I'll never hurt her."

You'll destroy her, just as you've destroyed the others. You burn whatever you touch. Red blood and White blood, they don't mix well. Fire is in you, just as it's in all living things, but there's more of it in you. It's burned, burned deeply. Your brain turns to ash. Hammu. That's where the story ends.

"Pshaw. Doom, bite this cur."

You don't want to believe it, that's all. Be logical, Isaac. Look at yourself—now, even now, how you attempt to bathe yourself in self-pity. You wallow in the appearance of emotion, disgustingly.

"Why in Gawd's name should I listen to a green fellow with the head of a song-dog? No man in his right mind would pay attention to anyone in such a get-up, even if the words were pure wisdom. Socrates didn't wear a mask. Why don't you take yours off?"

I say the fire has burned you. You're marred and therefore dedicated to me for as long as you live....

"That's truly a stupid costume, *Oleli.* Take off the dog-head and wash away the green stuff while you're at it. What happened? You went to the whorehouse at Mustang and had the neighborhood professional use a spray can on you? Clean up your act, and then we'll talk."

I created the mountains and plains and birds and fish and all the animals, damn it. I created you, too, a weak bear with no claws and no fur....

"What about the trees? Did you also create the trees?"

Yes, those too. All but Ootimtsaa, Tree of Creation.

"Well, I've seen some mighty peculiar-looking trees, all right. Twisted up, double tops, branches growing out at crazy angles. Let's face it, you're simply incompetent."

I get careless sometimes.

"I figured that might be the case. What about death—and after death?"

Let's not speak of foolish matters.

"But you've told me before...."

I've told you many things, Isaac, and you've listened. Listen now: the leaves have fallen from the trees, now is the kingdom of frost.

"Now is the kingdom of winter storms, even though spring is here."

Now is the kingdom of driving rain.

"Now is the kingdom of heavy snows, falling, covering the earth, quieting. Glaciers are coming down from the high peaks—they're going to bury Sacramento."

Now is the kingdom of the iron lock of winter.

"Now is the kingdom of warm spring rains, the rising earth, buds breaking, swarmings of bees, the kingdom of grass."

You really suppose you can put me off this way, you excremental bit of human intellect? Didn't I in fact create you and all your kind?

"And gave us minds like your own. Hell, Dog-face, I've done been to grad-yoot school—passed my exams with distinction, by golly. Don't think you did, though. What do you know about winter? It's not your time of year. You're speaking outside your proper area of expertise, *Señor Homo latrans.*"

It's your area, right? Right, Isaac? And while I may speak with you, I'm not actually with you. It is yours alone.

"Then I reject the sonofabitch."

Oh, well, winter's all right. I catch rabbits then—or else I follow the mule deer and get mice where the big hooves have broken the snow's crust. The high peaks glitter and freeze in low sun....

"Listen, old friend. That's Doom chasing a deer through the wet woods. Talk to him about winter."

Are you speaking of your three-legged dog, or something else? Dumb Injun reads a few books, starts using heap metaphors. Act decent, and I'll give you a vision.

"You're good at illusions. Isn't that why I'm out walking tonight? I've trusted a part of your vision, at least. But I think you're overly fond of destroying things. Okay, you've got a light-show for me?"

I need a better disciple, Last Bear. That's your name, isn't it? You think too much. But observe: a long procession of the dead come up to drink blood. There's April Incendie—three times you attempt to clasp her, but she's like the wind, the air, insubstantial. Do you hear what she's saying?

"April, is it you?"

"We loved, Isaac, but that is gone now. You must return to the upper world and live out your life. Do you care for this new one, the yellow-eyed one?"

"I've never loved anyone else. You and I, April, we were only children—I was a different person at that time. Dearest...."

Then you see her no more. Now it's your father who comes to drink of the blood.

"It's all right, Son. Use that strength of yours, but use your wits as well. It's the mind, the mind which renders man his salvation. Tell me when you come next time just how the air smells at sunrise, whether the stream's changed its course, describe the wild grapevines tendriling out and clinging to air. I miss the sunlight. I miss the smell of rain-wet woods. Be careful now, you hear me boy?"

"Abram, my father, forgive me...."

They wander forever, Isaac. At best, the sleep is fitful. Well, Mixed-blood, What do you think of the conjuration? You'll admit I have a certain talent? Give me something in return.

"As soon as I left the island, a thunderbolt shattered my long black ship, and I alone survived, pitched headlong though I was into the dusty red sea. Yet I clung to the broken keel and was thereby able to ride out the horrible storm, drifting without food or water for days until I was cast ashore on the island where some young women were washing clothes in a stream. I heard their voices from where I lay, exhausted, my hands still bleeding from the rocks at the edge of the sea. I wondered if madness were upon me, knowing well that I more than others am vulnerable, liable. And I thought, 'No, let me pretend, let me believe, perhaps just believing will make it so, will suffice, for I've read of such things. I will lie in the thicket of manzanita and greasewood, will suck on white clusters of blossom for the faint, sticky taste of honey. Then I crept from my cover and observed them below, made note of just one in particular, her face oddly familiar. I watched them bathe and anoint themselves with olive oil and take their meal at the side of the stream. They lounged about, waiting for sunlight to dry the clothing they'd laundered. What should I do? Might I offer supplication and throw my brawny arms about the beautiful girl's slender waist? Or would such a gesture be misinterpreted? Thus I crept from beneath the bushes and broke off a bough to conceal my naked manhood...."

I like the tale, Isaac. I feel more at home with you now. Were there any grizzlies or tule elk on the island?

"Such a vision has created humanity—not to belittle your part in the affair, *Oleli*. You gave us your brain. Nevertheless, you'd best stay here at the edge of the forest, old urine-poster. I've got a job to do. Will you wait for me?"

You know that I will. What about jackrabbits, Last Bear? Were there jackrabbits on the island? And what about K-aima the goose and Moloko the condor?

"If not, couldn't you create some—and perhaps some coyotes as well?"

That's true. I can create whatever I want.

*

APRIL 29, 1975:
Diggins, California.

Newly installed electric lights, designed in imitation of gas lanterns such as those used at the turn of the century, gave a strange glow as misty rain continued to settle earthward. Dawn was still several hours away.

A tall, bearded man and a white dog—they walked up the town's main street, past *Bullardi Chevrolet/Cadillac* to a restored brick building that housed the office of *Deer Creek Park Realty*. The man looked up and down the deserted street, wondered idly where the town's police patrol car was, and then drew a pistol from its holster. Grasping the weapon by its barrel, he used the butt to break out a square pane of glass in a wooden door.

A moment later he was walking down the street, crossing to the opposite side, calling his dog. He strode ahead quickly now, turned onto a side street, and was lost from view.

Another minute passed, two minutes, a few seconds more....

Then the explosion, and the plate-glass front of *Deer Creek Park Realty* burst outward along with a great deal of smoke, the shattered remnants forming almost a perfect semicircle on wet black asphalt of the town's main street.

Lights began to appear in the windows of a refurbished Goldrush era hotel.

Other lights came on.

In the distance, the sound of siren.

*

MAY 5, 1975:

Isaac McCain struck fire to the mantles of a Coleman lantern. The sky to the west still glowed a thin yellow hue. Isaac detected a double pair of headlamps, a car coming down the road above the cabin. He reached for the Smith & Wesson in its holster on the shelf, slipped the gun onto his belt, and walked to the door.

The Cadillac pulled in beside Ginny's half-dead Volkswagen, stopped, and a tall figure emerged.

"Who goes there? This be private property, by God!"

"Ike McCain, that you? Hey, man, I just came up to talk—you pointing a gun at me?"

Isaac thrust his weapon into its holster.

"It's Burt the Bulldog? Sure. Come on in. What have we got to palaver about? Nobody with you, I take it? How the hell's April Incendie these days?"

"That's a bad joke," Bullardi said, walking slowly toward the door of the McCain cabin. "Naw, I'm alone. You haven't got a pistol pointed in my direction, have you Ike?"

"Not at the moment, old friend. Come on in, Burt."

Isaac hung his lantern from a nail in the ceiling beam. The two men sat down at the table, beneath the light. Doom, suspicious, lay on the floor, next to his master's feet.

"Well, Mr. Bullardi, what's on your mind?"

"I brought you the keys to your new Monza, Ike. Here. The damage wasn't too extensive. She's all straightened out, body work and a complete new paint job—baked-on enamel, same color. My shop insurance covered it, no sweat. It's a good thing no one was in the office, though. You sorta came right through the wall. Clutch on a new car isn't like the one on that old tank of yours. Ain't that the same damned car you had when we were in high school? Saw it downtown awhile back. Put a couple of thousand into 'er, get 'er all restored, you could probably sell it for eight, nine thousand. She's a genuine antique now, and there's people looking for them."

"Guess I did at that. Right through the damned wall...."

"Actually," Burt said, "my insurance has been taking a beating this past month. Add to everything else, some damned fool set off explosives in the real estate office last week."

"Sorry to hear it. There's a lot of vandalism these days, Burt. I'm told those hippies from San Juan Ridge—they mix dynamite into their marijuana."

"That's a new one. Another little joke? Funny as a damned crutch. Anyway, I've decided to do what I can to hold down losses. Your car's on the lot. All you have to do is come in and pick 'er up. Think you'll like that Monza. Even with your long legs, there's plenty of room, Ike. I'm sorry about the business last fall, and thanks for bringing the rifles. We had it coming, I guess. Abbot said he knew the girl—we didn't realize you was up there. Just fooling around. Frank and I finished off a bottle of Seagram's downcanyon a ways, so we'd had a snoot full."

"Well, the lady's gone now. Left me a week or so ago."

"That right? Sorry to hear it. Ain't that her VW out there? A pretty little gal. You serious about her, or you just been pokin' in fun?"

"No problem, no problem."

"You know, Isaac, a long time ago things were pretty much all right between us. We went fishing a few occasions below town. You remember that? You and me and Mack Madison, wasn't it?"

"Yeah, I can bring it all back. Not Madison, though. It was Tommy Pinello—killed himself in that car wreck. Then it seems like you and I got to hating each other's guts. I don't recall why, but nothing to do with Pinello."

Bullardi placed both hands on the table, palms up, and squinted at Isaac.

"Let's get down to cases," he said. "You're an educated man, I'm not. You know we're beating around the bush. We loved the same girl, and she wasn't true to either of us. It wasn't just you and me, either. She went out with both of us, and she went out on both of us, and we both knew that, too. So we hated each other instead of hating her, and we had us a couple of go-arounds. Horse-feathers, we were kids, empty-headed kids. When you're that age, you don't never think about consequences. Later a man starts contemplatin' practical matters. Well, Ike, I never got married. As bitchy as she was to me, I loved April. What about you— you been hitched? Kids maybe?"

"Can't say as I did."

"Old Mack, he got married not long ago. I saw the notice in the Auburn paper—I got a dealership down there too. What happened years ago wasn't anyone's fault. You were hit from both sides. It wasn't right about your father—people in town admit it now, the ones who are still around. Twenty years ago. Actually, it was a real jolt to me to find out you'd come back. You don't hold me responsible?"

"For Dad's death? You didn't have anything to do with that, did you? The town went crazy, and people needed a target. Pop was visible, too Goddamned visible. That's all."

"Some of the tomfool things he did, Ike. A lot of people figured he was crazy as hell, but I never listened to that stuff. At the time I pretty well had my hands full just trying to keep you away from my girlfriend."

"Don't give me any of that horsecrap. I know you, Bullardi."

"Shee-it, Ike. It was a long time ago, a different world. Diggins is a town filled with guilt—about a lot of things. It ain't even the same town anymore. You've seen that. We've been invaded by city types, longhairs, and artists, and God knows what all. The beards are okay. Hell, everyone's got one now except me. Yours looks good on you. And Jesus, there's a lot of money to be made. Real estate, Ike, that's where it's at. Better than selling cars. You wouldn't believe the prices we get for plain old brushland. A guy I know says the land won't grow corn any better than when it was going for twenty bucks an acre—that's funny, don't you think? I put in roads and fire hydrants, and I've got clients lined up halfway to San Francisco. Development improves the county's tax base, more money for the schools, government money to improve the highways and the canal system, REA money. Seems like half of California wants to move up here. It's a shame the goldmines went belly-up, but these are modern times—and a man has to adjust if he wants to get ahead."

"Dirt insanity, by God," Isaac replied. "But I see you've adapted to the new ways, ehh Burt? A genuine successful businessman, pillar of the community—and you've got an oil company behind you. Right or wrong? It's true, not so?"

Burt grinned.

"I'm doing all right for a country boy, but I don't really like the changes. Oh, some things are okay. To tell you the truth, though, I still haven't got used to that damned freeway through town. I guess it was necessary, though. What about you, Ike? Grapevine tells me you were an English professor up in Oregon, and you quit your job. What's next for you?"

"You've got a good grapevine. I've got one too, but it doesn't tell me much I don't already know. Damned thing howls half the night. You ever try to translate what coyotes are saying?"

Bullardi shrugged, looked puzzled.

"Too many of those damned little wild dogs around. They play hell with the sheep and deer. Saw one trotting down Broad Street early the other morning. They got no respect for nothing now there's not so much poison being put out. Government trappers aren't worth a plugged nickel these days, tits on a boar-hog. Guess we have to get rid of the coyotes, though, or hunting's going to suffer. Look, Isaac, I'd like to help you if I can. If you're still interested in teaching, as it turns out, I'm a trustee on the local college board. It doesn't pay me anything, you understand—just a kind of community service thing. I figure I owe the county a few hours of my time every month, that's all. Your friend Madison, he teaches down there, and with a little string-pulling, I imagine I could get you hired. Hell, you're plenty qualified—you've been a university professor, the whole ball of wax."

"Appreciate the offer, Mr. Bullardi, but I'm through with teaching."

"Guess you've got your reasons, but if there's anything I can do, just let me know. You figuring to stay around here? Not that it's any of my business."

"No, Burt, I don't think I will. Too many ghosts. I needed to come home, but I think I'll be hitting the road soon. Canada, maybe Alaska. I've got a place above Chester, but it'll be getting crowded up there before long I imagine. Too many folks wandering in the woods right now. Come summer, I suppose the place is crawling."

"For sure. Everything's building up. Have you been down to look at my Deer Creek subdivision? Going to put in hundred and fifty thousand dollar houses, and that's the absolute minimum. Big marina on the lake. It'll be damned nice. That's one reason I came up here tonight, in fact."

"How's that?"

"Well, if you're pulling out of McCain Flat, I mean if you're thinking about leaving in any case, I could make you a highly attractive offer. Including the original patented hundred and sixty acres, you've got total holdings here in the canyon of seven hundred and forty acres, plus or minus. I went through the county records, as a matter of fact. Whatever else your dad was doing, he was buying up land every chance he got. Deer Creek's a good place for development—doesn't get as much snow as the ridgetops, and the creek provides plenty of water. I haven't calculated the thing out, but there's enough money in it to keep you happy for the rest of your life, and...."

"Naw," Isaac said. "Land's not for sale. I've been thinking about putting a crew in here and working Dad's old gold mine. Let me show you something, Burt."

Doom startled awake as his master rose, then groaned, settled once more into sleep when Isaac returned to the table.

"Take a look at this, Mr. Bullardi. A hundred and five ounces, more or less, from just a few days of work. Hit a hell of a pocket. I think my Pa must have buried a big cache of gold around here somewhere, but who knows? In any case, there's a rich vein up there. When she's worked out, then maybe I'll think about selling. Land prices keep going up, and in a few more years...."

"You been fooling with dynamite, then? Ike, you got anything to drink around here? I could really go for a belt of something. What do you intend to do with the gold, just look at it? Someone could break in here, you know. Hey, I brought up a bottle of Jack Daniels. You'll drink with me? Stuff's out in the car."

"Guess I could go for a snort. There's a condition, though."

"What's that?"

"Arm wrestling. I've always liked wrist-fighting, the sort of thing an English professor from the hills indulges in. Us Half-breeds, we never get totally civilized. It's kind of a pretense that I haven't sold out completely."

"You serious?"

"Sure as death."

"You're on, then. I've tried the sport once or twice myself. Let me fetch that bottle first. Why don't you take the pistol off, Ike? It gives you an unfair advantage, I'd say."

Isaac laughed, nodded.

"Forgot I was wearing the damned thing. Go get that bottle, Burt old buddy, old Bulldog."

Bullardi walked out, leaving the door slightly ajar. He returned a few moments later, whiskey in hand. He poured two water glasses half-full.

The men drank.

Then they squared off, across the table, joined hands, adjusted for position. Doom sat on his haunches, just the tip of his tail moving. Isaac and Burt wrestled. Their tendons strained. Their mouths were locked hard. Feet slid for advantage. The gripped hands moved slowly, first one way, then the other.

"Give you a draw," Isaac said.

"I'll take it, I'll take it. Jesus, you're like rocks, McCain. I figured you probably went soft, being a teacher and all. I need another shot of that good stuff."

Isaac massaged his wrist.

"Burt, you must have been doing something besides selling cars and otherwise bilking a gullible public. We'll have to try this again sometime, but not now."

Isaac stood up, flexed his arm, poured the drinks. Doom half whimpered, half growled, jumped on his master.

"It's okay, *Señor Three-legs*. We'll get him next time."

"A rematch is definitely in order," Burt said. "You come down for dinner, Ike. We'll wrestle on my home turf. I know a couple of professional ladies we could have over for the evening. Real lookers—and kinky. What do you say?"

"This is strong brew, Mr. Bullardi. Look, I don't know which one of us April Incendie loved, but she got buried with your ring on. That ain't fair. It was like this wrist-rasslin' contest—no clear-cut winner. I think we ought to have her dug up, take that ring off."

Bullardi had been smiling, but the smile vanished.

"Good Christ, Ike! You're drunk. I'm feeling it too. That was a rotten thing to say, no offense."

"You're right, I'm drunk. Not used to this fire water. *Swithe dronkan*. Bad English. *Gehlystan*: listen. You know April was with me the night it happened. She said you two had broken up, and she wasn't wearing the ring. I believed her...."

Bullardi started to stand up, changed his mind. He remained seated, glanced at the dog, and then emptied the bottle into the two glasses.

"Long time ago," Burt said. "Let's be friends, Ike. She ran off on me, left the car downtown. The little bitch actually took off with my Goddamned '55 Chevy! That girl had a temper. I found the ring in the glove-box of my car the next day. When she died, I asked her folks to have the rotten ring buried with her. Who'd want it after what happened? It was cursed, so to speak. Come on, Ichabod Crane, it's no good to dig around in this muck. You remember how pissed off you used to get in grammar school when the kids called you that? *Ichabod Crane the Injun*. I think of the day you and Tommy Pinello got into it, then we all started fighting and got sent down to old man Bonner with his Goddamned razor strap. You have some coffee around here? I don't want to run my Caddy into a tree on the way up to Highway Twenty."

"All coffee does is make a wide-awake drunk."

"A wide-awake drunk is better. Ike, you didn't set off that dynamite in my freakin' real estate office, did you?"

Isaac broke out laughing.

"Old friend, how can you even suggest such a thing? Those long-haired kids around town are responsible. They're all smoking pot these days—or doing acid and coke and uppers and downers, shooting heroin, eating mushrooms and banana peels and morning glory seeds, whatever works. Drifting on cloud nine."

"Sorry. Didn't mean to say that. But I gotta hold down my losses. Sold a '71 Pontiac to a kid from North San Juan—he rodded it a couple of weeks and blew the engine. Brought the car back all scratched up and covered with mud, one headlight busted out. Wanted me to put in a new vee-eight for him, free of charge, and I wouldn't do it. Jesus Christ. Long-haired little bean-pole, he might be the one, holding a grudge. That coffee water ready? You wanta come work for me, Ike? A guy like you could sell a lot of cars. People just naturally trust you."

*

MAY 6, 1975:

Bullardi hadn't felt well all day—an ugly headache, likely the result of drinking on an empty stomach the night before. The combined odors of new carpeting mastic and recently applied varnish on the freshly cut pine frame of the large plate glass front window of the real estate office sent a wave of nausea through him. But as he watched Alicia Blevens, his pretty young secretary, leaning forward across the file cabinets to retrieve a dossier of first-mortgage notes, he felt better. Ms. Blevens was wearing a gray miniskirt, and the posture she'd assumed was extremely revealing. Nice stems. Nice ass.

He enjoyed having Alicia around. In the first place, she was extremely efficient, and in the second place she offered a degree of challenge. It had taken nearly six months for him to get into her pants. In fact, he had to let it be known in no uncertain terms that her job depended upon her full cooperation, good-natured and enthusiastic, in occasional early evening forays to the Golden Heart Motel in Marysville. At first she'd offered to quit but at length settled for a considerable raise in salary. "Battle pay," she called it.

After a short while he came to realize that she had something more on her mind.

As perhaps the most eligible bachelor in Diggins, he reflected, he wasn't a bad catch at all, and for that reason he was obliged to be careful in matters of the heart. It was easy enough to have the women he wanted. Money and status took care of that. All things considered, it was safer to pay for what one desired—value for value transactions, and make damned sure the ladies were on the pill—or else professionals, pure and simple.

Alicia, however, was another matter. He was actually growing quite fond of her, and besides that, she was hell in the sack. She actually enjoyed it—or else was one fine actress.

Of late he'd been thinking of children. It was time, maybe well past time.

Alicia, he mused, *would be good at bearing children. Holy cat-whiskers, what a fine little body....*

But at the moment his head hurt.

He was rubbing at his eyes when the telephone rang. Alicia sidled past him, picked up the receiver.

"Deer Creek Park Realty," she said, "Alicia Blevens speaking."

A pause.

"He may have just stepped out for a moment, sir. I'll check. What was the name again?"

She glanced across at Bullardi.

"For you, Burt. A Mr. McCain. Are you in?" she whispered.

"I'll take it, yes."

Burt pushed a button on his desk phone and said, "Bullardi here. How's that arm of yours, Ike?"

Burt, I just wanted to tell you I'm real sorry about smashing in the office at the car lot. No kidding, and I sure like that little red Monza. I'll be down in a few days to pick it up. Now listen to me—I've only a minute. I'm at a pay phone and don't have any more change—long distance from the Washington House. This is important. You listen. I know you did it, Burt, and now I've got proof—I mean absolute proof. You know. April. April Incendie. Yes, it was a long time ago, but I've got some papers, the evidence is absolute.

"What the hell are you talking about, Ike?"

No, you listen. I'll tell you what. I'm leaving the country, just like I told you—heading to Canada—I'll give you the papers, no strings attached. You just come on up to my place Wednesday evening. I'll let you have everything I've got. It was a long time ago, no sense spoiling a man's life. We were friends once. You listening now? Just one thing—we never had a chance to finish an honest-to-God fistfight. You come on up by yourself, we'll go at it. No matter who wins, the papers are yours. Alone now. You don't show up, I'll take the stuff to the district attorney, our old pal, Tom Bridger. You never much liked him, did you? Yeah. I sure as hell enjoyed our talk last night. Alone.

The phone went dead, and Burt slowly replaced the receiver into its red plastic cradle.

"Something wrong, Hon?" Alicia Blevens asked. "Somebody die or...? Your face is all white, Burt."

"Might say that," Burt nodded. "You got any more of that Midol in your purse, Babe? Look, will you? Just can't seem to shake this headache."

Ms. Blevens produced three oblong white pills and poured her employer a cup of coffee.

"So we don't have to go to the Golden Heart tonight?" she smiled.

*

MAY 7, 1975:

"We figured it right, Doom. The Bulldog's still trying to hold down his losses. He came a night early, and here we sit on a mountainside, watching his flashlight. He may have brought me a Fourth of July firecracker—part of him thinks just the way I do. Well, we'll find it by daylight, no doubt. We could slip down there and take him, just like shooting a damned deer. But he'll return—I guess he's satisfied for the moment, no one's home. Ginny's got the Buick—don't think it registered on him the other night that my car wasn't around, just the old Bug. He's leaving. The ice breaks tomorrow. Spring flood comes late this year."

Your father would have done differently.

"Hello, *Oleli.* I imagined you'd show up. It's all right, Doom, don't bite our guest. Yep, I suppose you're correct. Abram's way's not mine, not totally."

Your father would have smashed the man's head on a rock.

"Maybe you didn't know him as well as you think."

Now the flashlight's gone. Perhaps we can kill him later. There goes the car. You know, Isaac, it might be nice to scalp him. A full scalp, in the way of the Maidu, the whole thing, right down to the throat. Poetic justice, I'd say. What if that isn't Bullardi? From up here, who can tell? But Burt's the one who deserves killing. Except for the beard, Isaac, you two resemble each other. You've noticed that? Well, he owes us a debt, and it's overdue.

"The car down there—it might have been Mack Madison come to see what I'm up to—no, I recognize the sound of the engine, almost no sound. That was Burt's Cadillac, I'm sure of it. You know, Bullardi's right. The whole thing happened a long time ago. In a dream, I'd say. Me, I've been dead too long and have just awakened. Ginny will bear our child in a few months. The mist of years has absorbed, annulled all my fine anger."

The yellow-eyed girl? You've seen the last of that one. She has your money, and she won't be at Upper Eden. You're a coward, Isaac. I won't call you by your father's name. You could have buried Bullardi in a mineshaft. Men could comb these mountains for years and never find such bones.

"I feel a new tide of life within me."

Earth itself must shudder to its base, for what are we but raw emotion laced with cunning intellect, and that so slight our fingers trickle fire?

"You tormented my father, and you've tormented me as well. You're a good-natured fellow most of the time. I keep thinking about the cartoons with you and the roadrunner, Saturday matinees at the theater—when I could get into town. You have a long history of trapping yourself, *Oleli*—sex urge, vegetation spirit, trickster, Coyote-Head. You take that thing off when you go home to your burrow at night? I'll bet your wife won't sleep with you while you're wearing it. I know how to render you harmless...."

What have you learned, Abram McCain?

"You're clever, but you already know. Not everything passes from father to son. I've got my own identity."

You wouldn't banish me?

"I know as well as you do, friend Twitch-Whiskers, I can never banish you."

Then why should you believe yourself free? I live as I've always lived, under the fingernails, dark in the blood.

"It's no good, I tell you. I've won. I declare victory. Get thee off to the ridges, catch possums, howl at the moon."

Why am I still here? Answer me that.

"Did you match wits with my father this way?"

Your father was mine until his death.

"I don't believe you at all—you know nothing of logic."

Prove your freedom, then, Isaac McCain.

"All right. I accept you, *Oleli* the Clown. I accept you."

You can't do that.

"I can. I do. You're mine. I'm not going to resist you any-more, and thus your power's broken. I'm pure Indian at last; the poles have reversed. Think of me as a sheep in wolf's clothing if you like. Hell, I can wear a Gringo costume as well as the best of them and at the same time watch their world come tumbling down about their ears. *Ishi-Pano*, the last grizzly. I'm not one thing or the other, but I'm both. This is all theory, of course. You think I should actually...scalp...Bullardi?"

Brave talk from a coward. You would not have had the cour-age to run through the standing arrows. I would have rejected you in those days. I tell you, you're an inferior disciple.

"Maybe so, but I know when there are too many hogs at the feeding trough. I ken something else, too. My submission is pre-cisely what you've wanted all along, for that frees you as well. What do you say, Mr. Lift-leg the boundary-marker, have I not spoken well?"

You've discovered the medicine doll. I'll call you "Dances Four Times," and you'll be invulnerable.

"You can't put me off."

I'll send a buffalo skull to torment you.

"No damned bufflers in this neck of the woods since before *Estawm Yan* rose from the inland waters, but you get around. Cities, fences, highways—coyote population on the increase again. Maybe all the animals are coming back."

Possibly so, my fine disciple.

"You don't give in easily. Well, let's go down together. Where the hell's Doom gotten to?"

Come along, Isaac. I know where jackrabbits are easy to catch and mice are playing in the darkness. Maybe we'll plant a new Ootimtsaa tree. The Walems cut down the first one for firewood.

"So you've told me once or twice."

*

MAY 8, 1975:

Isaac didn't actually approach the cabin until morning, his rifle under one arm, a sleeping bag under the other. He peered in through a rear window, studied the room. Then he came around to the front door and lifted the hemp welcome mat Ginny had placed there a few months earlier, just before the snowstorm.

Nothing.

The door was slightly ajar. The previous night's visitor had apparently entered the building, for Isaac knew he had pulled the door tight behind him. He lobbed a chunk of stovewood at the entryway, which bounced open, the stick skidding on the floor. He looked inside, nodded, and then walked around to enter through a side window. He searched the house carefully but found nothing—not even a note on the table.

Didn't think he'd leave a confession, did you?

"I suppose not. What did he leave?"

Don't use the outhouse.

"That figures. I'll go look."

You really think the Bulldog's going to fall for that bluff about absolute proof? You have no papers, only an old man's memory. Burt's story's different, but so what?

"You were with us the other night, I gather, or close by. If he isn't guilty, then why did he come up here? Besides, you yourself insisted Burt was the one."

True, but I'm not to be trusted. Someone was here last night; that's all you know. You saw only a flashlight, and you claimed to recognize the sound of a brand-new automobile.

"There's also the tail-light configuration. Us White boys, we knows about cars. You brought all this out of my memory, you sonofabitch, and now you plant doubts?"

They were yours all along.

"Suppose they were. But not at present. Now I'm certain. I'd best check that outhouse—and the VW as well. It's strange how the mind works...."

Ginny's car had not been touched. The tracks of Burt's cowboy boots were quite distinctive, but none near the battered-up Volkswagen.

Yet those same tracks, two or three sets of them, were visible along the path to the outhouse. Isaac found explosive taped under the padded toilet seat Ginny had installed, along with a pressure-release button mechanism and a metallic wafer battery.

"Clever," he mumbled as he carefully removed the device, teased the capping out of a wad of plastic explosive, and then placed the charge in the hollow under an old, rotten oak stump. He fired from twenty paces.

Concussion, bits of wood singing through the air.

"Glory be to God, Doom, that stuff's better than dynamite," he said to his startled dog. "Best we look around some more."

*

Isaac fixed breakfast, fed the dog, and then went out with burlap bags to gather dry leaves and pine needles. Two hours of work produced a dummy, his own old clothing stuffed. He tied the mannequin to the rocking chair, put a battered hat on its head, and then went outside to see if the image were visible. He checked his pistol and rifle, called Doom, and climbed the path to the mine-shaft. He had a clear view of both cabin and road.

An hour before sundown, and no one had arrived. Isaac circled the meadow, Doom sticking close to his side, sensing something special was afoot, and then to the cabin.

Thinking: *Not a lantern. The place has been burned twice already. My big six-celled flashlight—that will cast a shadow.*

When he was finished, he locked the doors to the house and printshop, walked again to the mine entrance, and resumed his vigil.

No moon. Better that way. I know these woods, and he doesn't. He'll come himself, or will he send someone else? Well, we'll see."

Then darkness, night shotgunned with stars.

Isaac lay on the hillside, stared upward intently, caught himself on the dim edge of sleep.

"Doom, for Christ's sake, I can't doze off."

The dog sat next to his master, growled softly, and nipped at Isaac's beard.

"Three-legs, we've never gone night hunting, have we? Well, this is big game. You stick with me now, damn it, and maybe we'll get through in one piece—what's going to happen. A dog's got a right to a master. What would you do without me, hunt deer and run with the wild brothers?"

Below, in the darkness, Isaac detected a beam of light.

"Doom, he's come alone, just hisself, the big Bulldog. I didn't think he would, but it makes sense. No witness. Keep your own counsel, trust no one. Guess I'd have done the same. Let's watch and see what happens."

The light moved slowly.

"He came down from the highway on foot, White Brother. He's a hunter, by Gawd. In a minute he'll see my double through the window—then what?"

Isaac smoothed the fur over Doom's shoulder muscles, waited.

It came.

A series of shots echoed the canyon—then another, a final round. The flashlight again, moving toward the cabin. But a moment before Isaac squeezed the trigger of his rifle, the light went out. He fired anyway, and a second time.

A rifle flared from below. The noise echoed, trailing off.

Isaac felt his way along a dark path, acrid-sweet odor of wild lilac, rich night smell of spring growth.

He'll hightail it now—up the road to where he's left his car. I'll get there first and wait for him.

At the creek he stopped suddenly.

Someone was near.

Isaac slipped behind a big liveoak and waited.

Footsteps, faint but certain, downstream.

"He's not heading for his car, then...he's looking for a place to cross the stream, doesn't want to slip and get his rifle wet...Burtdog wants to finish the job."

The glow of a flashlight, shielded, thirty yards downstream, was barely visible through a tangle of wild grapevines.

Isaac McCain leveled his thirty-ought-six and fired twice at the dim light.

Vanished.

Return fire.

Isaac moved toward the ridgecrest, stopped, fired again into darkness. He could see light flare from a gun below. Then silence. He crouched low, hissing at his dog, ran, came once more to the mineshaft. He pushed loose some debris over the edge of the tailings pile—a clatter of stone.

Once more a rifle coughed, and the slug struck rocks on the slope at the terminus of the mine dump.

Isaac fired where the flash was—then nothing.

"Doom, you son of a piebald jackal," he whispered, "don't you run off now—it's okay."

The dog was trembling, close to his master.

"What are you, a cross-eyed cocker spaniel pretending to be a hunting dog? Burt's climbing the hill. I hear noise in the brush. I guess he means business, all right. Car salesmen are persistent. Come along, Doomer dog, let's get up on the other side of Dad's old vent shaft—a good pile of rocks there."

Isaac fired when he heard footsteps slipping on loose shale. Then, half-running, his flashlight held low to the ground, he moved uphill above the mine opening.

Several shots followed him.   One spit bark from an oak, and the smell of raw sap was close.

Isaac grabbed Doom's collar, skirted carefully around the vertical shaft, and then scrambled to the pile of football-sized rocks beyond it.

A thrashing in brush down the ridge, followed by another volley of shots.

McCain laughed and shouted, "You're shooting deer, you slobbering idiot!   I'm over here.   You might as well come on up.   You're a dead man anyway!"

One more round, close this time.

"That's better, Bullardi—you're on target now!   Answer me, you sonofabitch!"

An interlude.

Isaac stared off into darkness, could see three lights to the north.

Someone's at Crooked Pines.   Maybe the foreman's moved up already.   It's been almost twenty-one years since Bandino, Lugie, Madison, and I first put on forest service hardhats, kids who wanted to fight fires.   Here I am now, shooting at shadows that are shooting back."

For a moment a vision passed before his eyes: a big Whiteman and a small, intense-eyed Maidu woman, riding together, directing an attack against a camp of miners.   Whoops and cursing, arrows singing through darkness, thudding reports of cap and ball rifles, pistol fire, barrels of black powder exploding and a silver-red column of fire, eruption as a building blew apart, a rain of flaming shingles into the air, spotfires starting....

Ben Goffe and Acorn Girl, maybe they would have appreciated what's happening right now.   Those two and an old mountain man from the fur trade days, the Irish Vulture, Dad called him.   Wonder who he was?   In H.V. Olivo's Journal, an account of him there, nowhere else—except that Grandpa True Bear also knew him.   Well, McCains have always enjoyed fireworks.

Across the canyon coyotes were wailing at the sky, their cries resonating in the dark.   Isaac scratched Doom behind the ears, whispered, "It's almost over, Three-legs.   Just hang on tight, here it comes...."

He heard movement below, fired.

An answering shot shattered rock next to him, a sliver of stone stabbing into his forearm, lodged against bone.   A jolt of pain ran up into his shoulder.

First blood, you crap-eating Bulldog....

He pulled out the splinter, used his teeth, felt them grind on a jagged piece of quartz.

"That's close, Bully-boy!" he yelled and fired twice.

The night was utterly silent now between bursts of rifle fire, and the air smelled of burned powder. That and gun-oil and perspiration.

Another shot hummed near. Isaac screamed, a long wail, and didn't fire again. He lay close to the rocks and waited.

Did the yell sound right? Will he buy it? Jesus, what if it's not Burt at all, but someone else? Maybe some worthless sonofabitch he's hired to do the job for him? That won't wash—the bastard's too persistent. A professional hit man would have returned later, next week, next month—or he'd have followed me off somewhere and tried it. Aren't they supposed to use pistols with silencers? That's how it is in the movies—who the hell wrote this script? Possibly it's a friend of Burt's—Abbot, maybe. Someone close to him he might have told about my phone call? Whoever it is, there's only one reason for him to be here. Mad Mack, where the hell are you? I need moral support—you're the one who got me juiced up just before the last of my doctoral exams. Whoever's down there, he has to be the one who raped April Incendie, and he owes me....

Then a voice, out of breath, half screaming:

"Maa-Caaa-ain!"

Whose?

Burt's. It's the garbage-eating Bulldog....

But was he certain?

Again the shout:

"McCain!"

It was Bullardi, without question.

Know it's impolite, but by Gord I don't believe I'll answer him just yet.

Isaac waited, his eyes were used to the dark: he searched it. A form, dim, barely visible, was moving upslope toward him. He steadied his rifle against a rock, drew down on a vaguely perceived target, and then thought, *No, this is better. He's right there, next to the vent shaft—he can't see it....*

Isaac fired high, and the shadow leaped forward and down—a sudden scream and the clatter of stones dropping into the deep shaft, a heavy weight, muffled, thumping twice.

Isaac rose, his entire body trembling now. He stared out into night, from the shadow of Harmony Ridge northward to the stars, to the Wain, and then across the freckled blackness to Polaris. His hands shook as he lit a cigarette, continued to shake as he stood there, as he breathed heavily, sucking in air. His shirt was damp and cold with sweat.

There's my boy. That wasn't so bad, was it? Yet you had him dead center—why let him fall into the hole? You could have taken his head off.

"You think the bastard's dead, then? That shaft's at least a hundred feet deep. I'd better look."

Be cautious, Isaac.

"My own trick? Not likely. At the very least, he's fairly well broken up."

You could blast the mine entrance, seal him in there.

"I've got a better use for the dynamite, old fellow."

Isaac stood at the rim of the vent, beamed the flashlight down. A slight bow in the shaft caught his light. He moved to the opposite side.

At the bottom lay the sprawled form of a man in a green plaid jacket, face up, head against a shoulder, the butt of a rifle protruded from under the motionless body. And dim, dim in the beamed illumination, puddled about the open mouth, the red-black of blood.

                                        *

MAY 9, 1975:

Nothing has changed. It's still the way it always was, except that this time it's for keeps. Isaac McCain, they've been dead for nearly twenty years. Abram, my father, sometimes I can't even remember what April Incendie looked like....

The music, louder.

Scene distorted.

The notes screamed life, overpowering, rank in the air, crushed vegetation, spider-webbed dew. Oleli Man perched atop a boulder, flames issuing from his ancient, yellow eyes, his muzzle atwitch, ears pointed. A young woman clung to his paw.

"Iphigenia Singares," Isaac said. "After all this time, am I not innocent? The earth exacted atonement, not I."

Clarion. Percussion. Stringed instrument. Angels with soft warm breath, their wings enfolding. Coyote-Head's phallus erect, monstrously swollen, engorged with blood, projecting from buckskin breeches.

A dog was baying—was it Doom?

I ain't no more a figment than you are, McCain. Did you think you could resist me? I've been under your skin all along. I live in the genes, I'm yours by birthright. Have you forgotten everything? Welcome home, dumbass.

"I think perhaps I should walk up to Crooked Pines—that direction, in any case. Someone's either waiting for the Bulldog, or else he's left a rig there."

Perhaps there's a posse—they'll chase you with dogs.

"Your memory's bad."

I have no memory, Abram McCain.

"Have you forgotten your friends—*Tsayempi, Waima, Pano, Sumi, K'aima, Ene, Yelime, Moloko?* You see, I've got this unfortunate habit—I read books. Clever trick, ehh? You and I, *Meta*, we've danced the *Hesi* together this night. Can't you bring to consciousness that first time at *Onolaitotl*, when all the animal people met in conclave? Even *Wakwak* and *Doritu* were there? Since that time I've lived with *Omeya*, the pain. Now it's purged, *Oleli*, and I'm free. I am *Kuksu*, First Man. I tell you, there's a future ahead. But first I'd better see about that car. There may be one or two others to put under—possibly you'll get a scalp out of this yet."

You're good at speeches, but the test's in the living. It's far easier to say a thing than to do it. Isaac, couldn't we set at least one fire? I dream an inferno that wipes the mountains clean of all these Walems. They set traps and poison. They shoot at me.

"You're never satisfied, Old Man Coyote."

It's not that. But things need to change. Too many people and not enough animals. Your friends down town, they'll come for you now. Your great-grandmother took the grizzly totem, and you're her egg. There's no room for an Isaac McCain in the civilized world.

"Perhaps I've spent too much time reading books, but I'm not a damn fool. I learned cunning from a good teacher. In any case, these woods are dangerous after dark, the hills are riddled with holes. A man poaches deer with a flashlight, he'd best watch where he's stepping. The one link's his car, but if he came alone, no one will look for several days. If someone's waiting for him, then that's another matter. A few more complications to deal with. But Burt wouldn't have done that—he liked to keep his own counsel, that's true. And he meant to murder me, let's not forget. Think I'll go board up the cabin window and burn some leaves—do that in the morning, I guess. First I need to take a walk. Tomorrow there's some dynamite to get rid of. Christ, the sun's coming up already—well, it's a fair sign. Where the hell's my dog?"

Close your eyes, Isaac. You'll see the crest of a grassy rise in the Diggins cemetery, a towering redness eastward over the Sierra. The dead sleep well—two graves that all these years have been inside your skull. A wind comes from the east, from high snowfields and dark crags. It's a chill wind this morning, but a clean wind, Isaac, a pure wind.

"Yes," McCain agreed, "wind shivers the leaves of the wild grape, and our coyote brothers and sisters dance in tall grass along the streamside. Listen to them."

*

A four-wheel drive Bronco with *Deer Creek Park Realty* and a logo on its doors was indeed pulled in beneath low-hanging cedar boughs at the most remote of the Crooked Pines campsites. The vehicle was locked, and the campground was otherwise deserted. Only a wisp of smoke rose from the chimney of the foreman's quarters.

Isaac nodded, turned, and strode away in the direction of McCain Flat.

Once more on his home ground, he entered the cabin, rubbed Doom's fur the wrong way, put on a pot of coffee, and asked the remains of the stuffed dummy in the chair if he'd like some.

The scarecrow didn't answer, and Isaac replaced the batteries in his heavy-duty flashlight. Then he drank coffee, put the empty cup into the sink, carried the dummy outside, doused it with kerosene, and set fire to it.

"You served your purpose, *Kakini Busda*, my man," he said, pushing the flaming remnants into a more compact pile. "A burned offering—myself to myself."

A section of weathered plywood was sufficient to cover the shattered window, and Isaac quickly drove half a dozen six-penny nails.

"Doom!" he shouted. "Where the hell are you? We've got a two, three hour walk ahead of us. Too bad Ginny's bucket of bolts isn't operational."

*

A large, bearded man and a dog.

They moved quickly up the main street of Diggins, stopped in front of Bank of America. The man gestured to his dog and went inside. The dog lay on the sidewalk, ignoring humans who passed by him. But his hackles rose at a black hound on the other side of the street—he growled and thumped his tail on the concrete.

His master returned, counting a handful of hundred dollar bills.

"Doomer, we've got some business to take care of. A date to keep, and it's too far to walk. We've done enough walking for one day. You just heel, damn it. That black mutt doesn't want to fight."

At *Bullardi Chevrolet/Cadillac* Isaac talked to a different salesman this time—an old acquaintance.

"Abbot, Frank Abbot, how the hell are you? You and Burt kicked in any doors lately? Where's the Bulldog—he around today? Well, I came in to pick up that little red Chevy of mine—I see it out there on the lot."

"Hello, Ike. The boss said he'd talked with you. I'm sorry as hell about that scene last fall, okay?"

"Sure, Frank, all's forgiven. Burt says you know Ginny?"

"Naw. Just talked to her once when she was a waitress at Five Mile House. Your car's ready to go—you've got the keys?"

"I've changed my mind. The old Studebaker pickup at the rear of the lot, how much is it?"

"Damned if I know—only filling in here since the real estate office got blown apart. Burt should show up right after lunch, at least for an hour or so. The truck's new on the lot—I think he wants five hundred, maybe six. What are you saying? You want a work truck to go along with the red bomb? Probably got need for one up there, hauling wood and the like. She's supposed to have a rebuilt engine, from what they tell me. Not many of them old Studeys left. Good trucks, though. I think it's a forty-seven. You wanna take 'er for a spin around town?"

"Mack Madison's dad used to have one just like it—only gray, not tan. You remember? Frank, if it runs, I'll make you a hell of a deal. I suppose the transmission's all right? Put on a new set of six-ply, and I'll trade you straight across for the Monza. That red car's not my type. Look what happened the last time I started it up—damned near killed myself."

Abbot laughed.

"So I'm told," he said. "You're out of your mind, Ike. So, we'll buy the Monza, sell you the Studey if you want. Can't give you what you paid for 'er, not after you smashed it up. She's a used car now, even if no one could tell it. We'll give you top blue book, though."

"Mr. Abbot, you're a businessman. You should know a good deal when you see one. I'll sell the Monza to you personally for the cost of that pickup, providing you'll put on some new tires for me."

"Hell, McCain. Burt wouldn't like it at all. We don't take advantage of our customers, and besides, I'm not even a regular here. You just bullcrappin' me, Ike? All right, then, we'll work something out."

"Bullardi won't mind," Isaac grinned. "He knows I don't have good sense. Us Injuns are heap dumb *bastardos* when it comes to cars. You'll be three thousand ahead, Frank, more or less, even after the margins are taken out. Customer's always right, isn't that so?"

"You ain't putting me on, then? I think you're loony, but let's get those tires mounted before you change your mind. I'm not going to look a gift horse in the ass. I'll have to owe you one, Ike. I'll buy you lunch, anyhow. We can sign up the papers when we get back. Hell, Alicia can take care of them, for that matter. She's running the office today. You get a chance to meet her? She's the brains behind the real estate operations, to tell the truth. Just between you and me, Ike, I figure old Burt's going to end up marrying her. She's got him pussy-whipped, but don't say I said so. Damned well wrapped around her little finger...."

"In the mouth, Frank. *Never look a gift horse in the mouth.* But is that so? The gal in the wire-rim glasses and the miniskirt? Pretty lady. The Bulldog's a lucky man, by golly."

"Always lands on his feet," Abbot agreed. "What'd you do to your arm, anyway, if you don't mind my asking? That crazy white dog of yours get hungry?"

"Rusty nail out in the printshop. I turned around, and it caught me a good one."

"Might be beneficial to have a tetanus shot if you ain't already—play it safe. Come on, Ike, let's walk on over to the Spare Rib. We can talk about old times."

*

It was just past five.

Isaac patted Doom on the head and watched as the Bullardi construction crew headed out, up the new road that led from Deer

Creek Park Estates to Highway Twenty. Below him was the wide meadow—*Coyote Meadow*, as he'd always thought of it. Once, as a boy, he'd walked down the creek from his father's place and spent the night here—he and Tom Pinello, whose father had brought him up to McCain Flat for the weekend. The boys built a fire just before sundown and cooked some dinner—beans and a piece of deer meat and some fried potatoes. Yes, that's how it was. They'd just finished their meal when they heard the first bark. Then more. Yapping and wailing.

Coyotes.

Eyes, all around them, reflecting firelight.

He and Tommy realized then that they were trespassing—the place was a hunting ground, a good spot for squirrels, rabbits, and mice. The coyotes had come to hunt by twilight, only to find their special preserve occupied. The brush wolves were attempting to frighten human intruders away. Half that night was devoted to the serenade, and Ike and Tommy fell asleep with sad and outraged music in their ears.

Now the meadow was changed—a new housing development in progress. The network of roads had been added to since Isaac's last visit, and brightly painted red fire hydrants punctuated the area. Up over the hill and crouched under some pines was a concrete reservoir, roofed over. Two houses were under construction. Sites had been marked off, survey stakes neatly ribboned. Several stacks of lumber grew from the earth, like cube-shaped mushrooms. The grass was still tall in places but already going yellow, beaten down in large areas by human traffic. A bulldozer. A flatbed truck with *Bullardi Enterprises, Inc.* painted on its doors. Telephone poles, as yet unplanted, were stacked to one side of a large electrical generator, diesel drive, on wheels.

Thinking: *A likely place to leave this dynamite. One big charge up at the reservoir, and another next to the bulldozer, right under those fuel barrels....*

He set the charges, used up an entire spool of fuse.

"We'll have plenty of time to get reach the ridge," he informed Doom. "Be able to watch our fireworks from there."

The dog went on point as a small greensnake slithered away and disappeared into a gopher hole.

Almost as an afterthought, Isaac took a steel pry bar, rolled a fuel barrel into dry grass next to a stack of lumber, and punched a hole in the metal. He waited for the contents of the barrel to gurgle out. The wind was just right, headed down-canyon, toward Diggins.

He smiled, shook his head.

They'll have the borate bombers over here from Loma Rica in a matter of twenty minutes or so, he thought, *and it's seven, eight miles to town. A man can hope, though. A man can't predict how a fire'll burn this time of year....*

He lit a cigarette and tossed the match into some dry grass, watched. Flames began to move toward the spilt gasoline. It would take a few minutes. Then he lit both fuses, nodded, laughed, called his dog, and walked away up the hill.

He hadn't yet reached his Studebaker pickup when the first explosion went off. He grinned and looked back. He couldn't see the meadow from here, but a good plume of smoke was rising—apparently flames had found the gasoline-soaked grass.

Then another explosion, a smaller one.

"Fuel barrel," he explained to the dog, whose tail was wagging. "When's that reservoir going to pop?"

He reached the summit where he'd parked the Studey at the terminus of an old logging trail. He looked downslope, could see the meadow. Everything was burning nicely.

The reservoir blew, and Isaac was surprised at the loudness of the explosion. A sudden balloon of debris and smoke rose from the hillside. A gusher of water poured down the little ravine toward Deer Creek.

Isaac got into the tan-colored pickup, scratched Doom's ears, and drove back along the unused logging road. When he reached the highway, he could see a column of smoke, rising blue-black and angry, drifting westward, toward Diggins. The fire was apparently running through thick manzanita and beginning to crown amidst low stands of pine and fir: a good, healthy fire. The smoke cloud gained, poured upward. In waning light of late afternoon, the plume took on almost animal form, the shape of a great dark-furred wolf or coyote.

McCain smiled as he turned eastward and sped past Crooked Pines Camp and on toward Bear Valley and the high country. All in all, the previous twenty-four hours had been extremely enjoyable. Last Bear's revenge....

"Wolf or coyote," he grumbled, "whatever ye be, go eat them all...."

*

Night found him in Reno, Nevada. In one of the coffee shops
in Harrah's Club, he ate dinner—an undercooked cheeseburger and
a paper cup full of French fries, several mugs of strong coffee. He
browsed through a day-old copy of the *San Francisco Chronicle*,
paid particular attention to an editorial concerning failure of negoti-
ations for arms limitation, talks that had been going on in Geneva
since January 31st. United States and Soviet delegates had failed
to come to conclusion with regard to any of the important specifics
of the general areas of agreement reached the previous November
in Vladivostok, by Brezhnev and Ford.

Thinking: *Population limitation would be more to the point.
The football player and the guy with the bushy eyebrows aren't
going to play catch with their big firecrackers. A few more years,
another century at most, and they won't have to—there'll be millions dying of starvation, yes, and the whole world's going to run
crazy. Oh, maybe it'll take a century and a half or more, but then
Oleli will howl in pure joy and probably make wise pronouncements
about grizzlies and buffalo returning. Possibly the Big Dreamer in
the guise of Anubis will wake up in time and reduce the population
in some completely painless way. Well, that's not likely, is it?. Or
perhaps technology will save our sorry asses, increase the food
supply, postpone the inevitable.*

He thought of the year 2025 or thereabout and wondered what
the human condition would be by then. And his own condition?
Dead, more likely than not. If still alive, he'd be almost ninety in
the autumn of that year—an old, old man at the time of the very
end of his human tenure. And what about Madison—would he still
be around? Most likely the wordy bastard would live to be a
hundred and still be writing self-indulgent poetry. Mack could even
preside over the time of the implosion and write a few good lines
for a questionable human future.

Isaac ordered another hamburger, paid for it, and took it out to
Doom, who was curled up on the seat of the pickup. The English
setter groaned at being disturbed, caught scent of proffered food,
and sat up quickly. He inhaled the hamburger, including pickles
and lettuce, in one gulp—then stared eagerly at Isaac, hoping for
another.

"But I'm afraid you won't be with me in that distant time,
Doomer," he said, scratching the English setter's ears.

McCain walked the crowded streets, grudgingly admired the art
of neon sign-makers, and now and again entered a casino and frit-
tered away two or three dollars worth of nickels.

A bell went off, and coins rattled into the receiving tray of a
machine operated by an old man with a crutch and just one leg.
Amazingly enough, the white-haired gent was able to do what
appeared to be a modified hornpipe.

Isaac made his way over to Harrah's, ordered another cup of
coffee, and chatted briefly with a waitress in her fifties—a lady who
gave the air of having previously made her living as a professional
in the numerous Nevada bordellos.

"Age," she said, "betrays everyone at last."

Lights began to flash on the opposite side of the casino.
Someone had won a big pot on the dollar machine.

*What the hell am I doing? Wasting time, afraid, maybe, that
when I reach Upper Eden, Ginny won't be there? Why didn't I
listen to Mack? Burt could have married that girl with the glasses,
and the world would have spun on quite nicely for another half
century. It will in any case, and by then I'll either be the oldest man
alive, other than Madison himself, and blind as a bat—or else
sleeping soundly and not overly concerned whether they put the
tides in harness or don't, whether they build cities on the moon.
Human things are not very important—when a man gets right
down to it. The problem lies in living, here and now, and in going
out with his principles intact. Well, maybe that's why I had to goad
the bulldog into visiting me again. Ginny, damn you, you're probably in Washington state by now and thinking about finding a man
who's at least halfass sane. And no doubt you'll sell my faithful
forty Buick to some highschool kid who'll have it painted taxi-yellow
and then wrap it around a big Douglas fir.*

Isaac finished his coffee, left a ten-dollar tip on the counter,
winked at the waitress, and worked his way across a crowded floor
filled with slot machines and automaton-like gamblers, almost a
scene from Dante; then he exited, walked up a side street to where
the Studebaker was parked.

"Doom!" he shouted as he unlocked the door, "by golly, let's
head north, what do you say?"

Halfway to Honey Lake Isaac pulled off onto what apparently
sometimes passed for a road and bounced a mile or two into the
desert. He parked beside a wind-battered juniper and got out, the
dog leaping past him and streaking three-legged away into a darkness of sage and sand, yipping furiously.

"The slowest jackrabbit in the world," Isaac grinned, "and you still couldn't catch him."

Flashlight in hand, he threw down his sleeping bag, gathered some dead sage, and lit a fire. The flames danced in the night, and the warmth felt good.

In a few minutes Doom returned, his tongue lolling.

*

MAY 10, 1975:

The six-cylinder Studebaker engine hummed satisfactorily, resonating from a rusted-through spot in the header pipe, and the broad surface of Honey Lake, full this time of the year, drifted away behind him. He passed through Janesville and then across Little Susan River and into the town of Susanville, where he had eggs over easy, hash-browns, toast, and coffee for breakfast—again ordering a hamburger for Doom.

"That dog eats better than I do, "he muttered as he sipped the last of his coffee.

*

Forested area now as the Studebaker growled its way upslope to the summit of Fredonyer Pass and on into Chester, close by the head of Lake Almanor, and thence to Childe's Meadows and the headwaters of another stream called Deer Creek, the one where Ishi's people once lived—then up a winding cinder road that led to the old McCain Ranch at Upper Eden, over a rim and at the foot of the maze of volcanic formations around Mt. Lassen—*Wahgalu, Waganupa*, the sacred mountain of the north, its crown fixing the extent of Maidu territory—the joining point of *Yana, Atsugewi*, and *Maidu* cultures in the days before the coming of the Whitemen—the long-vanished mountain of *Tehama*, now a great caldera wherein sulphur springs boiled and fumed into the air, a United States National Park that attracted relatively few visitors.

Isaac crested the rim, gazed north to the snow-streaked crown of Lassen, and felt an inexplicable chill run along his spine.

Beautiful country, he thought. *Maybe....*

The pickup rattled and bounced its way downslope, transmission howling in second and strongly suggesting the presence of a couple of badly worn gear teeth; Doom stared straight ahead, ignoring the mountain, and concentrating on a jackrabbit that went bounding in zigzag fashion before turning sharply and disappearing into a thicket of young Jeffrey pines.

Isaac was nervous.

He gripped the steering wheel, relaxed his hands, first one, then the other.

"What's the matter with me?" he asked his dog. "She's not here, hell no, and I don't blame her, either. I should jolly well have explained. I couldn't do that. I'll spend an hour or so with Mack and Sandy and then start looking—but where do I look? Seattle's only a wild guess—because her parents live there. Maybe she headed for the Bay Area or Los Angeles.... What's a coyote-girl to do?"

He attempted to envision Iphigenia living in Los Angeles, but no mental picture came. He shook his head. The road wound its way down to the old ranch, metal roof of one of the outbuildings glinting in sunlight. Smoke rose from the chimney of the ranch house, Madison's green GMC pickup parked conspicuously in front of the building.

Where was the Buick?

"Might be parked behind the tack shed," he explained to his dog—though the sinking feeling in the pit of his stomach suggested strongly enough that he was grasping at straws.

Doom sighed and thrust his head out the window.

McCain pulled in behind Madison's truck, shut off the engine, and got out—Doom leaping past him, dancing about in sunlight after the long drive, and pretending to be a pup again.

Isaac saw Mack Madison walking toward him, a dozen chunks of split cedar in his arms.

"Dr. Hamburger!" Madison shouted. "I was wondering when the grandson of old True Bear himself was going to get here. Another few hours, and I was ready to drive south and haul your ass out of the canyon. Hell, man, I'm a couple hundred pages into the masterpiece—not bad for having to labor under handicap of an ancient manual Underwood. Come on in, and I'll read the whole thing to you. Don't want your damned criticism, just a pat on the head."

How'd Mack know I was supposed to be here today? Unless....

Then a yellow-eyed, auburn-haired young woman in Levis stepped out onto the front porch of the house, and Last Bear McCain fought to control a sweet laughter.

ABOUT THE AUTHOR:

Bill Hotchkiss was born in New London, Connecticut, in 1936.
After World War Two, the Hotchkiss family moved to Griffin
Creek, Oregon (raised chickens), and then to Grass Valley,
California (raised strawberries, raspberries, and more chickens).
Graduating from Nevada Union High in 1954, the future author
matriculated at University of California, Berkeley and took his B.A.
with honors (1959), followed by an M.A. at San Francisco State
University (1960).   He subsequently received the M.F.A. (1964),
the D.A. (1971), and the Ph.D. (1974) from the University of
Oregon.   He has spent most of his teaching career at Sierra
College in Northern California, with stints at both Shasta College
and at Rogue Community College in Southern Oregon.   Critic,
novelist, editor, publisher, poet, and occasionally an amateur
carpenter, he lives alternately at his cabin in Woodpecker Ravine in
the foothills of the Sierra Nevada, Nevada County, California, or at
his place on Munger Creek in the Southern Oregon Siskiyous, near
the hamlet of Williams, close by Grayback Mountain.   Other novels
include *The Medicine Calf, Ammahabas, People of the Sacred Oak,
Dance of the Coyote, To Fell the Giants,* and *Sierra Santa Cruz.*
Collections of verse include *The Graces of Fire, Climb to the High
Country, Who Drinks the Wine,* and *I Hear the Coyote.*   Critical
volume: *Jeffers: The Sivaistic Vision;* contributing editor for
Perspectives on William Everson and for the Black Sparrow editions
of Everson's *The Residual Years* and *The Integral Years*—as well as
for Bob Whisenant's *Of Sand and Dreams* and Stan Hager's
Autumn was our Season; publisher for volumes by Edith Snow,
Cornel Lengyel, Robinson Jeffers, Randy White, K'os Naahaabii,
John Berutti, Ken Hancock, Hazard Adams, William Everson, and
James B. Hall.

✳

Colophon

The text was set in Souvenir 10,
with Stonehenge heads and Classica
running heads, via MSWord for Windows™.
The book was printed by
Highland Publishing of Grants Pass, Oregon.